Bateman was a journa... ...oming
a... time writer. His first n... ...the Betty
... Prize, and all his nov... ...ave been critically acclaimed. He
... ...e the screenplays for the feature films DIVORCING JACK and
... D ABOUT HARRY and the popular TV series MURPHY'S LAW
s... ...ing James Nesbitt. Colin Bateman lives in Ireland with his family.

... ise for Colin Bateman's novels:

'T... e funniest crime series around' *Daily Telegraph*

'... sharp as a pint of snakebite' *The Sunday Times*

... metimes brutal, often blackly humorous and always terrific'
Observer

... delightfully subversive take on crime fiction done with love and
...fection. Read it and weep tears of laughter' *Sunday Express*

'... n extraordinary mix of plots and characters begging to be
... scribed as colourful, zany, absurd and surreal' *The Times*

'... joy from start to finish . . . witty, fast-paced and throbbing with
... enace' *Time Out*

...wisty plots, outrageous deeds and outlandish characters, driven
... a fantastic energy, imagination and sense of fun' *Irish Independent*

...ateman has barged fearlessly into the previously unsuspected
... ddle ground between Carl Hiaasen and Irvine Welsh and claimed
... for his own' *GQ*

...xtremely funny, brilliantly dark, addictively readable' *Loaded*

FIRE and BRIMSTONE

Colin Bateman

headline

First published in Great Britain in 2013 by
HEADLINE PUBLISHING GROUP

First published in paperback in 2014 by
HEADLINE PUBLISHING GROUP

1

Cataloguing in Publication Data is available from the British Library

ISBN 978 1 4722 0121 8

Typeset in Meridien by Palimpsest Book Production Limited,
Falkirk, Stirlingshire

Printed and bound in Great Britain by
CPI Group (UK) Ltd, Croydon CR0 4YY

HEADLINE PUBLISHING GROUP
An Hachette UK Company
338 Euston Road
London NW1 3BH

www.headline.co.uk
www.hachette.co.uk

FIRE and BRIMSTONE

Prologue

She was out of her head, a whole world in shadows and fog, sliced by jagged glimpses of neon.

She didn't know where she was going or who she was really with; somehow she'd fallen in with them in a club and she went along even though deep down she knew, she *knew*. God knows they'd yelled it at her often enough. But her guards were stultifying killjoys and she loved giving them the slip. And it had been so, so easy.

Harry was cute – olive skin, black hair, killer smile and those eyes. He wore a cracked leather jacket and black boots, and he talked like he was street, but she could tell he really wasn't. He came from money. You couldn't hide it that easily. But he had saved her from someone, who definitely *wasn't* charming, at the bar, and they'd gotten talking. She'd told him her name was Katya and before she knew it his crew was surrounding them, laughing and joking, then Harry knew a place they could all go, he'd other friends there, there'd be no trouble, big party and, if she was good, something extra for the ride out, and she'd just gone along with him like it was the most natural thing in the world.

A whole posse of them left the bar, roaring and singing, but then the gear hit and soon everything went hazy and she thought maybe it was stronger than usual or it was the judder of the train or not having eaten, but – whatever – her legs would hardly support her and she was sick and the rest were for leaving her but Harry got her up and walking and told her she'd be OK once they got to the party; there'd be something to bring her down. He supported her along the street and she remembered the taut, miserable faces of the female New Seekers in their pristine white and comical wimples, glaring at her as they went along the other side and everyone laughing as she screamed abuse at them.

Then they were at a raucous party somewhere; maybe two hundred people packed into the terrace house, spilling outside, front and back. But now, Christ, her head was banging, banging, banging and Harry was shaking her, asking if she was OK, did she want to lie down and she said, 'Yeah, sure,' thinking he was going to lie with her, but he carried her into the room upstairs and laid her on the bed, and she threw up over the side and everything was upside down and sideways, and she was shivering so bad. He said he'd go and look for the cure and she said no, she was fine, she just wanted to sleep, so he rolled her up in a quilt and then threw coats on top of her and kissed her head and stroked her cheek and told her she'd be OK. After a while she must have drifted, despite the music blasting up the stairs. She had crazy pink dreams and then she woke with her head like lead and her throat ragged and she tried to pull herself together, struggled up, then lay down again. She slept some more and, the next time she opened her eyes, the music was quieter and she could actually hear voices now, drifting up from below, indistinct yet comforting, and she wondered where Harry was and who he might be with and she felt a pang of jealousy over a boy whose second name she didn't know and who she had never seen before. There was a skylight above her, and a hint of pink dawn.

Katya wanted out. She wanted *home*. She liked Harry, but not enough to go looking for him. She wanted her people to come and get her, *now*. She rolled off the bed, tried to steady her pounding head, then stumbled around the bedroom looking for her bag, her phone, but they were nowhere. She tried to think if she'd had ID in it, but no, she never carried it because mistakes happened; people couldn't know who she was. She made it into the en-suite bathroom, shielding her eyes from the fluorescent with her hand until they recovered enough for her to blink at the stark image in the mirror: nineteen years old, blond hair all over the place, eyeliner streaked, her lips chapped and her skin pallid.

Like any squalid junky.

She wanted to cry. Instead, she dry heaved into the sink. She drank from the cold tap, even though it was tepid, brown. The plumbing clanked and hissed. When she used the toilet, it barely flushed. Flies. What was she even *thinking* coming here? She had to get out, home, but she'd no idea where she was, and she wasn't stepping foot outside, not alone, not out there.

She made it to the bedroom door, steadied herself and opened it. The voices were mostly quiet now, nearly everyone sleeping it off. They were lying in the hall, on the stairs, in the other bedrooms in various states of undress, not bothering to close their doors. There was still music, but no beat. Orchestral. She moved down the stairs, looking for someone with a phone; she lifted handbags and patted down jackets, but no one, no one . . . then on the bottom step a girl, asleep with her head against the railings and one breast hanging out of her top, was clutching her phone in her dead grip. Katya opened her fingers, one at a time, and pulled it free. She retreated back up the stairs, into the room, closed the door and slipped down against it, steadying her head again.

The number – they'd drilled it into her, time and again, but now it remained frustratingly elusive. Her head was a sieve and everything she knew was leaking out, floating around her, but blurred, taunting her.

Concentrate.

She did as she'd been instructed. She pictured the pink room – home, loved ones, the apartment, Harry

Potter, her oh-so-dull flatmate – as she tried to calm herself down, but flashes from this night, from earlier nights kept cramming in, dissipating the numbers every time she tried to grab at them. She put the phone against her forehead and thought of combinations of places – home, pets, parents, nice things, good things – but she just couldn't grab hold of the figures she needed.

Outside, engines, doors slamming.

They've found me! Thank God!

They tracked the phone!

She felt woozy again, sucked in some air. She just had to let them know where she was, maybe keep them outside so that they wouldn't embarrass her by escorting her out. She made it to the window, more deep breaths to stop her heaving again; it was an attic room, so she had to drag a chair across and haul herself up so she could get a proper look at the street below and shout down, stopping them in their tracks. But when she got there she was confused, because, if they were coming for her, they'd have come in the usual Land Cruisers, not the ragtag of disparate vehicles below. A dozen men were gathering beside them, getting orders. Then they were crossing the road. They split into two groups, one going up an alley and around the back, the other for the front door; then, with the angle of the roof, she lost them.

OK, at least they're here, and in force. Just get me out of here.

She stepped off the chair and hurried to the door.

She yanked it open and hurried down the hall. She began to move back down the stairs; there was a loud crack from below as the door was kicked in.

OK, don't stand on ceremony, get in and out quick.

And then a burst of gunfire and screams.

Christ, some idiot off his head has stood up to them and they're trigger-happy with concern for me.

But there was more shooting, and it just didn't stop. She peered over the banister to the hall far below. She saw the girl she'd taken the cell off standing with her hands raised; the man before her, a bandana pulled up over his mouth and nose, just raised his gun and shot her in the head and she went down.

And suddenly she *knew*, because she'd read about it, heard about it, it was exactly what they'd warned her of: what they will do to you, what they will do to anyone; how they kill and they kill and they kill, like cats marking their territory in blood. They're not coming for you, they're coming for *everyone*.

She bolted back to the room, slammed the door and locked it, aware of how pathetically inadequate it was as a defence. Old, thin, cracked wood with a tiny lock. They'd walk through it. She leaned against it, breathing hard – and then suddenly there it was, right in front of her eyes, floating: the number. She keyed it in and she was screaming: 'Paladin! This is Paladin! Please!' There was no response. The gunfire was closer, coming up the stairs. The screaming, the *screaming*. Her heart was going to explode. 'Please! It's me! Paladin! Paladin!'

A cold voice, remote, uninterested: 'This is not Paladin's phone.'

'I lost it! This is Paladin! They're killing . . . Help me! *Please* . . .!'

'We have a number of security questions, please answer them as fully as . . .'

'NO!'

She threw the phone down and looked about her in desperation. She could hear them calling to each other, probably on the floor below, or coming up the stairs. There were two or three rooms along the hall before they got to this final one. She heard doors being kicked in, more shots.

They're going from room to room. They're killing everyone.

She could plead with them, tell them who she was, what she was worth. She had a duty to survive. But they weren't taking the time to ask questions. They were on a mission to slaughter. It didn't matter why. All she knew was that she was next.

She flicked the light switch off and raced back to the window. She clambered on to the chair. It was an old skylight, with the catch painted over; she pulled and pulled at it, but the drying paint had welded it shut. She stepped back down, lifted the chair by two legs and swung it up at the window. The glass shattered. Most of the jagged shards fell back towards her; all she could do was hold her head to one side and pray she wasn't impaled. She kept hold of the chair and moved it from side to side along the frame, clearing out as many of the remaining pieces as she could, then stood on it again and hauled herself up, wincing as fragments cut into her hands.

Behind her, there was a pull on the door handle, then a kick at the door. When it held firm, there was a thud as a shoulder was put to it. She was balancing precariously in the skylight now. A fraction of a second before the door was shouldered again, forcing it off its hinges, she lowered herself down until she was hanging by just her fingertips while her feet scrambled for purchase on the slippery tiles of the sharply angled roof. But there was none to be had.

The light went on behind her. She stopped moving. She held her breath. Her fingernails tried to dig into the paintwork of the frame, but it was no good. There were footsteps on the wooden floor, getting closer.

Please God, please God, please God . . .

Her face pressed into the tiles. She couldn't bring herself to look up at her doom. There was noise from below. She peered down and saw the killers steaming out of the house and crossing to their vehicles. The engines were starting up.

It's over, it's over, it's over, oh my sweet Lord, it's . . .

She glanced up at the window, wondering if she had the strength to pull herself back up.

And in that moment, she knew it didn't matter. There was a young man in the frame, staring down at her, just his head and shoulders; she knew he was standing on the chair, leaning one arm on the inside sill for support, a gun clutched in his hand. He had a red bandana across his mouth and nose. Even in the gloom she could see that his eyes were the most dynamic blue. He raised his other hand and pulled down the bandana and gave her a wide smile.

Please.

And then he brought the butt of the gun down hard on her fingers, and she could do nothing but let go.

She sailed out, silently.

The first light of day was just breaking through, daggers of revelation over Belfast. She loved her city, and she hated it. She thought of home, and her parents, and everything she had once had and had now lost forever and ever, Amen.

1

Just that morning I had been promised riches beyond my wildest dreams.

I was idly speculating on what the four million, three hundred thousand dollars could do for my lifestyle – including getting me a mint condition EMI vinyl copy of the Sex Pistols' *Anarchy in the UK* and something to play it on. I had imagined that acquiring such a rarity would eat well into my new fortune, but was both relieved and stressed to discover that it was currently only valued at twenty-five pounds. My first and only wife Patricia had melted my original copy in a toaster many years before. Now the toaster was probably worth more than the record, because nobody had yet worked out how to download toast for free.

I had been promised the money by the wife of an Exxon Mobil executive who'd been killed in a plane crash in Qatar with eight other oil workers. He'd left the money in a private account to which only she, Mrs Fatimah Abd-Al-Hamid, had access, but she had encountered various difficulties getting the money out of the country. By a process of elimination or blind luck she had heard of my good works and deep spirituality and was going to transfer all of her money into my bank account – all I had to do was open up a different account in Malaysia and pay a little bit to her up front, just to cover the paperwork. It seemed like a roundabout way to do it but, nevertheless, a good deal. It would certainly get me out of the private investigations business. Although I had some aptitude for it, I had no real desire. I had no idea what I actually wanted to be doing, but I knew it wasn't poking my nose into other people's business, because other people's business usually sucked.

I had exchanged several emails with Mrs Abd-Al-Hamid during the course of the morning; I felt increasingly close to her and found her charming, although suffused with old-fashioned formality. Even though our acquaintance was short, and I found myself occasionally distracted by a Twix, I think I was beginning to fall in love with her a little bit, a feeling which was soon allied with concern as she revealed further unsettling details about herself and her circumstances. Not only could she not get the money out of the country without my help, she was also terminally ill and might not see the week out, so it was doubly vital that I get the bank account set up immediately or the money might be lost forever. She was thinking of others, even though she was dying! How could I *not* love her?! She wasn't just asking me, she was beseeching me, which is something I don't get a lot of, unless you count my late wife Patricia's beseeching me to pay her maintenance by direct debit rather than via the handfuls of grubby bank notes I sometimes pushed through her letter box on the way home from the pub. And when I say 'late', I don't mean that Patricia had departed this mortal coil. No, absolutely not. Patricia was too stubborn to depart from anywhere until she was good and ready. By 'late' I mean that she was no longer officially Mrs Starkey. Following two years of separation, friendly negotiation and internecine warfare, our divorce had finally come through, which made everyone happy, with the exception of the late Mrs Starkey, and yours truly.

But I was fine.

Really.

I was footloose and fancy free.

I had my apartment, I had my office, I had the deep regard of my lover, Pamela Hand, and I had the boundless optimism that comes with middle age. Things couldn't be better. Honestly. And I had Fatima, at least I did have her until I made the devastating discovery that Mrs Abd-Al-Hamid was not being entirely faithful to me, and had been offering her riches to at least one other of my Facebook friends – that is to say, a complete stranger who had friended me because we were both called Dan, and I was that desperate I accepted. And then, the more I looked into it, the more suitors to her fortune were revealed and it began to dawn on me that

Mrs Abd-Al-Hamid was being unfaithful to me not just with my friends but with many thousands of other poor lonely souls. There was even the possibility that, not only was she being free with her cancer-ridden charms, she might even have been attempting to scam me out of my non-existent savings. Shocked and horrified as I was, I still retained enough composure to draft a dignified email to her which not only gave her notice of my intention to withdraw from our arrangement, but which also made it absolutely clear that my feelings had been badly hurt by her deceit. I wasn't the first and I wouldn't be the last, but at least I was letting my feelings be known. I was standing up for all men who had been led astray by the attentions of a beautiful woman with a master plan.

Don't get me wrong. I may have had a problem with the late Mrs Starkey, and I very definitely had issues with Fatimah Abd-Al-Hamid, but generally I love women. Always have. I love beautiful, mischievous women; I love women with raucous laughs and withering put-downs; I love the way their eyes dance when they're happy and their smiles are so alive they jump around like mackerel in a net, how they can make you forget everything and remember everything simultaneously, how they make you want to stand up and be counted. Women are the difference between life and living, they give a reason to be, a reason to endure and they give me hope. I hate to disappoint them, but I always will. I was poor and unemployed, and neither of the women I loved wanted anything to do with me; beyond Fat and

Trish, I had enjoyed several affairs in the past year which had ended badly. Another man, in a similarly singular situation, had told me, when I had most recently split up with Trish, that there were thousands of similarly middle-aged women out there who were dying to meet someone new and shag them senseless; he had failed to inform me that most of them were as mad as a box of frogs and came with more baggage than Dumbo's circus train.

As I checked over what was sure to be my final email to Fatimah Abd-Al-Hamid, I began to sing to myself, quietly at first, but then gradually building: Motown hits with delicate hip movements on my swivel chair. I should have been miserable and lonely, but it was such a rare and glorious day that my sadness was hiding behind a parasol and I felt unaccountably happy. I intended to shut up the office, pick up my regular sandwich across the road and adjourn to the Botanic Gardens with a six-pack. I would call up a couple of old friends and we would lie in the sun and discuss football and music and marriage, and burn ourselves in the sun in a way that only the Northern Irish can: red raw. I smiled at the thought of it while continuing to blast out my memories of taking the 'Midnight Train to Georgia'; though strictly speaking it wasn't Motown, it felt like one of their finest tales of heartbreak and hope . . . I was singing so loud, in fact, that I wasn't even aware that the office door had opened, or that there was a tall man in a smart suit standing there, at least not until he cleared his throat – and Gladys died in mine while still considerably short of Georgia – and he gave me a nod and said, 'It's good to see someone happy in their work.'

'Never knowingly happy,' I responded, 'and never heard of knocking?'

He said, 'I did.'

His accent was Belfast, but he spoke with the clarity of someone who'd spent a lot of time in England, wanting to be understood.

I said, 'But I didn't buzz you in, downstairs. I have a system.'

'Can't say I noticed,' he said.

'You have to press the buzzer before the system kicks in,' I said. 'I suspect you outfoxed it by waiting for someone to come out, and then slipping in before the door closed properly.'

He said, 'Correct, though I wasn't waiting, the fact that someone was leaving was fortuitous.'

'And with that,' I said, 'the Maginot Line was breached and millions died.'

'Hopefully not,' he said, and stepped fully into my office. His eyes flitted around it, taking in the desk and my comfy leather swivel chair and the two white plastic efforts from Homebase I kept for clients, although they were sometimes one too many, and often two too many. Business had not been good of late. He noted my laptop and filing cabinet and the skylight, which I occasionally propped open in our Ulster summer and through which it had once, rather memorably, snowed. Today it was actually boiling, and the little air that was getting in was doing nothing to relieve the heat. His gaze lingered for a moment on the rubber plant in one corner, which had neither thrived nor foundered since Patricia had presented it to me as a peace offering six months previously, and about which I was coming to the inescapable conclusion that it was in fact a rubber plant made of rubber. Apparently satisfied with our surroundings, my visitor then reached across the desk to shake my hand. We were both firm and manly about it.

'Michael Finn,' he said.

'Dan Starkey. But then you probably know that.'

He smiled. He had good teeth set in a good face, with a good complexion. When he faced himself in the mirror in the morning he probably felt pretty good about how he looked. He was maybe fifty-five years old. I hoped I looked that good when I got to fifty-five – ah, who am I kidding? I'll never get to fifty-five. His face was the kind you see in adverts for BUPA health care, gated communities and SAGA holidays: it glowed with robust good health, with vim and vigour, and displayed no hints of the doom which awaits all of us. His features were sharp, his skin smooth and his hair immaculate. When I indicated for him to sit, and he slipped into his chair, I caught the slightest hint of aftershave off him and a sharper whiff of recently consumed coffee. He had a small leather satchel with him, which was somewhere between a briefcase and a man-bag. There was a logo on the side, which I had a brief glimpse of before he set it at his feet, and which looked familiar – probably one of the designer labels that my late wife would have liked to have become more familiar with.

He said, 'I should have called ahead. But I was on the way to the airport when someone suggested you as a last resort, and I thought I would take the chance. You're some kind of private investigator.'

'Some kind,' I agreed.

'I mean no disrespect.'

'None taken. A last resort is still a resort. You're just leaving the best till last.'

'I mean, you don't have "Private Investigator" on the door, or downstairs on the buzzer. In fact, there's no name at all down there.'

'That's the way I like it,' I said. 'Last time I had my name out front, someone blew the door off with a bomb.'

He studied my face for some indication of humour, but there was none to be found. He gave a sad shake of his head. 'For a long time I thought this place had changed,' he said, 'and I told everyone at home it was safe to come here. This last year, it's gone to the dogs.'

'Bad as it ever was,' I said.

We both pondered that for a bit. He had slumped a little in his chair – pondering Ulster's Troubles can do that to you – but he became aware of it and straightened himself.

'You don't have a website,' he said, 'and, as far as I can determine, you're not in the phone book and, if someone goes pressing on the only buzzer downstairs that does have a name attached to it, they're not going to get you, they're going to end up with a Thai massage.'

'It says "Thai",' I said, 'but I'd say the closest they've been to Bangkok is the curry house on the corner. And I'd add, by way of caution, that if you were looking for anything other than your Wee Willie Winkie stretched, you're probably pressing the wrong buzzer.'

'I'll bear that in mind,' he said.

'Long gone?' I asked.

'Thirty years. I understand you—'

'I offer a boutique, bespoke service for important people with difficult problems.'

'That's what I heard. And also that you sometimes piss people off. Enough to want to blow you up, it would seem.'

'I try not to encourage that,' I said, 'though with mixed results.'

'The man I work for admires individuality, but demands discretion.'

'The man I work for provides both.'

'You *are* Dan Starkey?'

'If you're wearing a suicide vest, I'd have to say no.'

'The man I work for has a good sense of humour, but not in this case.'

'It's my experience that anyone who says they have a good sense of humour hasn't actually much of one at all.'

Mr Finn clasped his hands. 'You get results,' he said.

'Not always the ones you're looking for,' I said, 'but usually some approximation of the truth.'

'That's all he's looking for,' said Finn.

'That's what they all say,' I said.

He had been reaching down for his bag when I said it, and it caused him to hesitate. He pursed his lips and then nodded to himself, clearly coming to some decision. He lifted the bag on to his lap and unzipped it. He took out an iPad, tapped the screen and then placed it on the desk and pushed it across to me.

'This is our standard confidentiality agreement,' he said, 'I need your electronic signature before we can continue.'

'No,' I said, without looking at it.

'No?'

I raised an eyebrow.

'Mr Starkey,' he said, 'we—'

'Before you get into it, can we save ourselves some time by jumping to the point where I say no again?'

'My client,' said Finn, 'is a very rich and important man.'

'I'm very happy for him.'

'He—'

'Confidentiality comes as standard,' I said, 'unless you count my Facebook updates. I don't charge extra for it. Now you've already said you don't have anywhere else to go, so do you think we could stop fannying around and get to the point?'

I said it with a smile, which usually defuses the impact. Usually. Finn took the tablet back. He studied the screen, though I could see that his pupils weren't moving, so he wasn't reading it, but again just taking a little time out to think. I glanced at my watch. It was almost one. The café across the road had a sandwich with my name on it. I had gotten to the stage of life where food had assumed a greater importance than almost everything else, including my sex life and Liverpool, although perhaps only because they were both experiencing a disappointing early-season form. There was blue August sky visible through the open skylight. I had my jacket off and the sleeves of my white shirt were rolled up. It was hotter than July. I had spent the last three months largely working on a novel, which I knew would never be finished. I had no cases, no clients and the closest I'd come to a meaningful relationship with a beautiful woman was the lovely Fatimah, who had turned out to be not so lovely after all. The rent on my office and the mortgage on my apartment were badly overdue. I needed to work. If he'd pushed it, I would have signed the damn thing.

But he didn't.

Instead, he said, 'I work for Thomas Wolff.'

'The novelist?'

'No, not the novelist.'

'Good thing, he died in – I don't know – 1938? A different Thomas Wolff?' And then it clicked: I knew why the logo on his man-bag had looked familiar. The head of a wolf: the corporate logo of – 'Thomas Wolff, as in Wolff TV, movies, newspapers, computers, games, all that . . .?'

'All that. Yes.'

Wolff was an East Ender who'd gotten his start in

porn – publishing and sex shops – and he still kept his finger in, so to speak, with a dozen late-night soft-core channels, and he'd built them into a media company with interests on every continent. He loved the limelight, was always pictured with a cigar and a pretty girl; he had taken over on *The Apprentice*, hiring and firing with a rugged charisma.

'Very good. Very impressive. You know, when I was younger, I was convinced his first name was Billionaire, because every time—'

'Yes,' he said.

'. . . and you've heard it all before.'

He nodded.

'So, what can this private investigator of last resort do for Billionaire Barrow Boy Thomas Wolff?'

Finn tapped the iPad screen again and then turned it round to show me the photo of a very good looking young woman, possibly eighteen or nineteen, posing in what looked like the Caribbean. She had short blond hair and a wide, happy smile; she was wearing a white top, tied at the navel, and short cut-off jeans; there was a turquoise sea and a beach curving round behind her with a palm tree dipping down into the water.

'This is Alison Wolff,' said Finn, 'his only daughter. She went missing in Belfast nine months ago. She hasn't been seen since. He wants you to find her – dead or alive.'

2

My office was getting hotter and stickier by the minute, so, as we were still deep in discussion, I suggested retiring to the roof terrace. Finn was both surprised that I had one and relieved to get out into the fresh air. More than once he had said he blamed himself for what had happened to Alison Wolff – or, indeed, Katya Cummings, the name she'd been living under in Belfast. I could hear a little catch in his voice each time he said it. He made a quick call to someone, in which I definitely heard the words, 'Hold the plane.'

I had been renting my ill-lit box for more than a year, but I had only recently discovered that, if I went along the corridor and stepped into the cleaners' store-room, there was another door giving access on to a flat roof which afforded a wonderful view of the city. Standing there, however, was not without its risks.

There was a definite slope to it, and no guardrail, so a good gust of wind or an overnight frost could have you over, but, if you were careful, it was well worth it. It probably broke the Trade Descriptions Act for roof terraces, but I loved it. This day, there was barely a breeze. Finn had a bemused look on his face as he carried his plastic chair through the storeroom and up the stairs. I set my chair facing out across the city, and indicated for him to do the same. This wasn't only for the view, but to allow him to talk more freely. Even when you're a corporate vice president like Michael Finn, it can be hard to get the words out if the subject is personal as well as business.

'Beautiful,' he said, nodding up at the Cave Hill. 'The times . . .' He smiled at the memory of something, but then quickly sucked it back in. 'I do have a fondness for this place. When it came to choosing a university for her, I suggested Belfast. Everyone was against it, but when we looked at the figures, it wasn't only one of the safest places in the UK, it was one of the safest in the entire world. She needed to go somewhere she could let her hair down, without security all over her or the paps shadowing her every step. She needed to be someone other than Thomas Wolff's daughter. London was out of the question. For a while it was New York, but her dad wanted her close by so it was easier to see her. And, in my defence, Belfast had been quiet for—'

'I know,' I said. 'I remember it fondly.'

'Anyway – she took some persuasion but, once she

was here, she loved it. We gave her a new name, background, and she enjoyed all that. She had her own apartment, lots of friends. Her security detail was always there, but not so obvious that anyone could tell. And then, when things started to get a bit sticky and we wanted to pull her out – well, she refused. She was settled – friends, exams coming up. She just said no.'

'And Daddy said . . .?'

'Mr Wolff wasn't happy, but, you know kids, they have a way of—'

'Tell me about it,' I said.

'So we upped her security, she was well briefed on where she could and couldn't go, and the importance of giving us advance warning. But, then . . .' He shook his head again. His eyes roved out across the city. The Europa Hotel had company these days: bigger, flashier joints that had sprung up as part of our peace dividend. I wasn't sure if we were supposed to give them back now that we were killing each other again. 'We know she was in a bar in east Belfast, that someone gave her or slipped her crush. She had a bad reaction, but made it to this student party on William Street. We know she made a call to her security team about the time the shooting started but, when they got there, there were bodies all over the place and no trace of her.'

For a while William Street was up there with the classics – Enniskillen, Omagh, the Miami Showband, Ballykelly, Teebane, Kingsmill, Greysteel: a list of shame, a list of butchered innocents, all of them regarded then and now as own goals because the bloodiness of their execution had hindered rather than helped their originators' stated intent, had lost them political or popular support, had cost them funds and damaged their precious PR. There had been a war going on back then, and then it was over, and now it was not. We were back in a world of carnage, but the rules had changed so much that eight teenagers shot dead at a party at William Street only managed to hold our attention for a few weeks, until it was supplanted by another, deadlier massacre, and another.

Same balaclavas, different heads.

No matter what they claimed, it wasn't about the politics any more. It had *never* been about religion, but within the terrible violence there had always been a political agenda. They had all dipped their toes in gangsterism along the way to fund their campaigns, and some had enjoyed it so much they'd ventured in right up to their necks, but always with that default setting that they were fighting the good fight, and they had their flags and slogans to prove it. But now, now they hardly even bothered with all that. They were calling them 'gang-bangers' now. And the gangs had names straight out of Dickens or Holmes: the Ramsey Street Wheelers, the Donegal Road Retrievers, the Church Hill Regulars, the Reservoir Pups, the Strand Road Agitators. There were dozens of them now, carving up the city. William Street wasn't the first and it certainly wouldn't be the last. Nine builders on a bus. A flower shop raining petals and limbs. And how much worse if you stuck your pretty little head up and complained about it? A nine-year-old south-Belfast girl, Stefani Wilkinson, began a YouTube blog detailing how drugs were devastating her nice middle-class school. The Retrievers told her to shut it down, but too late. It went viral. Half a million hits. Comedian Ricky Gervais re-tweeted it to his three million followers. She appeared on *Newsnight* and, via Skype, on *The Late Show with David Letterman* on CBS. She had charisma and guts, he said. The next day, they stopped her mum's Land Cruiser on the school run and shot the little girl in her gutsy guts. She was airlifted to safety in England like she was being spirited out of some remote fucking Third World outpost.

Yes, indeed, it was all going to Pol Pot. It was no surprise that Alison's disappearance wasn't very high up the Police agenda. If they'd known who she was, they'd have thrown more at it, but that was Wolff's call.

'The advice we had at the time from our own experts,' said Finn, 'was not to reveal her true identity to the police or general public. If whoever had taken her knew who she was, we knew they would soon be in touch. If they didn't, then it would make her too valuable a commodity, increase the risk to her, if she was being held. So we waited, and we waited, but no demands, and then, as time went on, the perception was that, if we suddenly named her, then Mr Wolff would come across badly for trying to keep it quiet, that his judgement would be called into question, which would . . .' He raised his hands. 'Well . . .'

'Affect the bottom line?'

He took a deep breath. 'Nine months on,' he said, 'and Alison's now nothing more than a false name on a digital file.'

'And if you had to take a wild guess? What's your gut instinct?'

His shirt was still done up tight, despite the heat, and there were drops of sweat on his forehead. He took a handkerchief out of his trouser pocket and dabbed at them. He gave me a half smile and said, 'Old fashioned, I know. But Mother insists.' He crumpled it into his hand. 'Police say she's most likely just a runaway, got spooked by the massacre and has dropped out of sight or gotten out of the country. But I know her; well, she wouldn't . . . Her passport, credit cards – all untouched. I think it's more likely it got out who she was through her friends, or someone recognised her, or she let it slip when she was crushed. They tried to kidnap her but they screwed up and she was accidentally shot and died later, or she tried to escape and was killed. Either way, they took her with them and buried her somewhere. Mr Wolff is pretty much resigned to that; he just wants her back so he can do things right, not have her lying in some fucking field somewhere.' There were suddenly tears in his eyes. 'Sorry,' he said.

I had lost one too. One that wasn't mine. I knew the feeling.

'I've been with Wolff for a lot of years,' Finn said, 'and I might have been international head of this and that, but sometimes I was chief baby-sitter as well. We were close.' He looked out across the city again. 'This fucking place; it does my head in. I love it – but, Christ, I could never live here again.'

'Ah,' I said, 'it gets in your bones.'

'Cancer gets in your bones,' said Finn.

3

Finn said he would email everything he had on Alison as soon as he got back to London. I gave him my bank account details and he promised to transfer my fee. It was not insubstantial. When he told me exactly how much, I said, 'Great, that'll keep the wolf from the door.' He didn't smile. He said he would be opening a separate cash account that I could draw on to cover my expenses.

He said, 'Mr Wolff is not short of money. If you need to spend it to find out what you need to find out, then spend it.'

I said, 'OK.'

He shook my hand at the top of the stairs and wished me good luck. I had warned him that I might not be able to physically find Alison's body because we had a long history of disappearing people for good, quite often in peat bogs, but that I should at least be able to find out what had happened to her. He said, 'That would be something.' He nodded and turned away, but then swivelled back and said, 'The police really came to a dead end on this. How're you even going to . . .?'

'I'd thought about maybe putting posters up on trees.'

He took a deep breath. 'Sorry. I know. I'm just . . . But, absolutely. Just . . . do your best. She's . . .'

'I'm on it,' I said.

He nodded gratefully and turned back down the stairs. He got about halfway before I said, 'One more thing?' He stopped and turned again. 'Who the hell came up with "Katya Cummings"? It sounds like a porn name.'

'She did.'

'Right. OK. Makes you think, though.'

'No,' said Finn, 'it doesn't.'

He gave me a warning nod and, by way of trade, I gave him a grin back. He was about to say something else, as if he didn't want to let a dog he'd only recently purchased off the leash, when fortuitously my phone started to ring from the office and I thumped back towards it. He raised a hand, understanding, and finally continued on down and out. For someone who was vice president of this and vice president of that, he seemed quite vulnerable, and I supposed it was because he cared for the girl so much. You didn't have to be a blood relative to be devastated by a loss. I knew that much.

I hurried back to the office and picked up my mobile and saw that it was Patricia calling. I briefly considered not answering. I was already late with her money. She had a wide vocabulary of swear words she liked to employ when this happened. I was in good form because I now had a well-paying job, but I wanted to enjoy actually having the money for a while before handing over so much of it to her. I would maybe treat myself to a beer or three and a new pair of shoes.

But I answered it anyway.

I always do.

I said, 'Hello, babes; what's happening?'

Patricia said, 'I want you to come home.'

'I knew you'd cave in eventually.'

'Dan – I need you to come home right now.'

'Even better . . .'

'Oh, for fuck's sake, will you just get round here?! Bobby's gone and fucking done it this time!'

She cut the line.

I had only just been thinking that you didn't have to be a blood relative to be devastated by a loss, but now I realised that you *did* actually have to be one to care about the fate of a surly, one-legged teenager like Bobby. Bobby, who had attached himself like a leech to my family, was at least partially responsible for replacing me as the man of the house. Bobby wasn't my son, stepson, adopted son or foster son, but had been bequeathed to me by someone I barely knew. He was an unwanted gift, an unasked-for gift, but nevertheless one that couldn't be returned to the shop for a refund, or even exchanged for something useful, like a hammer. He was a drug dealer who'd run foul of the paramilitaries. When his mum stood up to their threats, they had burned her house down, with her inside it. He seemed to think that my tenuous contribution to his mum's demise made me somehow responsible for his future well-being. Because I am, as Fatimah had rightly deduced, big of spirit, I had reluctantly taken him under my wing for what was supposed to be a very brief period; he had used this rare outbreak of charitable behaviour to ruthlessly inveigle his way into Patricia's affections and under her roof, the very same roof, incidentally, under which I was no longer welcome, mostly because the late Mrs Starkey had come to the conclusion that I was not only a wanker, but an irredeemable one. That was, of course, just her opinion. Opinion is subjective. If it becomes two people's opinion, then it moves towards being a consensus. Shortly after Patricia put forward the motion that I was indeed a wanker, Bobby seconded it and it was duly carried.

It was only a five-minute drive to her house – *my* house – or one hour and five minutes, if you stop off for a pint first. Or two hours and five minutes if you throw in a game of pool and the last ten minutes of an early-afternoon football match televised from Serbia and featuring one British team I had no love for and the best team in Belgrade, which wasn't saying much. But I watched it nevertheless, because it was football and, no matter what Patricia wanted or Bobby had done, it couldn't have been that urgent if they were turning to me to deal with it. It was not only in matters of private investigation that I was often the last resort.

The match was on a Wolff TV channel. Nobody else

seemed to be watching it. The bar, on Botanic Avenue, was busy enough, given the sweltering conditions outside. A crusher with big zonked eyes sitting beside me, as pale as an albino's corpse, clutching a Guinness in a skeletal hand, said, 'This would be a great wee country if we had weather like this all the time.'

And I said, 'This would be a great wee country if we stopped shooting each other.'

And he said, 'A bird in the hand is worth two in the bush,' and asked if I would buy him a pint. When I said no, he said, 'Paedo,' and when I shrugged, he said, 'Gay,' and I bought him a pint anyway because, for the moment, I was flush and bouncy, neither of which could last. When he staggered to the toilet, I moved to a different part of the bar.

I picked up a *Belfast Telegraph*. There had been another few shootings around the city overnight. The worst was a drive-by at a bus stop on the Malone Road, which left half a dozen seriously injured. Crime reporter Sara Patterson's report was sober, concise, yet detailed, and blamed it on a feud between the Strand Road Agitators and the South Belfast Flying Squad. The story name-checked several other gangs who coveted the prosperous Malone Road. If I hadn't exactly told Finn that I had insider knowledge of Belfast's sordid underbelly, I had inferred it, and actually I had also kind of believed it. But even a brief glance at the paper reminded me that my knowledge was old knowledge. I had heard of some of these groups, but only with a vague kind of nodding awareness you pick up second hand. I was like a football manager who'd been out of the game for several years being suddenly catapulted back into the Premier League, only to find that the techniques and tactics that had once brought him so much success were hopelessly out of step with the modern game.

The crusher came back from the toilet. I saw him looking around the bar for me, but I kept the paper raised high. He drained the pint I'd bought him and moved towards the door. I flicked on to an inside page. An opinion piece was reflecting on the mounting demand for British soldiers to be brought back into Belfast to help quell the violence. We had 'enjoyed' our own Assembly and a reasonable amount of autonomy for many years, but the perception was that if the violence escalated much further then there would be no alternative but to bring in the troops, which would cause the Republicans to walk out of the Assembly, which would cause it to collapse, thus kicking off the whole civil war again. There were those who believed that the upsurge in gang violence was being orchestrated for exactly that purpose. I had been around for a long time and floundered into many conspiracies, so I supposed it was possible. But what was going on didn't have that feeling about. It stank of money and greed.

When I lowered the paper again, the crusher was standing right in front of me.

'Do I smell or somethin'?' he growled.

'Yes,' I said, and departed.

* * *

'You're late,' Patricia snapped, 'always late.' She ushered me in through her (my) quarter-open front door, as if she didn't want the neighbours to know I was calling. 'Kitchen,' she said. 'This way.'

I knew which way it was. I had walked it ten thousand times and, several times, crawled it. The hall was dark from the wood panelling we'd inherited and which we had always sworn we would rip out but never had. The kitchen door was half open and I could see Bobby at the table, swinging back on his chair. He was in a tracksuit. He'd put on weight. As I entered the room, I said, 'Don't swing on the chair, Bobby, it'll break.'

He snorted and kept on swinging. There was a girl at the end of the table. She was also wearing a track-suit. She had a lovely face, but it was spoiled by a cigarette.

I said, 'Don't smoke in the house.'

'Christ!' said Bobby.

The girl showed me the cigarette and said, 'It's electric; I'm tryin' to give up.'

I shook my head and said, 'How old are you?'

'Fourteen.'

'Christ!' said Bobby again.

'I'll fill the kettle,' said Patricia, and started.

I looked at Bobby. He looked away. I looked at the girl. She studied the table.

'Right,' I said, looking from one to the other, 'you've either been done for shoplifting, drugs or she's up the bubble.'

'*Up the bubble*?' said Patricia. 'Christ!'

'Christ!' said Bobby.

The girl just nodded and said, 'I am up the bubble.'

'Yours?' I asked Bobby.

He shrugged.

'Don't shrug at me, Bobby; have you—?'

'What the fuck's it got to do with you?'

'While you're under this roof you—!'

'Stop!' Patricia turned from the sink, her hand raised. 'Stop shouting. Believe you me, there's been enough of it in this house these last few days. Dan – sit down. We're going to talk this through calmly and see what we're going to do.'

'We,' I said, under my breath, as I pulled out a chair.

'I heard that,' said Patricia. 'Now do you want a cup of tea?'

'No,' I said. I'd barely sat down, but I was up again and opening the fridge. There were many pots of yoghurt, several leeks and six bottles of Corona in a cardboard holder. I took the box out and set it on the table. I lifted one of the bottles and handed it to Bobby. He raised the neck to his mouth and twisted the cap off with his teeth before handing it back to me. He had his uses. I said to Trish, her back to me and pouring from the kettle, 'Do you want one?'

'No, I'm off it.'

I tutted.

She said, 'I heard that.'

I took a second bottle and held it out to Bobby. He shook his head. 'You off it too?'

'No. But Corona is so gay. You're gay.'

'Good to know.'

He looked at Patricia. 'We have any Bucky?'

'I don't think so, Bobby,' said Trish. 'Especially as *Bucky* seems to have played a starring role in getting us here.'

Buckfast. Nectar of the fucked-up Gods.

'It's not funny,' said Patricia.

It was, though. My one-legged leech had gotten his one leg over, and now I had absolutely no doubt that he, he and she, he and she and her, were about to ask me to somehow take responsibility for the consequences of that.

I offered the second bottle to the girl.

Patricia said, 'Do you think that's appropriate? She's fourteen and eight months.'

'And up the bubble,' I said, 'so she's advanced for her years, and months.'

She took the bottle. She bit the cap off with her teeth, just like her beau. It was sweet that they had something in common besides tracksuits and parenthood. She spat the top out on to the table. It slid along a bit then fell over the edge and on to the floor before rolling away. We all followed its progress.

When it finally stopped, I said to the girl, 'Aren't you going to pick that up?'

'In my condition?'

But she said it with a smile as wide as the Sargasso Sea, cheeky and charming in equal measure, and suddenly I knew exactly why Bobby might have fallen for her, if indeed he had.

I took a deep breath, the first of what would surely be many to come, and put my hand out.

'In case you don't know,' I said, 'I'm Dan.'

She took hold of it and said, 'And, in case you don't know, I'm Lolita.'

My eyes flitted up to Patricia. She nodded.

'Christ!' I said.

4

And, verily, there was a great wailing and gnashing of teeth.

And that was just Patricia. She had become attached to Bobby in a way that I had not. But then, she had lost a son many years before, a son who would have been Bobby's age now. Any two-bit psychiatrist could make the connection. Patricia's son had not been my son, though I had raised him as such; his loss had nearly destroyed me, nevertheless, but it had been one million times worse for her. She had been locked in a bunker with him and forced to watch him die. And I was the reason that she had been locked in that bunker. Our relationship had always been rocky but, since our loss, it had foundered on guilt and blame. It said a lot that she now seemed to prefer the company of Bobby, a teenage druggy who had only narrowly escaped prison for stabbing someone to death, to mine. There was nothing on paper, but in reality she was now his stepmum. She had taken him out of his old school and, after a brief flirtation with a butchery apprenticeship, she had steered him into a local college. Lolita, or Lol as she was known, was in his former school and a year younger. When I asked how long they'd been going out, they both shrugged; when I asked how many dates they'd been on, they sniggered; Patricia did too. She said, 'Get with the programme, old man,' and then they sniggered at her too.

'Lol,' I said. 'Lol. I prefer it to Lolita. And I hope it stands for what there is between you two idiots.' They looked at me, confused. 'Lots of love,' I said, to clarify.

More sniggering, a snort and a guffaw.

'Laughs,' said Patricia. 'It's "lots of laughs". Even I know that.'

'Laugh out loud, *actually*,' I said, and as she made a face I tried not to think about the *Sorry for your loss, lol* card I had recently sent to a widowed friend. 'So, what do your parents think about this?'

'They don't know,' said Lol. 'And they're not going to.'

'Don't you think—?'

'No.'

But still with that smile. It could stop traffic.

'So,' I said, 'do you want to tell me how you got yourselves into this situation?'

I was aware of Patricia rolling her eyes.

'Sex in the front seat of a Renault Laguna,' said Lol.

'Great,' I said.

'We would have used the backseat, but someone else was using it.'

'They were blootered,' said Bobby, and they both giggled.

'I told you a million times to use protection,' said Trish.

'Ah, sure, they were carried away with the romance of it,' I said. 'And by-the-bye, where did you get a Renault Laguna?'

'Dan, that's not really relevant,' said Trish.

I was still looking at Bobby. He shrugged.

'Stolen,' I said. 'And, at the very moment of conception, he's already a thief.'

'Or she is,' said Lol.

She took a long swig of her bottle. She was trying to appear smart, cocky, in control, but it was a front. Had to be. Even fourteen-year-olds who know everything, actually know nothing. She had to be scared.

Patricia said, 'Lol wants to have a . . . She wants to get . . .' She waved her hand rather than said the words. 'She is only six weeks gone. Our boy –' and she indicated Bobby – 'is more in favour of her keeping it and—'

'And how exactly are you going to manage that?' I asked.

Bobby shrugged.

'Well,' said Trish, 'one possibility is . . . we could . . .'

'Right,' I said.

'Dan, don't dismiss something before . . .'

I looked at Lol. 'Do *you* have a plan?'

'I can't have it . . .' she said. 'I'm too young. I want to do stuff.'

'You can still do stuff,' said Trish.

'Right,' I said.

'*Dan* . . .'

'I'm just saying, when you're fourteen, nine months is like nine years. And that's just you getting to the starting line.' I nodded down the table. 'Do you really think this fella is ready to be a dad?'

'I can do it,' Bobby said, looking at me properly for the first time.

'Really?'

'People do it all the time. Since the Stone Age. You don't need a fucking degree.'

'Watch your language,' I said.

'Watch your own fucking language.'

'In the Stone Age,' I said, 'they went out and caught their food, you couldn't catch a KFC.'

'Dan,' said Trish, 'there's no need for that.'

'Well,' I said.

Silence descended. Bobby and Lol smirked at each other, which was, I suppose, a good sign.

Lol took a drag on her electronic cigarette. 'Look,' she said, 'I appreciate youse inviting me round and all that, and I've listened to what you have to say, Patricia – and, to a lesser extent –' she nodded at me – 'but I know what I have to do. And the sooner . . .' She raised her hands. 'I've looked into it; it's just a question of . . . you know . . . money.'

'Which is where muggins comes in,' I said.

'It's not just about the money,' said Trish.

'It's exactly about the money,' said Lol. 'Your son . . .' And she indicated Bobby.

I said, 'Uh-huh . . .'

'It's about making the right decision,' said Trish. She had been leaning against the sink, nursing a cup of tea. Now she set it on the table and sat. She reached out to take Lol's hand, but Lol held it back. 'We know you've made your mind up. But please believe me, what seems absolutely right and certain now, in a couple of months you might see that it's not right, and you'll hate yourself for what you've done. Doing this, there's no going back.'

'I can have another,' said Lol. She nodded at Bobby. 'We can have another, if you like.'

'I'd prefer this one,' said Bobby.

'I'm not going to school like a fucking whale,' said Lol.

'You could take time out,' said Trish.

'Go to the country for a cure,' I said.

Lol and Bobby both looked confused.

Trish just shook her head at me. 'If you've nothing sensible to say—'

'OK,' I said. 'But, look, we want to be sensible here. She . . . *You're* not the first girl this has happened to. And the solution is tried and tested. It's quick; it's efficient. Ticket to London, fly in, get it sorted, fly out. Generations of good Ulster girls have done it . . .'

'Dan . . .' Patricia began.

'I'm serious; it's like joining the Brownies and getting legless on Vodka: it's a rite of passage.'

'You're not helping. Please. And that's not how it's done any more.'

'Why, is it suddenly legal round here?'

We were, and always had been, behind the times.

'No,' said Trish, 'and yes.'

'Well, I'm glad we cleared that up.'

'There's a new clinic opened. The Braxton—'

'They can do it,' Lol cut in suddenly, 'if I'm no more than twelve weeks and it's causing me distress, or if it's necessary to save my life or dangerous to my mental health. And it will be, believe you me.'

'OK,' I said.

'And it costs four hundred and fifty pounds.'

'And we're back to muggins. But good to save on the air fare.'

'It is the best place to go. They give advice,' said Trish, 'they can tell you your options . . . They absolutely want what's best for you.'

'So you've both checked this out?' I asked.

'Of course,' said Trish. 'That's why we've called you. We've an appointment tomorrow afternoon.'

'And you want me on hand . . .'

'For moral support.'

'. . . to sign the cheque.'

'Exactly,' said Lol.

Bobby was staring up the table at her. 'You're not killing my baby,' he said.

'She's just going to talk to them,' said Trish.

'You're not killing my baby,' said Bobby.

5

Trish asked me to give Lol a lift home. I said I wasn't going in that direction. Trish asked about her overdue maintenance and I said now I was going in that direction and that I was just waiting for a cheque to clear. She said nobody sent cheques any more and fixed me with a look. Lol got up and headed to the front door. Bobby remained where he was, at the table, but became aware that I was looking at him, in a successful attempt to change the subject.

He said, '*What*?' in that very high-pitched whine only opera singers and teenagers can achieve.

My eyes shifted to the departing Lol and my eyebrows rose, but he just looked confused, so I said, 'Aren't you going to see her out?'

The '*Why*?' that came back at me was dripping with disdain.

Trish rubbed my arm and said, 'Leave it; I'll talk to him. And thanks.'

'My pleasure,' I said.

Lol lived in south Belfast. She didn't say anything for the first five minutes of our journey. Then I caught myself in two minds about whether to run a red light and decided to go for it, only to get a blast of horns and a near miss for my trouble, and she said, 'You shouldn't be drinking and driving. Baby on board.'

'I'm not drinking and driving,' I said. 'I had one Corona.'

'You had four, I had two; the carton was empty when we left.'

'If you insist. Anyway, Corona is like flavoured water, no strength to it at all. But it takes the edge off the heroin.'

She smiled.

I said, 'So, you and Bobby . . .'

'What about us?'

'Having a baby.'

She sighed. 'He says you give him a hard time.'

'I try to keep him on the right path.'

'And how's that working out for you?'

'He's a work-in-progress,' I said.

We turned into her street and she pointed at her house; I let out a low whistle. It was a terrace, but one of the old ones which seemed to go up forever, and probably had about nine bedrooms. There was a long, sloping garden which was putting-green trim.

'Brothers, sisters?'

She shook her head.

'Mother, father?'

'Mother. Dad's away.'

'Sorry.'

'I'm not.'

'Are you sure you don't want me to come up and have a word?'

'Certain,' she said, and got out. She started to walk away, then stopped and came back to the car, leaned in the open window and said, 'Thank you. My mum would go through me if she knew.'

She turned and hurried up her garden path.

I sat and drummed the wheel. I knew from sad past experience that, once you started lying about something or covering it up, it seldom ended well. I was armed with knowledge which could dramatically change the girl's life, but already drawn into a conspiracy of silence. I briefly debated whether I should go and knock on the door and tell her mum about the trouble she was in. What if something happened to her in the getting rid of the baby, something I might have been able to prevent, if I'd only informed on her? Or if she kept it, at exactly what stage would her mum find out, and would that not poison our future relations? Bobby wasn't a blood relative, but Trish cared deeply about him and, because I cared deeply about her, I had by association to consider Bobby's future, his girl's future and their baby's future. And I suppose I had to admit that I cared just a tiny, minuscule bit about the boy. I had gone through hell to ensure his survival. Bloody hell. He had been screwed up by life; meeting Trish had started him on the right road; who was I to say that having a baby wouldn't help him complete that journey, even if he was a couple of years short of legal?

As I thought about this, I became aware of two young women moving up the street towards me, dressed in the increasingly familiar garb of the New Seekers with their little cross logo with a blazing sun behind. I sank a little lower in my seat, praying that they wouldn't spot me and feel the need to stop and convert me.

They were becoming a real hassle. Some genius had come up with the marketing idea that what the increasing numbers of happy-clappy born-againers around Belfast really needed to help push their message was a *uniform*. *Here*, in the land of the paramilitary! What they'd come up with sat somewhere between a nun's habit and *Thunderbirds*. And all in brilliant white. When they started off, it seemed like there were just a handful of them, curiosities to be stared at or to hurl abuse at, but they seemed to be multiplying in direct response to the upsurge in violence. Now it felt like they were everywhere, on every corner, just waiting for an opportunity to collar you and ram their beliefs down your throat, because they were, actually, quite aggressive, and all with the tunnel thinking and conviction which usually comes with being a righteous zealot. Originally, they had been tied to an umbrella organisation of local churches before going their own way, and they had boasted an unwieldy name until someone sarcastically christened them the New Seekers. It had stuck, and they had quickly embraced it. A comedian had dubbed them the military wing of the Presbyterian Church, and I suspected he was not far wrong. But they had the last laugh; shortly thereafter, he was knocked down by a car. But it was just an accident.

These two were as young and innocent looking as any of them, but it was a mask that hid steely conviction. I held my breath as they came up close to the car, hoping they would be fooled by my inspired decision to lower the sun visor, and then cursed under it as they stopped beside me. I was all set to fire the engine and take off before they could smash in my window and haul me out for crimes against the soul, when they turned into Lol's driveway. I eased back up in my seat and saw that they were moving, arm in arm, up the steps to her front door. They might have been cold calling – it's something they're obliged to do to spread the message and make new recruits – or perhaps their divine radar had detected an unplanned pregnancy. They knocked and I had a brief glimpse of a woman with short dark hair, in a grey shirt and blue jeans, who answered the door with a smile and quickly ushered them inside. She looked, very briefly, towards my car, before closing the door.

I kept looking up at the house. I drummed my fingers on the steering wheel. Lol was nothing to do with me *at all*. I'd only known her half an hour. But I knew I was already getting protective. Lol had a gob on her. I liked that. You can just tell who's smart and who isn't;

it's not about exam results or jobs, it's about the fire in your eyes. I've no time for zealots of any conviction, and now Lol's mum had just invited two of them into her house. If they found out Lol was pregnant, they would prevent her from getting rid of it because they believed in the sanctity of life. And then they would also probably stone her to death.

I wanted to go straight up and whisk her out of there. I actually had the door half open. But I slammed it shut again because I was self-aware enough to know that my interference in any given situation has *never* helped. Destruction and despair follow in my wake. Professionally, it sometimes helps. In reacting to me, bad guys sometimes reveal themselves. *That* was where I needed to focus: on the job in hand, not on my one-legged teenager or his knocked-up girlfriend with the killer smile. Let Patricia do the running. I should content myself with signing the cheques. Lol and Bobby were at a difficult crossroads, but at least they were alive, they could make their choices. Alison Wolff – or Katya Cummings – was dead. Almost certainly. Nobody disappeared without trace, not for nine months, not in a city this size. She was the only daughter of one of the richest and most powerful men on the planet, but in an attempt to forge her own personality and build her own future, she had chosen Belfast, of all places, and Belfast had repaid her faith in it in its usual style. I had no connection to her at all, but I had a huge connection to Belfast. I loved it and loathed it in equal measure, but I was part of it and it was part of me, which meant that in some stupid, fucked-up way I was as responsible for Alison's disappearance as any man, woman or child walking our shotgun streets. We hadn't pulled the trigger, but we had colluded in it. So I was getting paid to find her, but it was also a responsibility. I would discover her fate, and in so doing I would be standing up and saying on behalf of everyone else who hated what was going on:

This is not what we are.

We are better than this.

6

Although it had been nine months since the massacre at William Street, I supposed that there would still be some evidence there that it had happened – a plaque on a wall in memory of the dead or even a bunch of flowers left by a grieving relative – but there was nothing. I had to stop and ask a woman, shepherding her children in from a Range Rover, which one it was, and she pointed it out, but then quickly added, 'Or maybe the next . . .'

The street smelled of freshly mown lawns, barbecues and newly laid tarmac. Number eighteen had been recently painted and had what looked like new double-glazed windows. It was three storeys high, with a skylight in the roof, and had recently been converted into apartments. There was a *For Rent* sign attached to the wall. It was a little after six p.m. I had just come for a brief recce but, seeing as Michael Finn's files weren't due until the morning and I'd nothing better to do with my time, I decided that there was no time like the present, so I rang the only one of three bells with a name attached. An Indian guy answered, peering out at me with his eyes scrunched up against the sun. I said I was interested in renting an apartment; he said it was supposed to go through an agent. I said I knew that, but was just passing by and spotted it and was hoping for a quick look round. Was he, by any chance, the owner? He opened the door a bit wider and took a proper look at me. He said, 'Two flats, newly converted, no sublets.'

I said, 'I don't intend to.'

He got some keys. He had the ground-floor apartment, which was open, to the left. He led me up the stairs. 'Eight hundred a month,' he said, 'bills on top.'

'Lived here long?' I asked.

He shook his head.

'I heard something happened here.'

He said, 'Long time ago. People come round looking for it cheaper because, but no way, Jose.'

I said, 'I don't suppose you looked for a discount when you bought it?'

He said, 'What's sauce for goose, is sauce for gander,' and I was still puzzling over that when he opened the door into the first-floor apartment. It smelled of Dettol and wallpaper paste, not carnage.

I said, 'You ever meet the owners? They must have been pretty badly shaken up.'

'No,' he said. 'Emersion heater, gas central heating and cooker.'

I said, 'Eight dead. Is that what it's like round here?'

'No, never; respectable area, not a single trouble since I moved here.'

I said, 'You would say that.'

He said, 'Swear; ask the neighbours.'

So I did. I knocked on a few doors, told them I was thinking of moving into the area, and they pretty much agreed. William Street was close to Belfast University's campus, but most of the houses were still family owned and occupied rather than broken up into student flats, as they were just a few streets away. It was to one of these ordinary middle-class homes that Katya and her friends had come in search of a party thrown by two boys whose parents were out of the country for the weekend. It was just supposed to be for close friends, but word had gotten out. Hundreds laid siege to the house. One of the neighbours told me there'd been a near riot when people couldn't get in and then started fighting amongst themselves. The police had broken it up, made arrests, but, as soon as they left, the party started up again. The neighbours seemed to think that the massacre had been the work of some of those people who hadn't been able to get in and who'd then been attacked outside, coming back to take revenge – with the two brothers finally paying with their lives, along with six of their student friends. The brothers' broken-hearted parents had sold up almost immediately, with the Indian indeed getting the house at a knock-down price and then converting it into flats, which hadn't gone down well. Finn hadn't mentioned anything about a riot outside the party, though it was probably in the paperwork he was sending.

I drove to my apartment at St Anne's Square, which was located in what has become known, thanks to heavy marketing, as the Cathedral Quarter. There was indeed something that looked like a cathedral, and called itself a cathedral, right next door to me, but technically it wasn't a cathedral at all because, although it served two dioceses, it was the seat of neither and therefore it didn't have its own bishop. But it did have a forty-metre high stainless-steel spire called the Spire of Hope protruding out of it, which, although it was nice to look at, had thus far failed to inspire hope in me. But it was good to know that God was so close at hand.

As soon as I got in, I kicked the bills out of the way and opened the curtains and then the French doors on to the veranda – it makes it sound way plusher than it is – to let some air in. I opened a can and went to sit outside in the cooling early-evening sun. At this hour, the square below would normally have been quietening down, but this night it was buzzing because of the weather. The cafés had shifted most of their tables outside and there was music and chatter drifting up to me on the first floor, all mixed and indistinct but also somehow comforting. Clusters of theatre-goes were drifting towards the MAC complex in the far corner and, to my right, I could see the third-floor gym of the Ramada Hotel. I had joined the first day I moved in. I used it for three hours that day and hadn't been back since, though I was still paying them thirty quid a month for the pleasure of not going. Joining the gym was not my only concession to getting fit: I also had a window box now, in which I was endeavouring to grow a tomato plant. I had never knowingly consumed a tomato in its original, rounded, tomatoey state, but, if this plant managed to actually produce one, then I had resolved to radically alter my diet and actually consume it, raw. From further afield there came the crackle of a hugely amplified blues guitar. The Open House Festival was setting up for a weekend of gigs.

The square, the theatre, the hotel – all busy, all relaxed, all enjoying the unfamiliar sunshine, and none of the people in them yet so deterred by the upsurge in violence that they were afraid to venture out. But that day was coming. I was old enough to remember Belfast in the darkness of the seventies when the city centre literally shut down at the end of the working day.

Nobody wanted that now.

But then nobody had much wanted it then.

I sipped my drink and checked my phone to see if Finn had managed to email the files across, but there was nothing yet. I lifted the paper I'd taken from the bar and studied the lead story again. I had always thought I had my finger on the pulse, but now I could barely detect it. I needed to talk to an expert. I phoned the *Telegraph* and asked for crime reporter Sara Patterson in editorial. After three rings, a man with a slightly camp south-Belfast accent said, 'Sara Patterson's phone.' I asked for her. 'Can I ask who's calling?'

'Dan Starkey,' I said.

'OK, right, Dan Starkey. From . . .?'

'From . . . I used to work there. As a reporter.'

'Really? I'm not long here. Recently, is this?'

'Not that long ago,' I said.

'Dan . . . Starkey. Was it under Mr Devine, our editor?'

'No, before him. Is she—?'

'Mr Todd, then.'

'Before him.'

'Right. I see. I think that was . . . old Mr Jennings? They always say *legendary* Mr Jennings.'

I cleared my throat. 'Before him. Now do you—'

'*Before*? When was this exactly?'

'I don't exac . . . Ahem; ninety-three, if you must know. I finished in ninety-three.'

'I was born in ninety-three!'

'Could you just put her on the fucking line?'

There were several moments of shocked silence. And then, 'I'm afraid Ms Patterson is not on duty this evening.'

'Right. Then could you possibly take—'

He hung up. And then I became aware that someone was saying, 'Hello?' and I looked around, confused, and then it came again, and this time I peered over the railing and there was a rotund man standing there, looking up. 'Oh – hello,' he said, 'you can hear me.' He had a camera round his neck. And an equally rotund woman standing beside him. 'You live there?' he asked. He was American.

'Yes,' I said.

'You're so *lucky*,' said the woman. She was also American.

'We were wondering,' said the man, 'the piazza is so beautiful and, with the sun going down, the way it's lighting up the cathedral, could we maybe come up and take a picture from your apartment, so we could get the piazza and the cathedral, and the whole quarter beyond?'

I stood. I nodded down at them.

'It's not a fucking piazza,' I said.

The man's brow furrowed. 'Excuse me?'

'What did he say?' the woman asked.

'It's a fucking square. And it's not a fucking cathedral, because there's no fucking bishop in it. And it's not a fucking quarter at all, because that's just fucking marketing shite, OK?'

'So could we come up and take a photograph?' the man asked.

'I don't understand his accent,' said the woman. 'What's he saying?'

'No you can't,' I said. 'Now FUCK OFF.'

And they did.

7

I had a strange, unsettling dream about a baby, on an island off the coast, and how one moment he was dead and the next he was brought back. It was as vague as that, and yet so familiar. He was little Stevie, the child born of Patricia's brief affair. I had come to love him as my own. I had had the dream several times in recent weeks. It always began as a nightmare before being happily resolved, yet it still left me edgy and drained each time I woke, with the joy of it only lasting as long as conscious thought took to reassert itself, and leaving in its wake a residue of regret and loss.

I showered, grabbed my laptop and walked to Starbucks for breakfast. I have nothing against multi-national chains. Familiarity is a comfort. I have a lot against idiots who stand in the queue in front of me and consider every single option on the menu for an eternity before giving their order. But I restrained myself. I was aware

I was becoming less tolerant as I grew older. I had seen it in other single, middle-aged men. It had to do with loneliness and bitterness and betrayal and the death of optimism. I did not like it but could do precious little to deny it. When I got my coffee, I found a quiet corner and fired up the computer.

True to his word, Finn had sent the Alison files through, as well as my fee to my bank account and an account number from which I could draw what appeared to be limitless amounts of cash to spend on the case. He asked me to keep receipts, but I'm not really in the receipts business. I am not unscrupulous, but I planned to live well for the next few weeks. Those plans included a second coffee. I flicked through the attachments as I sipped. Finn had sketched to me the sequence of events which had led to Alison's disappearance, and the police and private investigations into it that followed, but there was greater detail in the files: names of her friends who had accompanied her to the party; the address of her apartment and the name of the girl who'd shared it with her, but who hadn't gone to the party; copies of police statements from around a dozen kids who'd been at the party; newspaper clippings reporting the massacre and its aftermath, the outcry and the funerals; a list of the courses she had been taking and her lecturers and tutors; two separate reports by private investigation companies, one based in London, which seemed to be a rehash of what the police had discovered, and another in Belfast, which was a little better and gave me at least the name of a boy Alison was known to have been chatting to on the night of the party – 'Harry'. One of Alison's friends said she thought he had been killed at the party. I checked the list of the dead that Finn had included and, sure enough, there was a Harry Breen there. This second company had also recovered her phone, which had been fitted with a tracking device, from amongst a dozen that had been recovered from the party house.

I called Sara Patterson again, although not before practising my Scottish accent in case camp-boy answered again. But no, this time a woman answered with a crisp, 'Sara,' and I told her my name. There was a slight pause before she said, 'Yes?'

'I used to be—'

'I know who you are.'

'Good. I—'

'You're the fella who was verbally abusive to my assistant, Jeff.'

'Maybe he needs to grow a pair,' I suggested.

She hung up.

I drummed my fingers on the table. The guy with the need to read every single item on the menu was up at the counter, doing it again. The morning was still cool, but the sky outside was bright blue with no hint of a cloud. People were wearing shorts. Many of the legs passing the Starbucks window were bright red with sunburn. It was not pretty, but Belfast legs rarely are.

I phoned her back. When she answered, I said, 'We seemed to be cut off.'

'No,' she said, 'I hung up.'

'Oh. Well. I'm sorry if—'

'What can I help you with, Mr Starkey? I'm busy.'

'Well, as you may know, I used to be a reporter there . . .'

'No, I didn't know that.'

'. . . and I was just wondering if there was any chance of picking your brains about—'

'No.'

'No?'

'No. Way too busy. Since everything kicked off again, I get half a dozen requests a day for background briefings, mostly from foreign correspondents. I'd never get anything done.'

'I'm not a foreign correspondent.'

'What are you?'

'I'm just working on a story. The William Street massacre?'

'Uh-huh.'

'There was a girl went missing? She was at the party one minute and then the attack happened and she was never seen again. I've been engaged to find out what happened to her.'

'Engaged?'

'Hired.'

'To write a story?'

'To find the body.'

'You said you were writing a story.'

'I am. I will. If I find her.'

'Who are you writing it for?'

63

'No one yet.'

'But you said you were engaged to write it.'

'Hired to find the body. Look, what I'm trying to say is, I'm out of the loop a bit, I really need someone to bring me up to scratch and I don't mind paying you for your time and trouble.'

'Thanks, but no thanks.'

'The money is not an insignificant—'

'Too busy, too much bullshit, don't care.'

She hung up again.

I was beginning to suspect that we had gotten off on the wrong foot.

I headed across to my office. I spent ten minutes spending some of the money Michael Finn had paid me to settle my outstanding debts. When I was done, and back to black, I sauntered up the Lisburn Road, down University Street and crossed into the Holy Land, the nickname for the phalanx of streets with names like Jerusalem, Cairo, Palestine and Damascus, which bordered on William Street and which was mainly given over to student flats. Most of the houses on Palestine were rough and ready, but Alison's apartment was part of a recently converted three-storey block. It didn't appear luxurious by itself, but it definitely was in comparison to those surrounding it and it was altogether more suited to the teenage daughter of one of the world's richest men.

It was summer and most of the students had migrated home. I rang the bell, though mainly out of politeness.

When there was no response, I used the first of the access codes Finn had provided and let myself into the building. I took the lift to the second floor. It opened on a simple pine door with a camera above it and a similar keypad. I keyed in the second code, the mechanism clicked and I let myself into a spacious and fragrant hall. There was a telephone stand to the left, but no phone. There were three unopened letters sitting on top, one addressed to Katya Cummings, Alison's adopted name, and two to Sharon Quigg, her flatmate. Katya's letter appeared to be a reminder from Specsavers. I set the other two back down and proceeded down the hall into a well-equipped kitchen, which smelled of disinfectant. There were no dishes in the sink. The fridge was empty. The sun coming in through the window sparkled off the work surfaces. Sharon Quigg had probably given the apartment a thorough clean before going home for the summer break. There was a lounge area, with two sofas and a large-screen television with various digital and games boxes attached. The remote controls were in a neat line on a spotless coffee table. Thus far it did not feel much like a typical student flat. But that all changed when I stepped into Alison's room, which Finn's notes had told me was to the right.

As soon as I opened the door, I was assailed by opened or upturned drawers, unwashed clothes and the stink of rotting food. It looked as if it had been turned over by secret agents in search of a missing tape, but was probably just in the chaotic state that a teenager who was not expecting visitors might have left it. I stepped inside, picked my way carefully across the floor to the window and threw it open. As I turned back, I stepped in something sticky, which, on closer inspection, appeared to be the remains of a kebab. I peeled it off my shoe and rubbed my sole on the only clean square of carpet I could find. I moved to her bed, which was a large queen-size. The continental quilt lacked a cover and was tossed back, revealing a somewhat threadbare, but otherwise clean-looking sheet beneath. There were framed posters on the wall for *Lawrence of Arabia* and *The Muppet Show*. There were sets of drawers on either side of the bed, but the reading light was on the right, so I guessed that her more personal belongings would be in those ones. I knelt on several glossy magazines, which were dated eight months previously and, allowing for the fact that magazines generally bear cover dates one month ahead of when they are released, they fitted in with the timeline of Alison's disappearance. The top drawer was open and filled with half-full bottles and other containers of make-up, unopened whiskey and brandy shorts, revision notes, sweetie wrappers and a vibrator as slim and metallic as a Parker pen. It seemed impolite not to press the on switch, but there was no life in it at all, which suggested either over-use or lack of use. The bottom drawer contained a diary. I hoped for information about boyfriends or relationships, possibly with a side order of salacious revelation. She was a rich teenager on the loose in Belfast; if she hadn't gotten up to mischief, I would have been surprised. But it was blank from front to back. I checked that no pages had been removed, but the binding was perfect. An unwanted gift, probably. These days, diaries are digital and rarely private, but Alison's minders had forbidden her from using social media. I put the diary back and transferred my attention to a small alcove, which Katya had set up as a study area. There was a desk with an Apple Mac with a huge screen and her college textbooks in uneasy piles on the shelves below. I sat on her chair, switched on the computer and flicked through her books while it powered up. When I returned my focus to the screen, it was still dark but for a small box demanding a six digit password. As I optimistically began to type in her birth date, I also became aware of an almost ghostly image moving across the screen from left to right. I was just trying to understand exactly what it was when I realised, too late, that I was an idiot and that it was the reflection of a figure moving swiftly behind me. In the very act of turning to confront it, the side of my head was clattered hard with something blunt and heavy, which swept me on to the floor. The force of my landing was only slightly diminished by Alison's carpet of discarded clothes. It not only felt like my skull had been cleaved in half, it felt like it was on fire as well. I could *smell* burning flesh and knew it had to be my own. As I lay half blinded by the blood cascading down my brow, I became dimly aware that someone or something was standing over me, but I couldn't tell if they were animal, vegetable or mineral.

I whispered, 'I'm only—'

There was a very brief moment where I thought they were reaching down to help me up, but instead I was whacked again with the same blunt force.

And I was out like a light.

8

A girl was wailing, 'Oh my God, oh my God, oh my God – I've killed him!' and I was throwing up into a pile of unwashed underwear, and blood was dripping from my brow, and there was an arm around my shoulder, a man's arm, in a rough green material that smelled of disinfectant.

I said, 'I'm dying.'

And the man said, 'No, you're not; it's just smelling salts, like you'd give to a boxer; sometimes the old ways are the best.'

And I said, 'Oh, fuck off . . .'

And he said, 'Seriously. Now, let's take a look at you,' and he turned me gently on to my back and shone a torch into my eyes. He then turned my head and said, 'Ouch! She didn't half catch you.'

Behind him, the girl was beginning to take shape: a mousey blonde with her hands clasped around a damp tissue and her face tear-stained and her eyes panic-stricken. 'Is he going to die? Is he going to die?'

And the man said, 'No, he's got a tremendously thick skull, but that's not to say there isn't a crack in it, and there's a nasty burn which will need looking at . . . What on earth did you hit him with?'

She said, 'I was in my room, ironing, and I had my headphones on, and I came into this room to borrow my flatmate's charger cos, even though she hasn't been here for forever, I've always put it back when I've borrowed it before so she won't be angry when she does come back, and he was sitting there at the computer and I didn't know if he was a burglar or a rapist and I panicked and I still had the iron in my hand so I hit him with it, and then when he tried to get up, I hit him with it again. I called the police and screamed at them to come, but then I went through his pockets and found his card and realised he would have needed the codes to get in, so he mustn't be a rapist or a murderer, so I called the police back and they screamed at me for wasting their time and . . . is he going to die? There's so much blood!'

The man rubbed a sponge across my face and my vision cleared a little. I saw that he was a paramedic and that his green sleeve belonged to a green jumpsuit. He wore longish hair and a smirk.

I said, 'How long was I . . .?'

'From what she says,' said the paramedic, his eyes flitting up to the young woman, 'about an hour. I'm a rapid-response unit; I would have been here in five if she'd called, but she didn't make it until—'

'I thought I'd killed him! He was bleeding everywhere!'

'You're lucky.' The paramedic grinned. 'He seems to have had a pint to spare.'

I would have throttled him, but I didn't have the strength.

I'd been ironed.

Instead, I said to the girl, 'You're Sharon, Sharon Quigg.'

She looked surprised. 'How would you know that?' So I explained who I was and what I was about, all delivered like gossip at a funeral. And she responded with, 'Oh, holy fuck!'

I managed to sit up.

The paramedic said, 'Easy there.'

'I'm fine. Really. You and your colleague have been very good.'

'*What* colleague?'

'Joke. Really, I'm—'

'How many fingers?'

'Three,' I said.

'Two,' he said.

'Three,' I repeated.

'Three,' he agreed. 'You still need that X-rayed.'

'Later,' I said. 'For now, I just want to sit here.'

'I have the car outside; we'll be at the City in five . . .'

I shook my head and was surprised when it didn't roll off my shoulders, down the stairs and start making its own way to the hospital. Over the years, I had been beaten around more than most professional boxers and seemed to have developed something of a thick skin and skull. I felt sick and woozy, but experience told me that I would recover, and that the bruises would fade and I would only be left with the depressing memory of having been blindsided by a girl with an iron.

The paramedic tried to persuade me some more, but I was firm. He helped me up and out of the room and to a seat in the kitchen. I dripped blood the whole way, with Sharon following behind me dabbing at every drop with her damp tissue.

She said, 'Coffee?'

I said, 'A wee whiskey would probably—'

She said she didn't drink.

The paramedic suggested water and gave me painkillers and, after taking a closer look at where the blood was coming from, he said it wasn't as bad as he thought and I might get away with a couple of staples. He gave it a saline wash, a spray of an iodine antibacterial, which hurt like fuck, and some cream for the burn, and then he stapled me. It wasn't half as sore as I expected, but twice as sore as I could bear. Blood swept down my face again as he did it. He gave me another sponge off and Sharon squeezed kitchen roll into my hand. The paramedic gave me one last chance of a lift to the hospital and then left with a final, 'On your own head be it,' and departed.

When Sharon returned after seeing him out she hovered in the doorway and said, 'I'm *really* sorry.'

'Never worry,' I said. 'It goes with the job.' Then I clutched my head and said, '*Fuck*.'

* * *

The recovery process included tea and biscuits and Nurofen Plus. Sharon sat at the kitchen table watching me. She said, 'I can actually literally see the colour coming back into your cheeks.' I began to slowly open and close my jaw until it loosened sufficiently to allow me to speak words with several syllables. Sharon said, 'I'm really sorry, it's just funny living on our own, and then with Katya . . . It just scares you.'

'I need . . . to ask you . . . some questions about her,' I said.

'Because you're some kind of private detective.'

'Some kind.'

'I've never met a private detective before.'

'We're a . . . rare breed,' I said. 'Now, I have to ask you some questions. Did I say that already?'

Sharon nodded.

I pressed fingers into my brow. There was a metallic taste in my mouth. 'Questions like . . .' And I groped around for them. They were *there*, just out of reach. Eventually, I skewered one. 'How come . . . you're here rather than . . . away home with the rest of them?'

'Well,' she said, 'I'm on a three-year course, but I'm trying to squeeze it into two. So I'm studying over the summer to try and get ahead of the pack.' She nodded back towards Alison's room. 'I said to her dad about her stuff, whether I should box it up or tidy it, but he said no, leave it exactly as it is, like he expects her to come back. He keeps paying the rent, and doesn't charge me so I'll keep an eye on her stuff. Hence the . . .' She indicated my head.

'You've met the dad?'

'Yes, of course.'

'And when did you speak to him last?'

'Yesterday, actually. He's still really cut up.'

'Know the feeling,' I said.

I'd never met the man, and probably never would, but I knew he was big, with a shiny bald dome, loud suits and Havana cigar, like he'd sat down and planned out how to look like a media mogul. Still, I was surprised that, when he was supposedly trying to keep the fact that 'Katya' was his daughter under wraps, he had dropped his cover so easily with Sharon. I wondered if he'd been sitting outside my office while Finn had been hiring me. If I'd known, I would have invited him up top for a beer. When I described him as 'the big man in the big suit', Sharon's brow crinkled. A couple of simple questions later and I knew she was talking about Finn.

'Tell me about Katya,' I said.

'Messy,' said Sharon. 'Messy and funny and a bit of a pain. She didn't know she was coming to Belfast till real late and wanted to flat-share, but by the time she got here most people were sorted. Don't think she would have picked me otherwise. We're kind of opposites. We got on fine, like, but I think she thought I was a bit of a Holy Joe.'

'So you didn't party with her?'

'No, not ever, really. I'm not here to party.' She gave a little shrug. 'We're all different.'

'She had friends, though?'

'Yes, of course. But . . . well, I suppose you're looking for who she used to hang about with, who might have a better idea of what happened to her? But, the way I remember it, she didn't really have anyone you could say, "That's her besty." Do you know what I mean? She hung about with different groups, like, but never really got close to them. I mean, she never brought anyone back here.' Sharon gave a short laugh. 'I think she knew better.'

'Even though it's her flat?'

'I have my rights.'

She smiled. She was nice and nerdy. Nothing wrong with that.

'What about boyfriends?'

'Plenty. I mean, I'd see her in the Student Union and there was always someone with their arm round her. She looks fab, doesn't she? Like a model. But she didn't have anyone special that I know of.'

'No sleepovers then?'

'Sleepovers?'

'Was she having sexual relations with anyone?'

'I really wouldn't know. But not here.'

'What about Harry?'

'Harry?' She thought for a moment. 'No, I don't remember a Harry. Unless you count –' and she paused, and must have noticed a slight shift in my anticipation, and her eyes sparkled for a moment – 'your man with the glasses. Harry . . . Potter, I mean. She definitely had a thing for him. Now that is one thing we did bond over. She has all the books under her bed. We both agreed we would do him, if we had the chance, though not, of course, the early, underage version.' She let out a dirty giggle and I smiled with her, even though it hurt. 'But no, that's the only Harry I'm aware of.'

'OK,' I said, 'I'll put the young wizard on my list. What about the neighbours? Much to do with them?'

'Downstairs has been empty since I moved in. Upstairs, there were another couple of students – *mature* students, I should say.' She made a bit of a face. 'They took a shine to Katya, that's for sure, though she didn't have much time for them. Always turning up wherever she was, I noticed that. I used to joke with her that they must be listening through the floor when she was making arrangements. They moved out soon after . . .' Her brow furrowed. 'You don't think . . .?'

'I'm sure they were checked out by the police.'

I already had their names and their reports. For bodyguards, they had been remarkably unobservant and spectacularly unsuccessful. They'd probably been promoted. I was thinking about this, and then about how much my head still hurt, and that meandered into how stupid Bobby was for getting a girl up the bubble, and how awful to be carrying a baby around when your mum was a born-again nutter, when I saw that there were tears rolling down Sharon's cheeks, even though she had shut her eyes tight in an attempt to stop them flooding out.

'Sorry,' she said and dragged her arm across her face and then dug the heels of her palms into her eyes to clear them. After a bit, she said, 'She's not coming home, is she?'

I said, 'Probably not.'

'Will you find her . . . body?'

'It's unlikely, Sharon.'

'Will you find out who killed her, and make sure they are punished?'

'I don't know. Possibly not.'

'What, then, is the point of you?' she asked.

It was, I thought, a very good question.

9

I had the names of three bars Alison had visited prior to the Wellington Street party, from the few statements given by her friends to the police and to Wolff's own investigators. I visited each in quick succession, which was easy enough as they were all next door to each other in Ballyhackamore, an oasis of middle-class pretension in otherwise hard-as-nails east Belfast, halfway between the city centre and the suburb of Dundonald. With the passage of time, and the vagaries of shifts, there wasn't much point in seeking out individual staff. Instead I spoke to the managers and trusted that it would trickle down. I handed over a business card and showed them Alison's photo. I told them I was looking for information, any information, whether it was to do with the girl, who she was with, or who might have supplied her with crush. I gave each of them two hundred pounds and said there was plenty more where that came from. It was an incentive, and an investment, and an announcement.

I took a taxi back into town with the intention of going back to the office, but I diverted it to the red-brick *Belfast Telegraph* on Royal Avenue. I might not have worked there for twenty years, but I was not completely out of the journalistic loop, and a couple of calls from the backseat quickly established where I would find Sara Patterson at this hour of the day: in the Costa just opposite. In the old days, with the story done, or even while working on it, we would have retired to a bar; these days, it was all baristas and double decaf. The café was mostly empty, and she wasn't hard to pick out. She dealt with gang-bangers every day, so could – perhaps should – have kept her face out of the public eye, but there was a photo of her with nearly every story she wrote. She was good to look at. The publishers must have loved the combination of glam and guts and what it did for sales; from a health-and-safety point of view: not so hot. But sometimes you had to play that game and let trouble come to you, like you were drawing the pus. Sara was wearing a tartan shirt, black jeans and stilettos. She was sitting on a sofa, reading a paper, with her mobile sitting on top of a notebook on a table. The sofa opposite was empty. I asked if anyone was sitting there; she shook her head without looking up. I sat down. After a full minute of staring at her, she said, 'What do you want?'

'A cup of coffee and a bun would be nice,' I said.

Her eyes found me for the first time. 'Funny,' she said.

'I'm—'

'I know who you are.'

'Ah, my celebrity precedes—'

'No; the fella you phoned to ask where I was, then phoned me to tip me off.'

'OK. Then I can surmise from that that you must be interested in talking to me, otherwise you wouldn't be sitting in the place the fella told me you'd be sitting in.'

'Or that I'm not going to change my routine because some washed-up old soak won't stop annoying me.'

'Old? Washed up? *Soak*?' I shook my head. 'Two out of three ain't bad.'

'What do you *want*?'

'I told you what I want: to be brought up to speed on who does what and where.'

'Don't you read the paper?'

'Of course I do. I want what you know but can't print.'

She studied me and said, 'Who's the girl?'

'Katya Cummings.'

'I mean, who is she that you would be engaged to find her?'

'There's money in the family. Beyond that, I don't know.'

'Really? That doesn't sound like the legendary Dan Starkey.'

'Ah, so you have checked me out.'

'Yes, and, like all legends, I imagine most of it's shite.'

She turned a page of her paper.

I said, 'I've been following your articles. They're very good.'

'You would say that.'

'Well, no, actually, I wouldn't.'

She seemed to look at me properly for the first time. Her eyes narrowed. 'What happened to your head?'

'A girl hit me with an iron.'

'OK. Why did a girl hit you with an iron?'

'Because she thought I was a rapist.'

'You're doing yourself no favours here.'

'I'm aware of that. So are you going to help me out on this or not?'

'I haven't time. I'm due to meet someone.'

'Here?'

'No.'

'Where?'

'Is that any of your business?'

'No, but I could come with you, you could fill me in on the way.'

She snorted. 'You don't lack for confidence, do you?'

She stood and drained her coffee. She set it down and picked up her notebook, paper and handbag. She looked at me and shook her head.

I said, 'Look – I'll be no trouble, honestly. I just need some guidance.'

'She's been gone the best part of a year; what's the rush?'

'She somebody's daughter.'

'Well, maybe somebody should have gotten their finger out back then.' She pursed her lips. 'Fuck it, then. If you want to trail along, I'll answer whatever questions you have on the way – but that's it.'

'Brilliant.'

'And on one condition: you make a donation to Whitespots at the end. It's an—'

'Animal sanctuary. Though it hasn't been called that in a quarter of a century.'

'Yeah, well, it'll always be Whitespots,' she said.

We were out the door and trying to cross traffic to the company car park. She glanced across at me and said, 'You know she's dead, right?'

'Right.'

'This isn't the kind of place where miracles happen.'

'Know that,' I said.

10

We were driving along the West Link to Turf Lodge; it was an eight-minute journey, which was as long as she would spare me. But then almost immediately we hit traffic. There were police lights flashing up ahead near the Boucher Road. Sara gave me a look which suggested she thought I'd somehow organised it. She said 'fuck' a couple of times, before sighing and settling back. She said, 'So?'

'So, are you married?'

'What?'

'I don't see a ring, but what does that mean these days?'

'It's none of your business, Starkey.'

'Dan . . . Dan. I'm always Dan: Dan the Man.'

She rolled her eyes.

'So, going steady, is it, then?'

'I . . .'

'I know, none of my business. But, in our line, it's hard to maintain a relationship. You have to be able to not worry about other people. You're dealing with these trigger-happy morons, you don't want to be thinking about what they could do to your kids. On the other hand, lesbians.'

'You *what*?'

'Nothing to be ashamed of. Some of my best friends are gay.'

'I . . .'

'Actually, that's a lie; friends are in short supply right now. But, if I had friends, statistically—'

'Starkey, could you just cut the crap?'

'Absolutely, and Dan, please. And yes, sorry – I get nervous in the presence of beautiful women.' She kept her eyes front. 'For clarity,' I added, 'I'm talking about—'

'Just stop it. I've heard all about you. You want to know about the gangs, I'll tell you about the gangs. Nothing else. *Nothing* else. OK? Or you can get out now.'

'OK,' I said.

'Right.'

'This car smells of dog; you must have a dog?'

She sighed.

But, as the hold-up continued, I did eventually start on the questions, and she seemed to know her territory. The picture she painted was both more unpleasant and more depressing than I had imagined. I had hoped that the fairly recent removal of the Miller Brothers as the brutal joint heads of the UVF – to which I had made some small contribution last year – might have signalled the end of organised paramilitary activity in the province. Certainly the police had clamped down hard on the few remaining figureheads, but it soon became clear that the Millers' departure had left a power vacuum. It was like when Saddam got knocked off his perch in Iraq – everyone suddenly realised that, despite being a despotic monster, he had actually been doing a good job keeping a lid on things because, as soon as he was gone, everything went to shit. The seventies had seen bloated pomp rock knocked off its throne by thousands of kids embracing the DIY ethos of punk rock by forming their own bands; something similar had recently happened on the streets of Belfast, but instead of bands there were gangs, and instead of three chords and the truth, there was crush, the little orange pill that was cheap, powerful and highly addictive; the little orange pill that was the bastard son of MDNA and crack cocaine; the little orange pill born in a Chinese lab and exported the world over; the little orange pill whose secret recipe was worth more than Coke and KFC combined, at least until some anarchist chemist posted it on the internet so that any fucker with an A level could make it in his back bedroom. The Pistols had sung about anarchy in the UK, but crush had brought it.

'It's just revolutionised everything, and in – what? Less than a year? It's crazy.' I gave her my punk-rock analogy, and she responded with, 'How old are you, exactly?'

'Old enough to remember that, while everyone might

have wanted to be in a band, not everyone could afford the instruments, or master even one of the three chords; and, while they could all have made their own records, very few of them actually did and, of the ones who did, not many of them are classics.'

'Well,' said Sara. 'I don't know much about punk rock, but I imagine the principle's the same – there's always a few who know how to work the system, who rise to the top because they're a bit more savvy or they have access to the right equipment, and that's what's happened here. Everyone *could* manufacture their own crush, but how much easier just to go out and buy it cheap and sell it on! I mean, this isn't unique to Ulster, it's actually pretty close to how it works somewhere like Mexico. We're getting there on the killings for sure, but, while it may look like total anarchy, there's actually a pretty smooth business model at work here.' She began to count off on her fingers. 'You have manufacture, wholesale, retail and the customer. You think of the gangs as your corner shop; their clientele is almost exclusively local. Business is good, demand is growing, but then someone sees that and opens another shop just on the edge of your area, and pretty soon they're at each other's throats.'

'And that's what happened at William Street?'

'Most likely. William Street falls within the territory of the Botanic Boat Crew – I know, don't ask – not a huge outfit, pretty vicious when it has to be, but that hasn't been very often because the area it runs was until recently pretty well known and accepted by the other gangs. But last year, because we were at peace, there was an influx of students to the University, the Holy Land where they traditionally rent has gotten overcrowded and, as a result, it started expanding into the likes of William Street. So the Riot Squad, which controls the Holy Land, now stakes a claim to the upper end of William Street, and then, as the houses get converted one by one, they start rubbing shoulders with the Boat Crew. Something has to give.'

'So, for my girl, I'd need to be looking at the Boat Crew and the Riot Squad.'

'They're the most obvious, sure, but then everyone covets students because they usually have plenty of money. So if a student doesn't live in the Holy Land, but parties there, buying stuff in one area, transporting it to the next – like your girl getting crushed in Ballyhack – the lines start getting confused.'

Traffic finally began to rumble forward. When we got as far as the Boucher Road off-ramp, we were halted temporarily at traffic lights, which gave us just long enough to study the cause of our delay: a car smashed into the side of the barrier to our left with firemen trying to cut their way into it. There were police vehicles front and back and an ambulance blocking one of the two lanes. There was a woman police officer guiding cars into the outside lane; as we waited for her to let us out, Sara rolled down her window, flashed her press card and asked what had happened. The policewoman seemed to recognise her and crouched down beside her. I remembered that as a nice buzzy feeling. 'They pumped about thirty rounds into it,' she said, 'killed the girl, and her fella's pinned to the fence.' Sara thanked her, the cop nodded and moved away. Sara quickly raised her phone and took half a dozen photos of the crashed car with the firemen working at it; there was blood and glass all over the road.

I said, 'Do you want to stay and . . .?'

She shook her head. 'It's a paragraph on the front, nothing more.'

'That bad,' I said.

'If this is what you really want to get into, Starkey, this is what can happen, and probably will. They don't give a shit about anyone.'

'Bear it in mind,' I said.

11

We parked on the Springfield Road beside a ribbon of shops so recently built that the footpath outside hadn't yet been laid. We were just opposite Turf Lodge. It had once been a farm, but was bought over in the late fifties for low-grade public housing. By the time Elvis sang 'In the Ghetto', it was one. During the Troubles it was a fertile recruiting ground for the IRA. Fort Monagh, the army base on the estate, was considered to be one of the least desirable postings in the British Empire. As a reporter, it had been a nightmare to work in and, even now, looking at the estate from the relative safety of Sara's car, it still maintained an almost tangible aura of threat and menace, even in the hazy warmth of a summer's afternoon.

Sara lifted her laptop from the backseat and opened it. She pulled up a colour-coded map of Belfast. 'OK, Starkey, nearly done. This is something I put together that you might find useful . . . This is where we are now.' She touched the screen. 'Used to be solidly PIRA, now it's Turf Lodge Dragoons. And a vicious bunch they are.' She tapped again and an information box came up, showing who ran the Dragoons, how many members it had, and links to previous news articles they'd featured in.

'There must be . . . how many gangs?'

'There's nearly forty on here, and they're only the ones I've had direct dealings with. There're probably twenty others. And gangs within gangs – a big estate like Turf Lodge might sub-divide into three to cover the whole area, but will still answer to one chief, at least until someone cuts his head off.'

'Literally?'

'Oh, yes. Internal or external, that's the way it goes.'

'You have . . . about half of the gangs in red and half in green – the old religious boundaries . . .?'

'Yeah . . . yeah, that's how I started doing it, because the early pattern was that, if there was any kind of trouble, the Prods would stick with the Prods, and vice versa. But I'm thinking about changing it. They're getting younger; most of them don't even know the local history, just want to make their money and anyone who messes with that is fair game.'

'OK, so you've red and green – and then you've this long swathe of blue. That would be . . .?'

'Blue is the River Lagan.'

'Right. I should have known that.'

She shook her head and mouthed *idiot* under her breath.

I said, 'Can you send it to me?'

'Sure. It's not a secret. We published a version of it a few weeks back, names and all.'

'And how did that go down?'

'It was never going to be a problem. They all love the publicity.'

She began to close the laptop cover, but I put my hand out to stop her.

'Could you send it to me now?'

'I'll do it when I—'

'I'd appreciate it if you'd do it right now. We might fall out later.'

She half-laughed. 'Happen a lot, does it?'

'It does,' I said, 'though it's never my fault.'

She gave me a look, and I gave her my defusing smile and my email address and watched as she sent it.

'OK,' she said, 'You maybe want to be ordering a taxi or something to get back?'

'I thought I could maybe get a lift back with you; we could talk some more. You're the fount of all gang-banger knowledge.'

'I have a meeting,' she said. 'And that's your lot, Starkey.'

I gave her my big eyes and said I could really do with the lift back to town, and that we didn't need to talk about the gangs any more if she didn't want to. She said no, no, no and no, and eventually, yes, as long as I stopped looking at her like that and kept my mouth shut on the way back.

'Bloody hell,' she said as she opened the door. 'I'll be twenty minutes, half an hour max.'

As she was getting out, I asked if she could leave the keys so I could listen to the radio. She said no. I asked if she could leave the window open so I wouldn't suffocate. She said no. She got out, closed the door and started to walk towards a café called 'The Fruit Loop'. But then she stopped and came back to the car. I thought she was coming to open the window, but instead she reached in and lifted her laptop out. I said, 'I wouldn't dream of—'

She said, 'Just taking temptation out of your way.'

She entered the café. There were about a dozen tables, with just a sprinkling of customers. She chose one away from the window, which I could just about see. A waitress brought her a bottle of Diet Coke. After about five minutes, a small guy in a black bomber jacket approached the door, paused while he took a final puff on his cigarette, then threw it down and entered. He sat opposite her. They started to chat, and were still at it as I walked up, pulled out a chair and parked myself beside Sara. I set down a notebook and pen and smiled at both of them.

The fella, pudgy face and tiny eyes, said, 'Who the fuck are you?'

'Your worst nightmare,' I replied.

His mouth dropped open a bit.

'He's only winding you up,' said Sara, giving me the evil eye. 'He's no one. I thought I told you to wait in the car?'

'I'm not six,' I said, 'or a dog.' I put my hand out to the guy and said, 'Hi, Dan Starkey.'

He looked at it suspiciously. And then at Sara. 'What the fuck?'

Before she could answer, I took my hand back and said, 'Don't worry, I'm not a cop.'

'Why the fuck would I be worried if you were a cop?'

'Exactly. I work with Sara. But just pretend like I'm not here.'

He glared at Sara. She gave a resigned sigh. 'Sorry about this – sometimes they send the old fellas out of the back office on stories, just to remind them they're still alive. He's nothing to worry about.'

'Supposed to be just you and me,' her pal said.

'I know that; I know that – but, honestly, he doesn't even—'

I cut in with, 'I'm interested in some specific information. Do you remember the massacre in William Street? Lot of kids murdered, right?'

'What the fuck would I know about that?' He looked at Sara. 'Why the fuck is he asking me about that? You know why I'm here, and that's not why I'm here. What the fuck?'

'I'm sorry,' I said. 'What's your name?'

'What's it to you? I'm fucking out of here.'

He made as if to move, and Sara said, 'Don't, Tommy.'

'Tommy,' I said, flipping the cover of my book back and making a note.

'Fuck this,' he said, and this time he stood up.

'Wait,' said Sara, 'please. He doesn't mean—'

'This is fucking Turf Lodge. What the fuck do I know about Wellington Street?'

'I'm not saying you do,' I said, 'but you might know someone who does, or they might know someone who does. All I'm saying is I'm in the market for information.'

I took out my wallet. It was nice and bulky. I opened it and began to count out twenty-pound notes. Tommy's eyes widened. 'Take a seat,' I said, 'this might take a while.'

When I got to a hundred pounds, I started a second pile. When I got to two hundred pounds, I started a third. I was halfway through it when Sara brought her hand down on mine and squeezed hard. 'Could I have a word with you?'

'Of course,' I said.

'*Outside*.'

We went outside. We stood in the shade. It was very pleasant, right up to the point where she poked me in the chest and said, 'What the fuck are you playing at?'

I said, 'Don't; and I think it's pretty clear what—'

'You just barrel in and start throwing money around like—'

'It's usually the best way to get infor—'

'Don't you see what you're doing, you stupid prick? You're killing him as a source! I buy him a cup of coffee and a bun and I get to pick his brains and when we're finished I have to make sure I get a receipt otherwise I'll never get it back, but you just slap down wads of cash and now he'll never open his mouth to me again unless I do the same. You stupid shit. I told you to stay in the car!'

'I was only—'

'Why would you even do that to me?! I go out of my way to help you and you just fuck it all up!'

'Listen, relax, just tell him it's a one-off payment and—'

'Don't tell me to relax you . . . fuck!' But she wasn't looking at me. Her eyes were fixed on the café and the table where we'd all been sitting, which was now empty, and the money I'd purposefully left sitting there, which was now gone. Tommy had legged it, as I had supposed he would. Of course he was of no use to me as a source, but he would not be able to help himself spreading the word that there was someone out there looking for information about William Street who was prepared to really pay for it. It was all about dissemination.

Sara was saying, 'Brilliant, just fucking brilliant.'

I said, 'Sorry. I suppose I'm a bit rusty when it comes to . . .' I blew air out of my cheeks. 'Still, you can't win them all. Maybe on the way back you can tell me some more about—'

'Oh, fuck off.' She turned for the car and fumbled in her bag for the keys. And then her eyes widened and she swore again before darting back to the café. She charged through the door and up to our table. She looked around it and below it, and then approached the counter and spoke to the waitress. She came storming back out and stood before me. 'And he took my fucking laptop!'

'Bummer,' I said.

'Fuck!'

She spun back to the car, unlocked it and jumped in. I moved around to the passenger door.

For some reason, she didn't open it.

She started the engine. I tapped on the window. She ignored me. She backed out of the parking space. When she stopped to change gears, I knocked on the window again and said, 'Do you want to . . .?' I indicated the lock.

Sara kept her eyes front and, in her anger, struggled to find first gear.

I said, 'What about Whitespots?'

'Fuck Whitespots!'

She found the gear, and the car sprang forward. She hit a speed bump hard before turning on to the Springfield Road and roaring away. I smiled to myself. People were really ridiculously easy to wind up.

As I stood watching her go, my phone began to ring. I turned it in my hand and saw that it was Patricia.

I answered with a breezy, 'Hi, hon; what can I do for you on this lovely summer's—?'

'Where the fuck are you?!'

'I—'

'You promised you wouldn't let me down! We're in enough of a state as it is without you making us late!'

'Sorry, where am I—?'

'The clinic! We're supposed to be there in fifteen minutes! Dan, if you—!'

'Relax, Trish – I'm on my way; in fact, I'm nearly there. Be with you in five.'

'OK . . . OK . . . OK . . . OK . . . Sorry; I'm just up to high dough . . .'

'I know; it's fine; be there in a wee mo.'

I cut the line and took a deep breath. Five minutes wouldn't be a problem, once I found a mode of transport and a wormhole in the space–time continuum.

12

The Braxton Clinic had, somewhat appropriately, been open for exactly nine months, and for every one of those nine months it had been picketed all day every day by a motley assortment of protestors, united only by their desire to have it closed down. Devout Catholics clutching rosary beads stood shoulder to shoulder with free-range hippies, and straight-laced New Seekers, chanting in unison, all standing behind council-provided crash barriers on the opposite side of the street. Their positioning was supposed to be a compromise – allowing prospective customers access to the clinic, while not overtly interfering with the protestors' divine right to cause a racket. But the clinic was on Little Victoria Street, which was narrow and gloomy and made up of mostly shut-up small businesses that hadn't survived the recession, which meant that, if you were in Little Victoria Street at all, you had only one of two reasons to be there: either you were visiting the second-floor Braxton Clinic to consult on a possible abortion, or a sexually transmitted disease, or to get rape counselling – basically you were a dirty stop-out – or you were there to visit the ground-floor Madison Bakery, which had been churning out bread, cakes and pastries for exactly one hundred and twenty years and which was theoretically still going to be doing that long after the clinic was chased outta town; which would not, surely, be long. There was a separate, side entrance to the clinic, but it was impossible for the protestors to know if anyone approaching the building was there because they had a bun in the oven or because they wanted to purchase buns, so they tended to abuse everyone. Many, many of the clinic's prospective clients lost their nerve as they entered the eye of the storm and simply ducked into the bakery rather than reveal why they were really there. Sales were way up.

We weren't going to take that option. They had made their bed – a Laguna – and were going to lie in it, whether they liked it or not. I steered Lol down Little Victoria, one hand on her arm, and keeping her firmly on the inside, with me beside her and Trish and Bobby on the outside. She was barely recognisable as the tracksuited teen who'd sat in *my* kitchen the day before – she was wearing a short dress, killer heels, a blond wig and sunglasses that made her look like the Fly. It was a combination of hiding in plain sight and a *fuck you* to the protestors we all knew would be there. As we approached the building, they ramped up the singing and chanting and pointing and yelling.

'Stay calm, ignore it,' I said as I reached for the clinic's intercom button.

A voice said, 'Braxton Clinic.'

'Name of Starkey; we have an appointment – two forty-five – we're a little late, traffic was—'

'You'll need to answer the security question.'

Behind me the volume went up. When I glanced around, I saw that Lol and Bobby had stepped into the road and each was giving the protestors the finger. Trish was trying to pull them back on to the footpath. Several of the protestors, including a New Seeker, had climbed over the barrier and were shaking their fists at them. One was holding up a poster of an aborted foetus and screaming, 'Murderer! Murderer!' Another was yelling, 'Whore! Whore-bag!' Lol yanked up her skirt a little further to show off her black stockings and a suspender belt. She was *fifteen* for fuck's sake.

I said, 'Fire away, but it's getting ugly out here.'

'Mother's maiden name?'

'Brady.'

'No, that's not it . . .'

'It definitely is—'

'Did you make the appointment?'

'No, I think my ex-wife made the—'

'Then it would be her maiden name . . .'

I looked at Trish. She had Bobby by the arm and was pulling him back on to the pavement. Lol was doing a weird little dance, which would not have looked out of place in a pole-dancing club.

'Morrison,' I said.

'No, that's not it. Are you sure . . .?'

One of the protestors, a small man in a black suit with white socks, came right up to Lol and started yelling abuse in her face. Bobby was being held back by Trish, but he quickly shrugged her off to push in front of the protestor. He raised a finger to his face and spat venom.

'Do you think we could do this inside?' I said to the intercom.

'I'm sorry, but they've tried this before. Could it be the client's mother's name?'

'Lol! What's your surname?'

'No! You fuck off!' she was yelling. I shouted the question again. She shook her head, confused. 'McBurney!'

'McBurney,' I said.

'No . . . that's not—'

'For fuck— Trish! Security question!'

She looked daggers at me and stormed across and spat out, 'Jesus! Let a grown-up do it.' And then, 'Yes, what is it?' into the intercom and answered with, 'Waters.'

And the door buzzed and I pushed it open. I yelled, 'Bobby! Let him go!' because he had the black-suit-white-socks guy by the throat. Bobby just threw him to the ground, growled something over him and then gave the crowd the finger as he grabbed Lol by the hand. They walked haughtily past me and into the foyer. I ushered Trish in after them and then closed the door and waited for the lock to click. The baying of the crowd was suddenly cut dead. The door was probably bullet proof. All over the world, it was a life-or-death business, in more ways than one.

Trish said, 'Fucking hell.'

Bobby and Lol giggled.

Trish pushed the button for the lift. I said, 'Waters?' and Lol said it was her mum's surname and McBurney was her stepdad's name, which they preferred her to use, but she rarely did. I didn't really care one way or the other, but I did care about nearly getting lynched. I said, 'It's not good to antagonise people, even morons.'

'You not hear what they were saying?' Bobby asked.

'Yes, I did, Bobby . . .'

'Someone said that to Patricia, wouldn't you stand up for her?'

Trish snorted.

I said, 'There's a difference between standing up, and punching someone in the face. That's exactly what they wanted you to do.'

We got into the lift. Lol took Bobby's hand and smiled at him. Trish looked at me. 'And that was the easy part,' she said.

There was no Dr Braxton, in the same way that there was no Ronald McDonald or Colonel Sanders. It was a generic name, plucked at random and applied to a chain of clinics across mainland Great Britain. Over there, nobody blinked an eye. Over here, they tried to poke it out. A receptionist took my credit card details, then Dr Ciara Macceabee came and introduced herself. She must have come in at just under five foot. She wore a smart blue business suit and, when I checked, heels, which probably knocked a couple more inches off. Her face was soft and rounded and clean of make-up. Lol was the only one of us she actually touched, lightly, on the arm, and it came with an encouraging smile. She said she wanted to take Lol in first and, as soon as she said it, all of the bravado seemed to drain from the teenager. She blanched, swallowed and suddenly looked tearful. She pulled off her wig and handed it to me before stepping forward with trepidation. Ten minutes later, Bobby was called in, and then Trish. Nobody seemed to be interested in explaining things to me. I was just the ATM.

From the window in the waiting room I could see the ranks of protestors below. There was a big security guy called Terry who, after their intercom and thick door, was their third line of defence. I asked him if they'd ever managed to get up this far and he said, 'Once, but they were so surprised at getting in, they didn't really know what to do. I roared at them and they ran away, but it could have gotten nasty. They're just scum. At least your girl seems like she has good support.'

I nodded back down at the protestors. 'Must put a lot of girls off.'

'Nightmare. They end up trying to do it themselves,

and you really don't want to see the results of that.' He shook his head. 'But they won't drive us out.'

'Sounds personal,' I said.

'Yeah, well.' He got that faraway look people get when they're about to launch into a story. But then he just said, 'Yeah,' again. He turned towards me, peered a little closer. 'Starkey, you said?'

'Aye.'

'Dan Starkey? You used to write for the papers?'

'Aye. Long time ago.'

'I remember. You wouldn't have let that lot get away with what they're doing, would you? You'd have torn their bollocks off.'

'Metaphorically speaking,' I said. 'But probably. Someone should.'

He nodded.

I nodded. 'Is there a back way out? Don't particularly want her to run the gauntlet again.'

'There is, but it lets you into an alley, and they've people out there too. You get trapped in there, they'll likely tear you to shreds.'

'Christians,' I said; 'they're always doing stuff like that.'

He laughed. He said, 'Anyway – wouldn't recommend it. You'd be better bringing the car round the front, then they can just step right into it.'

Terry went to check on the time of the next appointment. I sat and studied several of Finn's files on my phone for twenty minutes, until Trish appeared out of the consulting room and crossed to a water cooler. I joined her and said, 'How's it going?'

'Tears,' she said.

'Is Bobby being an arse?'

'No. Why would you say that?'

'Experience.'

'Just . . . *don't*, OK? It's hard enough for him without you always winding him up.'

She was filling three plastic cups to take back in. I told her about bringing the car round and she said, 'Anything to avoid going through those bastards again.' We agreed on mutual texting, which was about as exciting as it got in our relationship. She walked me to the lift, balancing the cups in her hands, and told me to be careful.

I pushed the button. As she was turning away, I said, 'I don't mean to be hard on him. It's just like . . . banter.'

She pursed her lips. 'Dan, love, one man's banter is another man's . . . not banter.'

'Really?' I said, as the lift pinged and the doors opened.

'You know what I mean,' said Trish.

I was still thinking about it as I arrived on the ground floor. Maybe she had a point. I released the lock, pulled the clinic door open, hunched my shoulders, put my head down and started walking. Perhaps the protestors were more intent on scaring women, or they were aware of my ultimate irrelevance, but the bays and taunts and threats weren't half as loud as I left. A good brisk pace and I was at the corner and turning into Bruce Street, heading towards the space I'd nabbed behind the Dublin Road Movie House.

I was just about to cross the road when a voice behind me said, 'Hiya.'

I stopped and turned, and there was a New Seeker standing there: a girl, small, maybe seventeen, her face as pale as her uniform, but her eyes as bright as the day.

I said, 'Sorry?'

She smiled and said, 'You were in the clinic.'

I said, 'I'm in a hurry. I get the message; bear it in mind.'

She said, 'Are you happy?'

'That's a big question. But generally, yes, though Iran keeps me awake some nights.'

Her smile didn't falter. She said, 'Maybe we can do something about Iran, if we all get together.'

'Sounds like a plan,' I said, 'but, right now, I've more important things to be worrying about.'

'You should invite God into your life.'

'If He can cancel parking tickets,' I said, 'He's more than welcome.'

She said, 'You hide behind your humour.'

I said, 'You should try it sometime.'

I gave her the thumbs up and stepped out into the road. There was a screech of brakes and a blast of a horn and a Volvo missed me by a fraction of an inch. I waved apologetically at the driver as he pulled out around me and gave me the finger as he passed. I made it to the other side of the road, steadied myself on the pavement and then glanced back at the girl, who was still standing there.

'So did He send the car to warn me, or to save me?'

'Maybe both,' she replied.

I shook my head and said, 'Right; good one.'

As I walked off, she called after me, 'Be careful, Dan.'

I waved back at her, but had only taken a few more steps before it dawned on me that she'd used my name, and that she couldn't possibly have known it. But when I turned to pull her up on it, there was no sign of her at all.

13

Lol was adamant that she wanted rid of the baby, but the clinic insisted on a fourteen day cooling-off period before she went ahead. They were efficient, like a car finance company, and as empathetic as Samaritans. It was an odd combination. Lol was chatty as we left, relieved that a dreaded confrontation was over, irrespective of the result. I could tell from keeping an eye on Bobby in the mirror that his mind was working overtime. I suspected that what was troubling him wasn't just the words of wisdom from Dr Macceabee, but the abuse from the protestors outside. It had been purposefully virulent and literally graphic. He did not come from an area where threats and insults were taken lightly. Posters with extremely upsetting images had been pushed into our faces as we rushed out to the car. I had music on loud to drown out their yells. As soon as we rounded the corner, Patricia turned it down and suggested taking Bobby and Lol to McDonald's. I said they weren't bloody kids any more, and was then outvoted. I made the excuse that I had work to do and dropped them off downtown.

I was on the way to my office, but stuck at lights on the Dublin Road, when I remembered I'd put my phone on to silent while I'd been in the clinic; there were two messages. The first – technically, the second – had come in less than five minutes before: a south-Belfast accent saying his name was Jonathan and he was a part-time barman in Culchie's Corner, a gastro pub in Ballyhack, that he'd heard I was looking for information about 'that' missing girl and, if I wanted to call in to see him, he was working from six. The second message, coming just as the lights changed, caused me to fluff the gear change and stall the engine.

It wasn't the content; it was the voice: distinctively deep and cigar heavy. Billionaire Thomas Wolff.

He was unmistakable, and he knew it, because he didn't need to identify himself. All he said was, 'Mr Starkey – you're looking for my daughter. She means everything to me. Whatever you need, just call me. I know you can do this.'

And that was it.

Smooth. Efficient. Supposedly inspiring. It was a little surreal to have him on my voicemail, because he was so famous. He was a self-styled man of the people. He owned a Premier League football club and every year he discarded its manager, just because he could. He was flash and coarse, and didn't care what anyone thought of him; he believed money could buy everything and everyone, and he had just bought me. Which was fine. I needed the job. I was neither inspired nor diminished by his call. It was a novelty. In better times I would have played it to Patricia and she would have responded with, 'Well, you've gone down in the world.' That said, I wouldn't have minded a pint with him.

I kept thinking about him – and what I would do with his kind of money – as I turned the car round and drove out to Ballyhackamore. I found a space in the car park behind Culchie's Corner, overlooking its beer garden, which was just losing the late-afternoon sun. There were a couple of guys in T-shirts, with tattoos on their tattoos, sitting smoking at the pine tables. They watched me as I moved between the tables towards the back entrance; they probably didn't see many faces like mine, with an iron-shaped swelling on one side. I gave them a nod, but they didn't return it. I tried not to feel too put out. I stepped into the bar proper and stood for a moment while my eyes adjusted to the gloom. I pulled up a stool, ordered a pint and lifted a paper. I was early yet. But, even if I hadn't been, I sometimes like to suss people out before I engage with them; it's amazing how different they can be when they're not on their guard, or after something.

Jonathan came in, bang on six. I knew it was him as soon as he opened his mouth, and also the badge on his shirt said *Jonathan*. He was of medium height, skinny with a pinched face, which was a little too sharp to be handsome. His skin was pockmarked, but with a very slight tint to it, as if he'd raided his mum's make-up and applied a very thin layer of foundation to cover up the worst of it. He wore a regulation black short-sleeved shirt, black trousers and shoes. He had a small backpack over one shoulder, which he stowed behind the bar. He bumped knuckles with the girl who had been working and she quickly disappeared. As he coded himself into the cash register, I drained my pint; when he turned, I asked for another. I said, 'It's still boiling out there,' as I ordered and he said, 'Tell me about it,' without meaning it. There was a TV playing above the bar, showing news coverage on a Wolff channel about the shootings I'd passed on the way to Turf Lodge with Sara Patterson. I said, 'It's mad out there.'

Jonathan said, 'Aye.'

As there was hardly anyone else on the premises, Jonathan took a book out of his backpack and moved to the end of the bar to study it. When he moved the cover up, I could see it was a psychology textbook.

I called down the bar, 'Do you have any crisps?'

He folded his page and said, 'Aye; Pringles.'

It was that kind of a bar. I said, 'I mean proper crisps, in a bag.'

'They are proper crisps, but in a tube.'

'At twice the price.'

'That's what we have.'

I held up my hands: *no thanks*.

When he'd settled back into his studies, I said, 'What flavours?'

He looked down the bar and told me.

When he'd finished, I said, 'No cheese and onion?'

'No,' he said.

I held up my hands again: *no thanks*.

When he'd settled a third time, I said, 'So, Jonathan, this missing girl . . .'

If he was surprised, he did not show it. He closed his book over and moved down to me and, on the way, he lifted a small tube of Pringles and set it before me. 'On the house,' he said.

'There is no start to your generosity,' I said.

'Well, I hope I can't say the same about you. What're you after?'

'Whatever you have.'

'Are you going to cross my palm with silver?'

'Depends on what you have. How'd you hear about me?'

'Bar round the corner – I do afternoons there – manager said.'

'And it struck a chord.'

'Yeah, kind of.'

'Kind of how?'

'Kind of not about the girl . . .'

'It would kind of need to be . . .'

'More about this fella who used to hang around . . .'

'This is the girl,' I said and showed him the photo.

'. . . trying his luck. Good looking fella . . . Nah, don't remember her, but this guy . . . he'd get them crushed and then he'd have the knickers off them. He was in and out of all the pubs round here – I know, cos I've worked in them all – and it used to break my heart cos the girls would come back looking for him, weeks on end they'd come in but he always stayed one step ahead. And you could just see them going downhill – you know, like they get when they're proper crushed, their faces all bloaty and their looks away to shit?'

'You remember what he was called?'

'I do.'

He looked at me, and I looked at him.

I said, 'How much were those Pringles again?'

I took out my wallet and began to count out money. He was attempting jaunty indifference, but I could see his eyes widen as the pile mounted. I stopped when I got to two hundred, and pushed it across to him. He took it and folded it and put it in his back pocket.

'His name was Frank,' he said. 'Sometimes Harry. Sometimes Pat, or Mickey, or Sean. I'm not winding you up; he used all kinds of different names, different accents. One night I overheard him, he was Ramon, Spanish exchange student, and you could believe it, cos he had, like, quite dark skin . . . Not a black fella, if you know what I mean, but not . . . dead white, like a local would be. Anyway, I was thinking, if anyone knew what happened to your girl, it would most likely be him.'

'So where would I find Frank or Harry or Pat?'

'Well, I've a rough idea, but I could probably find out exactly, if you give me five minutes.' I opened my wallet again, but he surprised me by raising his hand.

'No, seriously – I didn't expect more than twenty quid.' He patted his back pocket. 'This'll keep me in fegs till term starts. Hold on . . .'

He turned away and raised his phone and began to tap out a text. I opened the Pringles. They looked like crisps. They tasted like crisps. They *were* crisps. But in a cardboard tube. It was just wrong.

Jonathan came back and said, 'Aye, I was right – didn't think he was local – just off the Ormeau Road. Must have come up here cos there was good pickings.' He studied his phone and said, 'Deramore Avenue; it's either sixty-six or sixty eight . . .'

'That's pretty precise for someone you don't know.'

He studied me, just for a moment, and then said, 'Aye, well, I suppose you're entitled.' He glanced towards the beer garden, and the tattooed guys at their table, and then leaned on the bar. His voice dropped to a conspiratorial whisper. 'Truth is, they don't give a fuck who Frank – or Harry, or whoever walks through those doors – hits on; that's why guys come to bars. They don't even care if he gets them crushed. But they do care if they don't get a cut of it; that's disrespecting the neighbourhood. So they dealt with him.'

I thought of Sara's map, which she'd sent to my email, but which I'd found much easier to study on her laptop in the car park outside. I'd bought it off Tommy, her runaway informant, for another hundred quid. If she'd hung around for five minutes, she would have seen him emerge from behind a set of bins at the side of the café. He wasn't the slightest bit bashful about ripping either of us off. According to her map, Ballyhack fell under the sway of two gangs operating on either side of the Newtownards Road: the North Road Clan and the Belmont Rievers. They had a couple of dozen members each. She didn't have their leaders' names.

As if I knew what I was talking about, I said, 'So that would be the Clan or the Rievers; these bars must be pretty lucrative for them, so they don't like free-lancers coming in.'

'Exactly. We're on the North Road side, so the Clan dealt with Harry – followed him home.' He raised an eyebrow.

'And gave him what? A stern telling off?'

'Yeah, right.'

'When was this?'

'Not sure; six months ago, maybe?'

'Did this stern telling off involve killing him, or is he likely to still be around?'

'Haven't seen him since, but beyond that . . . no idea. Sorry.'

I thanked him for his help and said, if he thought of anything else, I'd appreciate a call. I finished my pint, gave him a wink and turned for the beer garden.

He called after me, 'You forgot your Pringles.'

'No, I didn't,' I replied.

14

I swallowed more tablets with a few knock-backs from
a wee flask of Bladnoch I kept in the glove compartment for emergencies, and sat in the Ballyhack car park
with the window down, enjoying the cooling of the
sun, observing the two muscle-bounds in the shade of
the beer garden, still sinking pints and smoking their
fegs and laughing, and I tried to remember the last time
I'd done that with a real, proper friend, rather than
one I'd mistakenly acquired for the night while out on
a solo session and whom I would never want to see
again, nor recognise if I bumped into again. It went
back to Mouse, who had been murdered seven or maybe
eight years before. He had been my best man, and
nobody had replaced him. With Trish gone, there
was nobody I could call just to shoot the breeze with,
or talk into a night on the tiles, or get up to mischief
with. There was me and there was my empty flat in

the heart of the city's happening theatre and entertainment quarter – and my only problem with that was that, every time I heard the word *culture*, I had to reach for my Strongbow, and that never ended well. Maybe Thomas Wolff could be my friend. I'm sure he could show me a good time. I listened to his message again and thought about yachts and beaches and trashing a karaoke machine. After a while, I must have dozed off because, when I next opened my eyes, it was dark and there was loud music coming from the crowded beer garden. I shook myself. Dark, friendless, head sore, Alison missing, wife departed, fake stepson in a quandary.

I started the car and headed back towards the city centre before swinging left on to the Ormeau Road. I called Trish and asked her how Bobby and Lol were doing and if they'd said much in McDonald's or later, and she said not really, but that they were now locked in his room upstairs and there'd been raised voices for the best part of an hour. She related as much as she'd picked up of their argument and I said, 'Uh-huh,' a lot. I liked her voice. I loved when she shared things with me and we discussed our kids, even though they weren't our kids. After a while, she said, 'And how are you?' I told her I was working and looking for a missing girl, but not who she really was. She had steady and fixed views about Wolff TV. She had once said that all women hated Wolff TV and I had asked if that included the ones who were well paid to get nekkid and she said especially them, and she was pretty sure they weren't well paid. She asked me some questions about the case and what it involved and then let out a sigh and said, 'It's getting so I don't even want to go out at night, there's so much trouble around.'

I said, 'You go out at night? Who with?'

'Don't, Dan.'

'No, seriously, it's fine; if you've met someone else, I'm genuinely happy for you.'

'Really?'

'Of course not. I will track the cunt down and kill him.'

'Don't use that word; you know I don't like it.'

'If the cap fits, in a strictly non-gynaecological sense, wear it.'

'I'm just saying, it's dangerous out there and, if I know you, you'll be up to your neck in it in no time.'

'It's the nature of what I do, Trish.'

'It's the nature of what you choose to do, Dan. You know, you could easily go back to journalism – that's what you were born to do, not . . . you know, getting shot at and beaten up.'

'There's more to it than that, babe.'

'Of course there is. I was forgetting how you always manage to drag me into getting shot at and beaten up.'

'And that was just our marriage.'

'We had good times.'

'I remember that day.'

'Ha,' she said.

'Ha,' I said.

'*You* seeing anyone?'

'Of course not. I keep myself pure for you.'

I was easing the car along Deramore Avenue, looking at the even numbers, and came to a stop at the semi-detached sixty-six and sixty-eight.

Trish said, 'I'm worried about you. You don't look well.'

'Someone has just hit me with an iron. Maybe I'm just depressed. De-*pressed*,' I added for emphasis.

'I mean,' she said, ignoring it completely, 'that you looked tired and have done for a while. You know, we're not twenty-one any more.'

'We're not?'

'We can't go at everything a hundred miles an hour. Sometimes we have to recharge the batteries.'

'I know that, Trish.'

I was peering at the two houses, identically built, but one brightly lit, with a neat garden and apparently well maintained, the other with the dull light of a single bulb shining upstairs, and the garden running wild. There was a small bush growing out of the chimney, and the guttering on the right-hand side was hanging off.

'OK, sorry,' said Trish. 'I'm not your mother.'

'That would render many things we've done illegal.'

'But take it easy, OK? Go home, have a quiet night. Get your five a day.'

'Just arriving home now,' I said.

She said goodbye.

I said, 'Love you.'

It was a throwaway, deliberately short of '*I* love you'

because when I'd said *that* she'd always respond with, 'I know,' or 'Uh-huh,' or a pregnant pause long enough for the Titanic to slip past, but a simple 'Love you' was relatively meaningless and easily thrown back with the false chumminess of a McDonald's burger slapper's 'Have a nice day'.

'Love you too,' said Trish.

'Yeah, yeah,' I said, and cut the line.

I was trying to decide between the two houses – which one might be inhabited by a crush dealer with a smooth line in seduction. Bearing in mind that he had, at some point in the fairly recent past, been dealt with by the North Road Clan, I plumped for the dilapidated-looking one in semi-darkness.

The gates were closed, with a rusting bicycle chain looped over the bars to make it more awkward to enter. I slipped it off one side and the gate creaked as I walked it back. The driveway was thick with weeds pushing up through the tarmac. I moved towards a glass-fronted porch while holding my phone up ahead of me for light. It allowed me to see the accumulation of free newspapers and what appeared to be junk mail within, and to then locate the doorbell, which I pressed. I couldn't hear it ringing, so I knocked as well. When there was no response, I stepped back into the garden and looked up at the one room that was lit. There were no curtains, but the angle was too acute for me to see anything else. I gave the bell and door-knocking combo another go. I peered up again, and this time something moved. I also noticed that one of the windows was open slightly.

I waited, and I waited. When there was no further movement, I called up: 'Hi! Hello . . . Ah, I was trying the bell there but it might not be working . . . My, uh . . . Is there any chance of a word?'

Nothing.

'I . . . Uh . . . Is that you, Harry? Or Frank? You, ah, used to frequent the bars up round Ballyhack till the gang-bangers chased you out? Maybe eight, nine months ago? Nothing to be worried about; I'm just looking for some information. Happy to pay for it.'

Nothing.

'My name's Dan Starkey, I'm just trying to—'

'Fuck off!'

The voice was raspy, the words spat out.

'I'd be happy to, but I'd be even happier if you could just—'

'Fuck off, I said!'

There came the sound of someone clearing their throat, but not from above. I glanced to my left to see a man standing in the open doorway of the adjoining house.

'Oh – hi,' I said. 'Hope I wasn't . . .'

He raised a finger to his lips, and then quickly used it to beckon me over. I gave the upstairs window another look before pushing through the jungle of grass and weeds to a low dividing wall. I stopped there, expecting that the neighbour would meet me halfway, but he beckoned again. I stepped up on to the wall and jumped down on to a lawn that could have hosted Wimbledon. As I approached the door, I saw that the man standing there had a beard which was equally well maintained. He also wore tortoiseshell glasses with fashionably large lenses. His sandy hair was cut short and what little I could see of his teeth suggested that they were Mormon white. He was wearing a collarless shirt and brown cords. He looked like a young academic, striving to look older. There was a grandfather clock visible in the hall behind him and framed film posters lining the walls.

I said, 'I was trying to get a word with Harry . . . or Frank . . . or . . .'

'Fuck. Off.'

'Sorry I—'

'That's what we call him: Fuck Off, or Mr Fuck Off. Because that's all you ever get out of him. You could be the Pope or the President and he'd still tell you to . . .' He thumbed behind him. 'Sorry – I didn't mean to interfere . . . but we've just got the kids over . . . and their window is right beside . . . so we don't like to encourage him to interact . . .'

'Yes, of course,' I said, 'absolutely.' I moved a little closer and lowered my voice. 'Do you mind me asking – has he been like this . . . long?'

The neighbour gave a firm nod and stepped past me into his own front garden so that he could look up at the next-door window. 'Yes, indeed he has. Ever since we moved in, in fact. So, best part of a year. He's not, as you might have gathered –' and he raised his voice considerably – '*quite right* in the head.' He glared up, but there was no sign of Fuck Off. He turned back to me, shaking his head. 'Of course, they didn't tell us there was a nutter living next door. Look at the state of it. Whole place gone to wrack and ruin and the property prices all about here with it.' He took a deep breath and then slowly let it out. 'Anyway, sorry, you weren't to know. Yes, he's in there, but he doesn't take visitors. Is there anything I can help you with?'

'His real name would be useful.'

'Well, that's not a problem. Harry Frank.'

'Harry . . .?'

'Yeah, it's like two first names, but that's what it says on his mail. They deliver it here rather than go through the hassle of unchaining the gate. And I let it sit until there's a pile, then just hop over the wall. He never thanks me. He just says . . .'

'Fuck off.'

'Exactly. If you don't mind me asking – you said you were Dan . . . Dan Starkey, was it?' I nodded. 'You don't look much like a bailiff, which is what he usually gets. You were asking about . . . Ballyhackamore or . . .?'

'Yeah, well, actually, I'm trying to track down a young girl – a student who went missing about nine months ago. I was told she may have been in the company of someone who lives at this address, with the name Harry, or Frank . . . but he sounds like he's about ninety years old; my guy would only be in his early—'

'Twenties, I'd guess. Aye.' He nodded back up at the window. 'Reason he doesn't go out, doesn't see anyone, is his face is all burned, his throat . . .' The neighbour screwed his face up and ran his hand down one side of it. 'His voice . . . sounds like it's half melted. I think that's probably your man, but whether you'd ever get any sense out of him . . . I don't think so; he's away with the fairies.'

'Lookin' that way,' I said.

I thanked him for his help and he walked me to his gate. I got back in the car and sat watching Harry Frank's upstairs window. Two or three times, the neighbour looked out at me, but Harry Frank kept out of sight. After twenty minutes of observation, I got fed up. I took out one of my business cards, wrote on the back of it and then slipped it through Mr Fuck Off's letter box.

It said: *No, you fuck off.*

15

My phone rang. I tried to find it in the quilt. When I
finally located it inside a crisp packet, I growled a hello
and heard Trish's dulcet tones: 'You sound like you just
woke up!' I saw that it was just after dawn, or ten a.m.
as the clock preferred to put it. I said, 'No, actually, I'm
just back from my jog.'

She ignored that and said, 'Guess what?' all pleased.

'I'd prefer if you just—'

She cut me off with, 'I got you a job!'

I sat up, rubbing my eyes, and said, 'I have a job.'

'I mean a case; I got you a case!'

'I have a—'

'One case is a hobby, two cases is a job, and I got
you one! I don't hear a thank you . . .'

'Thank you, but I've no idea what you—'

'I volunteered you! Strike while the iron is hot – that's

what I say, Dan Starkey – so get up and about, you, and get down there; they're expecting you.'

'Who is?! Who? And where? And – what the fuck, Trish? Let me call you back.'

'No! You—'

I cut the line. It was *way* too early. I got up, turned the shower on, padded into the kitchen, filled the kettle, poured my Honey Cheerios, spooned out the coffee, switched the telly on, returned to the shower, which had now run to hot, showered, dried, dressed, returned to the kitchen, poured my coffee, added milk to it and the cereal, and carried both to my armchair where I sat and consumed my breakfast while watching the sports news on Wolff. My life was perfectly ordered. When the cereal was done, I drank the milk from the bottom of the bowl. I then washed the bowl in the sink. I checked my appearance in the mirror. I went back into the bedroom and changed my shirt because I'd dribbled milk down it. Satisfied, I faced the world, and Trish.

She said, 'Never fucking hang up on me again.'

I hung up on her.

Then I phoned her back.

She answered with, 'You are really fucking—'

I didn't get to hear her finish because I'd hung up again. I could be really annoying. I knew that.

She phoned back ten minutes later. She said, 'You love taking the wind out of my sails, don't you?' I didn't respond. 'I don't know why I go out of my way to help you, because you always throw it back in my face.'

I said, 'You're the one wanted the divorce. Now, what job are you talking about?'

'It was divorce or murder,' she said.

'Murder would have been cheaper,' I said, 'and you'd be out by now.'

'I still haven't ruled it out,' she said, 'you fucking eejit. So, listen, they want you down there as soon as.'

'*Who*?'

'The clinic. Dr Macceabee. They're in a bit of a state after last night . . .'

'Last night what?'

'The fire; the . . . Dan, do you not even listen to the news?'

'I was working late. What's—?'

'The clinic was firebombed last night, totally burned out.'

'Oh,' I said. 'Tell. Anyone hurt?'

'No, but scary biscuits. They've set up temporary premises, and one of the nurses was on with me an hour ago to rearrange Lol's appointment. I got talking to her, and then I got talking to Dr Macceabee herself, and the upshot of it is that they want to hire you to find out who did it.'

'Did they ever think of looking out their window?'

'Not the dummies out front – whoever's pulling their strings.'

'How do they know anyone's pulling their strings, or if there are even strings?'

'Dan – don't ask me. But will you go down and see them?'

'I suppose,' I said.

I asked her where and when, and then she said, 'I'm waiting.'

'For? Oh – thank you.'

'No; my percentage. If I'm going to be getting you work, I'll be looking at – what? – fifteen per cent?'

'Good one,' I said, and hung up.

Dr Macceabee was outside the clinic at Little Victoria Street, talking to insurance people. The whole building was burned out, including the ground-floor bakery. The air still smelled of smoke, with a hint of cinnamon. The protestors were noticeable by their absence. There was still a fire engine parked nearby and police had cordoned off the street. They weren't letting anyone through, and were singularly unimpressed by my business card. I had to stand waving for five minutes before I finally caught Dr Macceabee's attention and she came across and ushered me through. I looked at the charred wreckage of the building. I said, 'Lucky no one was killed.'

Dr Macceabee said, 'The people who did this would say that all the killing took place before the firebomb. They think we run some kind of abattoir. They have no *idea* how many lives we *save* here, on a daily basis.' She shook her head and spat, 'Bastards.' I nodded beside her. She had things to get off her chest. 'Do you know what's going to happen now? We're talking about young girls here, school girls, who can't just disappear to England for a couple of days. We'll be back to coat hangers and hot baths, and if they don't kill themselves doing that, they'll end up swinging from the rafters because that's what they do. We have the figures. It's just heartbreaking.' She turned to me. Her face was pale and her eyes red rimmed, either from crying or the smoke, or more probably both. 'We have clinics all over the UK, and there are protests outside every single one, but nothing like this. Nothing like this.'

'It's Belfast,' I said, 'and we don't do things by halves.'

'We will not be chased out by these barbarians.'

'OK,' I said.

'Mr Starkey – your ex-wife speaks very highly of you, which is, I think, a first.' She smiled, briefly. 'We would like to engage you.'

'Happy to be engaged,' I said, 'though I'm not half as cheap as my ex seems to think I am.'

'Money,' said Dr Macceabee, 'will not be a problem. We've found in the past that, while the police might pursue individuals – say, whoever actually threw this bomb at our premises – they rarely venture beyond that; they don't seek to discover who orchestrates such attacks. We, on the other hand, would prefer to pursue the organisation rather than the individual.'

'You're presuming that it's not just a one-off nutter.'

'Mr Starkey, there are plenty of what you call "nutters" out there, but our experience is that they rarely act without guidance. No, we're interested in whoever is behind this attack.'

'You want me to dig for dirt.'

'Exactly.'

'And what if there is no dirt available?'

'I'm sure if you look hard enough, Mr Starkey, you will find it. Now, I've work to do. We're moving to temporary premises in the retail park in Dundonald. Near the cinema? That's where you'll find me if you need anything, and the numbers are all the same; give my office a call to sort out the money and terms. I trust that you're capable of working on your own initiative?'

'Absolutely,' I said. 'I'm going to start with the Pope and work my way down.'

She gave a slight shake of her head. 'I don't think it's the Catholics we need to be worrying about,' she said, and raised an eyebrow. Before I could respond, she said, 'The girl, yesterday – Lolita – don't worry about her; she has her head screwed on. She'll do the right thing.'

'Depending, of course, on what the right thing is.'

'The important thing is she's armed, now, to make that choice. That's what we're about, Dan: choice. You take away choice, you've nothing left but a dictatorship based on fear and guilt.'

I said, 'What about my son? What about his choice?'

'He may have parked his car in the garage, but it doesn't mean he owns the garage.' I was still thinking about that when she added, 'Do you want this job or do you not?'

I was feeling pretty pleased with myself. In the space of twenty-four hours, I had gone from being penniless and unemployed to two potentially high-paying cases, which could quite possibly keep me busy for weeks, if not months. If I wasn't careful, I would soon have to start employing staff.

I *deserved* a coffee and a doughnut. I picked them up at the café opposite my office and sauntered across. I let myself in and sat in my chair and put my feet up on the table. I unfolded the morning paper. The lead story was about the firebombing. There was a photo of Dr Macceabee standing in front of the burned-out building. She looked both steely and grim. She gave some defiant quotes about refusing to be driven out of the city and it being business as usual. There was another short piece on the front about the shootings in west Belfast and an opinion piece following the release of the latest unemployment figures. It seemed I was bucking a trend. I was just turning to the sport when I heard the sharp click of high heels on the stairs, and then, with the office door open for the breeze, I had a good view of Sara Patterson as she approached along the corridor. I swished crumbs off the desk and ran my hand through my once-luxuriant hair. As she drew closer, I saw that her face was set harder than cement.

She stopped in the doorway and snapped out, 'You bastard.'

'You bitch.'

'*What*?'

'You can't just walk in here and call me a bastard without getting a little something in return.'

'Jesus! What sort of a despicable little shit are you?'

'Well, that's a matter of—'

'Just shut your cake hole and give it back to me.'

'Give—?'

'Just give it up, Starkey. I spoke to Tommy; he told me you cornered him and took my laptop.'

'And you believe *him*?'

'Yes.'

'That's *outrageous*.'

'Nevertheless.'

'Sara – I may be many things but, Christ, I'm still a journalist at heart; we're in the same business, and there's a certain responsibility there, a certain loyalty, whether we're colleagues or rivals. I came to you for help and I'd like to think I could still ask you for it despite our wee falling out, so why the hell would I want to jeopardise that by taking your laptop? And why would you believe a sneaky little two-faced tout like Tommy, who not only stole your laptop in the first place but also swiped my money while he was at it?'

'My laptop was fitted with a tracking device. I tracked it here.'

She folded her arms and, without speaking, dared me to come back from that.

'Sara – you know I'm not as dumb as I look.' I opened my desk drawer, took out the laptop and set it on the desk. 'Tommy stole it. I went out of my way to get it back for you. I just haven't had the chance to deliver it. So I think a thank you is in order?'

She stepped across and lifted the computer. She said, 'You're an unscrupulous scumbag, Starkey, do you know that?'

'I have scruples,' I said.

She swore again. She turned the laptop over to check for damage. Satisfied, she glared some more and, when I didn't wilt, she blew air out of her cheeks and pulled out one of the two garden chairs I'd returned from the roof terrace, and sat down.

She said, 'Do you really think there's a tracking device in it?'

'Uhm,' I said.

'But that's not the only reason I'm here.'

'It'll be the charm and good looks then.'

'Who's the girl?'

'Who's what girl?'

'The girl you're spreading Monopoly money around for. I've had three different calls tipping me off to what you're doing.'

'She's got well-off parents who want answers, that's all.'

'Katya Cummings.'

'That's her.'

'There are only three families with that surname in Northern Ireland – none of them with a daughter called Katya.'

'Maybe they left. With all the trouble, people have been doing that. It's hard to keep track of their Cummings and goings.'

'Do you know, Starkey, if you were half as funny as

you think you are, you'd be twice as funny as you really are.'

'Funny is subjective,' I said.

Sara stood. 'I'll find out who she is. And, when I do, you can read about it on the front of the *Belfast Telegraph*.'

'I hope I do,' I said. 'In the meantime, you should think about something other than your surname for your laptop password; anyone could guess it.'

Her eyes narrowed. 'Have you made that donation to Whitespots yet?'

'You were serious about that?'

She still stood looking at me.

I said, 'For all that you have a problem with me, you seem very reluctant to leave.'

'Yeah. I was just thinking.'

'And, pray tell, what were you thinking?'

'Never meet your heroes.'

Sara gave a short, disappointed laugh and spun on her heel, leaving me sitting with my mouth hanging open and half a doughnut in my lap.

16

My paternal grandfather was a mean, joyless and surly character who ruled my father with a variety of big black books whose main rules for life could be summed up by the word *don't*. My father, thankfully, preferred *do*, and lived his life that way. Where my grandfather believed in authority and organisation, my father lived by chaos and anarchy, even if he might not have employed those words. I inherited the gene, much to the detriment, in retrospect, of my relationships and employment, but hey ho, let's go.

I had – and have – a certain understanding of – but not belief in – God, insofar as I can appreciate faith and devotion. Without being facile in the slightest (or, only slightly, or, indeed, quite a lot), the faithless cannot understand the devout because they just cannot comprehend uncompromising and unshakeable belief. Yet they blithely accept it in many other spheres of their life. Someone who lives and breathes Manchester United, who thinks about them every minute of every day, who genuinely despises non-supporters (especially those from Liverpool), who worships in their church (Old Trafford) or travels there with the same intense excitement as a pilgrim visiting Mecca, cannot claim not to understand the nature of religion and belief because it is virtually a mirror image of their own fanaticism. Jesus saves; Best nets the re-bound.

I was thinking these and similarly lofty thoughts about the New Seekers, and wondering about my best way into them. They were not my only suspects for the attack on the clinic but, because they were the ones I knew the least about and they appeared the most belligerent, as much Caliban as Taliban, I needed to know how much of a leap it was from fire and brimstone to fire and firebomb. They described themselves as *an apostolic ministry, committed to global harvest through revival and church planting*. They had a Facebook page with over 70,000 likes and an even larger number of Twitter followers. I wasn't sure if it was God himself who was Tweeting but, if it was, He did not feel the need to endlessly quote himself. Many of the Tweets were about peace and love, turning away from violence. Laudable, but it didn't preclude their involvement in the attack. It has been known for Christians to indulge in torture, massacre and genocide. Sometimes it has been a requirement.

By lunchtime, I had read a lot about faith and belief and the great community work the New Seekers were doing, but discovered very little about exactly who they were. They attended ordinary neighbourhood churches and spread their version of the word from within: infiltrate, influence and gently assume control. They were tolerated, even accepted, because they brought fresh blood into an ageing, dying, shrinking church-going population; the New Seekers were vibrant, enthusiastic, optimistic young professionals. I liked the idea of them, but I'd also met them in the flesh and knew them to stink of cult and sanctimony. They also seemed to be multiplying like the norovirus on a cruise ship. What would actually have been handy, I decided, was a Sara Patterson style map showing how many churches in Northern Ireland they now controlled.

Bugger.

I had tried not to think about Sara, but now she was back, front and centre.

Never meet your heroes.

Who the hell did she think she was?

I blew air out of my cheeks, shut down my New Seeker research and shifted location to the café across the road. I ordered a sausage roll and a coffee.

She was, I guessed, about ten years younger than me. I supposed that, when she was wanting to be a journalist, I was on the front pages; I was campaigning and exposing and taking the piss. I wasn't everyone's glass of whiskey, but I could see now how I might have inspired a youngster on the rise; it wasn't something I would have been aware of at the time because journalists only tend to get negative feedback: nobody crosses the road to pat your back; they cross the road to punch you in the face or shoot you in the neck. It is a thankless job but a vital one. So it was lovely, even at such a distance, to know that I had been a hero to someone, and depressing that I had now sullied that legacy just by being me.

Never meet your heroes.

'Really?' Detective Inspector Gary Hood slipped into the chair on the other side of my table. 'First sign of madness, don't you know?'

'Don't you know?' I mimicked. 'What are you, a country gentleman now?'

He grinned and signalled to the waitress. As she came across, he set a padded envelope down on the table. 'I was just going to send them over, then I thought – what the hell – I'll bring them. You're very predictable, where you're going to be; you ought to watch that.'

He ordered tea and a scone. I paid for it; Gary registered his surprise.

If Sara Patterson was ten years younger than me, Gary Hood was nearer twenty. I'd met him last year when he'd been new on the force. He'd struck me then as officious and pious – a bad combination when you're still wet behind the ears. Maxi McDowell, my previous police confidante, had introduced us and had clearly seen something in him, but we had not exactly hit it off. It was a surprise, therefore, when he sought to keep up our fledgling relationship, even after Maxi had gone rogue. Since then, he'd been promoted from Detective Sergeant, and the more I got to know him the more I began to trust him and even to like him. He had loosened up some, which helped.

'So, never meet your heroes . . .?'

'I'd get those ears checked out, if I was you,' I said. 'I said, "No More Heroes" – the song, by The Stranglers. I don't expect you've heard of them – or were born when they were around.'

'Old man music.' He laughed. He began to cut and then butter his scone. At the same time, he nodded at the envelope and said, 'That's the best of what we have. From a Maxol garage just around the corner from William Street; shop camera; half the ones attending the party stopped off for sweets on the way to William Street . . .'

'Crush munchies,' I said.

'I'd a quick look; it's pretty good quality, about two hours' worth . . .'

'How far did they get with analyzing it?'

'They didn't. Wasn't considered pertinent to the main thrust of the murder investigation. Your missing girl wasn't exactly a priority, though she does seem to have become one. I'm hearing a few whispers.'

'That's the plan.'

'Tread carefully, Dan. Or invest in body armour.'

'That bad?'

'They're taking us out of civvies and putting us in Kevlar. That bad that we can't go out unless it's a convoy.'

'Yet you appear to be by yourself today.'

'I know. You're a bad influence.' He smiled and munched.

I said, 'Do you ever think of getting out of this fucking place? I mean, look at you: you're young; you could go anywhere.'

'It's home, Dan.'

'It's a broken home. You could go to Australia.'

'You looking rid of me, or something?'

I raised an eyebrow.

'Maybe you're the one wants to go. You could get a wee retirement home somewhere.'

'Fuck off,' I said.

'Sit in the sun and listen to your old man music and bore everyone with your adventures.'

'That'll be the day,' I said. Though I did have a sudden vision of sitting by a pool, sipping cocktails with Thomas Wolff and smiling across at his daughter splashing in the water with Trish. We were perfectly at home, part of the jet set now. And then I thought, *jet set*. I was *really* fucking old. 'So tell me,' I said, 'what do know about the Botanic Boat Crew? And the Riot Squad?'

'Enough to stay clear of them.'

'Which one do you fancy for Wellington Street?'

'Either. Both. Neither. That's how far we got with it.'

'But they were questioned?'

'Sure. We had Davy Blair from Botanic and Paddy White from Riot. Passed each other in the corridor; nearly tore each other's eyes out.'

'So no love lost. What did they say about the massacre?'

'Nothing. They didn't have to.'

'Were they crushed?'

'I'm told Paddy's into it. Davy not so much.'

Gary popped the last piece of his scone into his mouth. His fingernails were bitten to the quick. When he'd swallowed it, he said, 'This girl you're looking for . . .'

'Katya.'

'. . . Katya; I hope they're paying you well.'

'They are.'

'And how's your other girl?'

'Trish? Still playing hard to get.'

'She's bound to cave in eventually, man of your charm.'

'That's what I keep telling her.'

We both fell silent for a little bit. He stirred his tea. I looked out the window. There were a couple of New Seekers across the road, just walking along, smiling at people. Gary saw me looking.

'They're everywhere,' he said.

'Aye. But at least they wear uniforms; you can spot them coming and cross the road.'

'You think?'

He pushed his chair back and stood. 'Better hit the road.' He reached forward and patted the padded envelope again. 'Hope it's of some use. Like I say, tread carefully.'

'Will do,' I said. He was a couple of steps from the door when I said, 'And Gary?'

'Yep?'

'You know, if we stay strong together, we can really sort this place out.'

He nodded thoughtfully. Then he said, 'I think not,' and departed.

He was probably right.

We were beyond sorting.

But we'd die trying.

17

I spread some more money around the bars on Botanic Avenue, which bordered the Holy Land. Alison hadn't drunk there on the night she disappeared, but she definitely had on other nights. It was the hub of student drinking in the city, and the gang-bangers responsible for the massacre at Wellington Street more than likely hung out there too.

Nobody volunteered information. Several looked at my business card and nodded and smiled and promised to ask around, but probably binned it as soon as I left. It was a depressing trudge, with half the shops lying derelict and crush casualties slumped in doorways. At the far end, towards the university, the New Seekers had set up camp in a repainted Ulster bus, offering coffee and sustenance to addicts, alcoholics and chancers. I kept an eye on it as I moved from bar to bar, and an idea began to form. In the early evening, I ate a pizza in the Empire beside the Botanic railway halt and then watched another early season humiliation for Liverpool on their big screen. It was just a friendly, but still – a portent. I sipped whiskey throughout. When it got sufficiently dark outside, I ordered a final Bushmills and drank half of it. The rest I dabbed on my clothes and splashed behind my ears. I was half-cut, but wanted to appear fully cut.

When I left the bar, I was still walking normally, but as I drew closer to the drop-in bus I began to stagger, then to walk diagonally, and then it was the old two-steps-forward, three-steps-back. If anyone had been watching me the entire way, they would have seen a transformation as remarkable as Keyser Söze's. It was still well short of closing time, so the street was relatively quiet. Half a dozen New Seekers in their white robes were milling around dispensing smiles and encouragement to passers-by. I pretended to fall into a shop doorway just a couple down from the bus, then made sure they were watching before I righted myself against the barred door and sang as I peed. I emerged from a cloud of steam and lurched towards the bus. I stopped, put my hands on my hips, swayed back, swayed forward, steadied myself and demanded to know, 'What the fuck's going on here then?' of the little group of disciples.

One young man split from the group and approached me. 'It's just a wee drop-in centre,' he said, his accent Derry. 'Could I get you a wee cup of tea?'

'You could get me a wee whiskey and Coke.'

He beamed at me. He was clean-cut and handsome with dark hair and heavy eyebrows. When he wasn't saving souls, he probably worked as a male model.

'Well,' he said, 'we don't serve alcohol, but I could certainly get you a soft drink or a coffee. Do you want to come on board and grab a wee seat?'

I said, 'Nah, you're all right. What are youse like, in your wee dresses?'

'Actually, this weather, they're very comfortable. Sure, come on – I'll get you a Coke.'

I swayed some more. 'Once I get on,' I drawled, 'you'll try and convert me to . . . all that shit.'

'Absolutely not, sir . . . If you don't want us to say a word, we won't say a word. All we offer is a safe haven for a little while; maybe you want to wait here while you call a taxi? Or even just to take the weight off your feet?'

'I'm not drunk,' I said, 'though I fuckin' should be. Those bastards.'

'Those . . .?'

'Sure, what do you care? What does anyone care?' I held my chest and pretended to be fighting off a retch. My friend's smile remained vigorous. 'Aye, then,' I said, 'maybe a wee Coke . . .'

'Surely; come on then . . .'

I took a couple of steps forward and stopped again. I nodded at the bus.

'Is He on board?'

'Is . . .?'

'God: is He on the bus?'

'Yes, He is.'

'Does God drive your bus?'

'Nick drives our bus,' said the guy, 'but God inspires him to drive it well.'

'Answer me this,' I said. 'Does God, if He's driving your bus, does God use sat nav?'

'Nick uses sat nav, but God created the sat nav, and the roads and all of the people.'

'He's a busy little fucker, isn't he?'

Not even a hint of a falter.

'He is very busy, but He has time for all of us.'

I swayed back. He reached out to steady me and then guided me on board the single-decker. The usual two rows of seats had been stripped out and replaced with comfortable sofas and dark wooden tables and a soft but sturdy-looking carpet; it all smelled of Pine Fresh. There were three other pick-ups on board: one teenage girl crying into the arms of a New Seeker, who was patting her back and whispering consoling words; another grungy-looking fella was flat out asleep on a sofa with a plastic bucket on the floor beside him; and a third guy was sitting on the side of an armchair, rocking back and forth, clutching his knees, his eyes the size of Gollum's and repeating to himself, 'They told me to take one; I took four. They told me to take one; I took four. I can't feel my toes. They told me to take one; I took four . . .' There was another girl Seeker rubbing his back and telling him it would all be OK.

'I'm Simon,' said my companion, 'and I've to go back outside now, but Jane is going to look after you.'

Jane was a beauty in white, who approached with her hands clasped before her and a huge smile beaming out of her headdress.

'Fuck,' I said, 'you're lovely.' Her smile did not falter. I held up a hand. 'Sorry,' I said. 'But you are.'

'Never you mind; I'm Jane and *what's your name*?'

'Andy,' I said. 'Andy. *Andrew* Topping . . . Young, free, single and destitute.'

'Andy wants a Coke,' said Simon as he departed.

'We don't do Coke,' said Jane, 'but I could get you a nice wee cup of tea?'

'He promised me a Coke,' I said.

'Why don't you just sit down here,' said Jane, indicating a sofa, 'and I'll just *see what I can do*.'

I took the seat. I watched her move down the bus to a small galley. She looked good from the rear. The cut of the gown emphasised the shape of the wearer. It helped if you had a good shape to start with. All of the New Seekers on the bus were young and good looking, a New Testament mix of Abercrombie and Fitch. I was sure it was deliberate. They were trawling for lost souls, and it probably helped if your potential saviour looked like an angel.

Jane came back with a cup of tea. 'There you . . .' she began, but then stopped when she saw that my head was in my hands, and my shoulders were pumping.

I sniffed up and said, 'Sorry . . . Sorry . . .' through my fingers. 'It's just all . . . turned . . . turned to shit.'

She perched herself on the edge of the sofa and put her arm around my shoulders and squeezed. I was mostly concentrating on acting my socks off, but my mind kept drifting back to the fact that I could feel one of her breasts rubbing against me through the flimsy material of her gown.

It's just the nature of me.

Us.

'It's OK; it's all right, Andrew.' She shifted position so that she could put her own tiny hands on top of mine. She slowly peeled my fingers back to reveal my tear-stained and snot-smeared face. She gave me a sympathetic look and a tissue and said, 'Andrew, no matter how bad you feel, we can sort this out. Why don't you tell me about it?'

So I sat back. And she settled beside me. I told her about my failed marriage and how I'd lost my job and how my wife had – just that day – told me not to come home; she'd already changed the locks, and I'd no money and nowhere to go. I told her I had no hope, no future, and I might as well end it all. I'd spent my last few quid on drink, and now there was nothing to stop me jumping into the Lagan. I cried some more, and apologised, and told her how kind she was and I wished I could have her kind of breezy outlook on life, and she said I could, and I said no, not for the likes of a disaster – a failure – like me, and that started me off again. She asked me where I was staying and I said, if I didn't have the balls to kill myself tonight, I would maybe sleep out in the open because it was summer still, and warm. But everywhere I'd looked so far was already crowded with druggies out of their heads, and please God don't let me end up like that, and Jane said, 'No, Andrew, God doesn't want you to end up like that. Don't you see? That's why he sent you to us.' I told her I didn't believe in God, and she said that was fine, and it didn't matter, that I would always be looked after by the New Seekers, and I said they were one of the first bands I remembered and she nodded but I could tell she'd no idea what I was talking about because nobody under the age of forty-five ever does. She said, 'You're going to stay with us tonight, and that's the end of it. The bus will be leaving in about an hour; if you can just settle yourself till then, OK?'

I was going to slip away, but then I started thinking that, seeing as how I did not actually have anyone else in my life and nothing much to do on my other case until the money I'd been handing out did its work, it might be useful to follow these nutters back to their lair; it might help me get a better handle on them. So I made the snap decision to go with them. As soon as I told her, Jane took my hands in hers and said she could tell I was a good man who happened to have fallen on hard times, and she gave me a hug, and I could still feel her breasts pressing firmly against me and God damn me to hell for thinking about it, but hey ho, let's go.

The pubs eventually gave out and a few more were welcomed in for tea but, of those, only one was staying on the bus to God-knows-where. His name was Marty and he couldn't have been more than twenty. He had the heebie-jeebies: the first, easy stage of getting off the crush. After that you were better off in a hospital because, if you were an addict and withdrew it suddenly, it could fuck up your vital organs. As soon as Jane suggested taking him there, he got all manic and shouty and swore they were after his kidneys and thyroid (for some reason). So instead they wrapped him in one of those silver blankets they give to marathon runners and lay him on a couch and told him they had doctors at their place who could absolutely be trusted and that everything was going to turn out just fine.

When the bus finally started up and pulled out on to Botanic Avenue, Jane brought Marty a cup of tea and held it to his lips because his hands were shaking so much, but he threw it up almost immediately. He had the orangey hew some of them get in the latter stages of withdrawal. Jane held him to her bosom and told him that the Bishop would provide, and that the Bishop would heal him, but, before I could ask her which Bishop, there was a loud crack against the window beside us. Jane let out a scream and was thrown back as the bus lurched violently to one side. I just managed to catch her and, in the same movement, I grabbed on to a safety rail to support us both. Marty wasn't so lucky. He was hurled off his sofa and cracked his head as he hit the deck. The bus had mounted the kerb and was shaking madly as it careered along without dropping speed at all, until finally it crunched back down on to the road and roared away.

Nick, the driver, yelled back to see if everyone was OK. As they shouted, 'Yes,' and 'Praise the Lord!' Jane slipped out of my grasp and crouched beside Marty. The window beside us had a large hole in it with splintery tributaries running off.

Simon appeared at my side and said, 'It's OK; nothing to worry about; you can go back to your seat.'

I said, 'It was a brick.'

'I know – they do it most nights, but they haven't stopped us yet.'

'Who does? Why?'

'Kids, gangs . . . They think we should pay them to drive along their street.'

'Maybe you should think about going another way.'

'We do go another way, every night. But there's always someone looking to get paid. But what can you do?' He raised his hands and gave me another smile. 'And aren't we all fine? The Bishop protects us, the Lord protects us and we give thanks.'

Their relentless sunniness was really starting to get me down.

18

Fresh sea air rushed in off Strangford Lough through the broken glass as the drunk bus weaved its way along the Ards Peninsula to a happy-clappy New Seeker soundtrack, with the promise of a soft bed and salvation to come. I was lying on a sofa at the back, resting my pounding head on a cushion and debating the value of on-the-ground research over an internet trawl. I would rather have been at home in bed. In all my years of drinking, of throwing up in bushes and sleeping under cars, of dancing with album covers on my head and careering down stairs on biscuit-tin lids, I had never yet been reduced to a homeless shelter or sought the pity of the Church. But now I was about to embrace both.

Purely for work.

I was playing a drunk.

I am not a drunk.

I embrace the Ulster approach to drinking, that the weekend begins on a Thursday and, with the right planning, preparation and constitution, can be seen through at least until Tuesday. It is the way of us. But, also, I am aware that what seems wild and rebellious, full of spirit and character in a young man, is less to be admired in the aching, bloated body of one in his middle years. There is a thickening belly of division between charming and seedy, and I knew that I had been straddling it in a way that I had not much straddled anything else of late. I would never stop, but I would probably have to cut back, choose my moments more carefully. I do not much care how I am viewed by the world at large, but I do care what Patricia thinks – but, it would seem, just not enough to do anything about it quite yet. For now, I would make do with channelling my sodden lifestyle into my business: acting the drunk by becoming the drunk, bringing madness to the method. My job was to unmask who was behind a firebombing. If I'd been writing it as a story, I would have been tempted into the headline, *Fire At Abortion Clinic Saves Hundreds of Lives*. But I was no longer a journalist; I was a private eye for hire, going under cover, a half-cut Mr Ben, intent on infiltration and total immersion.

'Nearly there, now,' Simon said, giving me a little shake on the shoulder.

I gave him a grunt and sat up.

I'd expected a church hall in west Belfast or some grungy care-in-the-community setup, but we were bound for what Simon said was their country retreat in Ballyferris, which was halfway down the peninsula. I'd been there a few times as a kid, and later on had taken the odd romantic drive there with Trish and enjoyed a scenic fumble in its seafront car park. It was very much a one-horse town and, I supposed, perfect if you wanted to isolate vulnerable druggies and drinkers and convert them to the cause. After forty-five minutes of increasingly twisty country road, we finally pulled into its main street – and then continued on for another half a mile before our real destination unexpectedly presented itself: Ballyferris Park. This was a major surprise. Ballyferris Park was huge – over a thousand acres – one of the largest in the country. I knew it as belonging to Lord Danesfort, but it had now clearly changed hands – and, if the New Seekers had it, it spoke volumes about their spending power and ambition. There were two robed Seekers on the gates, who came on board and walked up and down, checking for God knows what. Then we were driven up a long, curving drive, which ended in front of the massive and imposing Victorian edifice that was Ballyferris House, all lit up and glistening against the star-studded sky. As we pulled to a stop, I had a very odd mix of sensations: part of me felt like I'd lucked into a free spa weekend at a luxury retreat; another part suspected that I'd cadged a lift on the night bus to Bedlam.

There were a dozen parking spaces out front, all filled. There was a working fountain. There were more Seekers waiting to greet us. We were shepherded off the bus, with the exception of Marty, who was carried off on a stretcher and taken inside the house. We weren't invited to follow, but instead Jane was one of a small group of smilers who escorted us around to a back yard and a row of somewhat dilapidated-looking Nissen huts. Three were in darkness, but the fourth had a light in the entrance, with the door open behind, so that we could see twin rows of camp beds, half of them already occupied.

Jane said, 'It may not look much, but it's warm and it's clean and secure. There's coffee and showers – but it's late and the others are sleeping, so maybe you should all go straight to bed? Then we can all have a lovely breakfast in the morning. We would just ask a couple of things of you: if you have a mobile phone, if you would be so kind as to let us look after it for the night; it's the only thing we don't really allow here, and there's hardly ever a signal, anyway – one of the drawbacks of being out in the country. And we also ask that you don't go wandering around during the night. We don't lock you in, of course – you are free to come and go – we just ask that you don't do it during the hours of darkness. I should remind you that this is a working estate and farm, and therefore there are all kind of dangers, from slurry pits that will suck you under to bulls that'll skewer you given half the chance, and our insurance is expensive enough without anything like that happening.'

Two of our group handed over their phones. I made a show of checking my pockets and then said, 'Fuckin' hell.' Jane raised an eyebrow. I said, 'What's your policy on swearing?'

'We don't encourage it.'

A second Seeker said, 'Matthew said it is not what goes into the mouth that defiles a person, but what comes out of the mouth.'

I nodded and said, 'He obviously never met my wife.'

He looked at me blankly, and I reminded myself that disciples of any religion were not known for their sense of humour. Or for appreciating that Jesus was a stand-up who needed better material.

I nabbed the closest bed to the door. I had intentions of hoking around the estate under the cover of darkness. The robes and chanting and general blinded-by-conviction demeanour of the New Seekers provided them with an image of secrecy, which I suspected they did not warrant; people knew so little about them only because they appeared so other-worldly and inaccessible. But if you reminded yourself that they were just ordinary guys and gals, that they were accountants and civil servants and farmers who peed and pooed along with the rest of us, who just happened to have a silly-clothes division, then their supposed secrecy became much more transparent and would, I hoped, be no more difficult, and possibly even easier, to breach than that of any other bonded group of mugs. They were, I hoped, in the business of trust. Maybe they would make it doubly simple by going along with the Amish and not believing in locks.

The hut smelled of sweat and beer; there was a

constant gurgle from the toilets at the back. Those already in their beds did not stir as we settled in. Jack, an emaciated chap with missing teeth and a barnacled face, took the bed beside mine. He didn't bother with taking off his clothes before climbing in. I slipped off my trousers and shoes and got in; the thin sheets were starched and refreshingly cool. I asked Jack if he'd been here before and he nodded. I lay back with my hands clasped behind my head and, after about five minutes, Jane reappeared and said a short prayer over us and then switched off the main inside lights on her way out. After the door was shut, the only light then came from the bathroom at the back, an illuminated rectangle around the main door itself from the outside light and the tiny but constant red glow from the corner of the ceiling above me. I wasn't sure if it was a smoke alarm, or something to do with the electricity supply, or if it was a camera to watch over us. I spent a long time studying it, and debating what it might be. So long, in fact, that despite all of my bad intentions I drifted off to sleep, and did not wake until I was shocked out of it by chanting – religious chanting, medieval religious chanting – booming out of what was now clearly not a smoke alarm or a camera, but a PA speaker.

We had not left Belfast until nearly two in the morning; the journey to Ballyferris had taken the best part of an hour, which gave us two hours of sleep before the August dawn was pierced by this incessant racket. I pulled the covers over my head and only peeked out when I felt movement around me and realised that, of the twelve of us poor wretches in the Nissen hut, ten were now rising.

I hissed, 'What the fuck is this about?' at Jack beside me.

'It's the call to prayer,' he said.

'Is it compulsory?'

'Nope,' he said.

He wasn't moving either.

It continued and, if anything, got louder. Sleep deprivation was probably part of the game. Break down their resistance. My inclination was to build a mountain of mattresses, to climb up them and to smash the speaker with my forehead. But I had to quickly remind myself why I was there, and that all knowledge was good knowledge, and knowing what they were up to would be useful, so I reluctantly threw back my covers and sat up. My head still ached, but it was low level. I rubbed at my eyes with the heel of one hand and felt around for my trousers with the other, and then I opened my eyes properly and actively looked for them, and my shirt, and my shoes, and then I became aware of Jack giggling beside me. I snapped out a *What?*

'They come and take them when we're sleeping,' he said, and pulled his covers back far enough to remind me that he was still fully dressed. 'You soon learn.'

'But what am I supposed to . . .?'

Jack pointed a bony finger towards the door, and I saw that there were robes hanging there, and sandals on the floor, and I muttered a *for-fuck's-sake*. I had gone to extraordinary lengths during my many adventures to solicit information, often involving me going under-cover and adopting disguises, but rarely had I had a dress code imposed upon me. I am of the punk genera-tion and favour black, and narrow trousers, and affect what I know will never be an aesthete's cool, except in my own head, but what I hope at least appears to be a little bit rock'n'roll: attitude with a hint of chaos. But white robes are nobody's idea of cool. They're hippy shit. White robes with a George-at-Asda black T-shirt underneath, together with a pair of washed-out black (now grey) knock-off Armani jockeys and a mismatched pair of black socks – one orphaned from a thoughtless M&S Christmas present and the other with a hole clearly visible because of the brown sandals – combined to make me look not only sartorially inelegant but a right buck eejit as well.

We filed out of the hut and towards a series of outbuildings, which had been painted white, but were old. There were country smells of shit. Other berobed folk emerged from the other huts, but there was no way of telling if they were converts or conscripts. Many more emerged from the rear of the house itself, and they all converged on the largest of the buildings, which had the outer appearance of an old barn but, as we entered, I saw that it had a wooden floor and chairs and a table at the front and a large but simple cross painted on to each of the four whitewashed walls. It was a church, but reduced to the bare essentials, and hardly big enough for what must have been about two hundred of us to squeeze into. We, last night's intake,

were somewhere around the back, and with no eleva-
tion we only had a very restricted view of what was
happening at the front. The chanting had followed
us as we walked to the church, relayed on speakers
attached to the exterior of the buildings or hung on
wires between them, and continued as we arranged
ourselves inside. Now it switched from being recorded
to live: there was a choir of some sort, and the quality
was not as good, but it was louder, bouncing off the
exposed brickwork. While heads were bowed in prayer
or swayed with the chanting, I caught glimpses of those
leading the service. I saw Jane there, smiling, singing
with gusto. Everyone was robed, but about half a dozen
of them at the front, facing the rest of the congregation,
were wearing different coloured ones, clearly indicating
that they held some kind of rank within the Church.

As the chanting ended, a guy at the front and left
– I could only catch glimpses of his red robe – launched
into a sermon in which he asked for absolute devotion
to the cause and resolution in the face of coming trials.
He was an old-school orator, voluminous and inspiring
in equal measure. There was also something vaguely
familiar about his voice, but I couldn't quite get a proper
look at him. Then, in trying to get a better look, my
eyes connected with another one of the rankers at the
front, and I recognised her instantly as the young girl
who had trailed after me outside the clinic, who
had somehow known my name. There was just a milli-
second of connection before I looked away and then
ducked down and moved sideways. I hardly dared to

check back to see if it had clicked with her who I was. I held my breath, but she did not scream and point or otherwise react, and ecclesiastical bouncers did not plough into the congregation in pursuit of me. So I stood and endured the rest of their interminable service.

Afterwards, we bus-drunks gathered in a group outside the church and were then led across to a prefab dining hall, which was otherwise empty. Jack, who had now joined us, said everyone else had already eaten. He sat beside me as porridge, then bacon and eggs were served. He used only one hand to eat, as his left was wrapped in a scabby-looking muslin bandage with a safety pin holding it in place. I had not noticed it the night before. I said, 'What happened to you?'

He grinned and gave me a wink and said, 'You'll learn.'

When we'd finished, Jane came in and said, 'Well, I hope you all had a good night's sleep, that you enjoyed the service and, of course, your breakfast. There is of course no charge for any of this, but the Bishop hopes that you will find it in your hearts perhaps to help out with some work around the estate while you're here.'

'Always a catch,' I said, probably louder than I should have.

But Jane's smile did not falter. She nodded at me and said, 'No one is compelled to work – but if you have something to offer . . . For example, are you good with your hands?'

There was an answer to that, but I kept it to myself. Foreplay, like comedy, is subjective.

I said instead, 'You wouldn't want to stand under a light bulb that I screwed in. It would fall out and smash on your head. So the short answer would be no.'

'But you could do dishes, surely?'

I looked at the table. Ten of us had been eating. Not so bad. I shrugged.

Jack said, 'I can help him.'

Jane gave a rueful shake of her head. 'Now, Jack, that's appreciated, but not with your sore hand.'

Jack looked disappointed, but then sneaked me his stupid grin. He did not have a sore hand, but he was an old hand, and had been dealt a bad hand, so fair play to him.

Jane invited me to follow her along a short, covered walkway that led into the kitchen at the back of the house, which boasted heavy ranges, marble worktops and what appeared to be every single dish that had been used to feed the entire congregation of New Seekers. They were set out in teetering columns on every available surface and, where they'd run out of counter space, they'd been stacked on the trolleys used to wheel the food across to the prefab in the first place.

'There's a lot of them,' said Jane. 'I should ask some of the others to—'

'No, really, they're fine,' I said. 'I like a challenge.' I was now in the actual house itself. If I was left alone for long enough, I would soon find a way to nose around. 'So, if you'll just point me in the direction of the dishwasher, I'll get stuck in.'

Jane said, 'We don't have a dishwasher.'

'Fuck *off*.' She looked at me. I looked at her. I was in character. '*Sorry* . . . but . . . no dishwasher? You need a fucking . . . sorry . . . industrial dishwasher for this lot. You don't believe in dishwashers? Or, for that matter, mobile phones?'

'We prefer—'

'I mean, I don't remember a verse in the Bible saying, *Ye shalt not Nokia, or sully thy hands with a Zanussi.*'

'Now, Andy,' she said, with a cheeky wave of her finger, 'of course they're not in the Bible. But the Bishop believes they are disruptive and affect our privacy, and so they are discouraged. The dishwasher is broken. It's away being fixed.'

'Ah,' I said. 'That's more like it. But nevertheless . . .' I nodded around the dishes. 'You want me to . . .? I'll be here for weeks.'

'That is our master plan.'

Her smile did not grow, or fade, but remained constant, so she was hard to read, but it was good to know there was a little spark in there somewhere – unless, of course, she was completely serious.

'Good one,' I said.

'Relax, Andy; you shall have help. Get started, and I'll see who I can drum up. If we get half an hour out of you, that would be good – then there will be time for your indexing and after that there's a bus back to Belfast—'

'Index . . .?'

'Yes . . . sorry, of course, it's your first time. So many of your companions are regulars here that I forgot. It's nothing to worry about; an index is like . . . a chat with one of our Sisters, to see if we can be of any help to you. We know you're at a very low point in your life.'

'I've been lower,' I said.

'Of course you have. And it's entirely voluntary. The bus doesn't leave till one; sure, why don't you have a wee think about it? But I have to say, many people have found indexing to be an extremely positive experience.'

'Good to know,' I said. 'I'll also be needing my trousers back.'

'Your trousers will be fresh, clean and pressed, waiting for you on your bed after you finish your indexing. Anyway, you get started and I'll go and get some help for you.'

And she was away, and I was left with the detritus of breakfast, one half bottle of Fairy Liquid and a mobile phone in my underpants. There had been no signal in the Nissen hut but, now that I was temporarily alone in the kitchen, I whipped it out and switched it on. The voicemail icon was showing that I had three messages waiting, but the signal wasn't strong enough for me to hear them. When I checked the call records, I saw that one was from Trish, the other two from numbers I didn't recognise. There was also a text from my good lady ex, pondering my whereabouts. I composed something about staying at someone else's place to hopefully get her jealous but, by the time I'd finished writing it, the signal was completely gone. I could also see through the kitchen window that Jane was returning with a couple of volunteers. I raised the phone high, hoping to catch the signal before they reached me, but no. Maybe if I got to the top of the building. Or maybe I had no idea about signals. I slipped the phone back into my pants, tightened my robe and plunged my hands into a sink full of foamy water. As they came through the door, I launched into 'Bringing in the Sheaves'. I stopped and feigned embarrassment. Jane urged me to continue, but I modestly declined, mostly because I didn't know anything beyond the opening lines. And actually, I had been singing 'Bringing in the Wreathes', which was something entirely different but much more appropriate for our little country.

19

Jane's volunteers were from our hut and the next one along. The ones from the other hut had, like us, been plucked from the streets, but they'd been in Ballyferris for four nights.

'Tell me,' I said, 'do you *ever* get your trousers back?'

Billy, a guy in his fifties, his rotundity emphasised by his robe, said, 'We choose not to get our trousers back.'

I nodded thoughtfully. You could take his words as deep as you wanted.

As we launched into the dishes, they all chipped in bits and pieces about their time at Ballyferris Park. At the end of their first week, if they still wanted to stay and had shown a willingness to work and be indexed, they would be invited to move to a third hut. There, the indexing would be ramped up and, after that, they would have the opportunity to pledge themselves to the New Seekers and become part of their global harvest.

Tony – late twenties, goatee beard and teeth all over the place – who took to the dishes with a manic kind of intensity, said he had absolutely found his place in life. He was going to stay forever. Three of the other five were right there with him.

I said, 'The Bishop's done a good sales job on you.'

They looked at me with barely concealed contempt.

Tony said, 'You'll see.'

Jack, with nothing better to do, had joined us in the kitchen. He was leaning against the back counter and concentrating his shaky hands on perfecting a roll-up. He said, 'Never stay more than one night, me; that way, they don't get their hooks into you.'

'You don't know what you're talking about, Jack,' said Tony, 'yet you keep coming back. You'll change; once the Bishop steps out, you'll change.'

'Steps out?' I asked.

'When the time comes,' said Tony, 'the Bishop will lead us to salvation.'

I said, 'I hope someone alerts the media.'

'The media will find out along with all the other sinners, they—'

'Joke,' I said.

Jack pushed off the counter and went outside to light his cigarette. As he passed, he indicated for me to follow. I looked at the others and said, 'Holy smoke,' and went after him.

We stood in the cobbled yard. There were farm workers moving about in mud-spattered robes. Jack was the odd man out with his tartan shirt and brown corduroys hanging off him like they were drying on a rail. He had a whiff of sweat and the charity shop about him. Instead of sandals, he wore tan leather loafers. When I looked a bit closer, I realised they weren't a pair. Close, but not blood relatives.

I said, 'Dishes! What do they think I am?'

'That's nothing,' said Jack. He gave a quick spit of loose tobacco. 'You should try the laundry. Don't know what genius came up with white robes for working on a farm! And they're rubbish quality – a couple of washes and they turn into, like, crumpled grey – but, instead of looking at a new supplier, they just buy in more. Nuts. They should take a look at their history books, understand what brought Napoleon down at Moscow, and the Nazis at Stalingrad: the quality of their clothes.'

'You should say to them; I'm sure they'd appreciate haberdashery advice from a down-and-out.'

'I wasn't always a down-and-out,' Jack snapped.

'Sorry,' I said quickly.

'But I sure as hell am one now.' He bared what was left of his teeth in a smile and then spat some more. 'You wouldn't do us a favour, would you? My hands . . .' He held out his tobacco and papers. 'Bit shaky.'

I took them off him and did my best. It had been a long time since I smoked. I said, 'I really didn't mean to—'

'Forget about it. It's the truth. Just scary how quickly it happens. This time a year ago, I had family and career – lecturer in politics at Belfast Uni.'

'Ah,' I said, 'politics will get you every which way.'

'Wasn't the politics; it was the crush. Takes about five minutes to eat you up. Weaned myself off it with whiskey and fags. Then the whiskey was the problem. But I'll get off that too, with the help of this lot.' He thumbed back towards the big house. 'Using them like a free Betty Ford. But I'm not stupid. Stay here for any length of time, they really will get their claws into you, so I break it up, do a couple of nights here, then back out on the streets. It's not so bad; it's summer; it's hot for once. Time autumn comes round, I'll be sorted. Those ones doing the dishes? Lost cause. Lost fucking cause.'

'They do seem pretty far down that road for only having been here a few days.'

'That's all they need. I've seen some of them turned in a day. It's the indexing; they break you down, then they build you back up in their image.'

'So you must have been through it?'

'Oh, aye.'

'So what's the secret of not being broken down?'

'You give them fuck all.'

'Fuck all,' I said.

'You don't give them anything they can hurt you with.'

'I don't *have* anything they can hurt me with,' I said.

'*Everyone* has something they can hurt you with,' said Jack.

20

We were most of the way through the dishes when they came for me.

It wasn't like they yanked me up by the hair and dragged me into a cell equipped with instruments of torture. They were very nice about it. Jane came back in and asked if anyone wanted to be indexed and, seeing as how I was the only one who hadn't been through it, they all looked at me. I held up my soapy hands and said, 'I'm clean. Nothing to confess.'

Jane tutted and half scolded me with a, 'It's nothing like confession,' and a roll of the eyes.

Tony handed me a tea towel and I dried my hands. I tossed it back to him and then said, 'Okey-doke, then – do your worst.'

She turned for the door. Jack, who was still hanging around, gave me a wink as I passed. We stepped out into a gloomy hall, lined with old photographs of the

Danesfort family, some dating back to the early days of photography. As we moved along narrow corridors, busy with Seekers going about their business but nodding and smiling as we passed, I became aware of how run-down the whole place was, with wallpaper peeling, paint chipped and an all-pervading aroma of damp and must.

I massaged the back of my head as I walked. I was probably still concussed. I was traipsing around a crumbling stately pile in a white robe and had thus far discovered nothing of interest. Meanwhile, I was neglecting my other, potentially more lucrative, case. I glanced at my watch. It was already twelve fifteen; I would need to get the indexing over with pretty quickly, then use the fact that I was in their main building to have a proper look round. Perhaps there would be an opportunity when they broke for lunch or another church service; failing that, it would have to be later, under the cover of darkness. If that didn't work then I'd have to think of another approach once I was back in Belfast, because there were calls to be dealt with and informants who could easily slip back into the murk if they were ignored for much longer. And if it meant I had to jump the estate wall later on, with or without my trousers, then that was what I would have to do.

Jane showed me into a library. Thousands of books and, by the look of them, none younger than a hundred years old. Dusty framed portraits of long-dead lords of the manor. There was a coffee table in the middle of the room with a laptop on it and two low red leather chairs on either side. I sat in the one nearest the door. At the very moment that Jane exited, a door on the other side of the room opened and the young woman who had approached me outside the clinic, and who knew my real name, entered.

I swore under my breath.

She was not grinning inanely like the others. Any slight hope that she had forgotten our first encounter, or that I had imagined our eye contact earlier in the church, vanished the moment she sat down opposite me and said, 'Dan Starkey.'

'That's me,' I said. 'And you've a good head for names.'

She ignored that and said, 'How are you finding it here?'

'Bit too much God for me, but fascinating. I like a good cult. How do you know my name?'

'You really don't know?'

There was something in her eyes: challenging, knowing, yet sparky with humour.

'Well, yes, I probably do.' I hadn't been thinking about it until that moment, but it was suddenly very clear. 'You have someone on the inside at the Braxton clinic.' She half raised an eyebrow. I warmed to my subject. 'Our appointment wasn't made in my name, but I gave it over the intercom when we were going in. So someone on the desk. Or the security guard; he remembered I used to work for the newspapers. Yeah – probably him.'

She shook her head and said, 'No. But good to know how duplicitous you think we are. Hopefully your time here will help you come to a different . . . appreciation of what we are about.'

'I think my time here might be up. And your name is . . .?'

'You can call me Eve. Why did you say you were Andrew Topping?'

'Well, Eve . . .' I spread my hands. She raised an eyebrow. I had no way of knowing how much she did actually know about me. She might only have been tipped off to my name. It was probably a regular device they employed when confronting family members. My turning up at Ballyferris might seem like a huge coincidence so soon after our encounter, but it might also play to a smug conviction that making it personal could be enough to instantly plunge me into a crisis of faith. If they *really* knew I was a private investigator trying to infiltrate their Church, they would surely not have allowed me to stay on site for so long. So I would brazen it out until exposed or stoned. 'I'm Andrew Topping because . . . Well, I'm sorry, but this is all new to me and I was kind of embarrassed about the state I got into, and plucked the name from thin air.'

'There's nothing to be embarrassed about, Dan.'

'I know that; I know that now. The whole clinic thing just came at a bad time; my life has been falling apart these past few months, but the one good thing to happen was my son and his girlfriend getting pregnant, and I thought becoming a granddad might help sort me out . . . but then they're talking about getting rid of it and I just don't agree with that, but what can I do? So that was all very upsetting and in the end I just went out and got very pissed . . . sorry, drunk . . . and, well, I suppose it's . . . how I deal with things. And then I saw your people on the street corner, and I'd nowhere to go home to, cos my wife has finally given me the boot, and I deserve it no doubt, but I was still kind of mortified about it all because I used to have money, and a big house, and everyone knew me from writing in the paper, but that's all gone and I'm broke now and I've nowhere to live and . . . well, here I am: in Ballyferris, of all places.'

I gave her a big sigh.

She said, 'Sad.'

I diverted my gaze to the portraits on the wall. None of the subjects looked happy. I said, 'I met Lord Danesfort a couple of times. Are you keeping him prisoner in the attic? Or stuffed?'

She smiled. I smiled. She was hard to read. She delved into the folds of her robe and produced two pear-shaped objects, the size of Sky remotes, in black plastic and handed one across to me.

'Hold this in your left hand. I take this in my right and –' she indicated the laptop between us – 'by the magic of technology, we are connected wirelessly. Is it slightly warm to the touch?'

I nodded. 'Is this . . .?'

'This is what has come to be known as indexing. It's nothing to worry about; it's just a chat, really, about what's troubling you. Is that OK?'

'Um – yes, fine. So it's like confession crossed with a lie-detector test?'

'You say it like it's a negative thing.'

She held my gaze.

I said, 'Well . . .'

'We value absolute honesty. Dan, in this world, people are conditioned to lie, they're brought up to lie; indexing brings you back to the truth. If you have no secrets, it reduces the need to lie.'

'OK. I understand that. But . . . I'm not sure I like the idea of you . . . recording what I have to say. What if you . . . well, you know . . .'

'Use what we discover against you, to blackmail you?'

'Well, I didn't quite mean, that, but . . .'

'Yes, you did. And I can assure you indexing is not about specifics. It records that you lied, but not the substance of it. Colour, not detail.'

'So if you want into the Church, you have to pass the test.'

'No, of course not. We are what we are. Indexing is extremely sensitive, getting to the very highest level is almost impossible. In fact, only one person has ever come through it with complete purity.'

'Would that be the . . . What do you call him? The Bishop?'

She nodded slowly.

'And would he also be the founder of the Church, and maybe even the designer of this . . . indexing . . . programme?'

'It's an app. And you are a very cynical man, Dan Starkey.'

'It has been said.'

'But we will cure you of that.' Said with a spark that masked what was otherwise a threat and a promise.

I said, 'Yeah, you and whose army?'

'Our army of salvation.'

'If this worked both ways, I'd now know if you truly believed that.'

'Yes, you would.'

'And you might run into copyright problems, with the old "Salvation Army" thing.'

'How long have you been a journalist, Dan Starkey?'

'So this is it starting, is it?'

She nodded.

I took a couple of theatrically rapid breaths and rubbed my hands together, ready for the contest. 'OK,' I said. 'Set. Since leaving school, yes.'

'Have you always told the truth in your stories?'

'As far as I'm aware.'

'Have you ever been put under pressure to not tell the truth?'

'Yes.'

'Do you drink to excess?'

'No. Yes. It's a matter of opinion.'

'Have you ever taken crush?'

'No.'

'Or other narcotics?'

'Not that I'm aware of.'

'Are you married?'

'No. Divorced.'

'When you were married, did you ever lie to your wife?'

'No, absolutely not.' And then, 'Only kidding. Yes. Frequently. And such was my downfall.'

'Were you unfaithful to your wife?'

'That too.'

'Do you have any children, Dan?'

'Not that I'm aware of.'

For the first time, her eyes left me and just briefly flitted to the laptop screen.

I realised the source of her concern and said, 'The boy at the clinic – he's not mine – we kind of adopted him by accident. He's an idiot. But we do love him so.'

She said, 'There are no blood children?'

'*Blood* children? No. Yes. Well.' I sighed. I didn't particularly mean to. It just kind of came out. I drummed my fingers on the edge of the chair. 'I mean . . . my wife had a son, a long time ago, because she was also unfaithful. It's complicated. I considered him to be my son, but he was not, as you say, my . . . blood . . . child.'

'You say, *had* a son . . . Is he still part of—?'

'He's dead. He died.'

'I'm sorry. Was this—?'

'He died violently.'

'Yes.'

'And it was . . . my fault. Fucking hell . . .'

I swore because, from nowhere, there were tears on my cheeks and a lump in my throat the size of a small horse.

'Were you . . . responsible for—?'

'No, I didn't kill my own son. And that's what he was. Yes. But he died because he was put in danger by my actions.'

She was nodding slowly. 'How old was he when this happened, Dan?'

'He was little. Toddling. *Fuck*.'

I looked away from her and wiped at my face. Behind me, the library door opened and I turned towards it, grateful for the distraction. I was absolutely mortified that she had, through no methodology other than asking very simple questions, so quickly and easily reduced me to tears. She had wanted the truth and I had determined to give it as a way of covering my lies. But now I was clogged with unexpected and unwelcome grief, and that was after precisely three minutes of an initial indexing, which Jack had warned me could last for up to three hours.

Jesus, she'll have the spine out of me yet.

But, as it turned out, she wouldn't get the chance.

Three men came through the door, two of whose dimensions suggested that, out of their robes, they would each fit quite nicely into a bouncer's tux. The other was the hooded man who had presided at the morning service, the one I had struggled to place. But now, as he dropped that hood, I saw his full face, straight on, for the first time.

I knew exactly who he was, and that my time was up.

A former finance minister at Stormont, whose downfall I had caused.

'Reverend Pike,' I began. 'Long time no—'

'Take him,' Pike cut in, and his men moved towards me. 'Take him and beat him like the dog he is.'

They grabbed me, dragged me up and began to trail me towards the door.

And all I could do was resign myself to the pain to come and marvel, not just at this unexpected revelation, but also at another sight, which confused me and, even in the midst of the drama, touched me: the girl, Eve, with her eyes closed, her mouth moving silently in prayer, and her peachy cheeks damp with tears which could only be for me and my loss and a guilt that weighed upon me heavier than the earth itself.

21

I was supposed to be an investigator, for fuck's sake; I should have done my homework properly. It had to have been out there somewhere that Pike was behind the New Seekers. *Had* to be. It may not have been directly relevant to the case I was investigating, but knowing that someone like Pike was involved would have made me more cautious, more suspicious, and probably less willing to rush into undercover mode. But instead of nailing it down – disgraced ex-minister re-invents himself as bishop of his own church – I'd gone off on my random little adventure and now found myself flat on my back on the courtyard cobbles for my trouble *and* getting a hiding from several angry men in open-toed sandals.

But I'd been kicked before.

And, on this occasion, it was comparatively easy to endure.

They were probably doing more damage to their toes than they were to me. So I lay there taking it and grunting and letting them think they were killing me. I'm like a jockey: fractures and falls are part of the business.

And I probably deserved it, seeing as how I had helped destroy his life. I couldn't really blame him for adding a little Old Testament vengeance to his regular fire and brimstone.

When he'd been taking the service earlier, I should have made sure I got a better look – that's why I was there, to *find out*. I had been partly thrown by the voice; he was known as a big, booming orator, who could shake the foundations of large buildings, but in the church it had not particularly stood out; firm and self-assured, yes, but it hadn't rocked like prime-time Pike. He was also a tall man and physically imposing, but he now had that slightly haggard look which comes with rapid weight loss and, while he remained imposing, his height now came with something of a stoop. Still – he was unmistakably Pike, and I had missed him, and I was stupid.

In the kicking and the rolling around with my arms protecting my head, my phone sprang out of my underwear and they grabbed it and smashed it on the cobbles. After this short respite, they returned to kicking me. I caught glimpses between my fingers of Seekers going about their work. They were paying no attention at all to my beating. They were either too scared to look, or they were well used to it.

When they were finally done, they picked me up and threw me into the back of a Land Rover. I lay there and did some groaning. It stank of dogs. My robe was filthy – and creased; Jack was right on that. They drove me to the estate gates. Two security guys opened them up and then came back to help drag me out. My sandals had already come off, but now they stripped the robe off me, so that I was just standing in my underwear. They made some cracks about my shape and six-pack and then pushed me through the gates and locked them. My knees were bloody and my lip was cut and the adrenaline, which masks immediate pain, was already wearing off, but nevertheless I stood and faced them, and crossed myself, and said that I forgave them. It did not go down well. When they started to unlock the gates again, I quickly limped away, and ignored the catcalls.

Country roads, in my pants.

I don't embarrass easily. And it would make for a great story. If they'd been doing it properly, they would have stripped my underwear away as well. But my snug-fit pants remained firmly in place and I strode past cows with my head held high and a new determination to stick it to Pike driving me along, at least until I was out of sight of the estate and I stopped to throw up, and then I could hardly take another step because my soft feet were already cutting up on the rough tarmac. I was also starting to shiver because the epic heat of the past few days had vanished and a late-afternoon chill was now coming in off the sea. As I limped slowly along, there was a peel of thunder from the bank of grey clouds rolling in above, and then it started to rain, *hard*.

I was half a mile from town, and I'd no phone and no money; I was already drenched and freezing and the chances of someone stopping to help a man in his underpants seemed remote. I was thinking about jumping a wall and entering a wood to build a fort out of twigs, when there came the sound of a car from behind and I put my thumb out, expecting that it would speed on past, or hurl me into a ditch, but instead it stopped – a blue Renault Clio with its wipers wiping furiously – and a window came down. I screwed my face up to explain – but then I recognised the driver and wondered if I was about to step from the frying pan into the fire.

'Terry?' I said to the security guard from the Braxton Clinic, who should not have been on this road if he was anything other than the man who had betrayed me to Pike and his New Seekers. 'I'm just out for a stroll, but I appear to have misplaced my clothes.'

'Get in, you fucking eejit,' Terry growled.

I was cold and wet and bleeding and in pain and had no other hope of salvation, so I did just that.

He had the bottom half of an old tracksuit in the back, which I pulled on, and a blanket he said he kept for picnics and emergencies, which I wrapped around my torso. He turned the heat up and gave me another shake of his head.

As we started along the road to Ballyferris, I said, 'Well, this is a coincidence.'

And he said, 'Not really. Your wife – your ex-wife – called Dr Macceabee all het up because she couldn't track you down. She said you had a habit of jumping into the deep end on things –' his eyes flitted across to me, and up and down my battered frame – 'and usually getting beaten up as a result of it, but you're not usually out of contact for so long, so Dr Macceabee asked if I could lend a hand and track you down. I went over to your office and had a wee look around—'

'You *broke* into my office?'

'No, I walked into it, because somebody else had already broken into it: the door was hanging off its hinges—'

'You serious? Who the—?!'

'Fuck should I know? Anyway, he, she or they trashed it—'

'My laptop—'

'Didn't see one. Anyway, that really got her worried, so we took her over to your apartment and she let me in—'

'She let you in? She has a *key*?'

'None of my affair; but, yes, she has a key. At first I thought somebody had been in there too, but your wife – your ex-wife – said no, it was probably in its natural state. Now, there definitely was a laptop there . . . and we kind of presumed that that would have been nicked if there had been burglars. Your wife – your ex—'

'Just say "Trish"; it'll be quicker . . .'

'*Trish* . . . said you were working on some other case you were being kind of coy about, so we thought we'd better take a look at the laptop for clues and . . . luckily she knew the password . . .'

'She *knew*—?'

'The date of the first release of *Anarchy in the UK* ? Absolutely. It means nothing to me, but that's "Vienna".' He gave me a big smile, which I didn't return. 'Anyway, for future reference, if someone else is going to be using your laptop, you might want to routinely delete your search history . . .'

'I . . .'

'None of my business and not me you have to explain it to . . . but, in this case, advantageous that you didn't, as the last few sites you visited were to do with the New Seekers and, fortuitously, you have find-my-phone software on your phone.'

'Have I?'

'Yes, it comes as standard, but you have to switch it on . . .'

'I've never—'

'Your ex did; she told me. Anyhow, it's connected to a GPS system and we kept trying it but couldn't get a signal . . . and then we got one just for a couple of minutes, but long enough to place your phone in this neck of the woods and, seeing as how everyone knows this is the New Seekers' national headquarters . . .'

'Exactly,' I said.

'Given the state of your office, we were worried you might have been kidnapped, so we put our heads together and thought it might be better to spook them. We gave them a call and, of course, they denied all knowledge—'

'You called them and *asked* for me?'

'Not exactly, but said we were looking for you . . .'

'Fucking hell. Never mind my safety; you got me a fucking hiding.'

'Were we to know? Anyway, we weren't about to take them at their word. I took a scoot down and was just trying to work out how I was going to get inside for a look round, when the gates opened and out you came.'

'Fortuitous,' I said.

'Aye, the Lord moves in mysterious ways.'

He gave me a grin and focused on the road ahead. I rested my head against the window and stared out at the passing fields. I wasn't at all convinced by Terry's explanation of his being there. Yes, he may have worked with Trish to uncover my whereabouts, but he had also probably tipped off the Bishop to my being there, in much the same way as he had informed Eve of my presence at the Braxton Clinic. I didn't believe that he just happened to be outside when I was ejected from the Ballyferris estate – he was definitely expecting me. No doubt the Bishop had called him in to make sure I didn't come to any harm, wandering mostly naked in the countryside, although not out of any concern for me, but to prevent any bad publicity for his Church or in case it drew unwanted attention to its headquarters. Despite Terry's collaboration with the Church, I didn't feel in any immediate danger. Killing me probably wasn't part of the plan – that would have been an extreme overreaction. All I'd managed to squeeze out of them was bed and breakfast. I was nothing more than an annoyance from Pike's past. His role as Bishop of the New Seekers might not yet be common knowledge, but it was hardly something he could expect to remain a secret; ordering my beating had been nothing more than petty vindictiveness on his part, not an attempt to gag me.

Terry clamped his hand down on my leg and I jumped.

'For fuck—'

'Here.' He was holding out his mobile phone. 'You should give her a call, tell her you're OK; she was going up the walls.'

'Maybe later,' I said.

We were already through Ballyferris and cutting across the peninsula towards Newtownards. I was thinking about the indexing and how easily Eve had reduced me to tears, and then about the timing of Pike's appearance. He and his thugs had burst through the door just a few minutes after Eve had mentioned my name. Could it be that he routinely listened in to the indexing, and that this was the source of his power? He armed himself with information from these confessions and then used it to wield influence, or, indeed, to blackmail? It was a definite possibility. If it was true, it might let Terry off the hook, though the timing of his appearance outside the estate still could not help but feel suspicious.

We didn't say much for a few miles. Terry turned the radio on and the dulcet tones of my old friend Jack Caramac came booming out. After our last encounter, the popular but controversial presenter had been shifted from his phone-in show to a more sedate afternoon request slot.

Terry said, 'Met him once: kebab shop, late on. Nice fella.'

I nodded. I didn't like that he had been in my office. He could easily have orchestrated or conducted the break-in himself. And I especially didn't like that Trish had led him to my home. She had also revealed my password to him. If he or the Seekers had earlier stolen the laptop from my office but hadn't been able to open my files – well, now they could, because, of course, I used the same password for everything. While I was doing dishes in Ballyferris, they were probably going through my files. There wasn't a tremendous amount of top-secret stuff on there, but there was enough to mess up the search for Alison, for a start.

'You want me to drop you at casualty?'

He indicated to our right, and the Ulster Hospital.

'Nope. Home. If you don't mind.'

'Okey-doke. We, uh, secured your office best we could, but you'll probably need someone to do it properly.'

The rain had passed almost as soon as it had started, and the optimists of Greater Belfast were back out in their shorts, even though the skies remained overcast. We passed the gates of Stormont and the long sweeping driveway up to our Assembly building. It had once been Pike's domain. He had wielded power and traded favours, with his bosomy wife, Abagail, by his side. She had fallen to coke, and dragged him down with her. He had held on by his fingernails for quite a while but, when his own party turned on him, he had no choice but to quit. He said he was quitting the business of government for good, but nobody really believed him. There were many second lives in Ulster politics. So there would be a barnstorming comeback, for sure; he was just choosing an unusual way to mount it. Pike had been gone for most of a year: if not quite long enough to slip from our minds entirely, then certainly long enough to no longer crowd our thoughts. Word was he had gone to a religious retreat, to a monastery in Italy and then on to France, but, by whatever circuitous route, he had ended up in Ballyferris, reinventing himself as the Bishop of a fledgling Church, and one that, judging from its headquarters and the number of robes on the streets, was growing at an incredible rate.

I said, 'Remember when Pike was in charge up there?'

'Oh, aye.'

'What'd you think of him?'

'I thought he was a bit of a cunt.'

'OK,' I said.

22

Terry wanted to come up with me, make sure I was OK, but I said no, I'm fine. He left me by my apartment block at St Anne's Court. He scribbled his number on a McDonald's wrapper, told me not to be a stranger and pulled away. The summer drinkers were still out in force, and would be until October. As I stood for a moment at the side of the road, in my bare feet, trackie bottoms and tartan rug, watching Terry's car recede and wondering if I'd gotten him wrong, one of the passing drinkers said, 'Goin' to a fancy dress, mate?' and I said, 'No, are you?' and he decked me. I sat on my sorry arse for a few minutes while he and his gang laughed and carried on and I bled a little from the nose.

I got up and walked to the entrance. I had known my access code off by heart, but now it wouldn't come to me. I tried many combinations – without luck. I pushed the intercom buttons for the apartments on either side of mine, but there was no one in. So I picked some others at random. It was a large complex, so there were plenty of responses, but the massacres around town had made everyone jumpy, so nobody was prepared to buzz me in. I sat down on the step. Huge apartment block, and nobody knew me. The only place roundabouts that I would be recognised was the Bob Shaw, my local pub, just a few hundred metres away. I would be recognised as soon as I walked in, and then I'd be thrown out, as I had lately been banned for having an opinion.

An elderly couple approached the door. I explained who I was and that I had forgotten the code because I had lately been smacked with an iron, beaten up by men in Jesus boots and then punched in the nose for being sarcastic, but they weren't of a mind to help, and when I tried to crowd in after them the man brought his walking stick down on my bare toes. I yelped and hopped back, and then yelled abuse at them for being miserable old fuckers, which did little to change their position. I raged on long after they were gone. I was furious at being defeated and denied by my own apartment block. I returned to the intercom and began methodically pushing every button, with exactly the same responses, until one woman cut me off mid-plead and said, 'Dan? Is that you?'

And I realised that I had accidentally pushed my own button, and it was Trish.

'Yes,' I said.

'You're alive.'

'Just . . . let me in.'

The door opened and I gave thanks. I took the lift up and Trish was waiting there when I stepped out on to my floor. She looked shocked but nevertheless happy to see me.

She even gave me a hug.

I said, 'You're a sight for sore eyes.'

'And you're . . . just a sight. Come on . . .' She led me by the hand into my own apartment. She closed the door behind me, but then stopped me where I was and said, 'Wait there a moment.'

She darted across the open-plan kitchen and lifted her phone from the counter. She came back and raised it before me and took my picture.

I said, 'What're you doing?'

'You just look so ridiculous; I should post it on Facebook.'

'For fuck's sake! I've just been—'

'I know what you've just been. Terry told me.'

'Terry! Trish if you—'

'Shut up! I was worried sick about you. If it hadn't been for Terry, I wouldn't have known what to do. And the real reason I took that photo? Because, if at any time in the future I find myself having those lovely old feelings about you, then I will remember to take out my phone and look at this photo – just so I can remind myself what a fucking wanker you really are.' She turned, grabbed her handbag and stormed past me to the door. She stopped there and nodded across to my laptop, sitting open on the coffee table. 'And by wanker,

I *mean* wanker.' She gave me a disgusted shake of her head, flung the door open, and was gone.

In the silence that followed, I stood there, wondering if any of it had actually happened, if by any chance it was part of some feverish hallucination caused by my recent beatings. If, indeed, I wasn't actually home at all but was lying on the cobbles in Ballyferris, getting a kicking. I was still standing there trying to work it out when there was a light knock on the door behind me. When I opened it, Trish was standing there. She stepped forward, kissed me on the lips, and then spun away again without a single word.

I refuelled on whiskey and pizza, more of one than the other. I had a shower and washed away blood and scabs and gravel. I applied ointments and plasters. I put on black jeans and a black T-shirt and located my spare phone and finally called to check my messages. The first was from Trish, concerned for my well-being. The second from someone called Joey, who said he'd heard I was looking for Katya and that he might know something. The third was from Jonathan, the barman from Culchie's Corner, but from a different number; he said he had something to show me and to give him a call.

Terry had said they'd secured the office as best they could, but I needed to check it for myself. I pulled on my black Harington jacket, lifted the spare keys and drove across town. I called Joey on the way. He took a long time to answer. His voice was young, reedy and suspicious. I told him who I was and he said, 'How much?' and I said it depended on the quality of his information. He said, 'Do you want the fuckin' girl or not?'

I said, 'What charm school did you graduate from?'

And he said, '*What*?'

I said, 'Joey, if it leads to the girl, then I've more money than you could ever dream of. If it's just the suggestion of a hint, then I'll settle for that too. Where do you want to meet?'

He shot back immediately with, 'Why do we need to meet?'

I said, 'So I can hand over the money?'

He snorted and said, 'Right-a-fuckin' nuff. This stuff makes me nervous. OK – OK. You know the Transport Museum? Meet me in the car park there.'

I said, 'OK. About an hour? Nine?'

He snorted again and said, '*No*.'

I said, 'You tell me, then, Joey.'

He went quiet.

I concentrated on turning on to the Lisburn Road.

'Ten past.'

'Ten past what?'

'Ten past nine; I can't get there by nine.'

'Right,' I said. I asked him what sort of car he would be driving.

He said, 'Who said I'd be driving a car?'

I said, 'Joey, do you work in the museum, by any chance? It closes at six, so you're probably in security but your shift finishes at nine?'

He snapped back, 'How the fuck do you know that?'

The Transport Museum was halfway between Belfast and Holywood. It wasn't exactly in the middle of nowhere, but it wasn't walking distance either. So I'd taken a punt. I said, 'I'm a private investigator, Joey; I know lots of things.'

After a pause, he gave me a rather crestfallen, 'Aye, well I know things too.'

I imagined he did. But hopefully not just what he picked up guarding traction engines. There were a lot of money-grabbing time-wasters out there, but I couldn't afford to ignore any of them.

I parked and entered my office building. The lights weren't working in either the front hall or the steps up, but there was just enough light coming in from the street to penetrate the gloom as far as the Thai massage parlour on the first floor. Someone had scrawled *Go Home Chinkies* on their door in thick black marker. I moved on up to my attic office, using my phone to light the way. The door was closed and appeared to be doing exactly the job it was designed for, at least until I actually touched it and it began to fall inwards. I caught hold of it just before it hit the floor, pulled it back up and then walked it inside. I placed it against a wall. The bulb overhead had been smashed, but there was enough light coming in through the dormer window for me to locate the reading lamp lying on the floor on its side, along with the desk. When I pushed the button, it lit up. I righted the desk and placed the lamp on it. Then I lifted my leather swivel chair – which had been sliced open, with the stuffing spilling out – and set it back in place. The filing cabinet was on its side, with the drawers open and various files scattered across the floor. There had not, in truth, been many files in there to start with. I righted the cabinet and was just setting the drawers back in it when I heard voices, and footsteps on the stairs, and I paused in my tidying to see if they were going where most footsteps in this building went – to the hookers below. But, unlike the hookers, they kept on coming and, given my recent history, I immediately began to regret not paying for an office with an alternative exit: at the very least, a fire escape or a helter-skelter. The access to my terrace and possible flight across the rooftops would mean somehow passing the three men who had now appeared at the end of my corridor. They might be potential clients, enquiring after my services, or workmen Trish had sent to carry out the repairs, but somehow, given the run of things, I doubted it. Whoever they were, whatever they wanted, I was trapped and would have to rely on my charm to see me through.

The corridor was narrow, so they had to approach in single file. The lead guy was tall, wiry and fresh faced with cropped hair. He was wearing a red zip-jacket with an anchor patch on the left arm and a gold hoop earring. He stopped in the opening, gave me a cursory glance and then examined the doorframe. He said, 'You have no door.'

'I have a door,' I replied; 'it's just not necessarily attached in the traditional manner.'

His brow furrowed. He entered the office, raising his foot as he did, as if he was stepping over some kind of invisible barrier. Behind him stood a slightly older man with dyed blond hair in a short-sleeved black shirt, tight black jeans and black trainers. He had a thin gold chain around his neck. He looked at the first man for a moment, and then smirked and stepped over the same invisible barrier. The third man had the same style jacket and earring as the first. His eyes were sunk back in his head. He just blundered on through the barrier as if it wasn't there.

I said, 'You guys, you always move in threes. Let me guess, you and you –' I pointed left and right of the black shirted man – 'you're the bodyguards, and you're the – what? The leader?'

He began to say, 'We were told you were a—'

'Do you want to be in my gang? My gang, my gang?'

'You what?'

'Oh yeah.'

Blondie's brow furrowed. He said, 'Are you *on* something?'

'High on life, my friend. High on life. If you want to talk business, have these two step outside and you take a seat.'

He said, 'You don't appear to have a seat.'

It was true. My two plastic B&Q chairs were gone. They were, clearly, of no value, which meant they had been taken purely for badness.

Sunken-eyes said, 'What's to say we don't smash your fucking face?'

His clone sniggered and said, 'Looks like someone already did. Eddie, you want us to knock his lamps in?'

Eddie shook his head. 'Step outside, like the man says.'

They looked mildly disappointed, and then did as they were told. It only involved them moving about five feet. They stood in the corridor, still looking in. I raised my hand and flicked the fingers out, indicating for them to move back.

Eddie said, 'End of the corridor. In fact, go across the road and get him a fucking Coke; he's out of it.'

Sunken-eyes said, 'I'm fine, I just . . .'

The other guy tugged at his arm and he turned reluctantly away.

Eddie moved closer – close enough to rest both hands on my desk and lean across. 'You know,' he said, 'those guys would shoot you as soon as look at you.'

'But you wouldn't. You're the voice of reason.'

He laughed, and pushed back, and let his eyes rove around my messed-up office. 'What happened?'

'You tell me.'

'Nothing to do with me, mate. But I have to say, you've got a lot of people talking.'

I gave him a shrug. 'So, Eddie . . . let me take a wild guess . . . You're high enough up in whatever gang to have your own security rockin' around with you, but not so high that they give you a pair who could actually look after you. At least one and probably both of them are crushed off their tits.'

'You care to put that to the test? I click my fingers they'll—'

'Ah, Eddie,' I said, 'settle down. You've been sent here to check me out, warn me off or offer me a deal. You're either –' I counted off on my fingers – 'North Road Clan, Belmont Rievers, Botanic Boat Crew or Riot Squad. Probably, judging from the anchor logo on your guys' jackets, you're Boat Crew.'

'No shit, Sherlock.'

'But you're not the boss. Maybe I should be speaking to him.'

'He asked me to speak to you. You don't speak to the boss, except through me.'

'OK; fair enough. Botanic Boat Crew. Nice name. And I like a nice name. Do you know what onomastics is?'

'Don't know, don't care, smart arse.'

'No, not that. Onomastics is about the genesis of names – where they are from.'

'So fucking what?'

'It traces their history through linguistics, anthropology, psychology, sociology, fuckology. It's really fascinating.'

'Are you fucking kidding me?'

'Partly,' I said. 'Botanic Boat Crew, comes from . . .?'

'Like it's a fucking secret. Our headquarters are in the old boathouse on the river. Still half their fucking canoes sitting around.'

'And now you've got lovely red jackets for uniforms with a nice insignia on the arm.'

'Aye. You have a problem with that?'

'Nope. You all look very smart. Except – the anchor's fine 'n' all – but you do know canoes don't actually have anchors? They'd probably sink if they did.'

'I'll let the boss know; I'm sure he'll be fascinated. But he'd be more fascinated by the twenty grand you're going to hand over to get your girl back.'

'Twenty grand?'

'Twenty grand.'

'That's a lot of money.'

'You want her back. That's how much.'

'What're we talking about here? A body? Or living, breathing?'

'Depends how much you fuck us around.'

'So she's alive now?'

'Now, yes.'

'You have any evidence of that?'

'You get the money, we hand her over: all the evidence you need.'

'Ah, right, OK, like an exchange – maybe in a damp warehouse or under a bridge at midnight?'

'What the fuck?'

'That would be the traditional way, wouldn't it? But, as attractive as that sounds, maybe this time I'll take a pass.'

'You what?'

'Nothing personal, but I'll have to say no. Not without evidence.'

'You want us to cut off her fucking fingers and send them to you?'

'Mmmm – it's a thought. But not all of them. Maybe just the one? That would be a step in the right direction.'

'Are you fucking cracked or something?'

'No offence, Eddie, but I should ask you the same question. Twenty grand? C'mon, mate, I've probably spread that much around town looking for info. Twenty grand? Christ, you could hardly get a Burton's suit for that these days. So, nice try; let the boss know I appreciate the effort, but maybe next time ask for more than I could shake out of my piggy bank. OK?'

His mouth was working, but no sound was coming out. He rocked back on his heels and then forward and finally said, 'I'll give him a call, tell him what a joker you are.'

'You do that. Now, if you don't mind . . . I've work to be doing.'

I nodded towards the doorway.

He looked at it, and then at me. He turned, but then immediately pivoted back and pointed a finger at me.

'You . . . I don't like you very much.'

'Good to know,' I said. He stepped out of my office. Before he'd gone very far along the corridor, I called after him. He stopped and turned. 'Are you not going to close the door?'

He threw his arm up dismissively. 'Aw, fuck off!'

23

By the time I pulled back out on to the Lisburn Road it was a little after eight fifty-five, which gave me fifteen minutes to get out to the Ulster Folk and Transport Museum and my appointment with Joey. Initially, I drove slowly so that I could keep an eye on the road behind me. No particular reason, other than the fact that someone had recently trashed my office and nicked my laptop and I had pissed off a Church cult and sent a jumped-up gang-banger away with a flea in his ear. But it all appeared perfectly abnormal. One benefit of the upsurge in violence was the roads were quieter at night, so it was easier to tell if you were being followed.

On the way, I called Sara Patterson. When she didn't answer her mobile, I tried the *Telegraph*. The switchboard asked who was calling and I told them. They said, 'Putting you through, Mr Pimpernel.'

Sara answered with, 'Sara's phone.'

I said, 'Hello, Sara. It's Dan. Don't hang up.'

'*Why*?'

'I thought it was time I forgave you. You said some very cruel things.'

'*I*—!'

'See how quick to anger you are? You're going to have to work on that.'

'What do you *want*?'

'God, that's such a big question. What does anyone want? Love? Is that asking too much?'

'I'm hanging up now.'

'Don't be like that, Sara; we've been friends for a long time; let's sort this out.'

'We've never been friends.'

'Babe, I've seen the glint in your eye, and I know we're going to be the best of pals, and maybe more.'

'You—'

'You know it. I was your hero once, remember? I can still teach you a thing or two.' I swear I could hear her fingers drumming on her desk. 'Anyway, what can I do for you?'

'You called me, Starkey.'

'Dan, please. And yes, of course, you're right. Listen – I know we got off on the wrong foot, so I thought, by way of recompense, I'd throw you a bone.'

A sigh.

'You know, I'm still looking for the girl. But I'm also looking into that bunch of nuts collectively known as the New Seekers.'

'Really.'

'Really, and I've just spent the night with them at their HQ in Ballyferris. One word answer: do you know who is actually behind them?'

'I don't know, I don't care and it's not my patch.'

'Not one word. But I can live with that. I think you'll be interested.'

She sighed again. 'Right. Try me.'

'So I have your interest now?'

'Not really.'

'Pike.'

'Pike *what*?'

'The good reverend, Dr Pike, is their leader. The New Seekers.'

'The good Reverend Dr Pike is in Italy. Or Germany.'

'Not any more, he's not. He's in Ballyferris. I've seen him.'

'And . . . so? He's home; why should I care?'

'Sara – you know why you should care. It's a story. He's heading up a cult that has thousands of followers—'

'It's a Church—'

'It's one short step away from a paramilitary organisation—'

'I think maybe you're exagg—'

'He had his disciples beat me up. Does that not tell you something?'

'It tells me quite a lot, yes.'

'Forget for a moment your personal feelings towards me, Sara; consider the bigger picture. Ex-minister sneaks back into the country, launches secretive but hugely popular Church with himself as the figurehead. It's like

Napoleon returning to France – and look how that ended.'

'In a very bad Abba song?'

'I'm serious about this, Sara. Not only did he have me beaten up, I have it on good authority he was directly responsible for the firebombing of the abortion clinic downtown the other night. You heard about that, right?'

'Yes, Starkey, I heard about it. Who's good authority would that be?'

'I'm just telling you, what he's doing down there is dangerous and, if you were any sort of a reporter, you'd be all over it like a rash.'

'*If* I was any sort of a reporter?'

'It's just an expression. I know you're a great reporter. I've told you as much. Look into this.'

'Is that it? Is that my bone? Pike's home and he's lobbing firebombs?'

'Yep, and all I want in exchange—'

'Christ, here we go . . .'

'Is anything you have on the Botanic Boat Crew . . .'

'You have the map and guide, I sent—'

'. . . and, in particular, whoever's running them.'

'Why?'

'It's girl related. And, yes, I have the file, but it's a little short of detail. Anything you have would be useful.'

There was a long pause. The city centre had been dead, so I'd whizzed through in a couple of minutes and was already on the outskirts of Holywood. I'd not only be on time, I'd be early.

Sara said, 'Starkey, we're not friends. We never have been and we never will be. Thanks for the tip on Pike, and I'll pass it on to someone who actually cares. I'll send you what I have on the Boat Crew and then that's us done, OK? I don't want to hear from you again.'

'Now you're just playing hard to get,' I said.

She hung up. I smiled. Job done. She was exactly like me, or how I had been in my pomp, before real life wore me down. There was no way she was passing it on. One sniff of a good story and she'd move heaven and earth to nail it down. There was a big difference between me poking my nose in and a reporter with the backing of a newspaper investigating. If Sara did what I hoped she would do, it would be like shaking a palm tree and waiting for the coconuts to fall. Most of them would bounce off the ground, but a couple were guaranteed to crack and leak. It was human nature; all she needed was a couple of disgruntled coconuts.

24

Everyone in Northern Ireland has visited the Ulster Folk and Transport Museum, mostly on school trips and miserable days out with the in-laws and grandchildren. It's split in two – ancient cottages and houses illustrating *the way we were* on one side of the main Belfast–Bangor road, and old buses, trains and trams showing *the way we got about* on the other. The Tourist Board spends a lot of money advertising it. They haven't yet used the slogan, *Come to the Ulster Folk and Transport Museum, let us bore the fucking arse off you*, but they should.

When I drove into the car park, there were two other cars sitting side by side against a fence at the far end and in the shadow of tall pines. One was empty, and the other had two heads pressed together in the front seats. They came apart as I cruised slowly past. Two guys, taking their life in their hands, still, here, now. I stopped in the nearest space to a set of locked, pink-painted wooden gates that guarded the museum proper. The giant hangars housing the main exhibits were visible beyond. I had barely turned off the engine when there was a tap on my window and a small, rat-faced guy in a blue uniform nodded at me and thumbed for me to get out. As a private investigator, I knew he must have been hiding in the bushes. I deduced this from the twig on his shoulder.

I brought my window down. 'Would you not be better getting in?'

'Nope; boss wants a word.'

'Boss of the Transport Museum? I know the car's past it, but still . . .'

'Aye, right,' said Joey.

He stepped back. I got out and looked about me.

'Is he in the trees? Or would that be Special Branch?'

'Aye, right,' said Joey. 'This way.'

He unlocked the gates and we walked together across a stone bridge. I peered over and saw the tracks of the main Belfast–Bangor railway line below. On the other side, we turned right towards the museum doors, which zipped open as we approached. We proceeded past the ticket desk and along a covered walkway decorated with huge black and white photos of shipyard workers building something titanic. We emerged on to a wide deck giving us a view over the floor of the largest of the hangars, which was crammed with locomotive steam engines and carriages, antique buses and cars. Beyond, I knew there were models of vast liners, at least one of which had managed to sink and launch an industry at the same time. The sound of trains puffing along at full throttle was intermingled with the twiddle of Irish folk over the PA.

I said, 'I hope you didn't go to all this trouble just for me.'

'Don't be a dick,' said Joey.

He led me down a curving disabled-access ramp to the hangar floor. From above, I'd been thinking, *Trains, so what?* It was only when you were right up close that you got a true sense of their size and power. We weaved our way through the exhibits until we arrived at a mocked-up railway halt with a *Warrenpoint* sign and a steam engine, painted green in the livery of the old Belfast and County Down railway, with attendant carriages was waiting to depart.

Joey said, 'Wait here.'

I considered saying something smart and train related, but he was giving me all the wrong signals. When he'd slipped away, I wandered along the platform and peered into the third-class carriage, which had all the facilities of a cattle truck, and then wandered on along to the private, first-class carriage, which featured a waxwork dummy in Edwardian duds leaning in its doorway, reading a book and spoilt for choice with a chaise longue and an armchair waiting behind him. You weren't allowed to enter the carriages, but you could step up to the engine. You could even pretend to drive it. So I did. Briefly, I became Casey Jones, and sang it. And then I caught myself. As I took a step back from the controls, my foot slipped on something and I saw a piece of card stuck to my heel. I peeled it off and was just about to drop it when I realised that it was one of my own business cards and that it must have dropped out of my pocket while I was driving the train . . . until I turned it over and saw there was writing on the back.

It said: *No, you fuck off.*

I was staring at it, thinking, *How the hell* . . . when a voice that wasn't Joey's but was still oddly familiar said, 'Irresistible, aren't they?'

I moved to the top of the steps and peered along the platform. I still had the card in my hand. Last time I'd held it was just before pushing it through the letter box of Harry Frank's house on Deramore Avenue. His neighbour had described Harry Frank as an abusive and reclusive burns victim, but that description didn't fit the man coming towards me, mostly because it was the very man who'd given me that description: the neighbour with the tortoiseshell glasses and the framed movie posters in his hall, who was more worried about the effect Harry Frank was having on his property value than concerned for his well-being. Or that, at least, had been the act. Now he stopped a couple of metres short of the steps and placed a hand on the big green engine beside him.

'You could just imagine thundering down Royal Avenue in this, couldn't you?' he said, his voice a cultured south Belfast. 'Flattening everyone in your path.'

'Traffic wardens,' I said, 'and charity workers.'

He gave a soft laugh as I stepped down on to the

platform. This, then, was the man Joey had referred to as 'the boss'.

'Mr Starkey,' he said, advancing with his hand out, 'we haven't been formally . . . Harry, Harry Frank.'

'Ah.'

'Sorry about the . . . pretence . . . It was very much spur of the moment. But once I checked you out, I knew you'd be back, so I thought I might pre-empt matters and set up this little meeting. Wonderful surroundings, don't you think?'

He was wrong. I hadn't given him a second thought.

He held on to my hand so long it was getting past the awkward stage. But there was a reason for it. It caused me to look away from his face and down at his hand, which I saw now was badly scarred. The skin around three of his fingers and part of his palm had been burned away. It did not look like a particularly old wound but, at the same time, he didn't flinch as we continued to shake and his grip was strong. As I clocked it, he clocked me clocking it and, point made, he let go. I had gone to the house on Deramore looking for a swarthy charmer and, naturally enough, focused my attention on the mad fella yelling abuse rather than his innocuous neighbour. There had been no reason to suspect him of anything then, of course.

'I love it here,' he said, nodding around our surroundings, 'and a suitably dramatic setting for our *entente cordiale*.'

'Uh-huh,' I said.

'But it's not entirely for your benefit . . . May I call

you Dan?' I nodded. 'I was here, anyway. Actually, I come here all the time – have done since I was a kid. My parents used to bring us all here. My brothers were always bored to distraction, but I couldn't get enough . . . Just the scale of them – kind of reminds us of how small we are . . . but how big we can become. Anyway, Joey's kind enough to allow me to wander around here when things are quiet. It helps me think, you know? C'mon . . . I'll give you the tour . . . We can talk as we go.'

We moved off the platform and on to the hangar floor. I'd presumed he was joking about giving me a tour, but he really wasn't. I learned more in five minutes about narrow- and standard-gauge railways than any sane person ever needs to know. He rubbed his hands together enthusiastically as we passed between engines and coaches, and he spewed out facts and figures like a besotted enthusiast who had landed his dream job. 'Oh, yeah; this one – constructed by Beyer-Peacock – ran on the Bangor line from 1865 . . .' He stopped, held his hand up and closed his eyes. 'From Queen's Quay, the halts were . . . Ballymacarrett . . . Victoria Park . . . Sydenham . . . Tillysburn . . . Holywood . . . Marino . . . Cultra . . . Craigavad . . . Helen's Bay . . . Carnalea . . . and Bangor West.'

'Very impressive,' I said.

'There's something about the old days – when everything ran according to plan.'

'Yep, like clockwork. Except, of course, clockwork trains never caught on.' I stopped because he was looking at me. I gave him my stupid grin and said, 'I'm only winding you up.' He was probably half my age but, with the beard and glasses and beige corduroys and brown Hush Puppies, he was in full old-fogey mode; nobody meeting him would ever have guessed that he'd been a low-level dealer with a penchant for getting students hooked on crush. 'Listen,' I said, 'this is all lovely, but I'm looking for Katya. It's none of my business if you were involved in what happened to her or not. I just want the girl, dead or alive.'

'And so do I, Dan,' he replied. 'So do I.'

We moved through a small Titanic exhibition and on into a second hanger, this one devoted to buses and trams, and then down another ramp on to a lower level, full of goods vans, sports cars and private vehicles. His eyes roved lovingly over the exhibits and he started to talk again, but no longer about the yawn-inducing history of transportation – about darker things, about drugs, revenge, murder and, darkest of all, ambition.

'You see, Dan, over these past months I've been through something of a transformation – and it probably started with Katya.'

'You were a dealer and she was your customer.'

'Yes, of course; but a little bit more than that as well. We were friends – yes, I suppose – but briefly. I never really did get to know her properly. She always had plenty of money, I know that, and she had loads of friends, so they were a good crowd for me to get in with. And I worked them, I really did. Good kids, out for fun. But they did like to move around the city – which meant I had to go with them to protect my business. And some people didn't like that. They thought I was encroaching on their territory and so they decided to teach me a lesson. They came to my house and they barged their way in and they held me down and shot me in the knees, but – not content with that – they also threw acid in my face and it burned and it burned and it burned, and the screams could be heard a mile away.'

'Except they got the wrong man.'

'Exactly. My brother, Rob, happened to be staying with me at the time, and we do not look dissimilar, and they were thugs who had only a vague notion of who they were looking for, so they grabbed him and did what they did, and the reason I know that his screams could literally be heard a mile away is because I know exactly where I was when I heard them, and I know the distance. Of course, I didn't know it was him until I got closer to home. Rob had crawled into our front garden, and that's where I found him. Those terrible screams, travelling so far, and yet no one came to help. Too scared. I did what I could –' he raised his burned hand – 'but, really, the damage was done. Now his life is destroyed, he will never walk unaided again and his mind . . . Well, he has good days when he's his old, sensible self, and other days when he's just . . . psychotic. It's so sad. I happen to own the house next door – quite the entrepreneur – and I was renting it out, but I've moved him in there now. But – you know something, Dan? – it didn't just change his life . . . it changed mine as well. It made me reconsider what I was doing with my time and how utterly powerless I was to protect my brother or even to get justice for him. I didn't even blame the men who did it; they were just . . . foot soldiers following orders; it was those who controlled them, but how was I ever going to be strong enough to take them on?'

He stopped and looked at me, and I realised it wasn't a rhetorical question.

'I don't suppose a regime of rigorous exer—?'

'Have you ever heard of Sun Tzu's *The Art of War*? It's a Chinese military treatise, much favoured by generals and business leaders—'

'And dictators and gangsters and rappers . . .'

'Yes! I tried it, wasn't for me. But I found another, less fashionable, book. Tell me, have you ever read Dale Carnegie's *How to Win Friends and Influence People*? It's really about being positive, getting your message across, and it promoted the benefits of networking seventy-five years before a word like "networking" even existed. And there's another one – Tony Robbins' *Awaken the Giant Within*. What a piece of work that is! Oh, it's wonderful, Dan; it's about harnessing your health and energy, overcoming your fears and how to master the art of persuasive communication. It's so life affirming! I listen to his tapes all the time; they're so inspiring.'

'Well,' I said, 'that's good to know: You've found – what? – redemption through self-help books? Peace of mind . . .?'

Harry Frank tapped the side of his head. 'What I've found, Dan, is a positive mental attitude. You really can achieve anything when you put your mind to it. I sort of blended the best of what I was reading about – from Carnegie, from Robbins – and I've kind of created my own personal philosophy to help me move forward. Do you know what I mean?'

I nodded vaguely.

'I looked at where I was – *poor me, look what the world has done to me* – and I did something about it.'

'Which was . . .?'

'Practical and pragmatic. My brother received a rather large sum of money in government compensation for his injuries, to be administered by myself as his closest living relative. I was to become his full-time carer. You know how it works: it gives me a living wage and allows me to adapt the house with ramps, stairlifts etc. so he can get around, and to pay for nursing support, respite care, that kind of thing.'

'That's commendable that you would—'

'But I discussed this all with my brother, when he was lucid, and we kind of agreed to take a different approach with it.'

'Uh-huh?'

'Oh, yes. And I'm telling you this on the under-standing that it will go no further, because we're going to have this client–attorney kind of privilege, aren't we?'

'Attorney? I hadn't—'

'Take it from me, Dan, we *are*. Anyway, the compensation

money – yes, we could have gone down the traditional route, but instead we decided to use two thirds of it to set up a lab to produce fuck-loads of premium-grade crush.'

'Ah,' I said, 'novel.'

'Absolutely. Almost overnight we transformed our business from a street-corner service, reliant on suppliers with an IQ of zilch, to being a manufacturer and a wholesale supplier. And it has taken off a treat. We have plans to expand our business and, within a year, with hard work and more investment, I expect to control two thirds of the crush being manufactured and sold in Ireland.'

'That's, uh, quite ambitious,' I said. 'And I'm sure the existing suppliers just welcomed you with open arms?'

'Well, no, of course not. But then we still had one third of the compensation money to play with.'

'Okaaaay, so you . . .'

'We used it to pay people to kidnap the men who'd ordered the hit on my brother. There were four of them, at different levels in their gang. Do you know what we did with them, Dan?'

'Did you read them excerpts from *How to Win Friends and Influence People*?'

'No, Dan; we dropped three of them, one after the other, and in ascending order of seniority, into a vat of acid. They dissolved, Dan. Like Disprin.'

I cleared my throat. 'And the, uh, fourth?'

'The fourth witnessed the dissolution and then agreed

to assume command of the gang, but under my guidance and paying what you might call a franchise fee. We supply the crush, the business advice, sometimes even gang uniforms. We might design a nice logo for them. It helps create team spirit, bonding and ultimately improves performance. We're like the KwikFit of crush, my friend: fast, efficient and, if we don't deliver on our promises, we shoot our sales director in the head and replace him with someone who can.'

'I'm not sure if KwikFit do that . . .'

'Dan, you want to know why I'm telling you all of this, and what it has to do with your missing girl?'

'I was wondering that,' I said.

'Dan, I've done my homework on you. I know exactly who you are and what you've done with your life.'

I sighed. 'Really? Does it make for depressing—?'

'You're a power broker.'

'Ex-squeeze me?'

'Dan, I know you're not much to look at and, as a business man, you're a disaster, and your personal life appears to be all over the place – but think about what you have achieved! You have brought down governments, Dan. You have exposed corruption, scandals and bad guys in powerful places. Your life has been a wonderful adventure, which has shaped this country we live in as much as anyone's has. It pays to have you, Dan, on side. And that's where I want you, as we go forward. I want you for me, not against me.'

He did appear to be deadly serious. I have often, usually under the influence of alcohol, reviewed the sordid facts of my life. The picture Harry Frank painted of my achieve-ments bore no resemblance to the one I have conjured on such occasions. My life is an unmitigated disaster, and anything I have achieved has come about accidentally. I have stumbled in and out of dire situations and survived only through blind luck, not skill or talent. Those who have chosen to become close to me have always lived to regret it, or, sometimes, haven't lived at all.

I said, 'Well, I appreciate the kind words, Harry Frank, but all I'm really interested in is finding the girl.'

'Which brings us right back to where we started. That's what I want as well.'

'Then, less about your life story and tell me what happened to her.'

Harry Frank nodded to himself and pursed his lips. I looked where he was looking and saw that Joey was sitting in the cab of a 1960s Co-op milk float, a dozen metres away. He said, 'Of course that is your main concern; that's understandable. Absolutely. Ask me anything you want.'

'Were you with her the night she disappeared?'

'Yes, I was. She was off her head.'

'And that would be whose fault?'

'It was a flaw in the system of production. There was no way *then* of telling the strength of the crush. That's one of the things I'm countering. You buy crush from me or my affiliates, you know what you're getting.'

'That's fine, then.'

'Don't be sanctimonious. We all have our own demons.'

'I generally know the strength of a pint of Harp,' I said. 'Nil.'

'Harp,' said Harry Frank, shaking his head. 'Anyway – they wanted to go to this party in William Street; I went with them, thought I might pick up a few customers, but everyone was already crushed up when we got there. Then Katya, she got pretty sick, so I put her upstairs so she could sleep it off – about as much as I could do. And then I got offside. You have to remember, they weren't really my friends; I was a couple of years older; I'd no particular urge to hang out at a student party if there wasn't anything in it for me. And . . . I got a bad vibe about the place, anyway; just something didn't feel right. So I went home; didn't hear about the shootings till the next morning.'

'And then . . .?'

'And then . . . nothing. I haven't seen her or heard anything about her since.'

'You . . . Sorry . . . am I getting hold of the wrong end of the stick here? Your man, Joey, called and said he had info. He passed me on to you. You've given me your life story in great detail, but nothing more than everyone else knows about Katya.'

'Nothing more than everyone else *cares*, Dan – and that's what intrigues me.'

'Nope – not getting it.'

'Dan, you're out there, throwing huge sums of money about, looking for her. You are being paid to do this, paid to care; it's a simple business transaction in the same way that getting her crushed was a business transaction.'

'Mmmm-hmmmm.'

'And there you go again. Dan, you've been around, you've seen things and done things, and you must be aware of how it's going; they've never been this bad before, have they? My dad grew up in the seventies – he was right in the thick of it – and he swears it's ten times worse now.'

'It's getting that way.'

'And we're less than a year into it, Dan. The police can't cope as it is; where are we going to be in another year, in two years?'

'Well, it—'

'Anarchy, Dan. Anarchy.'

'Anarchy in the UK,' I said.

He nodded beside me. 'This city is on the road to hell, Dan, the gangs are tearing it apart, but there *is* a way forward. It's not the right way for everyone, but I think it can work. Crush is here to stay; there's nothing anyone can do about it. So what do you do? How do you control it? How do you stop the gangs from killing each other and everyone who gets in their way? Who benefits there? No one. But what if, instead of fighting it, you embrace it? You know, when I was reading Carnegie and Robbins, I was also looking at how drugs work in other parts of the world, specifically in Central and South America. The cartels, Dan! The scale! And do you know what they do, Dan? They give back. They build, they educate, they employ – the economies they create are greater than those of the countries they live in. And some of them even pay their taxes! Imagine that! What we have now – to get back to your girl and that massacre – is gangs who actually kill their own customers! Where's the logic in that? How would Marks and Spencer survive if they treated their customers like that?'

'Well, some would argue—'

'Dan – strength through unity.'

'Indeed.'

'If I can create alliances between the gangs, fix a standard product and price and we agree territories, then there's no end to what we can achieve. I've started along that path now, Dan, but, with these people, to really make an impact, you have to invest in two things: violence and influence. Violence is cheap; influence isn't. You need a *lot* of money. I will get there, the way business is going, but it will take some considerable time. I would prefer to take a shortcut. And that's where you and your girl come in.'

'I . . . uh . . . lost me . . .?'

'Dan, whoever is bankrolling your little investigation obviously has it to spare.'

'It's someone's daughter; of course they're going to spend everything—'

'It's more than that. When I realised what you were spending, I started thinking about Katya again, and what I knew about her – or didn't. Even back when I was hanging out with her, there was something that didn't add up. She wasn't local, hardly knew her way around, she had an odd sort of mid-Atlantic accent, like she'd travelled, she always had money, but she was kind of secretive too. And I remembered, one day, making a delivery and meeting her upstairs neighbours, and they were very suspicious of me and warned me off, and I thought it was odd at the time, and how I'd always see them hanging around wherever she happened to be. I can even remember mentioning it to her that they were like her stalkers and her laughing it off, but – now that I think about it – they were always there, never far away. I think they were there to look after her: bodyguards. And that means real money. Wouldn't you say, Dan? Wouldn't you think that someone who can afford that kind of support would be prepared to pay a vast sum to have her returned?'

'It's a nice theory, Harry Frank, and it might even be true, but all I really know is that I've been hired to find her. Beyond that, I'm not interested.'

'Well, perhaps you should be.'

He studied me for a long moment before nodding to his left and I turned and saw that we had stopped beside a gull-winged DeLorean, sitting on a slanted platform with its stainless-steel doors raised and black leather interior displayed to the world.

'Tell me, Dan – what do you think of when you look at this . . . magnificent creation?'

'That it was built before you were born.'

Harry Frank smiled. 'The silver dream machine, they called it.'

'Nightmare,' I said.

It was a luxury sports car, financed by Maggie Thatcher and built by redundant shipyard workers three thousand miles from its main market. What could possibly go wrong? It stoked the hopes of a nation, and then pissed all over them. It was cursed from the start. For all I know, it also gave Michael J. Fox fucking Parkinson's.

'You are a cynical man, Dan Starkey,' said Harry Frank, and he was not wrong. Or finished. 'You've been worn down by life, depressed, bullied, violated. Whereas, as you quite rightly point out, I'm so much younger than you, young enough still to have dreams – and ambition. When I look at this, I see someone with a master plan, who dared to think big, who had the balls to put everything on the line, who was so devoted to his dream that he even contemplated trying to save it by dealing in cocaine – which he never actually did, by the way. And, at the end of the day, this is still a genius vehicle, and the only valid reason for its failure is because its launch coincided with the largest slump in the US car market since the 1930s. But for that . . . man . . . the DeLorean could have made this place.' Harry Frank stood nodding at the vehicle, before turning and raising his hand. He clicked his burned fingers and Joey stepped out from the milk float and threw something that Harry Frank plucked out of the air. There was a mischievous grin on his face as he slowly opened his fist to reveal a single key. He nodded back towards the DeLorean and said, 'Why don't you jump in?'

'You're not serious.'

'Am too,' he said.

Harry Frank stepped up the ramp, ducked under the gull wing and lowered himself into the driver's seat.

I said, 'Get away to fuck.'

'Joey – will you do the needful?'

Joey moved to some doors set into the wall of the shed and began to release a series of locks and bolts.

I said, 'It's a fucking exhibit; you can't just—'

He started the engine.

And it purred.

Ahead, Joey opened the doors on to a clear view of Belfast Lough and the setting sun.

The headlights came on.

I stepped somewhat hesitantly on to the platform and peered in at Harry Frank. He was pulling on a pair of leather driving gloves.

I said, 'This is ridiculous. You can't just drive a DeLorean. For one, it doesn't have a tax disc.'

He revved the engine. He said, 'Get in. I have a plan for getting you your girl back that might just be advantageous to me as well. To put it in motion, I need to take you somewhere and show you something. If I drive out of here alone, you'll never know.'

I stared at him, and then stepped back and studied, first, the vehicle and then the open hangar doors and the sea beyond. I had a strong conviction that nothing good could come of getting into a DeLorean, but it was nevertheless irresistible. If he had a plan for getting Alison back, and the only way of hearing about it was by going for a ride in the DMC-12, then I was duty-bound to climb in.

I climbed in.

I reached up and gripped the pull-strap attached to the gull-wing door handle. It came down as smoothly as it surely would have done thirty years before, and clicked into place.

Harry Frank said, 'Fasten your seat belt.'

I fastened my seat belt.

He eased the car down off the ramp and then along the floor of the hangar towards the gaping doors. We swung out into the car park and, with the main road ahead of us, he gunned the engine again.

He grinned across at me. 'Do you want to know where we're going?'

I shook my head. 'Please don't say it.'

But he did, he had to, for it was written.

We shot forward – one hundred and fifty horsepower, nought to sixty in an unbelievable eight seconds – as Harry Frank yelled, 'We're going back to the future!'

25

The DMC broke down on the other side of Holywood. Harry Frank had the boot up and was tinkering with the engine while drivers on the dual carriageway slowed down to gawk, pump their horns and yell what a wanker he was. I stood well back. 'I'd give you a hand,' I said, 'but my knowledge of cars stops at the petrol tank. I have to sell mine if I get a flat tyre, because I've no idea how to change it.'

Eventually, he stood back from it and said, 'No.' He made a couple of calls and, ten minutes later, Joey showed up in a tow truck and, five minutes after that, a taxi appeared. There wasn't much talk while we waited, and there was even less in the back of the cab. I was trying to work out what I actually thought of him: he was clearly ambitious but delusional, not quite Adolf Hitler but also well short of Charlie Cairoli. It was hard to reconcile his appearance and manner with his extravagant claims – he was like a history professor who'd taken LSD while watching *The Warriors*. On the one hand, he waxed lyrically and believably about railway gauges and self-help gurus; on the other, he'd spoken clinically about dissolving his enemies in acid. I had encountered many nuts in my time. Harry Frank was probably the most disarming of them all.

Which worried me.

I didn't catch the address he gave the taxi driver. Even when we eventually pulled up outside a house on Palestine Street, I didn't make the connection until we were actually out of the car and Harry Frank was pushing on the buzzer to Alison's apartment. The voice that told him to come on up did not belong to her roommate, Sharon.

As he pushed the door open, Harry Frank saw me hesitate and gave me a reassuring smile. 'It's fine,' he said. 'Remember – we're on the same side now.'

I followed him to the elevator. As we rose to the second floor, he said, 'Funny to be back here.'

'Aye,' I said. Last time I'd been in Alison's apartment, Sharon had clouted me with an iron. In the right light, you could still see the outline of it on my face.

There was a bulky, muscled fella in a too-tight T-shirt and shaved head, straight out of Central Casting, waiting for us when we stepped out of the lift. He nodded at Harry Frank and stepped aside so that we could enter the apartment through the open door behind him. As we passed, he gave me a hard look and I returned the same, though it probably wasn't. I had a notion that he was one of the two heavies who'd been sitting in the Culchie's Corner beer garden when I'd visited my informant, to whom I still owed a phone call, in Ballyhack, but I couldn't be sure – at least, not until I entered the open-plan kitchen–dining room and saw another fella who looked just as vaguely familiar. I guessed it was them, but it didn't really matter. What did matter was that he was standing behind Sharon Quigg, who was sitting in a chair, which had been pulled away from the kitchen table into the middle of the lounge, and that one of her eyes was punched closed and blood was flowing from her nose and mouth. She was in a vest and pants that were stained with blood and snot, and her bare legs had what looked like cigarette burns. She was shivering and crying and moaning.

I said, 'What the fuck—?'

Harry Frank said, 'Well?' to the guy behind her. He shook his head. Harry Frank turned to me and said, 'That's unfortunate. You'd think you'd at least know who you were sharing an apartment with.'

Sharon whispered, '*Please*,' out of her swollen lips, her one good eye fixed on me.

I said, 'Jesus . . .' and looked at Harry Frank.

He moved beside Sharon. He lifted one of her hands and patted it and said, 'I'm sorry, I really am. But there are things I need to know. Seemingly, you don't know them. But your friend, here, does.' He nodded at me. 'See, Dan, I think I'm quite good at reading people. Sharon – one glance, I can almost tell she's telling the truth; but of course I wasn't here – I was with you in the museum. You, yourself – not so much. I was watching you while I told you about my plans and dreams, and you had a look on your face that I see all the time: feigning interest, but with this air of smug condescension and disbelief, like I'm talking out of my arse. And so, sometimes, I have to make a point so that people will take me seriously. Sharon, here, for example. Or maybe one of your family. Divorced, aren't you? There's some kind of odd set-up with a teenage boy and his girlfriend too?' He smiled. 'Yes, Dan, I do my homework.'

'There's no need for this,' I said.

'No, there's not. That's why, if you had been honest with me, I could have phoned my chaps here and told them to lay off, that I had what I needed. But instead you tried to play me for a tube. Oh, no; you've no idea who's really employing you – just an ordinary little family, looking for their lost wain, who just happen to have millions to throw around. So, Dan, if you would tell me *now* who you're working for, that would be a start.' His eyes flitted to Sharon. 'And, I should warn you, I'm not in the habit of making threats.'

'It's not a problem,' I said. 'I just underestimated your interest. So it's all fine and I'll absolutely tell you who I'm working for . . . but would you at least let her go and clean herself up?'

He gave Sharon a sympathetic smile. 'Of course . . . But in a moment. Let's just see how we do first . . . Make sure we have all that fannying around out of your system, eh? *So* . . . you work for . . .?'

She was just a kid who loved Harry Potter. She didn't deserve this.

'Thomas Wolff,' I said. 'Billionaire Thomas Wolff.'

His eyes widened in surprise.

'Katya Cummings is his daughter – real name of Alison Wolff. They've managed to keep a lid on the fact that she's missing, but not, I imagine, for much longer.'

'Thomas Wolff,' said Harry Frank. 'Thomas *Wolff*. Oh my – that's a surprise! I was thinking some pop star's daughter or diplomat's niece, but Thomas Wolff . . . Jackpot, don't you think?' He gave an unappealing little laugh and said, 'And here was me going to ask for a million! He probably carries that in loose change. Well, thank you, Dan; that wasn't so hard, was it?' He moved forward and worked one of his gloved fingers under Sharon's chin and lifted it from where it had slumped on to her chest. 'And because of that, this little girl will be free to go, with just a bit of a thick lip to show for her terrible ordeal. Not so bad in the end, eh, love?'

She gurgled something indecipherable.

'That's right,' said Harry Frank, allowing her head to fall forward again. He moved right up to me. 'So what're we going to do now?'

'Do . . .? I'm not sure I—'

But he held up a hand to stop me, this time the leather finger actually touching my lips. 'Rhetorical question,' he said. He moved his finger off my lips. 'You see, Dan, I have plans, not quite for world domination, but you know what I mean. So I haven't time to go searching under every rock for Alison Wolff. Plus, once I get involved, and my people get involved, the word will be out there and everyone else will be looking for her too. Much better to keep this small, don't you think? To grow my business, it needs significant investment, and that's where you come in. You do what you do best: you find her, you bring her to me and then I can sit down with Mr Wolff and work out a suitable fee for her return. You'll still get paid – and I might even chuck in a few quid as well – and Wolff will get his daughter back. Everyone's a winner. How does that sound?'

'I'm not sure that Thomas Wolff would think—'

Harry Frank cut in with, 'Cypress Avenue, isn't it? Patricia, no?'

'If—'

'Oh, relax; they're fine. But you can't watch them all the time, Dan, and if I want to disappear them, then they will be disappeared. So what is it you're going to do?'

'I'm going to find Alison,' I said. 'But . . .'

He held up his hand. 'Don't "but" me, Dan; don't threaten or swear on your mother's grave because I will dig your mother up and throw her bones in your face. Just do your job and everyone will be happy. Don't you know, I'm in the happy business?'

He nodded behind me and the thug there kicked the backs of my legs so that they collapsed under me and suddenly I was on my knees on the floor. Before I could react at all, he had one arm round my throat. Harry Frank loomed over me. His hand delved into his jacket pocket and produced a clear plastic packet. He held it up and gave it a little jiggle. It contained about a dozen little orange pills.

'Oh, yes,' said Harry Frank as he opened the bag, 'I think it's important to spread it where you can, but it's like the driving test and sex, Dan: you can read the theory, but you'll never really understand or appreciate them until you do the practical. So what say . . .?' He nodded at the thug. He squeezed my throat harder and at the same time gripped my nose, which forced my mouth open as I gasped for breath. 'Will we try one?' Harry Frank shook a pill out into his gloved hand and popped it into my mouth. 'Or what about two?' A second went in. He stood back. 'Wait a minute – you're quite the party animal, aren't you, Dan? Excess is your thing, I'm told. Great reporter, lovely wife, but you really fucked yourself up by partying too hard. So a mere two is never going to satisfy you, is it, Dan? What say . . . the whole dirty dozen?'

He grabbed my jaw, his gloved fingers delving inside my mouth for grip, and he upended the bag. The pills cascaded towards the back of my throat. I brought my upper teeth down hard on his fingers and he yelped and tried to pull them free but I wouldn't let go; he started to scream; I could taste blood, even through the leather glove. The thug squeezed harder. I gagged, and the pills were gone. I couldn't breathe at all; my grip relaxed and Harry Frank yanked his bloody hand out and spun away clutching it to his chest and yelping like a dog. The other thug came round from behind Sharon and swung for me. Even groggy and breathless, I managed to move my head to the side and ride the punch. It struck, but not hard. I laughed and wheezed, 'You'll have to do better than that . . .'

So he did.

And everything went black.

26

I was on the island, so long ago. Our baby Stevie had gotten sick and died in the night and we had gone to bed with him lying between us. Then, when we woke in the morning, he was gone and we couldn't understand it. We tore around the cottage looking for him. There were others there – the doctor, the teacher, the priest with the protestant heart, the other mother, but not her daughter, her strange, otherworldly daughter, older than her years. She was gone with our dead baby and we had to search for her across the barren fields and peat bogs, and then I saw her in the distance, standing with our baby in her arms and I rushed up to her and tore Stevie from her and Stevie cried, and cried, and cried, because he was alive, alive, alive . . .

I opened my eyes.

There was a phone ringing.

Somewhere.

I was on the floor of the apartment, lying on my back.

A chair floated past.

I watched it for what seemed like along time.

The phone was still ringing, and also a siren. An ambulance. Or a fire engine. Or a police car. Or an ice-cream van. Or, possibly, Noddy.

I laughed and rolled on to my stomach. I felt great, but also . . . bad . . . somehow. I looked to the kitchen and saw that Sharon was sitting with her back to me, at the table, with a cup of tea or something steaming beside her.

I said, 'Sharon, are you OK?' But she didn't reply. I looked at the floating chair and saw that it was now at the lounge window, but instead of cracking into it, it passed straight through. I got up and walked to the window and put my hand through the glass and saw it emerge on the other side. It was some new kind of glass – transparent or translucent or transgender, but kind of cool. The chair was drifting away across the city. The phone was still ringing and I realised it was in my pocket. I put my hand in, but the pocket seemed to be incredibly spacious, and I pulled out what seemed to be a beating kidney, and a squirrel, before I located it. It was huge, like the one that comedian used to have on TV and shout into, so I yelled hello and a voice said, 'Dan – you're awake; how're you feeling?'

I said, 'Fandabidozi.'

The man giggled and said, 'Enjoy it while you can because, very soon, you're going to start feeling like shit and, after that, if you don't get to a hospital and pumped out, you're going to be dead. Do you understand me?'

'I understand French,' I said. 'And Polynesian.'

'Very good. You have a job to do. You better get to it.'

'Get to it I will.'

'Dan – do you hear that sound?'

'I hear many sounds. Kites and tractors.'

'And a siren?'

'Sirens. Many. Yes. Loud. They won't sell any ice cream going at . . .'

'Dan, if I were you . . .'

'Yes, sir . . .?'

'I would get out of there. Can't do your job locked up in pokey, can you?'

'No, sirree, Bob,' I said.

He laughed and cut the line, and I was trying to work out how the huge phone could get back into my now tiny little teeny-weeny pocket when I saw a police car pull up outside. Not one, but two. No, three. Policemen were getting out – in SWAT-team black. It was a very popular look that summer. Slimming too. They crossed the road.

I called to Sharon, 'You should come and see this; it's like one of those documentary series on Wolff TV.'

And something about that thought made me wince, and I closed my eyes and rested my boiling head against the glass. I thought I would fall through and float out after the chair, but it was hard and cool to the touch: refreshing. My head was starting to get sore and I wanted them to turn the sirens off, so I banged on the window and yelled at them, but there didn't seem to be a sound coming out of my mouth. I turned and said, 'Sharon – will you tell them to turn it down a bit?' But she kept sitting there with her back to me; plain rude. But then I remembered that she had been beaten and was probably sore, and a tear rolled down my cheek because it was my fault, and I thought about getting a T-shirt with *Why is it always me?* on the front.

I was still thinking about this, and how loud the sirens were and what the dream about our dead baby meant, as I crossed the room to her. I would apologise and tell her I would find her friend. I said, 'Sharon?' and put a hand on her shoulder, but, instead of looking up, she fell sideways and there was a hole where her eye should have been and she was dead. I staggered back. I yelled, 'Holy Fuck!' I pointed down and said, 'You know what you are? You're a lesson to me as to what will happen to my family if I don't get the ring back to Mordor.'

Though she was clearly dead, I thought it would be a good idea to be call an ambulance, mostly for myself, so I put my hand back into my jacket pocket for the phone, except it was the wrong pocket and, instead of the phone, I brought out a gun. It smelled of *use*. I understood that this had been planted upon me to make it look as if I had shot Sharon, and that it would be in my best interests to get out of there. So I ran to the door, threw it open and ran to the lift, but I could see that it was already coming up and I could also hear footsteps on the stairs. I put my hands up and prepared for arrest. Then I thought better of it and ran up the stairs to the apartment above. It had lain empty since Alison's useless bodyguards had shipped out. I tried the door, but it was locked. I ran along to the end of the hall. There was a fire escape. I pushed up the bars and stepped out and nearly fell over and to my messy death. But I held on and then thundered down them saying, 'Holyfuckholyfuckholyfuck,' over and over again, expecting at any time to be shot down or felled by arrows.

Then I was on the ground and there was a wall, which I threw myself at. There was jagged glass along the top, which ripped my hands, but I still got over it and landed in an alley and thought that I had done something similar many years before, so I stood and thought about Parker, the American journalist, but then I remembered that he had died a horrible death and that I might also do just that damn thing if I did not shift my arse. So I ran whatever way was opposite to where the police cars were and ended up in a nice street with students looking at me oddly because my hands were bleeding. I put them in my pockets to hide them, but instead I found my phone and I stared at it. I pushed buttons and Patricia said, 'What now? I'm busy.'

So I said, 'Fine by me, but I just want to say I love you, I may be unwell, I'm in . . . lemme see . . . Carmel

Street . . . but there's a garden here I'm going to lie down in, so that's goodnight from me, and goodnight from him. Goodnight,' and I lay down on the lawn, which was well kept, and died.

27

Shapes. Indistinct sounds. Movement. Closer. Focus. An elderly man rolling his sleeves down and trying to button them, saying, 'He'll live . . .'

And a woman, 'I can't thank you enough.' Standing over me. 'Sleep.'

'Love you, baby,' I murmured.

I opened my eyes and the world hurt. My throat was ragged, my nose blocked, stomach ached and, when I looked at my hands, they were all bandaged up. I was in a room I didn't know, in an unfamiliar bed; there were furry toys piled in a corner; a dinosaur mobile with a cobweb on it hung from the ceiling. The window was open and, I guessed from the sun, it was somewhere around midday. There was a small bookcase close by with children's titles, spine out: Enid Blyton and the Moomins. There was a bottle of water on a bedside table, which I guzzled down in one. I threw back the quilt and sat up. The world spun. There was a basin at my feet, into which I was sick. I lay down again. The door opened, but I was too busy retching to look up. I just said, 'Thank you.'

A woman said, 'You owe me.'

She wasn't Trish.

Maybe a couple of hours later, I struggled out of bed. I was naked. There was no sign of my clothes, but there was a woman's dressing gown hanging on the back of the door. I put it on and tied it tight and opened the door and looked both ways along a hall. I moved left, looking for the bathroom, but found another bedroom and an airing cupboard. I turned right and tried the first door, but it was locked and there was the sound of running water and splashing from within. I knocked gently. The splashing stopped. I said, 'I have no idea where I am or who you are, but I'm eternally grateful. Also, I can't find my clothes so I'm wearing your dressing gown.'

She said, 'Are you OK?'

'I'm dead . . . but alive. Who are you?'

There was more splashing. I crouched down to look through the keyhole.

I couldn't see anything through it, but was still in that position when the door suddenly opened. I straightened. I was looking at Sara Patterson. She was wrapped in an identical dressing gown, and she was shaking her head.

I said, 'You.'

She said, 'Me.'

I said, 'Why you?'

'Because I'm a frickin' idiot, that's why me.'

'But how did you even . . .?'

'Because you phoned me up and told me you loved me.'

'Yes, I do.'

'Don't you be a frickin' idiot. You thought I was your wife. But, nevertheless, you did sound like you were dying, and sometimes I go on instinct, and sometimes I live to regret it. This time, I hope not. Go into the kitchen, make yourself some toast; doctor said it's important to get food into you. I'll be there in a couple of minutes.'

'OK.'

I turned.

She said, 'And, Starkey? My opinion of you hasn't changed one bit.'

I nodded. 'Still your hero.'

'Still a wanker,' she said.

When she came into the kitchen, dressed in black jeans and a tartan shirt, barefoot, I was staring at the toaster, trying to remember how it worked.

She said, 'How do you feel?'

'Kevin,' I said. I looked at her and she looked at me, and finally I found the word I was looking for: 'Spacey.'

She told me to sit down. She would make the toast. She asked me if I liked jam and, after a while, I said I did. She asked me how I liked my toast and I said, 'Black. Like my men.'

She nodded.

I said, 'Belfast has the largest number of black men in the United Kingdom. And all of their wives are white.'

She nodded.

'Some of the black men are also Orange.'

She said, 'Uh-huh,' and concentrated on my toast.

After I ate it and drank her coffee, and then did the same again and again, I felt a lot better but still a little light headed.

'So,' I said, 'this is your house? Where's the kid?'

'What kid?'

'There are furry bunnies in my bedroom.'

'It's not your bedroom, and my niece stays sometimes. Do you want to tell me what happened?'

I said, 'Why don't *you* tell *me*?'

'OK. I'll go first. I found you lying in a garden. The owner of the house was prodding you with a rake and telling you to fuck off. I told her I was your carer and that you'd escaped from hospital and I'd take you back. You were rambling about trains and DeLoreans and someone called Lolita. As soon as I saw you, I knew you were crushed, so I was going to take you to the hospital, and started driving there, but then I turned on to Palestine, and saw all the action there, and I remembered, because I've been checking you out, that the girl you've been looking for lived there. So I made a couple of calls as I drove and found out a girl had been murdered and they were looking for a single white male, and I thought of you. And then I did something which might turn out to be spectacularly stupid and brought you here. I have a doctor friend. He's discreet. Retired. He got me off crush as well.'

'You were . . .?'

'One hundred per cent, but he got me off, and I won't go back, ever.'

'But you can be around people who are?'

'Like you? Yes.'

'Not like me. No.'

She looked at me. 'So, it's your turn to tell me.'

'It's kind of hazy. Maybe later.'

'Or maybe I should just call the police.' She smiled, but with threat and evil intent.

'If you know anything about me,' I said, 'you'll know I haven't it in me to kill someone. So feel free.'

'Crushed, you would kill the baby Jesus for a hit.'

'I wasn't voluntarily crushed.'

'A big boy did it and ran away?'

'More or less. Yes. Are they seriously looking for me?'

'No, they're doing it comically. Not by name. Not yet.'

'Fuck!' I said. And then I remembered, and said, 'I need to make a call.' I felt the pockets of my dressing gown. There was no reason why my phone should have been in there, but it was to emphasise the fact that I didn't know where it or my clothes were.

She said, 'Your clothes were in a state, so I stuck them in the wash. Unfortunately, your phone was in a back pocket I didn't check, so it's drying on the radiator. I'm sure it will be fine.'

'People are always washing my clothes,' I said.

'Well, it's a one-off for me. Now you need to tell me what's going on.'

'Call first.'

She studied me. Then she took her phone out of her jeans pocket and pushed it across the table to me.

'Always on call,' I said. 'I remember those days. Excuse me.'

I got up and walked back down the hall to the bedroom with the soft toys. I couldn't quite remember what threat Harry Frank had made to my family, but there had definitely been one. I sat on the bed and rubbed at my head and tried to get some sense into it. Patricia's mobile number wouldn't come to me. I passed some time reading Sara's texts and call history. Then it came to me and I called and I was too zonked to feel properly terrified when she didn't answer. I cut the line and fumbled for her home number. While it eluded me, I flicked through Sara's photos. The number arrived. I called and Bobby answered with, 'What?'

'It's me,' I said. 'How're you doing?'

'Fine.'

'Is Patricia with you?'

'No.'

'Do you know where she is?'

'Tesco's.'

'I tried calling her, but she didn't pick up.'

'Tesco's in the Connswater shopping centre; there's no signal if she's in the frozen-food aisles.'

'Good to know,' I said. 'What about Lol?'

'Fine.'

'Is she with you?'

'Yes. She's making Hungarian goulash. It's her Home Economics homework.'

I said, 'Has anything strange been happening? People hanging around outside, following, callers . . .?'

'Just you,' said Bobby. 'And . . . well, now that you mention it . . . I stayed over at Lol's last night; when we got back this morning, Trish was already away but the front door was open . . . Just thought maybe she hadn't closed it properly, but that might qualify as strange.'

'Fuck. Right. OK. OK. Now, listen to me. I'm really serious here. Are you the slightest bit keen on Hungarian goulash?'

'I've never had it.'

'It will taste like shite. Although taste is subjective.'

'Are you on something, or something?'

'That's for me to know and you to find out.'

'Right . . . OK.'

'So, listen to me . . . I'm going to make you an offer. Fuck the goulash, go to Pizza Hut. Eat as much as you want and I'll foot the bill. I'm celebrating – I've had a windfall – want to treat you.'

'Serious?'

'Straight up.'

'Excellent. But we'd prefer Domino's. We can order in.'

'No – I want you to go out to Pizza Hut.'

'Pizza Hut don't deliver; Dominos do. What's the point in going out?'

'The point *is* the going out; I want you to get out of the house.'

'Why? Are you coming round to go through Trish's—?'

'I've never done—! Just for once, could you do something without having to know the reason, because I'm asking you to do it?'

'Why?'

'Could you just . . . do . . . it?'

'Tell you the truth, CBA.'

'You . . . what?'

'Couldn't be arsed, granddad.'

'OK.' I pushed my fingers into my eyes in a futile attempt to diminish the pain of talking to a teenager. 'Then listen to this: I'm on a case; it has taken a very serious turn and there's a real possibility that someone will, in the very near future, try to harm you or Lolita or Patricia in order to get at me. I'm going to go and get Patricia now, but I need you to get offside; I need you to take Lol with you and I need you to go somewhere he or they won't be able to guess, i.e. not her mum's. Are you getting me?'

'Are you fucking serious?'

'Yes, I'm fucking serious.'

'Well, why didn't you say that in the first place?'

'I . . . Right, you're right, I should have. Sorry.'

'OK. So how are we going to pay for it?'

'Pay for what?'

'The pizza, *duh*.'

'Just . . . just fucking go there, Bobby, and keep eating until I arrive.'

'OK. Keep your hair on.'

'And, Bobby?'

'*What?*'

'Be careful. Go out the back way. Be careful.'

'Seriously, Dan . . . Are you seriously serious? Or winding me up?'

'I'm serious! Jesus! Get out of there, would you?!'

'OK! Always fucking shouting at me. And who am I even looking out for? What do they look like?'

'Killers,' I said.

I must have zoned out again. When I looked up, Sara was standing in the doorway, looking at me looking at her phone. I said, 'Sorry . . .'

'No – just checking; you'd stopped talking . . . What're you . . .?' She came towards me and took the phone out of my hands. She looked at the screen. 'Really?' she said. 'REALLY?'

'What . . .?'

She showed me the screen, and the photo of her in her bikini.

'Sorry, I didn't mean . . . but you do look good for forty.'

She said, 'You're fucking funny. Now tell me what the hell is going on or I really am calling the cops.'

I said, 'OK. Well . . .'

'Not in here,' she said. 'Inappropriate.'

She stalked out of the room and back to the kitchen. I looked at the bed and the fluffy toys and thought she was probably right. I waited for a bit, and then followed.

I had looked up her age when I was first checking her out, but that too was proving evasive. I moved along the hall and into the kitchen and stood at the table. I said, 'I want to thank you for everything, and now I need you to take me to Tesco's.'

'You . . .' She held up a hand. 'I'm going nowhere until you tell me what the fuck is going on. What happened at Katya Cummings' apartment? Who is the dead girl? What have you got to do with it? And why were you lying crushed in someone's front garden?'

'Thirty-five,' I said.

'Thirty-five *what*?'

'That's how old you are. Sorry, the old brainbox—'

'Talk. Talk to me about *this*.' She set the gun from my jacket – the one Harry Frank had planted on me – on the table. She had, I now realised, been sitting with it on her lap, wrapped in an Asda plastic bag. 'I suspect this is what the police will be looking for. It will most certainly have your fingerprints on it. So start talking, Starkey or . . .' and she raised an eyebrow.

'What's to say I don't take the gun off you and shoot you with it?'

'With those hands? You could barely lift the toast. What's to say I don't shoot *you* with it instead?'

'That would be murder.'

'That would be self-defence.'

'I need to go to Tesco's. My wife is in danger. Ex-wife, but nevertheless.'

'What kind of danger?'

'It's a long story, and I haven't time, just please—'

'Make time, Starkey.'

'On the way. I will tell you everything on the way.'

She stared at me. Then she sighed and stood up and said, 'For fuck's sake.' She shook her head at me and said, 'You look ridiculous. Right. I'll get your clothes. You better fucking well be worth it.'

She strode out; she strode back in. She handed me my black jeans and a tartan shirt – *blouse*, in fact.

'Your top is fucked,' she said.

I dropped the dressing gown.

'Jesus, Starkey!' She turned away. 'Pants! And work out once in a while!'

'Sorry, I . . . Fuzzy . . .'

She hurried down the hall and then came back with keys in her hand and said, 'Ready?'

I looked at her and she looked at me. We were dressed identically.

We both said, 'Fuck!' at the same time.

I turned for the door.

She said, 'Starkey.'

I looked back. She was holding out the gun in its plastic bag.

'Do you want this?'

'Trusting me, now?'

'Do you want it?'

'You bring it.'

'No. I'm a journalist. Journalists don't carry guns.'

I stepped back to her and took the bag and withdrew the gun. I'd forgotten how heavy they could be, and, conversely, how delicate. With my bandaged hand it was hard to get a proper grip and my finger just about squeezed in by the trigger. But I could do it. Whether I would was another matter entirely. I slipped it into my pocket. 'C'mon, Tonto,' I said.

28

Sara lived in south Belfast, not that far from my office. We had to cross into east Belfast to get to the Connswater shopping centre and Tesco's. That meant going through the city centre. Traffic was heavy and there were random checkpoints. Not looking for me, specifically. She gave me a camera to hold, then used her press card to get us through. I had tried Trish's mobile twice since setting out, but still no response. It didn't necessarily mean she was in danger. She could easily already be on her way home and wasn't picking up because she was driving. I had also known her to take seventeen minutes deciding between two identical bags of frozen vegetables, so she might still be in whatever part of Tesco's didn't have coverage.

Sara's Volkswagen still smelled of dog. 'Yet you appear not to have one.'

'Died,' she said. 'Recently. Haven't had the heart to . . .'

'Will you get another?'

'I think I just have. Now – talk.'

I had no reason to trust her. There is a camaraderie amongst journalists but it does not extend to sharing stories or keeping promises not to use information given on the Q.T. It's a dog-eat-dog profession. And, as we had already clearly established, I wasn't even a journalist any more. To her I was a source and a suspect. But I was embroiled in something that was threatening to overwhelm me and which had put my family in considerable danger and I needed her help. Harry Frank had killed Sharon, or at least given the order. The very fact of that gave credence to his claims about the crush business and his plans to organise and control the many disparate gangs currently running amok in Belfast. It also proved how ruthless he could be. He now knew about Alison and how rich and powerful her father was. He didn't have a clue where she was or about her fate after the Wellington Street massacre, but was expecting me to find her. If not, he would harm my family. My job description hadn't changed, but I had become *One Man, Two Guvnors*.

I said, 'There's a guy called Harry Frank; he's buying and muscling his way into crush but he's being stymied because Katya ran off with the secret formula—'

'*Secret formula*?!'

'For some new kind of crush which is guaranteed pure; it's the Holy Grail of crush and she ran off with it and has disappeared and he's desperate to get it back.'

'And how did Katya come to have it?'

'They were lovers, but he thinks she got a better offer and took off with it.'

'So there was only one copy of it?'

'I suppose. Yes.'

'Like, written on a piece of paper, or something?'

'Yes, maybe. I don't know.'

'Wouldn't the chemists who developed it have a copy?'

'Something happened to them, I think. You know what it's like.'

'So she's the only one who has a copy.'

'That's what he said.'

'And he wants you to find her.'

'Yes.'

'And you're already working for her parents.'

'Yes.'

'And what happened at her apartment, to the girl?'

'He killed her because she wouldn't tell him where Katya was, and to show me what he would do to my family if I didn't help him find her.'

'Why isn't he trying to find her himself? Why you?'

'He's tried, but he doesn't want to put it out there that there's a secret formula or everyone will be after it and her. So he wants me to do it on the Q.T.'

Sara was nodding. But then her nose crinkled and she looked across at me and said, 'Do you smell that?'

'What?'

'The smell of utter shite! Secret formula! For fuck's sake, Starkey, this isn't the fucking fifties! Secret formula, written on a scrap of paper, for fuck's sake! I'm trying to help you; I'm here, in my car, with a murder suspect who I've just given a gun to – for fuck's sake, what more do I have to do to make you trust me?!'

'Would a blow— OK, all right . . .' I put my hands up. 'I'm just . . . Let's get to Tesco's and then—'

'No!' She threw the car into the side of the road and cut the engine. There was honking from behind. 'Now!'

'OK. All right! I'll tell you, just please – keep driving. My wife's life . . .'

Her eyes narrowed. She shook her head. 'No.'

'OK. OK. All right. Off the record, OK?'

'No.'

'*No?*'

'No. "Off the record" is a catch-all for liars and hoods and charlatans to get out of taking responsibility for anything. I've helped you; I've put myself in danger; I'm risking my hard-won reputation; I could be sacked for being here for you, let alone arrested for aiding and abetting. I'm taking a colossal chance on you, Starkey, and I'm not doing that and getting nothing out of it in the end. So tell me what the fuck is going on or get out of the fucking car.'

'My wife—'

'Tell me!'

'Then you agree not to use it, any of it, until this is all over.'

'No. You don't get to make deals. You tell me, I use my best judgement.'

'OK. OK. I'll give you three words, then you drive; I'll give you the rest later.'

'Better be three fucking big words, Starkey.'

I nodded. She nodded.

'Thomas Wolff's daughter.'

Her mouth dropped open slightly; her lips formed up in the shape of the *wuh* of Wolff, but no sound emerged.

Then she started the engine.

Connswater was a medium-sized shopping mall with Tesco's as an anchor tenant. There was a large car park on three sides and one main entrance with a couple of side doors. I said, 'Drop me here, I'll go through the store and meet you at the back.'

'No.'

Nevertheless, I started to open the door, but she jumped to put the central locking on. I swore and she swore back. She pulled further into the car park and we cruised around. I spotted Trish's empty car halfway along our third row. We moved past it towards the drop-off zone, populated with large groups of smokers, old women with plastic bags at their feet, waiting for taxis, and then, at the back, half turned so he could keep one eye on the inside of the mall and the other on the car park, I saw the thug who'd held me tight while Harry Frank poured crush down my throat. I told Sara who he was and added, 'No Pinky without Perky.' Her brow furrowed. I shook my head and said, 'They've followed her here; *he's* keeping track; his partner will be in a car, waiting for the signal. Whip round again, see if I can . . .'

Two more rows – then I spotted him – the back of his head, really, elbow resting on the open window, chatting on his phone but apparently looking towards the entrance. Sara turned into the next row and stopped the car.

'What're you—?'

'Working,' she said.

She reached down and took the camera from the floor at my feet, then quickly and smoothly swung it up, shot off a rapid series of photos of the car and its occupant and then lowered it again.

'Biggest story of our career and you jeopardise—'

'Get over yourself, Starkey; I do this day in, day—'

'OK! Just . . . in here . . .' I indicated a space and she pulled in. 'Now you need to go in and get her.'

'Me? I don't—'

'If they see me approaching her, Christ knows what will happen, but they don't know you . . .'

'And I don't know *her*.'

'You can't miss her; she's . . . she's . . . tall, and her hair is . . .'

Sara rolled her eyes. She lifted her handbag and pulled my phone out of it. 'Here . . . It should be dry by now.'

'There's no signal in Tes—'

'Photo. You must have a photo of her?'

I switched the phone on – there were a few moments of suspense as we waited to see if it would actually start, but then it lit up, good as new. I'm not one for taking lots of photos on my phone – old school – but I had one good one of Trish. I cleared my throat. I showed it to Sara.

'Christ!' she said.

'You can still see her face . . .'

'That's not all I can fucking see! Put it away!'

'That's what she—'

'Stop!'

'OK – it was three years or three hundred years ago. But she hasn't changed much – you'll remember what she looks like?'

'Starkey – I will *never* forget what she looks like. Right. Wait here.' She took the keys from the ignition and opened her door.

I said, 'What are you doing? The keys.'

'Yeah, *right* . . .'

'What if we need to make a quick getaway?'

'What if you drive off in my car with my story?'

'What would be the fucking point in that?'

'I don't know, but you can be sure as fuck I'm going to protect myself against it. So shut up, sit tight and I'll be back in a few minutes. Probably.'

Sara shut the door and hurried away. As she approached the entrance, I could see the thug still looking into the mall rather than out. She moved through the doors and turned to her left rather than going straight ahead to Tesco's. She stopped on one side of the glass doors, with the thug directly opposite her. She raised her phone while facing away from him and appeared to be talking into it. But I knew what she was doing. In a moment, she would turn nonchalantly and take his photo. She did exactly that, talked on for several moments, then put the phone away and started walking.

I sat in the lifeless car and looked about me, feeling utterly helpless. I tried Trish's phone, but no response. I had a view of the back of the thugs' car, but not enough to see the driver. I had to presume he was still there. It was almost lunchtime, the car park was busy and the smokers out front appeared to be self-replicating. It was a disadvantaged neighbourhood and they clung on to the old ways with declining vigour. An old woman in a blue mac and white ankle socks pushed her trolley to a stop at the back of the grey Fiat opposite me. She put the keys in the boot and pushed it up. Then she struggled to lift a heavy bag of dry dog food. In trying to get to grips with it, she managed to push the trolley away from the car. She had to put the bag down again and push it back. She took a second run at the bag. She got it up and over the edge, but then she lost control and it fell, bumped off the back of the boot and hit the ground. She stood over it, breathing hard. Then she looked at the trolley. There were five other bags of exactly the same, apparently colossal, weight. She looked up the row of cars one way and then the other, clearly looking for help. Then her eyes fell on me. I looked away. When I looked back, she was still looking at me. This time it was harder to break the connection. I forced myself to focus on my mission rather than her watery old eyeballs and switched my attention to the mall entrance. When I glanced back at the old woman, she had suddenly materialised six feet from my window.

She said, 'Young man . . .?'

'No; fuck off.'

She stepped nearer and said, 'I'm sorry, I'm a little –' and she pointed at her ear – 'hard of hearing. Do you think you could give me a wee hand? They loaded them up for me in the shop, but I had a stroke last year and I've just not got the strength to—'

'Right. Fuck. Right.'

I got out of the car. She stepped out of my way as I stomped across to her trolley. I picked the bag up from the ground and put it in the boot. It wasn't that heavy. I turned to the others.

The old woman said, 'When I was your age, a gentleman would have volunteered his services.'

'When you were my age, the Kaiser was still hopeful of victory.'

She said, 'What?'

I said, 'How many dogs do you have?'

'Just the one.'

'Is he going camping or something?'

'What?'

I shook my head. My phone rang. Sara said, 'Found her in fish; she took some persuading. She's just paying for her groceries now, but I'm going to walk them out. I'll put them in my car, then she'll wait for my signal and come running out the side door to the left, and hopefully we'll be off before they can do anything. OK?'

'OK,' I said.

I looked back to the mall entrance. I could see the outline of thug number one, but I was too far away for him to realise who I was. In a few moments, Sara was going to emerge with the shopping and Trish would be waiting by the side exit. Thug number two, judging from where his car was positioned, would probably have a pretty good view of what we were about to do.

I moved closer to the old woman and said, very distinctly, 'I'm happy to help, love, but would you do me a favour? The wife's paranoid about having our car stolen; would you mind just sitting in the passenger seat, there, till I get these loaded up?'

'Why don't you just lock it?'

'She took the keys. Honestly, she'll only be a minute, but she'll be furious if she finds out I left it unlocked.'

The woman sighed. 'Well . . .'

'Thanks, love,' I said. She moved slowly across. I'd left the door half open. She stood by it. 'Get in,' I said; 'take the weight off your feet.'

She opened the door further and carefully lowered herself into the seat. She sat sideways for a moment, then, after a few moments of consideration, moved her feet in as well. I closed the door and gave her the thumbs up. Then I returned to her trolley and gave it a hefty push. As it rolled away, I reached up and pulled her keys out of the lock, slammed the boot shut, jumped in and started the engine. She watched it all, but couldn't quite work out what was happening. I backed out of her space and then drove down the row towards the entrance. Sara was now emerging from the mall and guiding a trolley, packed with groceries, towards me. I moved the sun visor down and cruised past her.

I pulled up by the side entrance. I glanced back at Thug Two, who remained in his car. Thug One was out of sight around the corner. I called Trish. She answered straight away and I told her to come out *now*.

She came charging out, but then stopped and looked straight at the old woman's car, and then to the left and right of it.

'Where are you?' she yelled into her phone.

'Straight in front!' I could see her looking, but still she hesitated. 'Trish!' I glanced back, and saw that Thug Two was getting out of his car. And Thug One had appeared around the corner. 'Trish! Now!'

'She said a Volkswagen!'

'Change of plan, you stupid— Grey Fiat, straight— I'm waving!'

She crouched slightly and squinted against the afternoon sun, then smiled and started to walk. The thugs were converging on her. I threw the car into gear and sped it up a slanted disabled kerb on to the paved walkway. I skidded to a halt beside her, leaned across and pushed the door open.

'Get in, for fuck's sake!'

She jumped in. 'What's the fucking panic?' she yelled as she slammed the door.

'They—'

Thug One was just reaching Trish's window as I gunned the car forward. Thug Two threw himself out of the way. The car clattered off a high kerb back down on to the exit lane. In the mirror, I could see the two thugs running uselessly after us. I glanced to my right and saw Sara standing stock still beside her car, watching us drive away. The old woman was out of the car and gesticulating madly at her.

'Knew I should have gone to fucking Asda,' said Trish.

29

I made a quick turn on to the Holywood Road, then on to Cheviot, Irwin and Lomand avenues. I threw the car into a space halfway along Lomand, outside a run of terrace houses with white doors and satellite dishes. I kept watching the mirror.

Trish said, 'So who is she?'

'Who is who?'

'The skinny . . . The woman you sent in to get me.'

'Sara? She's a journalist; she's helping me—'

'Aye. You and your floozies.'

'I'm not even going there . . .'

Trish shook her head and said, 'I forgot how much fun life with you was. And how you take a special delight in putting your loved ones in danger.'

'Loved ones? That's pushing it.'

She gave me a curled lip and I gave her one back. I said we'd better go and pick up Bobby and Lol, and that I hoped they were OK. I started the car again and drove back to the Holywood Road and headed into town.

I said, 'I know it's a pain in the arse, but you'll all need to go somewhere for a few days until I sort this out.'

She said, 'Jesus, Dan, I have a job; I can't be doing this every time you screw something up.'

'I haven't screwed anything, which is more than I can say for you.'

'You what?'

I gave her a sarcastic smile and a knowing look, all in one. 'You know,' I said.

'I don't know what the fuck you're talking about.'

'So, Bobby and Lol were at Lol's house last night, right?'

'So *what*?'

I gave her another look. She blew air out of her cheeks. She said, 'There's a girl I work with has a place in Bangor; maybe we could go—?'

I cut in with, 'So who is he?'

'Who is he who?'

'Trish, let's be grown up about this. Who is whoever you're fucking?'

'Christ! What *are* you talking about? Do you not think I've enough on my plate without—?'

'Just tell me. I *know*, Trish.'

'We're divorced, case you hadn't noticed.'

'Oh, I know it. So, are you not going to tell me? Are you *ashamed* to tell me?'

'Ashamed? *Jesus!*'

'Then what's the harm? Anyway, I just want to thank him for saving your life.'

'Saving? It's quite casual; I wouldn't say he'd—'

'I *mean*, if you hadn't gotten rid of the kids and then popped round to fuck him, then the guys who're after me would have taken you last night. If you'd been at home, we wouldn't be having this conversation – you'd be a hostage and they'd be sticking your face in a vat of acid to show me they mean business.'

'Thank fuck then,' said Trish.

We smiled sarcastically at each other.

After several minutes of silence, while we each tried to decide on the best method of renewing attack, Trish beat me to it with, 'So where is she now?'

'She?'

'*Sara.*'

'I don't know. She helped out; she's away on. I hardly know her.'

'I can believe that, because you're like a stray dog everyone wants to pet, but nobody particularly wants to keep once they discover you're not house-trained and leave your shit everywhere.'

'Thanks, Trish.'

I felt only slightly bad about dumping Sara. For one, the fewer people I involved in the mess of my life, the better for them. Harry Frank and his gang – and, at this point, I didn't know if his acolytes stretched to a thousand or just the two thugs charging after us outside Tesco – were undoubtedly ruthless and would think nothing of torturing her for information. As much as I wanted to trust her – as indeed, she had trusted me – she had the ulterior motive of wanting to get her story and she was enough like me for me to know that she would go to considerable lengths to get it. Yes, I'd told her about Wolff and his missing daughter, but it wasn't exactly evidence; I was an unreliable source, on the run for a murder I may have committed, while he was a billionaire, well used to being the focus of outlandish stories and to fending off nosey journalists. If Sara dared suggest his daughter was missing without any evidence to back it up, he would find a way to silence her. If she couldn't be bought, her paper certainly could. But he probably wouldn't need to go that far; he'd argue that running the story would threaten his daughter's safety and, if they didn't go along with that, he'd call in his legal team and rain down cash-sapping injunctions.

No, Sara Patterson was better off out of it. Which was exactly where I needed to place my ex, her adoptive one-legged son and his pregnant schoolgirl girlfriend. I'd been a bit on the prescriptive side on telling the kid where to wait, thinking they could amble to a nearby Pizza Hut, but the chain was going through stricken times and their closest sit-down restaurant was down-town in the Victoria Centre. The city was going all to shit, but Victoria was nearly always busy, mostly with aspirational gang-bangers, so the less time we spent in there the better. I took the off-ramp into the centre's two-tier underground car park. The old woman's car would have been reported stolen by now, so we dumped it there and quickly rode the escalators up to the food court. As we walked in, we saw that Bobby and Lol had finished eating their pizzas and were busy eating each other. We split them up with some difficulty and walked them outside. While I waved down a taxi, Trish explained to them that they were going on a surprise holiday for a couple of days. Their eyes lit up, and then lit down again when she told them they were going to get the train to Bangor, a dozen miles away. I gave Trish plenty of Wolff cash. Lol said she didn't think she could go without her mum's permission; I gave her some Wolff cash and suddenly her mum's approval didn't seem so important. Bobby put his hand out and said he didn't have his mum's permission either. I pointed out that she was dead and said she was with him in spirit, and I gave him some as well. I found it really easy giving someone else's money away. A taxi pulled in and Trish shepherded the kids into the back. They were going to Bangor, but it was probably better that I didn't know exactly where so that Harry Frank couldn't torture it out of me.

Trish moved around and opened the passenger door.

I said, 'So, good luck.'

She said, 'Cheers.'

I turned away.

She called me back, as I knew she would. Most of the time she annoyed the hell out of me, but I was also totally in love with her. We had been through hell together, but we could still make each other laugh. She swore like a trooper and sometimes fought like one, but she was still my anchor. She was still beautiful.

She grabbed hold of my jacket. She turned to Bobby and Lol, watching us out of the back window, and said, 'Look away.'

Bobby said, 'Aw, for fuck's sake.'

Lol just grinned and kept looking as Trish pulled me close and kissed me on the lips.

'You still love me,' I said.

'*Still*? That's just in case something happens to you. If you come out of this alive, you're not getting another one.'

'Yeah, yeah,' I said.

30

It was a little after three p.m. I was crossing Belfast on foot, heading for Botanic. Harry Frank's intervention had briefly complicated my life, but hadn't much changed my situation. He had killed a young student to show me how ruthless he was. I was not yet on the run for her murder, even though I was probably carrying the murder weapon in my pocket, but it would surely not be very long before I was blamed. The easiest thing would have been to clean it of fingerprints and DNA and then dump it – but I just couldn't do it. I have never been one for guns but, in this new, savage Belfast, it definitely made me feel safer to have it about me. And guns sometimes got questions answered where polite enquiry did not. My job was still to find Alison Wolff, dead or alive, and deliver her to her father. Harry Frank now knew who she was and, if he hadn't found her already, would have launched a search. He had the advantage of knowing the underworld of the city he was striving to control. My knowledge of it was second-hand.

Maybe it hadn't been the best idea in the world to jettison Sara Patterson so quickly, but at least I still had access to the gang info she'd sent me and, now that I was able to check my phone, I saw that she had also forwarded the background info she'd promised on the Botanic Boat Crew and, in particular, their leader, Davy Blair. I was reading up on him as I walked when my phone rang. I looked at the caller ID and saw it was Michael Finn, Wolff's right-hand man.

He snapped out, 'Starkey – what the hell's going on?'

I said, 'How d'you mean?'

'Starkey! The girl in the apartment!'

'What about—?'

'Don't fuck with me, Starkey! What happened to her? And what have you to do with it?'

'Relax, Michael,' I said. 'I've done nothing. But word's out on Katya's real identity. They tortured it out of her.'

'Christ! There's been nothing on the news about that.'

'It isn't the news you have to worry about. But I'm on it; I'm closing in.'

'What do you mean, "closing in"?'

'Getting there, on the cusp, there's light at the end of the tunnel.'

'Starkey! Tell me what you—'

'No. You'll just have to trust me.'

'Starkey – we expect results.'

'And you'll get results.' I didn't add the very obvious, *but not necessarily* . . .

'*Did* you have anything to do with the murder?'

'Am I going to answer that?'

'Christ!'

'Trust me. Have I ever let you down?'

'Starkey . . .!' He sighed. 'Mr Wolff is having kittens. Just . . . keep a lid on things. If you say you're closing in, then that's good . . . We will have to trust you. But it's vitally important there's not even the suggestion of a hint that there's a connection between this girl's death and any employee of the Wolff organisation. Do I make myself clear? Mr Wolff has a reputation that must be protected.'

'*Really*?'

'*Really*, Starkey. And, I'm warning you, if it comes out that you were within even a mile of this girl when she died, then you can consider our business closed. We will, at the same time, actively pursue you for breach of contract and all monies paid, which is, at least in your terms, a fairly considerable sum. Do I make myself clear?'

'Could you go over it once more?'

'Starkey . . .'

'Finn,' I said, 'let me also make *myself* clear: you hired me to do a job, and I'm trying to do it, but I don't need you threatening me – that doesn't help. And do you know something? This isn't just about a little rich girl and the share price of daddy's company any more. It's also about little, unimportant people, people who actually go under their own names, people like Sharon Craig who never did any harm to anyone. Sharon Craig wasn't "this girl" or "the girl in the apartment"; she was a living, breathing, Harry-Potter-obsessed nerd who died because of her connection to Alison. And, to tell you the truth, what they did to her fires me up more than any money you can pay me.'

'Very good, Starkey, very noble, and I'll remember that when it's time to settle your account. It's also good to know you've been affected so deeply by this girl's death. Perhaps it will indeed prove inspirational for you. But in the meantime, *do your job*. And, just one thing?'

'*What*?'

'Her name was Sharon *Quigg*. Not Craig. Quigg.'

'Same difference,' I said, and cut the line.

Sharon Quigg. Sharon *Quigg*. *Sharon Quigg*.

Her name may not have yet imprinted itself on my brain, but her dead-eyed face had. I was not to blame for her death, but I was in some part responsible for it. As I walked, I decided that finding Alison was no longer my only job. It was just the job I was being paid for. Getting Harry Frank, and making him pay for what he'd done to bookish Sharon Quigg, that was fucking pro bono.

I stopped in a café, just down from Botanic station, to finish reading what Sara had sent me on Davy Blair and the Boat Crew. I ordered a German biscuit and a Diet Coke. There were half a dozen students grouped around the next table having an urgent discussion about the New Seekers. They were arrogant and patronising and dismissive and I wished I had that little to be concerned with.

I'd hardly gotten started when a chair was pulled out opposite me and D.I. Hood sat down. I asked him where the fuck he had sprung from and he said he always had one eye on me because I was a shit magnet. And, also, he had been on the way back to base from a crime scene when he'd spotted me coming in.

'Oh, yeah,' he said. 'Nasty one – young student shot in the head. Looks like she had been tortured first.'

'Crumbs,' I said.

I flicked them off the table. German biscuits can be like that.

He said, 'Is that it?'

'What do you want me to say? *Crikey*?'

'Dan, you know who she is; I know you know who she is.'

'And how would you know that?'

'Because we've only recently discussed who you're looking for and now the friend turns up dead and I can get dragged into this because I gave you CCTV footage out of the goodness of my heart. Tell me you had nothing to do with it.'

'I had nothing to do with it.'

'Of course you had! So tell me what's going on or—'

'There's nothing to tell,' I said.

He studied me for a bit and then said, 'Are you in trouble?'

'When am I not?'

'I'm serious. If I can help you, I will. I know you usually try to do the right thing, that's why I don't think you actually murdered her, but if you turn down my help now and it turns out you were involved in some way, or were even there, then it's out of my hands completely.'

'I appreciate that,' I said.

I nodded; he nodded. We got into a staring match that only ended when his phone went. He snapped it open and said, 'What?' Then he said, 'Sir,' a couple of times. He closed his phone and said, 'This city,' shook his head and got up. He stopped long enough to say, 'I'm serious: give me a bell; let me know. OK?'

'OK,' I said.

'Again,' he said, 'this time with feeling.'

'*OK*.'

He gave me a nod and departed. I signalled to the waitress for another coffee and tried to concentrate on Davy Blair – hood, enforcer, dealer, and now gang leader. He was done for GBH in his mid-teens and had then graduated from Hydebank Young Offenders Centre to Maghaberry Prison with barely six months on the outside in between. Incarceration, according to Sara's notes, had not reformed him. Rather, it had trained him and enabled him to do bad things better. When he came out, he was harder, more ambitious, devious and better connected, but his approach was Marxist – he didn't want to be a member of any club that would have him as a member. So he took the route all headstrong and egocentric aspiring leaders take, from politicians to reverends – he set up a gang in his own image. He knew exactly how to wind new members in: a combination of his charisma, fear, money, women and crush. He too started beholden to offshore suppliers, then he got into production and wholesaling. He had a ground-floor office in a terraced house on Cromwell Road, where he hung out under cover of a taxi company, but, as the gang outgrew its damp terraced base, he settled on a new home on the Lagan and rechristened his outfit the Botanic Boat Crew.

The waitress finally brought my coffee. She set it down and started to turn away but then stopped and crouched down. She moved the chair opposite a little and picked something up. She said, 'Did you drop something?'

She was holding out a small gold cross, with a tiny sun halo behind it.

I shook my head and nodded at the students across the way: 'Maybe?'

She asked them, and they roared derisively.

She turned back to my table and set it down and said, 'They turn up all the time. The clasp is rubbish. You'd think God would have better suppliers. Maybe it was your friend's?'

I shook my head, but at the same time picked it up. It was indeed cheap and nasty. Had D.I. Hood been wearing it? Had he accidentally dropped it or left it on purpose? And, if he was now a Holy Roller, was his interest in me fully to do with the murder of Sharon

Quigg or was he giving me a subtle warning about leaving Pike alone? Or was the fact that so many people had tried to kill me over the years making me paranoid?

I drained the coffee and made a start for the river. I tried to stop myself from checking to see if I was being followed. And failed. It was a half-hour walk. By the time I was halfway there, I had a crick in my neck and a pain in my head from thinking about the havoc people like Davy Blair could cause.

In February, Ormo Rowing Club had staged a race with rivals from the Moyle Rowing Club on the north coast. It was just a friendly competition along the Lagan on a bright Saturday afternoon. Half a mile into the race, a hand grenade was lobbed from the bank, which blew the local boat out of the water, injuring two rowers. At about the same time, gunmen walked into the rowing club's social headquarters, just a few hundred metres along from the boat sheds, and sprayed the restaurant; it was mostly empty, but that wasn't the point. Two warnings in one day, and the club moved out. Davy Blair took control of the lease of the clubhouse, complete with bar and restaurant. He fired the staff and moved his own people in. They couldn't boil a fucking egg. But it quickly became party central. You wanted crush in south Belfast, the rechristened Botanic Boat Club was the place to go. All night long. The attic was converted into a series of tiny bedrooms, and hookers recruited locally or imported. Neighbours who complained about the music or finding the crushed unconscious in their front gardens very quickly stopped complaining. The police wouldn't go near the place. If Sara's files were to be believed, Davy Blair was one of the most ruthless gang leaders in the city. Given this reputation, there probably weren't many eejits brave enough to just walk up to the clubhouse gates on tree-lined Lockview Road with two cups of Starbucks coffee and demand an audience.

Probably just one.

The guy on the gates, in the flashy Boat Crew jacket, said, 'And who the fuck are you when you're at home?'

I told him my name and that the coffees were getting cold.

He told me they had a fucking restaurant inside; there was coffee on tap.

I said the coffees weren't just coffees, but also meta-phorical coffees, that I had churlishly rejected Davy Blair's first attempt to connect but now I was trying to make amends by coming to his door with the gift of hot drinks.

The gatekeeper took this on board and then said, 'Houl' on,' and phoned someone. He listened and nodded and said to me, 'You're to go on up.' He opened the gates. I went to move past him but he said, 'Not so fast. Stand a hoke.' He raised his arms. I raised mine. I laughed and he said, 'What's so funny?' I said I hadn't heard anyone say 'Stand a hoke' since primary school and he said, 'So the fuck what?' Then I warned him that I had a gun in my back pocket. He felt it and said, 'You'll have to check that.'

I said, 'Fine.' He went to take it out and I said, 'You better let me; I'm on the run for a murder *I did not commit*; you wouldn't want to get your shit on it.'

He looked at me like I was odd. He turned and gave a low whistle and two other hoods in shiny jackets stepped out from the front of the clubhouse, which was about fifteen metres back, and asked what the trouble was. The gatekeeper explained the situation. He referred to me as 'this joker' for some reason. They had their own guns. They told me to take mine out, but 'real careful'. One of them pulled out a Tesco bag and had me place the gun in it and then told me I would get it back *if* I came back out, and giggled with it.

The two that had come out escorted me to the entrance. Eddie, the dyed-blond-hair guy who'd visited my office and demanded twenty grand for Katya, was waiting at the bottom of stairs. He grunted at me and took the two coffees and threw them into a plastic bin. Then he led me up to the restaurant on the first floor.

There were nice views over the Lagan, twenty tables, but only one of them set, and Davy Blair behind it with a napkin tucked into his T-shirt and munching on a salad. He was wearing a black suit with narrow lapels. He was a big fella to start with, but run to fat. His eyes were bright and his face pink and smooth. He shook my hand and told me to sit and join him for dinner. Eddie handed me a menu. I asked Davy what he would recommend and he said, 'Full disclosure,' and we both laughed. A waiter came and took our orders. I ordered a steak. Part of me was thinking that at least I might then be armed with a steak knife. The other part was starving.

Davy said, 'My dad always said, "Eat every meal as if it was your last; make love to every woman as if you will never make love to another." He died screwing the girl next door. High cholesterol did it for him. I'm thirty-two years old and I'm already on statins for life. That's what I inherited from my old man: Christmas-cracker philosophy and fat blood. Theoretically, I could eat anything now because the statins control it, but I've embraced healthy eating. When I go at something, I go at it full tilt.'

My steak arrived. As I tucked in, he described his plans for the clubhouse like it was a legitimate concern, and maybe in his eyes it was. He talked about the fabulous chefs he was going to employ and how he was going to bring in top-drawer entertainment, the way Sinatra and the Rat Pack had rocked Vegas. 'That's what Belfast could be,' he said, 'the Vegas of the North. So what do you think? Realistic or pie in the sky?'

I said better chefs would indeed be a good place to start.

He looked at me and then sliced off a chunk of my sirloin and chewed on it, and chewed on it, and chewed on it. When he finally swallowed, he shook his head and bellowed, 'It's like eating a fucking bathmat!' in the direction of the kitchens.

Eddie, sitting three tables away, said, 'Gone through three in a month; we can't lose another one.' He got up and pushed through swing doors into the kitchen. There was some shouting. He came back out rubbing at his knuckles and said, 'The chef recommends the swordfish.'

Davy waved him away. I put my cutlery down, but kept my hand close to the steak knife. I said, 'So, Davy Blair, you heard about this girl I'm looking for, and you sent Eddie to make an offer, which I rejected, maybe a little too quickly.'

'You're some kind of private detective.'

'Some kind, yes.'

'Money in that?'

'Not much.'

'But there's demand?'

I nodded.

'Is it because the police are so fucking useless?'

'It's because I'm good at what I do. If you still have her, I'm happy to pay the twenty grand.'

'Twenty grand. I try to do a guy a favour – a guy I don't even know – and he slaps my face with it.'

'Like I—'

'Price has gone up,' said Eddie, back at his table.

Davy still had his knife in his pudgy hand. He jabbed it at Eddie and said, 'I do the negotiating.'

'I can go to twenty-two,' I said. 'That's all I'm authorised for.'

'Generous,' said Davy. He looked at Eddie again and said, 'Bring the dessert.'

Eddie went back through the doors.

Davy dabbed at his lips with the still-tucked-in napkin

and said, 'I was wondering who you thought you were, to tell me to fuck off.'

'I didn't exactly—'

'Cocksure, aren't you?'

'I'd been fielding a lot of calls about her, just sorting the wheat from the . . . others . . .'

'I come to you with a deal and you kick my bony arse.'

His arse, I was pretty sure, was whatever the opposite of bony was, but I nevertheless gave him a little smile and an apologetic shrug.

'But that's fine; you're a businessman; I didn't offer any proof. Far as you're concerned, I'm just some fucking chancer after a fast one. Then you do a little research, maybe find out I'm not just some neighbourhood clown, and now you're here for serious business.'

'Something like that,' I said.

'But you still don't really know. Probably you've hit a brick wall looking for her and now you're trawling through your rejects to see if anything sticks.' The swing doors opened again. Eddie came out carrying a covered silver platter. He set it between us and then hovered behind Davy. I didn't like the hovering, or the look on his face. 'And you remember Eddie and how you disrespected him, and how you made jokes about him sending you one of her fingers.'

Davy nodded down at the platter. He raised an eyebrow. I could feel a little rush of adrenalin. They were dropping broad, stagey hints that there was a finger under there and, if there was, it meant it had to have been freshly cut, because they weren't to know that I was going to suddenly arrive and ask for a meeting, which, horrific as it was, meant that Alison was actually alive, and quite possibly somewhere in this very building.

I said, 'I spoke rashly. It's important no harm comes to her.'

'Fingers grow back,' said Eddie.

'What he means,' said Davy, 'is that you keep it on ice, you can stitch it back on.'

We studied each other until my phone vibrated in my pocket. I said, 'Excuse me,' and took it out. There was a text from Sara Patterson saying, *Choke on this, fuckwit* and a link to the *Belfast Telegraph* website. I quickly pressed it and it brought up an old photo of me and a headline that said, *Ex-Journalist Sought in Student Murder*. I turned the phone over. I nodded at the platter and said, 'I'm here to make a deal. If there's a finger under there, I still don't know if it belongs to Katya. I'd need to take it away, do the match and, by that time, it's no use to anyone.'

'Shame.' He put his hand on the lid handle. He nodded at me. Then he lifted his hand off it again and held it up to me. 'Do you have any idea how many girls like your Katya feel the benefit of these fingers every day, every week, every month?'

'No,' I said.

'There's not a one that works for me isn't intimately acquainted with them, and your girl is no exception.

Soon as I saw her photo, heard the story, I knew she was one of ours. That house, the one on Wellington Street? It was quite the party house. They were warned about bringing in outside caterers but they didn't take it seriously and look what happened.'

'It was your people who attacked it?'

'What do you think? You let them get away with that kind of shit . . . Well. So we took away a few of the girls so they could work off their debt.'

'And Katya is one of them?'

'So it would seem.'

'Is she here now?'

'She was, briefly, but duty calls. She's working. These Russian girls . . .'

'Polish,' said Eddie, 'or Slovak.'

'These Russian girls,' Davy continued, 'they're not like Irish girls. They know how to work. Irish girls, they give it away for free; Russians make their cunts work for them.'

'Your experience of Irish girls,' I said, 'is clearly different from mine.'

Davy laughed. 'Nevertheless,' he said. 'She owes a crush debt, she's working it off. I'm not a charity. Interest mounts. She's done – what? – nine months on her back. She has another year to do, ten guys a day, fifty quid a pop. What's that . . .?'

'One hundred eighty-two thousand,' said Eddie, 'five hundred. Plus bed, breakfast and evening meal. Lunch, her mouth is usually full.'

'So what the fuck was I thinking,' said Davy, 'offering

her to you for twenty grand? One hundred eighty two thousand . . .'

'. . . five hundred,' said Eddie, 'plus board . . .'

'. . . is just me breaking even.'

'Not to mention the crush . . .' said Eddie.

'Ah, fuck, we throw that in for free.'

'Generous,' I said.

'Ask around,' said Davy; 'in this business, those terms are not particularly onerous. Not like they're fucking indentured for life. Indentured the right word?'

I nodded slowly. I said, 'Difference is, and I think you know it well, you have to wait a year to make that much and you never know what might happen in the meantime: she could run off, succumb to crush, kill herself, get killed – maybe the clients won't like her being a finger short. If she's crushed, how many good days are you really going to get out of her, anyway? Like I say, I'm cleared to twenty-two.'

'So, we compromise.'

'Compromise is good,' I said. 'It is, after all, what has brought peace to our divided nation.'

'One hundred and fifty thousand,' said Davy.

'That's not much of a compromise. Twenty-two and a half.'

'One hundred and sixty.'

'I'm not sure you're—'

'One hundred and sixty, and each day that goes past, we lop off another finger.'

'I need to speak to my people,' I said.

'Do that,' said Davy. He nodded. I nodded. Eddie shrugged. I got up from the table. 'Do it here, now.'

'OK,' I said. 'Fine. But I need a little privacy.'

Eddie pointed down the restaurant. 'Fire escape.'

Davy said, 'Aye.' He thumbed behind him. I stepped away from the table. As I moved past him, he put his hand out and caught my arm. He said, 'And nothing funny. You try anything smart and she gets it, ear to ear. I want the cash; I get to decide the swap venue; everyone walks away happy.' I nodded. I went to move on again, but he kept hold of me. 'And just in case you think we're fucking with you . . .'

Davy gave Eddie the eyes, and Eddie lifted the lid off the platter with a flourish. There was indeed a finger there, resting on a bed of ice stained red. It was a little finger – very little, very pale but with a hint of bone, torn skin and rendered flesh at one end and a minuscule nail painted pink with a tiny little star set in it at the other.

Would break your heart.

'Nice,' I said.

I stepped out on to the fire escape and sucked in some air: it tasted of dank river and deep-fat fryer. I gripped the railing for a moment. Alison had been a job, a well-paying job that had suddenly become real with the murder of Sharon *Quigg*. Now that had been dramatically reinforced by the sight of the severed finger – so delicate, petite, with the decorated varnish emphasising that, while she might be a spoiled little rich girl, she was still just a little girl, a student, studying in a strange city, giving us the benefit of the doubt and living or dying to regret it. The hell she must have been through over the past nine months – and all the while keeping up the charade that she was Russian or Polish or fucking Slovak – while waiting in vain to be rescued. Now, perhaps, was her time. One hundred and sixty thousand was nothing, *nothing*. I called up Finn's number. I was just going to push *connect* when the phone vibrated again and Trish's number came up with an invitation to connect over the iPhone's video FaceTime.

I pushed accept and, a few moments later, I was looking at panoramic scenes of Bangor: a children's playground, giant white swans on a boating lake, yachts in a marina, in the distance the Royal Hotel. But it wasn't just a view, there was a soundtrack of Trish, Bobby and Lol singing 'Day Trip to Bangor', although without any particular spirit, as if they were forcing themselves to enjoy a day out; a sarcastic sing-along at best. But I was smiling, because it was good – and bad – to hear them and know they were safe and on familiar territory. The view shifted back along the masts and rigging and moved slowly across Pickie Fun Park to Lol, singing sullenly, then on to Bobby with his usual lethargic contribution, before finally resting on Trish's deadpan stare. I was about to tell them to give themselves a kick, when I realised that the angle from which I was seeing Trish, together with her distance from the lens, made it impossible for her to have been actually holding the phone. And at the very moment that it struck, the image was flipped round, and I was suddenly looking at the grinning face of Harry Frank.

'I can't believe you put them on a fucking train!' he cried, and I knew then that they were fucked, and that I was too – sideways.

31

I was almost out on to Lockview Road when the gate-keeper called me back.

'Forget something?' he said, and held up the Tesco bag with the gun in it.

I told him I was always leaving it lying around and he called me a prick. I was just trying to be matey, but mateyness had no business at the Botanic Boat Club. I took the gun out, slipped it into my jacket and handed him back the bag. He dropped it and the breeze picked it up and carried it towards the river. I have always had a habit of poisoning and destroying things: Sharon Quigg, Alison, Lol and Bobby were just the latest additions to a list already topped by Trish and shortly to be joined by a choking duck.

I walked along, trying to think it through, while putting my head down every time a jogger or dog walker approached. My first responsibility was to

Patricia, then Bobby and Lol. Everything else was business. Had to be. Harry Frank was threatening from a position of overwhelming strength. He wanted Katya Cummings or Alison Wolff delivered to him and he was all the more excited about it when I told him that she was alive. He wanted details and I said no. He reminded me of what he could and would do and I still said no. I told him it was all very delicately balanced and that, if waiting a few hours was the difference between getting nothing and getting several million pounds, then, surely, it was worth taking that chance.

Davy Blair was less ambitious. To him, Katya was just a crusher converted to a hooker with a debt and anxious parents willing to pony up for her safe return. The swap was just another piece of business. I had returned from the fire escape saying that my employers were anxious that everything went smoothly, that they would need twenty-four hours to put the money together and they would be in touch, through me, as soon as they were good to go. That was fine with Davy. He had his fingers in many pies, some of which he was eating.

And then there was Finn and Wolff. All I had to do was work out a way of getting them to hand over a large amount of cash to me to give to Davy Blair for the return of Alison, but instead of handing her directly back to her loved ones, I would swap her for my loved ones and then I would have to convince them that Blair had double-crossed us and traded her to Harry

Frank, who was now demanding millions for her safe return. What could possibly go wrong?

I came to the Wharf, a bar on two floors overlooking the river, about a quarter of a mile along from the Boat Club. I entered somewhat tentatively, saw that it was mostly empty and ordered a drink. There was a television high in the corner playing the local news. I sat and watched it in trepidation that my mug was going to flash up, but there was no mention. Apparently there was enough going on in gangsterville without me. There were print editions of the *Telegraph* sitting unloved at the end of the bar – I examined the first few pages and there was nothing there either. When I checked their website on my phone, the story about me had been taken down. I drummed my fingers on the bar and wondered what that meant. Had Sara had a change of heart? Unlikely. Had Wolff brought pressure to bear? Quite possibly. I wondered what would happen if I was straight with him and Finn – that Alison was alive, but that it was more complicated than a simple payment now my family was under threat. Finn seemed like a decent enough bloke, but his first loyalty had to be to Wolff, so he wouldn't make a move without his approval and certainly wouldn't approve of anything that might extend Alison's imprisonment. And Wolff himself? He was ruthless in business and would be doubly so when it came to protecting his family. He wouldn't give a damn about my people. No – if Trish and Bobby and Lol had any chance at all, I would have to succumb to the blackmail and play everyone off against each other with the hope that, somehow, everyone might emerge unscathed.

I called Finn to give him my version of events and set my plan in motion.

The number came back as not being recognised.

I laughed and rubbed at my brow.

Now that word was out, he'd shut me down.

Very first step and the plan had fallen apart.

I looked at my call history and found the number Wolff had called from to leave me his inspirational message. When I tried it, it was no longer in service. I called up the banking app Finn had provided but was denied access. When I checked my own account, I saw that all evidence of transfers to it from the Wolff account had disappeared.

They had the power.

I ordered another drink. The barman remarked on the good weather. I remarked on the scarcity of customers and he said it had been that way since that lot had taken over, and he thumbed in the direction of the Boat Club. He said people were scared, that some nights it was mental down there – people lying every-where, blitzed on drink and crush, lasers in the sky, like they were searching for the Luftwaffe, and music blasting so loud the bass vibrated the whole river. He said, if you took a walk along it at night, you'd see the rats driven crazy, fleeing their nests and swimming across to the other side to escape, then they'd come back the next day because they were stupid.

I said I'd only wanted a pint, not a state-of-the-union

address and he looked at me oddly, but then I laughed and he laughed too. Right then, he was my only pal in the whole world, and he wasn't even my pal.

I sipped, and thought about Alison being alive after all – the fresh blood on the finger indicated that. Davy Blair hadn't known that I would suddenly turn up on his doorstep, so the finger must have been lopped off during the few minutes when I was introducing myself at the gates, before being ushered into the restaurant. When I'd suggested she was on the premises, he'd claimed she was already back out working, but I thought it was much more likely she was upstairs in one of the bedrooms, possibly bleeding profusely.

I did more drumming, and more thinking, and tried not to picture my loved ones in an acid bath. I tried not to think either about my own stupidity in not objecting to Trish catching a train when transport, especially trains, was Harry Frank's passion. He had guessed that I would try to get them to safety, and knew exactly who to call to keep an eye on the very limited options there were for getting out of Belfast. I ordered another pint, and crisps. I was pleased when they didn't come in a cardboard tube.

I went to the window with my drink and looked out along the river towards the club, which was just visible. It was now six p.m. I asked the barman what time things hotted up down there and he said it built up gradually until about midnight. I asked what kind of policy they had for letting people in and he said that, if I was young and beautiful and had money to spend,

I wouldn't have a problem. He grinned. He said the bouncers would go along the line picking who would get in; those who didn't make it hung around outside hoping for a change of heart. I gazed back along the river, thinking.

I called Sara's mobile. It went to voicemail and I asked her to call me back. I phoned the *Telegraph* and asked to be put through to her. Her phone was picked up and I recognised the dulcet tones of Jeff, the camp reporter I'd previously had a run-in with.

'Sar—' he began, then stopped himself and said, 'Editorial.'

I deepened my voice and asked for her.

'I'm sorry, Sara no longer works here. Can I ask you what it's in connection with?'

I hung up.

Before I took another sip, it rang again and Sara's name came up.

I said, 'Hey . . . I hear you got the boot.'

'I wasn't fucking fired, you scumbag,' said Sara. 'I resigned.'

I said, 'Do you want to talk about it?'

'No, I fucking don't!'

'*OK* . . .'

'But it's all your fucking fault!'

'Listen, I need a favour . . .'

'Fuck. Off.'

'Sara, c'mon, I really—'

'Starkey? Listen to me. Do you know what I am?'

'A damn fine reporter?'

'Yes, but beyond that? I wouldn't even claim to be much of a feminist but, first and foremost, I'm a woman. I haven't really had to battle to get where I am today; there's no glass ceiling any more – except when it comes to standing up for yourself; where a man is admired for it, a woman is suddenly defined as difficult, odd, weird, hysterical. And I will not be treated like that. I will not be fucked with.'

'OK,' I said, and almost meant it.

'OK,' she said, 'now fuck off.'

She hung up.

I gave it ten minutes and called her back.

She said, 'What?'

'I'm sorry for running off; I swear to God, I was only trying to protect you.'

'Fuck off, Starkey.'

'Swear to God. Tell me why you resigned.'

'No. Fuck off.'

'You wrote the story about me, it went live, and then it got yanked from higher up.'

'No.'

'You wanted to do a follow-up about my connection to the victim's missing flatmate, and how she was really Thomas Wolff's daughter, and you got shutdown.'

'No.'

'Sara, it's Wolff; he has more strings to pull than—'

'I resigned because I compromised my integrity.'

'You what-what?'

She let out long, exasperated sigh. 'Right. Starkey, if

you must know, by getting involved with you, I became part of the story. When I then tried to write it, I couldn't be objective. It's a shit story. I have no evidence, but they were prepared to run it because they trust me. It's an expression of anger and I let myself down, so the only thing I could do was ask them to pull it, and I resigned.'

'Well, that was fucking stupid,' I said.

'Yes, probably. Now, what do you *want*, Starkey?'

'I want to put the old team back together.'

'Oh, fuck off.'

'I'm serious. You and me . . . or *I* – I'm never quite sure.'

'No, Starkey . . .'

'I'm serious. Just listen to me for a minute, then . . . then it's up to you, but I really do need your help. Please.'

Another sigh. But she said nothing. So I told her about Davy Blair and the severed finger, about Harry Frank and my ex on their day trip to Bangor. There was no longer any reason not to.

When I'd finished, she said, 'So – basically, right from the start, you've been lying through your teeth and playing everyone against each other and now you've been caught out.'

'Yes.'

'And your wife and two innocent kids are possibly going to die because of it.'

'Exactly.'

'Although, because you've been lying all along, I've

no way of knowing if even this story is true or if Harry Frank exists at all. Because, not only have you lied to your enemies, you've lied to me as well . . .'

'You say it like it's a negative thing.'

'. . . but, despite this, you just expect me to forget about it because now you're stuck and have nowhere else to turn.'

I cleared my throat. 'Yes.'

There were, I now saw, two rowers on the river, just going past beneath me. They both appeared to be wearing crash helmets. The water looked stagnant.

There was a long pause before, 'Well, *Starkey*, as it happens, I do actually believe you this time, because I did some checking. I *found out* about Harry Frank and what he's been up to. And Davy Blair *has* been on my radar for a long time, so I know *exactly* what he's capable of, and all about the girls he imports and destroys. But you've burned me once before – twice, now that I think about it. How do I know it's not going to happen again?'

'You don't,' I admitted.

'Because your word is useless and you're a despicable human being.'

'Yes. But my ex-wife isn't. Sometimes I hate her, absolutely, but she is a wonderful, funny, beautiful, optimistic and loving woman who has done nothing wrong and does not deserve to end up in an acid bath and I will go to the ends of the earth, climb every mountain and ford every stream to save her life.'

'And what about the other two?'

'I can take 'em or leave 'em.'

There was, at last, a laugh.

'Starkey, this is probably the stupidest thing I've ever done . . . but, fuck it. I have a story already, but I suspect that, every time you get involved in something, that story somehow gets bigger and more important, and I want part of that. So – yes, I'm going to help you if I can. But no more lies; we work together; we work as a team.'

'Absolutely,' I said. 'There's no *I* in *team*.'

'But there's definitely a *u* in *cunt*, and that's what I will be to you if you try to fuck me over again. Do you understand?'

'I understand completely,' I said, 'and also, I'm slightly turned on.'

32

Sara came into the Wharf about an hour later. She was wearing a black T-shirt, a denim waistcoat and a red tartan skirt with black leggings. She looked at the two empty pints on my table and shook her head and I told her it was OK because I'd had crisps. She said that, when she came to write the story, she would probably describe me as a functioning alcoholic. I told her 'functioning' was the important word. Actually, it wasn't my table or glasses. I'd spent forty minutes walking the riverbank, considering my plan. But she didn't need to know that. I bought us both a drink and we sat by the window.

'You were right,' she said. 'My doc asked around. They use another struck-off guy – there's a whole network of them – he's on call to de-crush them and swat any bugs they pick up. He was only a junior when he got the chop. They call him the Chlamydia Kid.'

'And?'

'He was there this afternoon; one of the girls had an accident, lost a finger. She was crushed up, so wasn't particularly feeling any pain . . . He said they told him the finger was on ice and he would have taken her to hospital to try and get it re-attached, but, by the time he got there, they'd allowed the ice to melt, so it was just sitting in a pool of water, which caused it to shrivel. No use at all. The idiots.'

'They're probably not,' I said. 'They just don't care. But you showed him the photo of Alison? Is she the girl . . .?'

'Dan – he says there's a resemblance, but he can't be sure.'

'Well, if she's been on her back for nine months and crushed as well, she's not going to look like the princess she was when she went in. She's going to look like death warmed up. He spoke to her, though?'

'Barely, and what there was he thought was Russian.'

'She's acting. Out of her head and amputated, but still keeping it up until someone goes in there and gets her out.'

'Someone like you?'

She gave me the eye.

I gave it to her back.

'In case you haven't noticed,' I said, 'I don't come equipped with a SWAT team. Wolff and his minions and billions won't speak to me because of your story and even if I called the police they would arrest me for murder before they even thought about raiding the

Boat Club, and if *you* tipped them off they probably still wouldn't do it anyway because they never do, despite half of south Belfast being up in arms about it being party central, which suggests their focus is elsewhere or they're getting sweeteners or both. And none of which is going to help my Trish. I need the girl to get my wife back, and if the only way to get her is going in there myself, then that's what I have to do.'

'And how're you going to do that? Just waltz in?'

'I'm working on something.'

'I can't wait to hear. But if you find your ex and the kids first, and rescue them, then that at least removes Harry Frank's hold over you.'

'And how are we going to do that?'

'Well.' Sara sat back and sipped her white wine. She wasn't using the beermat that came with it for its rightful purpose, but was tapping it on the edge of our table as a kind of rhythmic aide-memoir. Then she abruptly sat forward again. 'Harry Frank may be a bit more ambitious than most gang-bangers, but I wouldn't be surprised if he shares many of their traits. They're like cats – hugely territorial. They put their mark down and don't stray too much. Sure, from time to time they'll nose around the neighbour's back yard, might even instigate a scrap, steal some food, but basically they like the comfort and security of their home turf. Harry Frank might covet the rest of Belfast but, until he actually gets there, I think we're going to find him exactly where he's most comfortable. Somewhere he knows the streets, the back-streets, escape routes . . . people he can trust . . .'

'In other words, he's not on a seesaw in Pickie Fun Park, he's back in town, probably back in Deramore Avenue direction.'

She nodded across the table at me.

'He'd want to keep them close at hand so he can move quickly – there's millions at stake.'

'Exactly. So, shouldn't we go take a look?'

'Yes,' I said. 'And no. Time is of the essence; much better to divide and conquer. So I think you should go after Harry and I'll go for Alison.'

Sara's eyes narrowed. 'You wouldn't just be looking to get rid of me again, would you, Starkey?'

'Funny,' I said. 'When you suspect me of something, I'm Starkey; when we're getting on like a house on fire, it's Dan. Sara, before this goes any further, you need to make your mind up who I am: Dan or Starkey?'

She tap-tapped the beermat while she studied me.

I reached across and took it off her and tore it in half, and in half again.

'You wouldn't just be looking to get rid of me again, would you, Dan Starkey?' she asked.

We were just crossing the car park when Sara saw the big guy leaning on her Volkswagen, arms folded, clearly waiting for us. She slowed, put a hand on my arm and said, 'Dan . . .?'

'Relax,' I said, 'he's on our side.'

Though I wasn't yet sure that he was.

Terry put his hand out and I clasped it. He said, 'I didn't recognise you with your clothes on.'

Sara looked at me and I said, 'Yep: my gay lover. He works security for the Braxton Clinic. And, as it turns out, he's ex-military.'

She looked at him suspiciously. 'And what has that got to do with anything?'

'He's going to ride along and make sure nothing happens to you.'

'I don't think so.'

'Yes, he is.'

'Not a chance. We didn't discuss this.'

'I was getting to it . . . Look, my wife and the kids have an acid bath hanging over them and I would really prefer if you didn't join them. Terry can look after you. He fought in Afghanistan.'

'For the Taliban,' said Terry.

'I don't care where the fuck he . . .' Sara started to say, but then she realised what he'd said and laughed involuntarily. 'Very good; but, really, I work on my own, I—'

'No *I* in *team* . . .' I said.

'Nevertheless, security's the kiss of death for a story when you want to talk to people and they see some big ape – no offence – hanging on your shoulder. They shut up like—'

'This isn't just a story, Sara, and I'm sure you'll be unobtrusive, won't you, Terry?'

'At least until I have to go and break things.'

'Please, Sara, it's just a bit of insurance.'

'Starkey – see this face? Gloriously unmarked. Try taking a look in the mirror sometime and maybe you'll understand which one of us actually needs protection.'

'Look, if you're as good a reporter as I think you are . . .'

'Don't patronise me, Starkey!'

'. . . and you find Harry Frank and where he's keeping my people, that's where you step out and Terry steps in. What else are you going to do? You said yourself you didn't like being part of a story, so you just work it like an investigative reporter and then get offside. Let Terry go in and get them, Sara. Please.'

Sara was shaking her head. She looked towards the river. She pursed her lips. She tapped her toe. Her resistance was weakening. She said, 'When did you work this one up? We only just agreed to work together – *again*.'

'He called me about half an hour ago,' said Terry. 'He's very persuasive.'

'Isn't he just?'

'And also he's promised me a large amount of money.'

I had. Wolff money I no longer had access to. But needs must.

Sara moved past me and unlocked the passenger side door. She reached in and pulled out her camera by the strap. She swung it up into her hands and then held it out to Terry. 'Take it,' she said, 'and then at least in my head I can pretend you're my photographer and not my bodyguard.' She moved back around to the driver's side and opened it. She looked back at me and said, 'Are you going to tell me what your plan is?'

I shook my head. 'Better not.'

'Is it something really stupid?'

I fixed her with my most serious look. 'Sara – will you give me some credit, please? A young girl's life is at stake here; not to mention my wife's life and the lives of two innocent kids. I'm not going to do anything stupid. It's a plan and it will work. So trust me.'

'Right,' said Sara. She got into the car.

Terry moved to the passenger door. I caught his arm and said, 'Look after her.'

'I intend to.'

'But, if it's a choice between her and my family . . .'

He smiled.

'I'm serious,' I said.

Sara backed out of the parking space. As she came alongside me, she gave me the thumbs up and then they drove away. I stood and watched until their tail-lights disappeared around the corner. Whatever they did now was out of my control. All I could do was trust that my plan was solid and that I would experience the good fortune I needed to see it through.

It was time to get my canoe.

33

One of the guys with crash helmets that I'd spotted from the bar had been using the grounds of the Wharf to gain access to the river ever since 'those bastards' had taken over the club down the road. It was six months on and he was still spitting blood about it. He didn't mind who he ranted to about it either. He loved getting out on the water. He'd actually moved to live in an apartment just a few hundred metres away so he could be close to the club but, since they'd moved in, he'd had nowhere to stash his boat. So he'd come to an agreement with the bar owners to keep it on a small trailer in their car park. He told me this as he patted it down with a towel, zipped it into its cover and secured it against a wire fence.

He was a small guy, about five foot, maybe forty years old with a weather-beaten face and a permanent scowl, which didn't change at all when I offered him a large amount of cash to hire his canoe. He said it wasn't a canoe, but a kayak of classic Eskimo rib and cross wooden frame construction, and no way was he renting it to a complete stranger. But I kept at him while feigning interest in his hobby and guessing that he would have the true enthusiast's desire to convert. He rattled on forever about the difference between a kayak and a canoe – double bladed oars and you sit with your legs flat out in a kayak; single blades but sitting with knees bent in a canoe. Canoes float on the surface; kayaks move just beneath, with their pilots sitting in a slightly raised cockpit – and insisted, in the face of common sense, that the differences were important. Man, he loved getting out and, although he favoured the kayak, he had nothing against canoes and, when he got together with his mates, they'd travel up and down the river in mixed groups having great fun and getting fit at the same time.

I nodded, fascinated. 'So these kayaks and canoes,' I said, 'do they ever breed?'

He looked at me for a long time, and then a big, booming, rolling laugh came from him, and he went from being mildly suspicious to insisting that lending me his *kayak* would be no trouble at all and he didn't even want to get paid for it.

I said it wasn't convenient for me now but I'd *love* to have a go in the morning. He said he would have to check it with his rowing partner, because they owned it jointly, but it shouldn't be a problem. So we agreed to meet up. He was about to leave the key to the lock back inside so that the staff could move the kayak if they needed to, but I volunteered to do that for him as I was on my way back in to meet someone.

And he agreed.

The fucking eejit.

I had another pint in the bar for luck. While I savoured it, I phoned the only cop I still knew and partially trusted. Gary Hood gave me a gruff 'Hello', and told me I should give myself up. When I finished laughing, I told him I needed a favour. I wanted him to arrest a perfectly innocent man and to hold him for as long as he could. He asked me why and I said I couldn't tell him right now, but that he would have to trust me. When he'd finished laughing, he asked me again. I wasn't for shifting, but told him to do it for the love of God. He hesitated and then asked what I was talking about. I told him that I thought he knew already. He said he still thought I should turn myself in for the student murder. I said how about I give you the name and address and you do what I ask and, when everything works out all right, I'll convert to whatever religion you want and he said he doubted if any of them would have me. But he took down the details and said he would have to think about it. I said that was all I wanted, and God bless him. He told me to wise up.

When I judged it was dark enough outside, I slipped down the stairs and into the car park. The floodlights, which might once have illuminated it, were broken and the few cars dotted about empty. The faint hum of music followed me out, but it was immediately drowned out by the bass throb coming along the river from the Boat Club. I moved across to the kayak and unlocked it from the fence. I stripped the cover off and then tried to ease it down off its trolley, but it was heavier than it looked and it quickly slipped out of my grasp and cracked loudly on to the gravelled tarmac. I stood beside it for a minute, waiting to see if anyone came to investigate the noise. When I was satisfied nobody was coming, I lifted one end of it up and dragged it across to the water's edge. I took the gun from my jacket and placed it inside the kayak. Then I folded the jacket and hid it under a bush, so that I was just wearing my black T-shirt and jeans. I gently lowered the kayak into the murky water and attempted to climb in. I miscalculated the buoyancy of the vessel and, with one foot in and the other on dry land, it began to move away from the bank, causing me to perform a mad dance to stop myself from falling into the river, but which resulted in my landing flat on my face in the mud. Somewhere beside me, creatures of the night scrambled for better cover. Fortunately, I had kept one hand on the kayak, so I was able to pull it back to the side and try again, this time successfully. I lifted the double-bladed oar, stuck it into the water and began to paddle away from the bank while being as far from comfortable in my abilities to properly command and control the vessel as it was possible to be. The river was neither fast nor particularly deep and, despite my clear lack of coordination, I defin-itely appeared to be moving in the right direction – that is, towards the Botanic Boat Club. My progress may have lacked style and speed, but I made up for it with determination. I had a plan and I was bloody well going to make sure it worked. I was going to take them from behind.

Sara's doctor's doctor connection had passed on what I hoped would be vital information about what I would find if and when I managed to breach the security surrounding the Boat Club and actually get inside the building.

The clubbing mainly took up the ground-floor bar area and, on busy nights, spilled into the first-floor restaurant. This, I had already observed, was where Davy Blair held court. The second floor was the attic, converted to brothel. There were nine rooms, reached via a single set of stairs, four on either side of a straight corridor that ran the entire length of the building, and with a fire escape at the far end. These rooms were open to paying customers or gratis as a reward for Davy's favoured gang-bangers. Sara's notes said that local politicians and high-ranking cops had been spotted up there, but she didn't name any names.

As I rounded the slight bend in the river, the Botanic Boat Club came properly into view. There was a series of crackles and then streaks through the air followed by explosions and the whole sky lit up with fireworks. There were dozens of them lighting up the night and giving anyone who cared to look across the water a perfect view of me approaching the club from the rear.

All I could do was trust that all eyes were on the sky. And, in truth, it didn't worry me half as much as the water, which was now very clearly leaking into the kayak. It didn't matter if the hole or crack had been there all along or if I'd caused it by dropping it in the car park; what mattered was it was there. My feet and trousers were soaked already and I could feel that it was beginning to slosh about. But, for the moment I was still moving through the water and, indeed, drawing near to the club.

And I remained unobserved.

I was able to pilot the boat right up to a narrow, scrubby area of the bank at the rear of the club and then I performed a better balancing act than before in getting out. I slipped the gun into the back of my trousers and tied the kayak up. I pulled myself up on to a low breeze-block wall and, all the while, the fireworks continued to explode in the sky above me. I could hear cheering coming from the other side of the building. There was a three-string barbed-wire fence on top of the wall, but it was old and sagging and I almost managed to duck between the strands, but then snagged one leg of my jeans. As I tried to free it, I felt it tear right through the material and across my knee. I would probably rescue the girl but succumb to septicaemia.

I dropped down into a back yard littered with discarded beer barrels and crates of bottles. It stank from rotting food spilling out of bins and skips. Glass cracked underfoot as I made my way to the side of the building and looked up the two flights of metal stairs that formed the fire escape. There were two doors. The lower one was very slightly ajar, with kitchen sounds coming from beyond it, and then above it the door to the second floor. I waited for a particularly loud explosion and slipped up the stairs, past the kitchen, to the platform at the top. I felt around the fire door for a handle, but there seemed to be no way of opening it from the outside. No, that would have been too easy.

The last few fireworks were drizzling down as I hurried back down the stairs. By the time I reached the bottom, the yard had been plunged into darkness again. I moved cautiously along the side of the building, guided only by starlight, until I had a view of the front of the club. Several dozen people were standing around in the slight haze caused by smoke from the fireworks but, as I watched, they began to drift back inside now that the show was over. They were having to shout at each other to make themselves heard over the music blasting out from within. Beyond them I could see the front gates, which were open but with bouncers standing guard just outside them, making sure that the small crowd, which had already been considered but rejected for entrance to the club, didn't try and squeeze past. At least I was already inside the perimeter.

I stepped around the corner and slipped nonchalantly in with those returning inside the club, holding my breath as I did and expecting at any moment to be exposed but, in the event, I made it inside unmolested. There were plenty of security men inside, but no one I recognised from my earlier visit. I was intending to buy a drink and then scope the place out but, as I nudged my way forward through the throng, I caught a glimpse of myself in the mirrored bar and realised that my face was smudged with mud from my fall on the riverbank. Because of the murk of the club, nobody had yet noticed, but that might not last, so I quickly made my way to the gents' toilets to clean it off.

They had an ingrained stench about them, which suggested they hadn't been properly cleaned in months. I was in there for as little time as I could manage, but it was time enough for three guys to try to sell me crush. Another tried to buy it from me. There was a boy who didn't look more than sixteen slumped in the corner, with vomit down his shirt. A pissed guy came in in a Hawaiian shirt, popped a pill, threw his arm round my shoulders and yelled, 'Bout ya, mucker! This place is fuckin' class.' I agreed. I asked him if he'd been upstairs yet and he yelled, 'It's full of fuckin' manky hookers! And yes!' I asked him what the procedure was for going up and he said you had to buy a ticket at the bar and they gave you a room number and a warning about what would happen to you if you didn't behave. I asked him if you had any choice of what hooker you got and he said, 'No; but any cunt in a storm.' He cackled. I asked him if there was anything specific I needed to say to the bar staff and he said sure, that I needed to know the magic words. He put his hands on my shoulders and shouted in my face, 'I want to fuck your hookers! Here's thirty quid!' He roared again before releasing me and staggering off into one of the cubicles.

Duly informed, and marginally cleaner, I exited the toilets and pushed through to the bar. I wasn't quite as graphic as my friend had recommended. I handed over the last of my cash. The barman checked his computer screen, printed off a ticket and told me to go to Tanya in room nine. I made my way to the stairs and was just about to go up them when a voice called, 'Oi! Not so fast.' I turned and saw a bouncer with an earpiece indicating for me to approach. 'Ticket,' he said. I handed it to him, he nodded, and then he raised his hands and said, 'Stand a hoke.' I smiled involuntarily as I realised it was the same bouncer who'd searched me earlier. He wasn't particularly looking at me as his hands roved across my body, at least until he came to the gun and then his brow furrowed. He pulled it out. He studied it. I didn't know what to say, or whether to make a run for it, but in the end he just handed it back to me with, 'Try not to shoot anyone.' I nodded and put it back in my trousers. 'Away you go,' he said.

I started to turn, but pivoted back to him. 'You don't mind me asking – if you're letting me take a gun upstairs, what exactly are you searching for?'

'I don't mind you asking,' he replied, 'and nothing specific. It's more of a deterrent than anything, in case you have any bad intentions, you'll know I'm not far away.'

'But you took one off me earlier?'

'I did. But then it was just you and the boss. If I tried to take a gun off everyone who came in here, they'd still find a way of sneaking them in and everyone would be paranoid. If everyone's armed then it's a level playing field.'

'OK,' I said. 'Noted.'

He clearly wasn't privy to my earlier business with Davy Blair and so had no reason to question my presence in the club. His hand went to his ear, listening to something. He gave me a nod and quickly took off into the bar to deal with something or someone more troubling than me.

I moved on up the stairs. I came to the narrow hallway the doctor had described. It was dully lit by a single bulb with the numbers on the rooms just about decipherable. Three of the doors were lying open. As I passed the first, a bone-white girl in black lingerie and lying on a double bed looked up from the magazine she was reading. 'You for me, honey?' she asked, with Eastern European inflection.

I looked at her hands, saw that she had ten fingers, and said, 'Nine,' which was the number I was looking for on both counts. She immediately returned her attention to the magazine and I continued on.

Door nine was at the bottom of the corridor on the right. I stood in the opening and studied a blonde girl sitting at a dressing table, combing her hair. She was completely naked and so thin I could almost see through her. A cigarette sat smoking in an ashtray beside her. She also had a full set of fingers. She said, 'Close door, give ticket, clothes off.'

I stepped into the room and pushed the door closed

behind me. I said, 'Tanya, you're not the girl I'm looking for.'

She put her hand out and clicked her fingers. I stepped across and showed her the ticket. Her eyes seemed to struggle to focus on the number. 'I am nine,' she said. 'Clothes off, take condom.'

I told her no, she didn't understand, I was looking for Katya. She shook her head vaguely. Crushed. I moved closer. Her breasts hung on her chest like sacks of flour. 'She's my regular girl,' I said and held up my hand. 'She's hurt her finger . . .?' I bent one digit back and comprehension dawned.

'Alexa,' she said. 'Alexa is seven. You have nine. We fuck.' I shook my head and stepped back to the door. Tanya pushed her chair back and stood. 'What's wrong with me?' she asked.

'Nothing,' I said. 'You're lovely . . . I just need to . . .' I stepped back out into the corridor and moved two doors up. I knocked on it.

A man's voice gave a querulous, 'Busy!'

I knocked again, harder, and said, 'Security! You need to open up.' There was shuffling behind the door and then it opened a fraction and a bearded man looked nervously out. He was naked, but holding his trousers to his groin. Beyond him I could see a blonde girl lying face down on a bed but with her hands bound and stuck by Velcro straps to the wall in front of her. One of those hands was heavily bandaged.

He said, 'I'm in the middle . . .'

I told him there'd been a mix-up downstairs and he'd

317

been assigned the wrong room. I held up my number nine.

He said, 'But I'm halfway . . .'

I told him to look at it this way, he was getting two for the price of one, and he thought about that and then grinned stupidly and went to gather the rest of his stuff. He quickly shuffled past me and out into the corridor. Tanya was still growling outside her room as he approached her.

I stepped into the room and closed the door behind me. The girl didn't look round. I said, 'Katya . . .' But no reaction. I moved to the bed and undid the strap on her injured hand and gently lowered it. I released the other one. I said, 'Alexa . . .' When she still didn't move, I put my hand on her shoulder and gently turned her until I could see her face. Her eyes were open and staring at me, her cheeks pinched and her lips dry and ragged. Sara was right: after so long in captivity, it was impossible to tell if it was really her. The doc who'd seen her had given her a sedative and painkillers, and her guardians had probably topped her up with crush. She was out of it, but not so out of it that she wasn't considered fit for duty.

They were monsters.

I told her who I was and that I was going to get her out of there. I hoped that some of it went in so that she understood as I went about dressing her. I got her to stand up, and then pulled her back to her feet when she immediately collapsed down again. I opened a wardrobe and pulled out a short skirt and zipped it around her.

There was a T-shirt and zip-up cardigan. There was nothing for her feet but thigh-length leather boots with stiletto heels. They weren't exactly built for a speedy escape over rough terrain, but then I remembered the glass in the back yard. I lay her back on the bed and pulled the first one on. I was just lifting the second when there was a thump on the door and the security guy from downstairs told me to open up. I told him to go away and he banged again and said I was in the wrong room. I told him I'd swapped but he said I couldn't do that, that punters paid extra for 'that one'.

'So put it back in your pants and open the fuck up.'

I stood behind the door and pulled it open. When he stepped in, I cracked him across the back of his skull with the butt of my gun. He turned and looked at me and said, 'What the fuck did you do that for?' I hit him again, this time across the forehead, which split and blood began to cascade down his face. Then he punched me hard and I went tumbling across the room. He came right after me. Before I could scramble to my feet, he kicked me and I went flat on my back. He stood over me and kicked me again. I still had the gun in my hand but, when I tried to bring it up, he brought his foot down hard on my hand and it sprang out of my grasp and skittered across the room. He put a foot on my chest and pressed down hard. His blood dripped on to me. 'What the fuck is your game?' he demanded. I tried to sit up and he slammed me right back down, and all I could think of, besides the pain of it, was that here was another classic Dan Starkey plan gone cataclysmically wrong. Then the bouncer suddenly lifted his foot from my chest. His mouth opened and closed, and opened and closed, and his eyes began to blink madly and I couldn't tell what the hell was up with him until he slowly began to turn and I saw that Alexa or Katya or Alison was standing behind him, staring at him in horror. The guard tried to raise his hand to claw at the back of his head, but he couldn't get it up far enough, and then I saw the reason why: the stiletto heel of Alexa's boot was embedded in his skull.

He slowly collapsed to his knees. I scrambled to my feet as the guard toppled forward again, this time on to his face. I stood over him. He wasn't moving at all. Her fuck-me boots had fucked him for sure. I reached down and took hold of the leather rim and tried to ease the heel out of his head, but it was wedged in hard. I put one foot on his back for leverage and had to yank at it twice before it came away with a squelching sound like a Cadbury's flake being pulled out of a ninety-nine. I turned, unzipped the boot and handed it, dripping, to Alison. I told her to put it on, but she just kept looking at it. I lifted her leg and yanked it into place, then knelt before her and re-zipped it. I picked up the gun and hurried to the door. I looked down the corridor. There was a punter just coming out of a room. And a girl in stockings and a woolly jumper at the top of the stairs, carrying a coffee. The punter nodded nervously at me; he couldn't see the gun, he was just nervous. I looked back at Alison and said, 'C'mon,' and waved her forward. She staggered to the door. I looked at her and said, 'I'm going to get you home.' And then added, 'Probably.' She replied in what I supposed was Russian. Her eyes were like pinpricks in the snow.

I took her hand and we stepped into the corridor. I turned right, towards the fire doors. I tried pushing the bar across them up but it wouldn't budge. Then I discovered why: padlocked. Not huge, but it didn't have to be. The Botanic Boat Club did not live in fear of a visit from health and safety. I struck the padlock with the butt of the gun without making any impression on it at all. I looked back along the corridor. Another girl was peering out of her room. 'Alexa? OK?' she called.

On the wall beside the door there was a fire-alarm panel. I cracked the gun into the glass and the alarm began to sound. I took Alison by the hand and walked her to the stairs. I peered down to the landing below. Another security guard was standing there, but he was peering down at the disco floor below. But then the music suddenly stopped, leaving only the piercing reverberation of the alarm and a lot of crushed-ups looking around wondering what had changed. I slipped the gun back into my pocket and held tight on to Alison as we descended the stairs and slipped past the guard. As we did, I glanced to my left into the restaurant and saw Eddie reassuring diners. We reached the bottom of the stairs and mixed in with the crowd now trying to squeeze out through the doors. Three security guys pushed their way past us and went charging up the stairs. As we emerged into the open air, everyone began to congregate around the entrance. I had hoped that the gates might have been thrown open to allow a mass exit but, with everyone determined to continue their night's entertainment, virtually nobody was trying to leave and the gates remained resolutely shut. If the guards didn't recognise me, they would surely clock Alison. Behind us the alarm stopped abruptly. Alison shivered beside me. 'It's OK,' I said. 'It's OK. There's always plan B.'

People were already turning back into the club. We went along with them as far as the doors, before slipping off to the side. I hurried her as best as I could to the corner and on into the back yard. We picked our way through the beer barrels and rubbish strewn around to the low breeze-block wall. I stepped up on to it first and then hauled her up. Just as I did, floodlights smacked on, illuminating the entire yard. There was immediately a shout from the second-floor platform beside the, now open, fire doors. Two security guards and Eddie, his blond hair so distinctive in the blazing light, were standing, gesticulating and shouting in our direction, but their words were blasted out by the resurgent music. They began to descend.

I forced the barbed wire apart and guided Alison through, but she didn't crouch down far enough and one strand ripped across her back. She didn't react at all. I jumped down on to the riverbank while keeping a firm hold on her hand and pulled her down after me. She landed badly, her left stiletto twisting under her. This time there was a small, involuntary yelp as she fell to her knees. I pushed her flat in the soft mud and grabbed her boots and pulled them off. I threw them behind me, pulled her back up and then supported her the few metres along to where I'd secured the kayak. When she saw it, she stopped dead and tried to back away, but I hissed at her that it was our only chance of escape. I let go of her hand and eased the boat into the water, then held it still with one hand while helping her, as she stepped into it, with the other. The weight of her, as she settled into it, balanced it for me to climb in after her; but our combined weights forced us lower in the water. I grabbed my paddle and immediately we struck out from the bank. As we eased into the darkness, the security guards appeared on the perimeter wall, silhouetted against the lights from the club. They had guns drawn, but they weren't shooting and I supposed that they could no longer see us in the dark. I thought, for a few blessed moments, that we were home free, that I could propel us as far up the Lagan as I liked until there was somewhere safe for us to land. But then I realised that the water that had seeped in earlier had not gone away, but was in fact deepening with our extra weight and was now up and over our ankles. The kayak itself was lying so low that the river was beginning to splash over the edge of the cockpit, adding considerably to the flooding.

We were up shit creek, with a paddle.

34

Daddy's little princess, crushed and doped and ampu-tated, couldn't swim. As soon as the kayak let out a great sucking noise and began to sink under us, I rolled it over and wriggled myself out before grabbing hold of Alison and pulling her up, coughing and choking but clear. My reward for this was a rake of nails down my cheek and a mad, thrashing maelstrom of arms and legs. She would have taken us both down if I hadn't batted her away. As she began to disappear under the water, I reached out and grabbed her hair and pulled her, face-up and backwards, towards the bank.

As we approached the Annadale Embankment side of the river, I pulled Alison closer to me and this time she nestled contentedly in my arms, but only because she was barely conscious. We had managed about a thousand yards along the river before abandoning ship and the club was still clearly visible. I could actually feel the music vibrating through the water.

Flashlights appeared on the opposite bank, scouring along. The authorities had done a good job keeping the river so neat that there was nowhere to hide – no overgrown bushes or reeds or tipped in washing machines – just water-smoothed brick, a walkway, a steep grass bank and the road beyond. I ducked back under the water and forced Alison down with me as the lights roved along towards us – but the shock of it caused another hysterical flailing, and the noise of that brought the lights right back to us. We floated there, frozen in full beam, for just a moment before I struck out for the bank. It was close enough and, in truth, the river wasn't that wide and, if they'd been truly committed, they could easily have dived in after us, but instead they chose to race back for their cars. We reached the shallows and then the bank and I dragged Alison out after me and up on to the walkway. We lay there for a moment, fighting for breath, but then we were up again and moving. They'd be arriving very soon – Lockview Road and on to Stranmillis Embankment, then there was a short bridge across to where we were on Annadale – two minutes, max, with the only slight thing in our favour being that the last section was part of a one-way system, which would be against them. It might add a minute to their journey. But it was late at night, there were few other vehicles on the road and they did not seem like the type of people who would feel obliged to stick to the Highway Code.

Alison stumbled and fell into my arms. When I pushed her back up, she flopped down again. I straightened her and slapped her face. It was supposed to wake her up, but it seemed to knock her out. She was waterlogged but whippet-thin enough for me to manage the fireman's lift. I struggled up the grass bank with her over my shoulder, and out on to the road. There was a car coming towards us; I tried waving it down, but it sped up instead and narrowly missed us. I thought my chances of getting a ride might be improved by me not having an unconscious girl over my shoulder, so I lowered her again and, instead, held her straight up and tight into my side like we were on the way home from a drunken night out. Two more cars passed us by, but then a taxi turned on to the embankment and stopped beside us. He lowered his window and said, 'Where you going, mate?'

I said, 'Cathedral Quarter.' Close enough to home without giving away too much.

The driver was in two minds. It was too dark for him to appreciate that we were completely drenched, but we must still have looked like a dubious proposition – my battered face, Alison barefoot and spaced – but we were a fare and times were hard and he decided to take the chance.

The back door clicked; I pulled it open and pushed Alison in ahead of me and then slipped in beside her. I thanked the driver as I buckled her in. He pulled out. I checked behind for signs of our pursuers. There were other cars, but it was impossible to tell.

'So, busy tonight?' I asked.

'No, it's dead.'

I turned to Alison and lifted her chin and told her we were nearly home. Her eyes fluttered and she muttered something I couldn't make out. When I looked up, the driver was watching me in the mirror.

He said, 'Good night?'

'Aye,' I said. 'Epic.'

He took a call from base as we turned on to the Ormeau Road and said where he was en route to, and then he switched the call to his earpiece. I didn't like that. I eased the gun out from the back of my trousers. It felt comforting to hold it in my lap. My phone was soaked through and wouldn't switch on. I had no way of knowing if Sara and Terry had been able to track down Trish and the kids, or if any of them were still alive.

It was more or less a straight two-mile run into the city centre. We drove along Victoria Street, and should have turned then on to Waring Street. When he didn't make the turn, I asked the driver why and he said there were roadworks and he'd have to take the long way round. I told him to stop and we could walk the rest of the way and he said he'd have us there in a minute. I said, no, we could walk. When he still didn't stop, I put the muzzle of the gun against the side of his face and suggested he reconsider. He pulled in near the top of Dunbar Link and said he was only trying to help and I said, 'Aye.' He looked at the meter and said that would be a fiver. I checked my pockets but my wallet was gone. I said I would have to owe him. He said that wouldn't do. I said that it would have to. I tried the doors, but he had the lock on. I tapped the gun against his cheek and said, 'I've never shot anyone in my life and, to tell you the truth, I've just been for a swim in the Lagan and the gun got soaked, so I've no idea if it still works, but this is a life-or-death situation, so if you don't open the doors right now I will pull the trigger and it will either blow your brains out through your eyeballs or it will click and I'll feel a bit silly. But it's up to you.'

The doors clicked. I got out and ran round to Alison's side, undid her belt and helped her out. She was awake again, blinking around her at the unfamiliar surroundings. I shut the door, tapped the top of the taxi and it pulled away. I walked Alison around the bend into Great Patrick Street and quickly along to Academy Street. When we got to that corner, I glanced back and saw that the taxi had stopped further up. I chivvied Alison along. Her feet were swollen and bleeding. About a hundred yards along Waring, I glanced back again and saw that the taxi was now idling at the top of that street.

'C'mon you,' I said. I'd an arm round her waist and was half lifting her with every step. 'C'mon . . .'

We moved around the slight bend in Academy Street and began to walk along the side of St Anne's Cathedral. Alison was really finding it hard going. I stopped and crouched down so that she could climb aboard for a piggyback. She wasn't sure what I was trying and, in the end, I kind of backed into her, took hold of her arms and pulled her up like I was lifting a bag of coal. I looped her hands under my neck and straightened; I grabbed her legs as I did and lifted her off the ground, then held on to them to keep her in position. Her bandaged hand, so close to my nose, smelled rotten.

'That's better,' I said. 'Now let's giddy-up.'

I upped the pace as we turned on to Donegal Street. Although it was late, the Cathedral Quarter was still busy with summer revellers spilling out of the bars and restaurants, and the air was thick with the clamour of drunken jabber. Taxis were double parked all along and vying for custom. Nobody paid any attention to us as we weaved through the crowds. The turn for my apartment complex was about a hundred metres along to the right, with the *Bob Shaw* beyond that again – and there my gaze stopped on four guys just getting out of a taxi: arriving, instead of leaving like everyone else. I have middle-aged eyes, but even at such a distance I still instantly recognised Eddie's shock of white hair. They started in our direction, walking in a solid group and forcing other pedestrians off the footpath.

They hadn't spotted us – yet.

I turned us in the opposite direction and we began to duck in and out of the throng again, Alison bouncing up and down on my back. And then, ahead of us, as we passed the cathedral again and entered the less populous part of Donegal Street, I recognised the taxi we'd only just climbed out of, pulling to a halt further up at the junction with York Street – and another car pulled in immediately behind it. Three guys got out of this one. One approached the taxi driver's window, bent down to it, and then straightened and looked straight at us.

We stopped again.

Trapped.

Of the two sets of hunters, only Eddie and his crew hadn't spotted us, and they were, just about, furthest away. I turned and began to walk towards them, still trying to decide what to do. The shops all about were boarded up; there were a number of entries that I knew, from sad past experience, were dead ends; the bars were already shut and the punters outside were beginning to dissipate. If it had been just me, I might have given them a run for their money, but I had an heiress to a billion-dollar fortune limp on my back and that fact was reducing my options to none at all.

Were they after her or me?

Well, I was pretty sure they were after both of us.

But if I cut and ran, they might just be happy with her, or they would at least stop for long enough to gather her up, and that might increase my chances of getting away.

To have so nearly gotten home and damp was maddening but, if they got her back, I would still be armed with the ammunition of knowing where she was; Davy Blair didn't know who she was and was only interested in protecting his investment. So I could pass that on to Harry Frank and he might consider that enough to release my people. It wasn't perfect, and it meant that Patricia's fate would be out of my hands, but he would surely know that I had done my best and almost delivered Alison as required. And, even if he didn't, I would still be alive and, as long as I was, there would still be some possibility, however minuscule it was, of getting my wife back.

I let go of Alison's legs and swung her round, off my back and on to her bloody feet. Her legs immediately gave way under her and she flopped down on to the footpath. I crouched beside her and took hold of her shoulders.

'Alison . . . *Alison* . . .' I shook her until her roving eyes focused on me. 'Alison – I have to leave you . . . I'm sorry, but I have to go . . .' I looked towards the guys coming from York Street, not more than a hundred yards away now. And then in the other direction, where Eddie had spotted us and was pointing, and the three good fellas with him were picking up speed. Alison's face had drifted towards them, but she was so still, so fucking out of it. I forced her head back towards me. 'Do you understand? I've done my best, and I will come back and get you. I swear to . . .'

I looked up again, but not towards our assailants. Up at the cathedral, looming over us, and the Spire of Hope, glowing against the night sky.

Sanctuary.

Fucking sanctuary.

I scooped Alison up and held her against my chest and whispered, 'Where there's life, there's hope . . .'

I hurried us up the cathedral steps to the huge

wooden doors. With my luck, they would be locked against gypsies, tramps and thieves.

But, no; I pulled at them and they opened, miraculously, and we slipped in. As I pushed them closed behind me, I looked back and saw the bad guys converging at the base of the steps. They quickly turned, drew their guns, and began to mount them. I looked about in vain for some way of locking the doors from the inside but there was nothing. I turned and dragged Alison after me down the weakly lit nave aisle. There *had* to be somewhere in such a massive building to hide, or some alternative exit. We were halfway to the high altar when it dawned on me that we weren't alone and, as my eyes grew more accustomed to the gloom, it became apparent that the pews were in fact filled with worshippers, that there was an organ playing and the air was thick with the smell of incense; we were stumbling through some stupid bloody midnight mass or other such nonsense. I looked back to see the men with guns arriving at the top of the aisle. I turned and urged Alison forward, but our legs got tangled and we fell over each other and tumbled at the very foot of the altar. I scrambled to my feet and tried to pull her up, but she seemed to have given up; it was like trying to raise a deadweight. They were now hurrying down the aisle towards us and I knew the game was up, that I had been incredibly stupid in not saving myself when I had the chance. There was nothing else I could do but what I did. I stepped in front of Alison and raised my hands and said, 'No, you can't do this in here; it's against the rules.'

But they just kept on coming, and I braced myself, and, in the same moment, embraced the insane notion I would not let them take her without a fight.

Although I was pretty sure there wouldn't be one.

They would just shoot me, and be done.

I was of no value to them, no significance.

'Dan . . . Dan . . .'

I didn't even turn, or consider how she might have known my name or recovered her senses, because they were raising their guns and I knew I was now facing a Botanic Death Squad.

'Dan – it's OK.'

Eddie and his gang-bangers stopped just a few metres short of me because one of the congregation had stepped out in front of them. And when they pushed him out of the way, another took his place. Then another. And another. And the Death Squad looked about them, confused, as more and more worshippers began to rise up and move defiantly into the aisle, blocking it, dozens of them sidling out in what I now saw was their New-Seeker robes. Very quickly, the bad guys were surrounded and pushed closer together and the buggers didn't know how to react, save by waving their guns about and yelling, but to no effect. Not only were they stopped in their tracks, they seemed to realise that they were in actual danger themselves, that they might be overwhelmed and trampled or worse.

They began to back away, pushing and shoving and still shouting their warnings while looking absolutely terrified. Soon they were squeezed right back up the aisle to the double doors and then out on to the steps. I didn't know what the hell had just happened – and I didn't really care, because we were still alive. I crouched beside her and she whispered something in Russian and I knew then that she hadn't spoken my name, but that it had come from above us, from the high altar.

I looked up there, and it was Eve, my petite, tearful interrogator, my indexer, smiling down at me, in a red gown, her face illuminated in part by a slight glow from the stained-glass window set in the curved chancel wall behind her. A window which, even the briefest glance showed me, depicted the story of the Good Samaritan. The metaphor could not have been more obvious if Reverend Pike, who I could now see standing to the side of it, had banged my head against it.

Eve moved down from the high alter, her arms wide and welcoming. 'Welcome home, Dan,' she said. 'Welcome home.'

35

There was a car waiting for us at the foot of the steps: a stretch limo, more used to hen parties than religious cults. We moved towards it through what I can only describe as an honour guard. Eve and Pike led the way. I carried Alison in my arms. As Pike and Eve passed, the Seekers bowed their heads. When they got to the car, a Seeker driver was standing by the open back door. He too bowed, then quickly raised his head again and said, 'Where to, Bishop?'

'Before we go anywhere,' I said, 'I need a phone.'

'You need a hospital,' said Pike, 'and a lawyer.'

Eve reached into the folds of her gown, produced a mobile phone and handed it to me.

'Is God's number in here?' I asked. 'Might be handy.'

Pike looked anxiously about him and said, 'Just get in the car, Starkey; it's not good for us to be seen with a murderer.'

'He's not a murderer,' said Eve. 'And give him time. Dan – put your friend in and make your call in private. She will be safe with us.'

I looked from one to the other. Pike, I would never trust, but Eve? Yes. And they had saved our lives. I manoeuvred Alison into one of the backseats, whispered reassurance and then stepped away from the limo. I had, by some miracle, retained Sara's number in my head. As I waited for a response, I looked up at the cathedral and the hundreds of New Seekers, now milling around outside, and wondered what the hell they were doing there at two in the morning. I checked up and down the street, but could see no obvious sign of Eddie or his gang-bangers. Of course, it didn't mean they weren't there. I was pretty sure they wouldn't easily let go of their investment, even if they weren't aware of its true value.

The phone was answered on the sixth ring. Before Sara could say anything, I said, 'Are they safe?'

There was a giggle, and then the unmistakable voice of Harry Frank exclaimed, 'Danny boy!'

He was, it seemed, destined always to be one step ahead of me. I swore, and asked again for the health of my family.

'Well, it's like our weather, Dan: it's changeable,' he replied. 'For now, yes, they're fine. But time and patience are running out. But it's so good to hear from you. What did you think of the photo, by the way?'

'Photo? What photo? If you've harmed a hair on—'

'Oh – right. I see: you're calling from a different

number. I sent you a wee pic. Sure, I'll send it to this one as well, eh?'

'I want my wife back, and my kids and Sara and—'

'Do you have the girl?'

I looked back to the limo. The back door was still open and I could see Eve sitting, stroking Alison's brow.

'Yes, I have her.'

'Dan the man! See, I knew with a wee bit of incentive you'd come up trumps!'

'I just want my—'

'You're so funny, Dan Starkey, do you know that?'

'What're you—'

'I had no idea who this pair were! Caught them sneaking around my warehouse, sticking their big noses in where they had no business, but, even though I had them battered, they didn't give anything away, so I didn't know they were from you until you called this number and jumped in with both feet. You're like one of those fucking Ninja Turtles, Starkey, do you know that? Brave, but also ridiculous. Do you get me? That's you, Dan Starkey: a hero in a half-shell.' He laughed.

I put the phone against my chest to stop myself from wading further in on the abuse. Eve caught my eye. I turned away, took a deep breath and said, 'What do you want me to do with her?'

I was walking back to the limo when the phone pinged and there was a message from Sara's number. I clicked and it brought up a photo. It was a picture of Terry, his face bloody and battered and a bloody hole in his throat. I lurched to the side and then stumbled forward against the car. Terry was clearly dead, and it was my fault. I'd casually sent him to protect Sara, and Harry Frank had killed him.

'Are you OK?' Eve asked from the backseat.

I nodded, gathered myself, slipped the phone into my pocket and got in beside Alison. She appeared to be sleeping, even though Eve had unwrapped her bandage and was in the act of replacing it with one from a first-aid kit. I had a brief glimpse of Alison's hand but quickly looked away. I didn't need to see any more poison, because the whole fucking city was suppurating. I just wanted to get Trish back – and Bobby and Lol, and now Sara – and put them all in a campervan and fuck off out of Ulster to somewhere quiet, where the sun shone, the beer was cold and the chances of murder, kidnap and carnage were remote. For that reason, once we got there, I would immediately abandon them there and piss off somewhere else, because murder, kidnap and carnage have a habit of following me around.

Pike closed the door behind me, then lent forward and spoke quietly to the driver. As we pulled out, I asked where we were going and Pike said, 'Nowhere.'

'I appreciate the help,' I said, 'but is there any reason I shouldn't be thinking I've just jumped from the frying pan into the fire? Seeing as how the last time I saw you, *Bishop*, you ordered your henchmen to give me a kicking?'

'*Henchmen*.' Pike laughed. 'You lied your way into

our Church, Starkey – a Church based on truth and honesty . . .'

'Two concepts that don't traditionally figure high on your—'

'Stop,' said Eve. 'Please.' She had just finished re-bandaging the hand and was gently setting it down on Alison's chest. 'Don't worry; we're not going anywhere. It's just better to . . . keep on the move.'

Pike nodded across at Alison. 'Who is she?'

'She's just someone in trouble I'm trying to get home.'

He laughed dismissively. 'You really expect us to believe that? You're on the run; who's to say this isn't just another of your victims? Look at her! This is you saving someone? *Really*?'

I angrily jabbed a finger at him. 'If you really want to know, *Bishop*,' I spat, 'fucking ask her! I'm sure she'd love to tell you all about it. But, for your information, for the past nine months, this girl has been held captive by the Botanic Boat Crew. Heard of them? Or is your head stuck too far up your own arse? She's been forced to work as a prostitute and kept docile on crush. According to Davy Blair, who runs the Crew, for all of those nine months she's been fucked ten times a day at fifty quid a go, and she'd still be flat on her back if I hadn't gotten her out of there. So I just want to get her home, if that's OK with you?'

He was nodding, but without sympathy or understanding. He said, 'Hold on there, Starkey, and we'll give you a medal.' He nodded across at Eve. 'If it wasn't for the grace of . . . we'd be handing you over now to the police. Remember, I *know* you, Starkey. I know what you do and the chaos you bring; why should we believe a word you say? Eve – you know the damage he's done to my family, my profession, and isn't he only after lying his way into our headquarters—?'

'I was on a case,' I said, cutting in. There was no harm in telling him, I supposed, as that investigation now appeared so minor – almost quaint – and not one, it now seemed, that I was destined to solve. 'The petrol-bomb attack on the Braxton Clinic? I was looking for evidence of your involvement.'

'My involvement!' Pike snorted. 'You think that's my style, do you?'

'As a matter of fact—'

'You have no idea what we're about! It's scum like you who—'

'Enough!' said Eve, her voice still small, yet firm. 'Enough.'

Pike glared at her for several long moments, but then something passed between them, which I didn't quite understand. Instead of the combative, argumentative and fake-pious Pike that I had known for years, he surprised me by meekly taking a deep breath and turning to stare out of the window as we continued our meandering journey through the city centre. When I looked back at Eve, as she gently stroked Alison's arm, I could see that a faint smile had appeared on her young lips.

And then I did understand, and I half laughed because it had been staring me in the face but, like anything, that is too close: it had been rendered out of focus.

'You,' I said to Eve, '*you're* the Bishop.'

The smile widened. 'Me? Little me?'

'*He* kowtows to *you*, and it kills him to have to do it, but he does it because you have something over him, or—'

'Or he believes,' said Eve.

'Believes?' I said.

'Believes,' said Eve.

Pike looked across at her and gave her an exasperated shake of his head. 'Believes, and can't quite believe that he believes, but, nevertheless, believes with all his heart and soul.'

I looked from one to the other, still confused. 'What the hell is going on here? Believes in *what*, exactly?'

'*Her*,' said Pike.

'*Me*?' said Eve, her eyes sparkling.

She was a beautiful girl, with a charm and humour about her that she could probably use to wind anyone around any one of her fingers with very little effort, including, clearly, someone as tough and unwieldy as Pike.

Or me.

'If you're the Bishop, how can you even begin to run a . . . I mean, you can't be more than—?'

'Sixteen. And precocious. And, frankly, Dan Starkey, you've a memory like a sieve.'

Her face lit up as she said it, and I kept staring at her: there was some wisp of something from my past, but I just couldn't grasp it.

'Starkey,' said Pike, 'open your eyes. She doesn't run the bloody Church. She *is* the bloody Church.'

And that simple rephrasing instantly unlocked the puzzle and the memory was released and I put my hand to my chin and open mouth and shook my head and said, 'No fucking way.'

And she nodded and said, 'Yes, way.'

'Christine,' I said. 'The fucking Messiah.'

36

It was long ago, and it was reasonably far away.

I was sent by the Catholic Church to the north coast, to Wrathlin Island, to investigate madness: priests who'd gone rogue and proclaimed a new Messiah – Christine, magical daughter of a single mum – and a congregation caught up in the mania. It had all descended into violence and bloody murder. Patricia and I, and her son, *our* son, little Stevie, had nearly paid with our lives. In the end, in my usual haphazard and accidental way, I had helped to save Christine's life. She had fled the island with her mother and set up home in Belfast and, although I hadn't met them since, I knew that Patricia had kept in touch, at least for a while. But they found it difficult to settle. They eventually moved on and dropped out of sight and, almost, out of memory. But they would always be in there somewhere, and when I did occasionally think of them, it was always with a mixture of horror and grateful thanks. Little Stevie had caught an infection, which brought him to death's door, on a storm-battered night when evacuation from the island was impossible. In fact, as far as we were concerned, and the local doctor confirmed, he had actually passed through that door. Somehow, Christine, just a little barefoot kid, had coaxed our boy back to life. We didn't know if it was divine intervention or extreme good fortune, but we would always be grateful to her for the extra time it gave us with him.

'And now here you are,' I said, 'all growed up.'

'I was sure you'd recognise me. *I* never forgot *you*.'

'Ah, but you're about three feet taller. And you outfoxed me by changing your name. Christine too on the nose, was it?'

She let out a little giggle. 'Exactly! Eve is . . .'

'Perfect,' I said.

She smiled at me.

'Moira?'

Eve shook her head. 'We had a tough time.'

'Your mum's . . .?'

'She died.'

'Oh,' I said. It was a shock, but a removed shock because it had been so long. Moira was nobody's idea of how the mother of the Messiah was supposed to be. She was a beery, sweary, beautiful and sexy live wire who didn't suffer fools gladly. Apart from me, of course. 'I'm sorry. That's . . . inadequate . . . But she was . . . lovely.'

'Yes, she was. I know you had something going on with her.'

'*Me*?'

'I might only have been a little girl, but I wasn't stupid. Also, I'm the Messiah.'

'Right,' I said. 'What happened?'

'We went to Europe, but it followed us around, the . . .'

'The whole Messiah thing.'

'Watch your tone, Starkey,' Pike shot across. 'Show some respect.'

'He's fine,' said Eve. 'It's his job to be cynical.'

'It's no one's job,' snapped Pike; 'it's a personality disorder.'

'Well, I don't mind it. Too much adoration does my head in.' She gave him the sparkly eyes before returning her attention to me. 'I was so sorry to hear about your son.'

'Yeah, well,' I said. There was something about the way she spoke about him that squeezed my chest. I concentrated on Pike. 'What about you?' I asked. 'Were you sorry to hear about him too?'

'What are you talking about?'

'Listening in to the indexing: that's how you get your power over people; that's how you knew to burst in and order me to be beaten up by men in sandals.'

He let out a throaty laugh. 'Really, Starkey? Seriously? As it happens, I've no interest in indexing. You were found out for two reasons: one, because you used your mobile phone and we have checks for that, and two, you stuck out like a sore thumb and three different people squealed on you. I don't much like touts, but it can go with the territory.'

I gave him a *yeah, right* look. I rested my head back against the seat for the first time. Dog-tired. I glanced out of the window at the City Hall passing beside us, a Union Jack flying proudly on one of the few days when it was allowed to fly proudly. Images that had lain neglected crowded back in: on the island with Trish, feeding hedgehogs; a caravan going over the edge of a cliff; the death of a Bill Oddie lookalike. And Moira, beautiful mouthy Moira, who had almost seduced me.

'It was a car accident, last year,' Eve said, unprompted.

She'd had that gift of *knowing* on the island. It was one of the signs the priests had picked up on. And it hadn't deserted her.

'They *called* it an accident,' said Pike. He looked to Eve for approval but, when she didn't react, he continued anyway. 'It could have killed both of them. What you call the "Messiah thing" does not easily sit with the established Church, and there are those who'd prefer—'

'It means I have to be careful,' said Eve. 'I have to protect myself, which is why I have to surround myself with all of this –' she nodded around the car – 'and people I can trust.' She reached across and touched Pike's knee. 'And I couldn't have done it without your help.'

'You do have form in setting up churches,' I observed.

Pike blew air out of his cheeks and glanced at his watch. Alison turned restlessly between us and her eyes fluttered. Eve stroked her brow and they closed again.

'She's not well,' she said. 'I can feel a fever on her. Her hand . . . They really did that?'

I nodded.

'Let's take her to Ballyferris, then. She can recuperate with us until she's ready to go home. We have doctors.'

I was pretty sure that she was good and kind – but she was also barking mad. She had been corrupted as a child by having the mantle of Messiah placed upon her by delusional priests and she had not only failed to shake it off, but had now clearly embraced it. I had a vague recollection of Trish asking at the time, 'If Christine is already a handful, what is she going to be like when she hits puberty?' We'd concluded that she'd either be locked up in the nuthouse or she'd rule the world. And, with her growing hordes of followers, it was the latter path she had clearly embarked upon. I knew she would look after Alison – but there was no way I was letting her out of my sight, not with Harry Frank waiting, my family in jeopardy and someone as wily and treacherous and ambitious and bitter and vengeful as Pike on the scene. Whatever he was building with Eve, I was pretty sure he planned, ultimately, to be the main beneficiary of it. If he got wind of who Alison really was, he would not hesitate to exploit her.

'I appreciate the offer,' I said, 'but her folks have

been waiting a long time to get her back. If you're heading for Ballyferris anyway, there's somewhere you can drop us on the way.'

Pike said, 'We're not a taxi service.'

But, in fact, they were.

As we headed out of the city centre on the main Bangor Road, Alison began to stir again. Her eyes opened and fixed on Eve. She whispered something to Eve, and Eve responded in the same language.

'You speak in tongues,' I said.

'Russian A-level at Methody,' said Eve. 'I took it when I was twelve.'

'Nobody like a know-all,' I said.

Eve smiled and looked at Pike. 'How do we go about recruiting him?' she asked. 'We could do with a voice of sanity in the camp.'

'Over my dead body,' said Pike.

'Beware of what you wish for,' I said. I nodded at Eve. 'What does she say?'

'That she wants to go home to her parents. That she has been kept as you have said she was.'

I raised an eyebrow at Pike, but he ignored it. I reached out and took Alison's good hand. I patted it. She looked at me the way she must have looked at a thousand men over the preceding months: blankly. She was in a wretched condition, and I was about to add to her misery by trading her to a killer. And she would come with me and do what was required, because it had been programmed into her to do what men in authority required of her. I was supposed to be her saviour in exactly the same way that Eve was purporting to be ours. It was truly a fucked-up world.

Ten minutes later, we pulled into the car park of the five-star Culloden Hotel, just outside Holywood.

'Swanky,' said Pike.

'Her parents are waiting,' I said.

I looked to Alison for signs of understanding or hope, but nothing. The limo pulled to a halt just short of the front doors. The driver got out and opened our door and I stepped out. As I began to help Alison out after me, Eve put a hand on her shoulder, leaned forward and gently kissed her on the cheek. Alison smiled.

Eve then looked at me. 'Dan,' she said, 'make the right choice.'

'Unlikely,' I said, 'but I'll bear it in mind.'

Somehow, by whatever talent she had, I was sure she knew that what I was about to do was cheap and scurrilous and ambiguous and self-serving and just plain wrong, but also that I had no choice, because you only go around once.

The driver closed the door but, immediately, Eve's window came down. 'Dan?' she said. 'My phone?'

I feigned surprise, checked my pockets and then handed it to her with an apology. Pike was shaking his head.

I leaned into the window and said, 'One thing: the cathedral, the fact that you were there so late at night – how come?'

'Because you needed us, Dan.'

'No, really,' I said. 'How come—?'

But her window zipped up.

Alison stood trembling beside me as the driver turned the car around and then eased it back towards us. It stopped again and the other blacked-out window, now on the nearside, came down.

'Eve says I should wish you luck,' Pike said flatly. 'So – luck.'

'That means a lot,' I said.

'You sarc—' he began, but stopped himself. He cleared his throat and said, 'Starkey, don't forget, I know you of old, and how you always manage to get hold of the wrong end of the stick. The incident at the clinic? As it happens, we were very aware that we might get the blame for it, so we looked into it ourselves. And do you know something? If you really want to know who did it, then maybe you'd be better off looking a little closer to home.'

He raised an eyebrow and kept what I could only describe as triumphant eye contact with me as his window moved up again.

The limo pulled away, pausing briefly at the entrance before turning left on to the main road and presumably heading for their headquarters in Ballyferris. I had no immediate idea of what Pike's cryptic comment meant, and possibly he was just stirring things for badness. And there was no time to think about it. I looked down at Alison and tried to give her a reassuring smile. It was the first time we had been truly alone and out of immediate danger since I had freed her from the Boat Club.

I said, 'Alison, it won't be long till your home; there's just one more thing we have to do. Do you hear me?' She just looked at me. 'You're just going to have to trust me. I won't let anything else bad happen to you; just stick with me for a little bit.'

It was a lie, of course.

There were huge mountains of bad things that could still happen to her.

But there was nothing else I could do.

I had to trade her in.

There was a cough behind us and I turned to find a burly hotel security guard emerging from the hotel's revolving door.

'Excuse me, sir,' he said, warily eyeing us up, 'but are you residents?'

'No,' I said, 'we're Protestants.'

I took Alison's hand again and we walked past him out of the hotel grounds and on to the main road.

37

The Ulster Folk and Transport Museum was just a two-minute walk away from the hotel – along a main road, largely free of traffic – but Alison was already finding it hard going. I stopped her and crouched down. She was still barefoot and her feet were black and bleeding and her ankle was up like a bap. The light breeze coming off Belfast Lough seemed to be blowing straight through her. I hauled her up into the piggyback again. She was as light as a down pillow, as bony as a crone or super-model. She groaned. The crush would be wearing off soon, to be replaced by the depraved pain of a thousand fucks.

In all the madness, I had forgotten about my car, but, as we turned off the main road and started down the incline to the museum car park, I could see it still sitting there, miraculously unvandalised. The gay snoggers' vehicle was also still in place, but it had now been joined by another, parked up tight beside it. Two's a couple; four's an orgy, and good luck to them.

It was three on an August morning and still a couple of hours shy of daybreak. But we were bang on time. I was pretty sure that Joey, Harry Frank's little rat-faced helper, would be lurking somewhere in the bushes ahead of us, letting his boss know that we had arrived with the prize. Inside one of the sheds looming large against the starry sky was, I hoped, my wife, and Bobby, and Lol, and maybe even Sara too.

Dan – make the right choice.

As I walked with Alison's stick-thin arms crisscrossed on my chest, my two hands clasping her thighs to keep her in place, Eve's words came stabbing through my brain. In this situation, what the bloody hell was right? The lives of what passed for my family, against a slightly extended imprisonment of a billionaire's daughter. She had been in hell for nine months; what difference could another few hours make?

And yet . . . And yet.

I barely knew Harry Frank, but I knew enough. He was a sadist, a torturer, and he was absolutely ruthless. If the bargaining didn't go his way, what further terrors would he inflict on Alison? Or what if he got the yips, or something went wrong with the exchange and he thought it better to destroy the evidence, to acid bath her and run? I had given her this little taste of freedom and she had come willingly with me. I was her only hope and I was about to betray her to a psychopath.

Dan – make the right choice.

Like a fucking tattoo on my cerebral cortex.

But what else could I do?

How else could I possibly get them back?

I had a damp gun in my back pocket and was possessed of the wit and wisdom of a washed-up, liquored-up ex-hack.

Harry Frank had his acid baths, his goons and he was within touching distance of millions, possibly tens of millions of pounds with which to finance his dreams of uniting the gangs and controlling my country. He was already contributing more than his fair share of violence to our fucked-up city; with virtually unlimited money to his name, he would be unstoppable.

We passed my car and I got as far as the security gate before I swore out loud, then backtracked to it. I eased Alison down off my back. I took out the gun and smashed the passenger-side window with the butt. I opened the door and reached into the glove compartment and took out the spare key. Trish had told me a thousand times not to keep it there, but I always did. A better man might have been able to manage something more showy, like pulling wires out and starting the car by jamming them together, but Trish and the world knew that I wasn't that man. I manoeuvred Alison around to the driver's side and opened it and helped her in behind the wheel.

I said, 'Do you know how to drive?'

She looked at me blankly. I put the key in the ignition and started the engine.

I closed the door.

Her brow furrowed through the glass. She fumbled around inside for a moment and then the window came down and she said something in Russian, her voice weak, her eyes suddenly wider and panic stricken. I supposed that she had been controlled for so long, including by me, that she didn't know how to cope with being set free, or she suspected that it was some kind of a trick and that all kinds of hell would rain down on her the moment she put the car into gear.

I waved towards the main road and said, 'Just fucking drive away before I change my mind. Go on!'

Still she wouldn't move, and I supposed that it was my close proximity that was stopping her going. So I turned and walked away. I slipped around the security gate and walked towards the small bridge leading down to the museum entrance. I kept walking, didn't look back, and after about ten seconds I heard the engine turn over again; there was a scraping as she struggled to find a gear, and then the sound of tyres on gravel.

She was away, and with her probably my chance of saving Patricia's life.

Or Bobby's.

Or Lol's.

Or the baby that ticked inside her.

Or Sara's.

Five for one, or one for thousands.

Or six.

Because the chances of me walking out of the museum alive were fuck-all squared in a box.

* * *

The two hoods from the pub, from the Tesco car park, were behind the desk. One of them looked at me said, 'Whoop, whoop. Lookee fucking here. Shouldn't you be with someone?'

'I am,' I said, and patted my pocket; 'she's just very small.'

They advised me of what a comedian I was, indicated for me to keep walking and fell in behind me. We moved down the curving ramp on to the darkened floor of the shed. The mighty engines loomed above us as we walked, all the more threatening now that they were robbed of softening light. I could hear our footsteps echo on the hard concrete floor where, before, they'd been masked by raggedy Irish folk music and a peaty accent enthusing over our glorious steam-driven history. I was terrified as to how this was going to play out. I'd set out with a hostage and a vague back-up plan, but now, because of something loosely related to a conscience or guilt or plain stupidity, I was only left with the back-up. As Harry Frank put it when he stepped down from a red double-decker bus,

'Haven't you got a brass neck on you?'

I just nodded.

He looked up at the bus. 'What do you think of the Guy Arab?'

'Gay Arab? Whatever turns you on.'

He had on a black shirt, open at the neck, with a large collar; he was wearing a gold chain, which is always a mistake. He stroked the side of the vehicle and said, 'Lancashire United Guy Arab double-decker motor bus, purchased by Belfast Corporation during the war, phased out in the 1950s and just brought back into service by me, with four special passengers up top awaiting exchange for the dearly beloved daughter of a porn baron. Starkey, they were getting their hopes up.'

'I had her,' I said, 'but I let her go.'

He laughed and he clapped his hands and said, 'And why the hell would you do that, when you know what will happen to your people?'

'I don't really know. But it seemed like a good idea at the time.'

He stepped closer to me. The hoods behind me stepped closer too. I had the waterlogged gun tucked into the back of my trousers but no way to get at it without asking for planning permission.

'You really had her?'

'About five minutes ago; about a hundred yards from here. But she's well away now. I was going to hand her over, I really was, and I went through all sorts of shit to get her, but then it came to me that you might turn out to be, as Oscar Wilde memorably observed, a bit of a cunt and might not stick to your side of the bargain. So I decided at the last minute to give her a chance and concentrate all my efforts on appealing to your good nature, and to throw in a bit of a charm offensive, as well – straight out of *How To Win Friends and Assassinate People*, or whatever it's called.'

He was looking at me as if he couldn't quite believe that I would be that stupid, that I had to have something else up my sleeve. Clearly, he didn't know me well at all. He moved even closer – toothpaste close.

'So,' I said, 'I was thinking, if you're taking over Belfast one gang at the time, you could probably do with someone who's worked in PR; you know, get the message out there you're not such a bad guy. We could do photo ops: you handing over cheques for charity or planting trees to save the world. That's what the cartels do in Mexico. Shit like—'

'Starkey, give me one good reason why they all don't just go in the bath, right now?'

'Because you have a heart; I know you have a heart. Let them go; someone has to take the first step on the road to sorting this country out, so you take it, Harry Frank, and then together we can start rebuilding this . . . No? OK. You threaten my family; I threaten yours. That's how it works here; that's how it has always worked here.'

'What're you talking about?'

'Your brother, Rob. He might be taking a bath of his own, if you don't let my people go-go.'

'You . . .'

'Yep; mad as a box of frogs, but completely at my mercy. Soon as I have them home safe, I'll have my guy let him go.'

'Bullshit,' said Harry Frank. 'There's no way you—'

'You forget: I've been to your home; you told me yourself he lives next door. Try calling him, you'll see.'

He took out his phone and called.

I said, 'Not so clever now, eh, Napoleon?'

I had asked D.I. Hood to arrest the brother. He had said he would think about it, so I had no idea if he had actually done it. He wasn't exactly a friend; he was hardly a colleague; he always played it by the book and I had some evidence to suggest that he had lately converted to the New Seekers. I had only the merest slither of a hope, but sometimes things just work out.

Harry Frank said, 'Jack?'

He nodded. He listened. He kept his eyes fixed on me. He listened some more. Then he said, 'I'll call you back.'

He closed the phone. I knew before he spoke, because he looked smug.

He said, 'So, seems there were cops called at his house and tried to get him to come out, but he's sitting tight. They're still there, but it's built like a fortress; they'd need a fucking neutron bomb to get inside.'

'Actually,' I said, trying to mask my utter despair, 'a neutron bomb would kill him and leave the house intact. That's why—'

'Is that it, Starkey? The best you have? Anything else you want to run past me?'

'No,' I said, 'although I'd like to reconsider the Napoleon remark.'

'Really? That's your final shot, is it?'

'No,' I said, '*this* is.'

And I would have whipped the gun out and shot him through the head before spinning to shoot his two cronies in the guts, except it got snagged in the back of my trousers and the cronies chopped me down and

I fell on my face. They kicked me until I rolled over. Harry Frank stood over me, with his gun – my gun, his gun again – in his hand.

He said, 'The mind boggles; the mind just fucking boggles.' He centred the sights on my chest. 'Ordinarily,' he said, 'I'd do the traditional thing of killing your family one by one, making you watch, just to prolong the agony, but I'm a great believer in efficiency. So, Dan Starkey, die in the knowledge that you fucked up big style, and know that all of your loved ones will be following straight after you and it's all your fault because you're such a fucking idiot.'

And the only final thought I could manage before he pulled the trigger was that he was indeed right about my foolishness, but at least I had tried, and God loves a trier. There was a loud crack and a bright light, which blinded me, and a complete absence of pain, and then I heard screaming. It slowly dawned on me that it wasn't me screaming, but Harry Frank. As my eyes grew used to the dimness again, I could see that he had reeled away and was holding his hand to his chest and crying in agony. Or, now that I focused properly, he was holding what was left of his hand, and that his two cronies were around him, trying to help, and I supposed that I had the glorious silt of the River Lagan to thank for my exploding gun.

I began to crawl along the cold concrete, hoping to get far enough under the Guy Arab to then make a run for it on the other side and possibly lose them in the dark, but then one of the cronies said, 'Not so fucking fast,' and I was caught by the ankles and dragged facedown backwards.

They got me about halfway back to where I'd started when they suddenly dropped my legs, and I was aware that there were lights on and the folksy tape had started up. Then there were hurried footsteps, quite a few of them, and there was some shouting I couldn't quite make out and then there were hands on my shoulders, gently turning me. I blinked up at Alison, and then beyond her to three men I didn't recognise with guns, who were holding them on Harry Frank and his cronies, who were returning the favour.

Alison helped me up into a sitting position, but remained crouched down beside me. She did not have the happy look of someone who had been rescued, while the new arrivals with guns did not have the look of men who received a regular wage from the government for keeping us safe in our beds. Harry Frank was upright and mouthing threats and curses at the newcomers, flecks of white spit in the corners of his mouth as he did it, and cradling his mangled, dripping hand. His gun – my gun, his gun – was on the floor, smoking, more relaxed than any of us. There were more footsteps and I caught sight of a shock of blond hair coming down the ramp and someone big and bulky behind.

Then they were there: Eddie coming in front, Davy lumbering along behind. The guys with the guns on Harry Frank didn't look round, so I guessed they were Boat Crew. Davy glanced at me and then faced Harry

Frank. Eddie came across and yanked Alison up and led her over to stand beside Davy.

Harry Frank calmed down as soon as Davy strode into view. They warily eyed each other up until Davy said, 'Bit of an accident, Harry?'

Harry Frank ignored the comment and said, 'Davy – what're you doing here? You know this is off limits. We have an agreement.'

'Well, you know what they say about agreements.' Davy put an arm around Alison and gave her a squeeze. 'Besides, you tried to take my property.'

'You getting maudlin over a whore, Davy? It's not like you.'

'I'm getting maudlin, Harry, over my investment . . .' He nodded at Eddie, beside him. 'How much does she represent?'

'Roughly, two hundred grand over a lifetime – or eighteen months, in real terms.'

Harry Frank shook his head. 'Look at her, Davy; you'll be lucky to get another month out of her. So, tell you what, I'll give you fifty grand for her. And then I'll take forty of that off as a fine for trespassing on my property. So take ten for her, Davy, and have done.'

'Ten grand? You'd really pay that for this collection of bone and nits? Really?'

'It's not for her, Davy; it's a piss-off fee for you. And I won't offer it twice.'

'Well, now . . . Ten grand . . . Fair enough . . . If only it was that simple.' He thumbed in my direction. 'See, Harry, it got me wondering why a loser like yer man would risk his life to get a whore back, or why he would just take *one* when we have a whole cattle truck of them. Then, when I looked into it a bit further, I wondered why you had the word out looking for her too. Got me thinking maybe she's more than the sum of her cunty parts, eh? Got me wondering just how far you'd go to get her back. Soon as my guys saw her outside – and we've been staking you out for weeks, anyway – they were all over her like the rash she definitely has. So, to cut to the fucking quick, Harry, you, through that dick –' and he thumbed at me again – 'trespassed on my property, took my whore and brought her back here. You stole. Anyone broke an agreement, it's you. And, case you hadn't noticed, I've four guns on you to your two, so I'd say it was in your interests to up your offer for the merchandise.'

'She's not merchandise,' I said.

They both looked at me.

'Shut the fuck up, Starkey,' said Harry Frank.

'No,' I said, and I slowly began to get to my feet. 'I don't think so.'

'What the fuck—?' Davy began.

'You do what you're told, fella,' Eddie said, moving across to me and placing the tip of his gun barrel against the side of my head. 'Or are we done with him?'

'Shoot away,' I said, 'but, Davy – if she's merchandise, she's fucking Harrods merchandise. You don't need to be trading for her like some fucking sack of Comber spuds. She's worth – what? – five million, if she's delivered home safe? That right, Harry?'

Eddie, finger on the trigger, looked to his boss.

Davy Blair looked to Harry Frank. 'What's he talking about?'

'He's slabbering,' said Harry Frank. 'Don't pay any attention—'

'Her real name is Alison Wolff,' I said. 'Her dad is Billionaire Thomas Wolff. She's worth a fortune. I was paid to track her down and Harry got wind of it. You give her up for anything less than five, you're a lunatic.'

'He's delusional,' said Harry Frank. 'Look at her! Does she look like—?'

Davy moved his hand from around Alison's waist to her hair, and quickly yanked her head back. As she let out a yelp, he snapped, 'This true?' into her face. Alison cried something in Russian. Davy pulled her hair harder. '*Is* it?!'

'She doesn't understand,' said Harry Frank, 'because it's bullshit.'

'She doesn't understand,' I said, 'because she's traumatised. But you look into it, Davy. Swear to God. Why else would there be so much money floating around looking for her? She's worth a fortune. Even with only nine fingers.'

Davy suddenly let go of her hair and she staggered back and collapsed to her knees. I moved tentatively away from Eddie's gun barrel to crouch beside her and Eddie didn't try to stop me.

Davy studied Harry Frank for what felt like a long time – and then laughed suddenly. 'Do you know something? I don't care if she is a billionaire's daughter. And do you know why, Harry? Because I'm happy with what I have. I'm not big league, Harry, not the way you plan to be. I do OK. But, if I go up against the likes of Thomas Wolff, if I try to bargain or blackmail, he'll spend his money well: he'll have the cops, the SAS and, for all I know, the fucking US Marines crawling all over me and I don't really need that. And if word gets out that I've been whoring her, well, that's not going to do me much good, either. So better just to put a bullet in her head now and disappear her, eh?'

He looked across at Eddie and nodded. Eddie moved behind us, the gun now on Alison.

'Now, boss?' Eddie asked.

Davy began to nod.

Harry Frank said, 'Don't! I want her, and I want her alive.'

'Then I'll be taking the two hundred grand in cash, and she's yours. I'm sure that won't be a problem to a man of your means, will it? Particularly when you have all those millions to come.'

'OK then, two hundred.' Harry Frank smiled. 'But, you know something, Davy? You know *why* I'm going to be running this city in a few months? Because of little people like you – small minded, lacking in ambition – people like you, who can see the bigger picture but are too scared to buy into it.'

'Whatever you say, Harry. Just give me the cash and we'll be off.'

'That's exactly what I'm going to do, Davy – but with a twist. I'm not going to give it to you; I'm going to give it to you guys.' He nodded at Eddie, and around the other Boat Crew. 'Yep, because, actually, Dan here is right: she is the Wolff girl, and she is worth a fortune, and that means I'm going to have money to burn. Some of that, I'm going to give to you guys: more money in a day than you could earn in a year with this fucking loser. All you have to do to earn it is shoot him in the head. That's right – go on – do it now, then come work for me and you'll have the time of your fucking lives.'

'Oh, for fuck's sake,' said Davy. 'If you're going to be like that about it, just forget the money.' He nodded at Harry. 'Eddie, fucking shoot him now.'

There was a brief moment of hesitation as eyes connected and cogs whirred and synapses snapped before all hell broke loose.

38

When the smoke began to clear and the raw clamour of gunfire echoing around the massive shed had receded, I saw that there was still one man standing: Davy Blair – with blood streaming down his brow from where a bullet had clearly grazed him, and with a hole torn through the right arm of his jacket and through which I could see ripped flesh and exposed bone. But he was, at least, standing, which is more than could be said for his three cronies – two plainly dead, one rolling around in agony, clutching his stomach. Or for Eddie, with the top of his blond head scalped and his brain exposed. Or for the Tesco twins, their bodies riddled like Tom-and-Jerry cheese. Or for Harry Frank, flat on his back, his arms and legs waving about like a flipped tortoise, trying to right himself but sadly unaware that it was a physical impossibility, that he was doomed to have the life drain out of him on the hard concrete floor, surrounded by the trains and buses and milk floats he adored.

Davy Blair, the only gangster who hadn't fired a shot in anger, reached down and picked up a discarded gun and walked the few yards across to his fallen rival and stood over him.

Harry Frank looked up, his eyes wide and filled with horror. He said, 'This wasn't supposed to—' while raising his ragged hand to protect his face. But Davy Blair shot right through it into his mouth, and his head slammed back into the concrete. But he was dead before it touched. Davy stood over him for a moment, shaking his head. He glanced back at me, crouching with my arm around a shaking Alison, and raised an eyebrow.

'Trouble with this place,' he said, 'it's full of clever clogs who try to run before they can walk. If he'd taken his time, he might have been OK, but these guys, they want everything and they want it now.'

He turned with the gun at his side and looked down at Harry Frank's two gunmen, nodded with satisfaction and then turned to his own fallen men. He studied Eddie for a moment, then moved to the only one who was still alive, squirming and looking in desperation at his boss for help. It came in the form of a quick dispatch: bullet to the head.

Davy moved across to stand over us. He casually opened his gun and checked how many bullets were left. He said, 'Sorry about this, but – this kind of setup – best not to leave witnesses. We can kill each other till the cows come home and the cops won't bat an eye, but, once you involve billionaires' daughters, people tend to take that seriously.'

'We won't tell anyone,' I said.

Davy Blair closed the gun and raised it.

'No, you won't,' he said.

I pulled Alison closer and brought my hand down over her eyes. She didn't resist. The shaking stopped. Perhaps she was all shaken out.

Davy Blair said, 'Any last words?'

There could have been many – perhaps should have been.

But I settled on, 'He's behind you.'

He smiled, and began to squeeze the trigger.

But he should have listened, because then his head imploded and we were sprayed with brain and blood and bone. What was left of Davy Blair collapsed to the floor, leaving little rat-faced Joey standing at the bottom of the Guy Arab stairs in his security-guard uniform and with a stupid grin on his face.

We, dripping, looked at him expectantly, and the expectancy was that the relentless cycle of violence would continue.

But instead he gave us a manic kind of a giggle and said, 'Fucking hell – this is going to take some explaining.' He dropped the gun to his side, stepped off the bus and just started to wander away without saying whether he was making a run for it or going for a mop.

As he disappeared behind the double-decker, I slowly regained my feet and then helped Alison up. She looked staggered and stunned, pretty much as she had from the start. I took her good hand and led her towards the back of the bus. I put my hand on the rail, but then hesitated. I had taken Harry Frank at his word that he'd been keeping my ex and the kids and Sara hostage on the top deck, but there hadn't been a peep out of them from the moment I arrived. They might easily not be there at all. Or be there and dead, just like everyone else. I was more terrified at that prospect than I was of anything else during the entire misadventure.

'Trish? Are you there?' I called, tremulously, up the stairs.

No response.

I called again.

No . . . but then there was a muffled thump from the metal floor above.

I pulled myself up on to the step and guided Alison up after me. Then I slowly led the way up the curving stairs to the top deck.

And there she was, all trussed up with the rest of them, mouth taped, terrified and trying to say things to me which I suspected might be unflattering. In fact, they were all at it, a nightmare chorus of strangled complaints, but more welcome than anything I would ever be able to think of.

I nodded around them and said, 'I just want all of you to know – none of this is my fault.'

There would, of course, be hell to pay – from Trish, from Bobby, probably from Lol, definitely from Sara and certainly from the forces of law and order. But for now all anyone was concerned with was getting out of there, away from the carnage, and home safe. Trish, almost immediately, took Alison under her wing. Sara, who had been beaten by Harry Frank's cronies, was helped down from the top deck by Bobby. We gathered at the foot of the stairs. I checked the bodies until I found a phone, then I gave Bobby the nod and he began to lead us through the carnage and then up the ramp and out of the museum. The air was early-morning fresh and the sun was just breaking through and illuminating a splendid view, which swept down across the manicured lawns and over Belfast Lough to the Antrim Hills beyond. We drank it in, but only for a very short moment, then turned and walked across the stone bridge with the railway line below.

When we reached the car park, I saw my car, sandwiched on either side by the two vehicles I had thought belonged to the late-night snoggers, but which had really been keeping watch on Harry Frank for Davy and his Botanic Boat Crew. They had nabbed Alison almost as soon as she had tried to leave, thus precipitating a gun battle which none of them had survived.

The keys were still in the ignition. It was a tight squeeze, but I got everyone in. I started us on the drive back to Belfast. Trish said, 'Who're we dropping off first?' I said I didn't really know. Trish said, 'Well, why don't we stop at the garage on the way home, and then I can make a fry?' In the mirror, I caught Bobby and Lol looking at each other. They both demanded McDonald's.

Trish said she was too tired to argue, so we headed for the closest, opposite the Ulster Hospital. The restaurant itself was closed to diners but the drive-thru was open. We joined the queue. There is always a queue. When we got to the window to pay, the cashier looked us over and said, 'Youse look like you've had a good night.' Ordinarily, I would have told him to stick his fucking multiple Big Mac Meals up his spotty minimum-wage arse, but I was too tired. Instead, I gave him a wide smile, which caused several of my cuts to open.

We sat in the car park facing the hospital.

Bobby and Lol ate, leaning on the bonnet. When they were done and had dropped their litter on the ground, Bobby had a cigarette. Lol sneaked a couple of puffs. When I got out beside them, she smiled guiltily and climbed back in.

I looked at Bobby and said, 'Some night.'

'Aye,' he said.

'Seeing people die,' I said, 'kind of makes you appreciate the sanctity of life.'

Bobby snorted. 'Aye, right,' he said.

'OK,' I said. 'None of my business.'

After a couple more drags, he said, without looking at me, 'It is your business. And we're keeping it.'

'Good,' I said. After another while, I said, 'Did you firebomb the clinic?'

There was an approximation of a shrug, then he turned and got back into the car beside Lol. I had put to the back of my mind, given what was going on all around me, that Bobby was a one-legged ex-drug-addict who had grown up rough in a ghetto, witnessed his mother being killed by gangsters and had murdered one of them in revenge. He was of the streets and had been bred to defend whatever was his. Lol's baby was partly his and, in his mind, a firebomb must have seemed like the most direct solution to a problem that had to be dealt with urgently. He had bought himself some time, and whatever had happened to them over the past few hours seemed to have caused Lol to reconsider. As he settled in beside her, he pulled her close and kissed her hard. She responded equally vigorously, the two of them impervious to the fact that their mouths were still slathered with mayo. Trish couldn't take her eyes off them. Sara found it more uncomfortable and climbed out to stand beside me. Her right cheek was badly swollen and her lip cracked. She said, at least partly seriously, 'I'll be wanting an exclusive on this.' She shook her head and said, 'Those bastards. I mean, I knew they were bastards going in, but, Christ! What they did to . . . what's his name?'

'Terry,' I said.

'Terry. Fuck. I should have remembered his name.'

'I hardly knew him, either,' I said.

She nodded back at Alison, her head resting against Trish's shoulder but her eyes open and resting on us with a casual vacancy. 'I tried talking to her,' said Sara, 'but nothing. That one's lost.'

'No,' I said, 'she's found.'

I took out my phone and wandered off to phone Wolff International.

39

'God love her,' Trish said, 'she's like a little baby.' She had led Alison to the shower upstairs but, when she seemed disinclined to step into it of her own accord, had basically been forced to take one with her. 'An emaciated, maltreated baby, kept in the dark for a year.'

Their hair was still dripping, but they were downstairs and dressed again, Alison in a T-shirt and jeans that Trish provided and which hung off her. There had been a couple of little smiles from the girl, but she was still reluctant to embrace her freedom, seemingly terrified of it being snatched away from her again. She was content, though, to sit in the kitchen and have Trish comb out and gently dry her hair. I tried telling her that her dad was coming for her, that Michael Finn was coming, that she would soon be back in familiar surroundings, her own bed, the bosom of her family. She nodded at me, but I wasn't sure if it was really going in.

Alison had to be in there somewhere, but I suspected it would take a better man than me to tease her out.

Bobby and Lol were in bed together, exhausted. Trish's phone had gone south when they were kidnapped by Harry Frank, but the home phone was crowded with increasingly panicked voicemail messages from Lol's mum. Trish did a fine job of soothing her fears and convincing her that it was all right for her teenage daughter to stay away from home for so long, especially considering that she had recently embraced the New Seekers.

When she hung up, I said, 'You sweet talker.'

'Enough from you, bollock-brain,' was her response.

Normally, at this stage of one of our adventures, we would collapse into each other's arms and swear undying love, but there was a reticence about her this time. When I did try to envelop her, she squirmed away from me with an angry, 'Don't . . .'

I thought maybe she was wary of Sara, pacing in the other room with our shared mobile phone, setting up a photographer to secretly record the delivery of the billionaire's daughter. She also had one eye on the live coverage of the massacre at the Ulster Folk and Transport Museum on our telly. While the body count wasn't unique, the setting was, and there was a sense that it was about something other than gang warfare, though nobody could quite work out what. Sara was primed to break the story. She just needed the happy ending.

When Trish saw me looking at her through the

dividing doors, I said, 'Don't worry about her; there's nothing going on there.'

'Do you think I give a shit?'

'Yes,' I said.

'Well, you are sadly mistaken.'

'Trish . . .'

'Too far this time, Dan. Too far.'

She gave Alison a squeeze of the shoulder and then walked out of the kitchen. I hoped that there might be a tear in her eye, a quiver in her voice, but no. It was summer outside and winter indoors.

Sara appeared in the kitchen doorway.

'Set?' I asked her.

'Set.'

'They better not see you.'

'They won't. My guy is very good. He's nearly here.'

I walked her to the door. 'Big story,' I said.

'Huge.'

'And after? Will you go back to them – the gangs? It hasn't put you off?'

'All the more reason to,' she said.

'In my day, they pretty much left reporters alone. It's all changed now. You could walk away. You *should* walk away. But you won't.'

'Nope.'

I opened the front door. Her car was just pulling up. I showed her my watch and said, 'Steps of St Anne's, exactly thirty minutes from now.'

She moved past me. Then she stepped back and gave me a quick peck on the cheek.

I said, 'If Trish saw that, she'd lamp you.'

'That's why I waited,' said Sara, with a smile.

St Anne's Cathedral was brightly lit in the midday sun. There were skateboarders using the steps for jumps and a couple of Seekers in the doorway. Sara and her photographer would be in position on top of one of the boarded-up shops opposite, preparing to record the handover – which was a pity, because it wasn't actually happening there. I'd agreed right at the start that there'd be no publicity and I saw no reason to change that now. Alison already had a mountain of problems to overcome and scrutiny by the world's press wouldn't help. I felt a little bad at the deception, but also suspected that, if she was half the reporter I thought she was, she should have second-guessed me, anyway. If she got us, she got us.

Alison was belted into the passenger seat. She sat there meekly and didn't even object when the radio began to play something by Phil Collins. I switched to a different station before any further damage was done to her fragile mind. Jack Caramac's oily voice then began to dissect the shootings at the museum, with the aid of his crackpot listeners. I turned that off as well and we drove the rest of the way to Ormeau Park in silence.

I parked up, got out, leaned against the bonnet and waited. The park was the oldest in Belfast and one of the largest. Trees, flowers, nature walks, bowling greens, tennis courts and football pitches, all bordered on one

Colin Bateman

side by the Lagan: scene of my catastrophic kayaking adventure. There was no helicopter pad but, when you were Thomas Wolff, you didn't really need one. You could land exactly where you fancied. After about five minutes, I heard the thump-thump of the blades, and the distant shape of what my research told me was his new favourite plaything: a state-of-the-art, sixteen-seater Bell 525 Relentless, which had the mouths of the twenty-two eleven-year-old soccer players watching as it landed hanging open in surprise and awe, particularly as it set down in the centre circle in the middle of their game. As the referee gathered the youngsters together at one end of the pitch, the doors slid open and a squad of security men jumped out and quickly set up a defensive perimeter. They weren't shy about showing off their weapons. A few moments later, I picked out Michael Finn as he stepped down and quickly turned to lend a supportive hand to corpulent Thomas Wolff.

I glanced back at Alison, who was looking at the helicopter with mild curiosity. I pushed myself off the bonnet and sauntered across the pitch towards Finn and Wolff. Before I got within twenty metres of them, two of their security guards stopped me, searched me and allowed me to continue.

The blades were still deafening as Finn bustled forward ahead of his boss. He took my hand and shook it and shouted in my ear, 'Starkey – she's here?!'

I nodded.

Thomas Wolff came up beside him, his eyes fully

focused on my car, and shouted, 'I can't thank you enough!'

'You probably can,' I said.

But he either ignored it or lost it in the rush of sound. 'Why isn't she coming?'

'Scared! She's not in great shape!' I had given them only the barest details over the phone: that she had been held captive; not that she had been used and abused for nine months. If it came out, it came out, but it wouldn't come from me. 'She'll need time!'

Wolff nodded. His tongue darted out to moisten his lips. For the moment, he was no longer Billionaire Thomas Wolff, but a dad.

Michael Finn handed a small briefcase to me. 'Tax free!' he said.

I nodded thanks and hurried back to the car. I put the briefcase in the backseat and then opened Alison's door. I undid her seat belt and helped her out. She stood, lost in Trish's clothes. Wolff had stopped halfway towards us and was standing with his arms open. I took Alison by the shoulders, gave her a reassuring smile and then gently nudged her forward. She began to walk tentatively towards her waiting dad. As she drew closer, the wind from the blades pressed her clothes back against her, emphasising her skeletal frame. Before she quite reached him, she stopped and glanced back at me. I gave her a nod. She stepped forward then and was quickly enveloped in Wolff's enormous arms. I wanted to shout at him that, if he wasn't careful, he might snap her in two. But of course I couldn't say it;

even at a distance I could see the tears rolling down his cheeks. Then his hand came and reached under her and lifted her up and he turned and began to carry her back to the helicopter. Finn gave me the thumbs up and turned to follow him. Behind him, the circle of security began to contract.

I leaned against the car again, watching as the chopper rose from the ground. The kids finally rebelled against their referee, charged toward the centre circle and began to jump up and down and yell while being buffeted by the down draft.

I got back into the car and started the engine. I wiped a tear from my eye. It had nothing to do with the death of Katya Cummings and the rebirth of Alison Wolff, or the pleasure of seeing a father, even a porn baron turned media mogul, reunited with his long lost daughter. It was the cold air from the helicopter. But, as I drove away, I thought to myself that there was nothing quite like a happy ending.

And, indeed, it was nothing like a happy ending.

I was halfway home, caught in traffic, when my purloined phone rang and it was Finn, spitting blood against the clatter of the blades.

'You bastard, Starkey!'

'I'm sorry; what—?'

'We're going to get every fucking penny back and make sure you—'

'What's wrong? Is he not happy to have—'

'It isn't Alison, you bastard!'

'What're you—'

'It's some Russian fucking halfwit!'

'No – hold on – it's her; she's just lost a lot of weight and—'

'And a birthmark? Has she lost that too? And her eyes: a different colour? What the fuck do you take us for, Starkey?'

'I—'

'You've made me look like a fool, and Mr Wolff is . . . is . . . furious . . . and embarrassed . . . Mortified! By God, Starkey, he's of a mind to just throw her out over Belfast and have done. What're we supposed to do with her?!'

I had a sudden notion that Alison . . . or Alexa, who was indeed, it seemed, a poor Russian girl who'd been lured to Belfast on the promise of a job and forced into prostitution, could possibly end up in Patricia's home for waifs and strays. But it didn't seem like the time to mention it, not with Finn's threats continuing to spray from my phone. So I cut the line and tried to concentrate on the traffic, but my eye kept being drawn back to the helicopter, barely a dot on the horizon, and I couldn't help but smile. I had done my very best to bring Alison Wolff home but, as Trish was always keen to remind me, my best was never good enough.

Epilogue

Thomas Wolff was a very powerful man, and he employed powerful men, but he would not get the briefcase of cash back from me without a fight. There were lots of phone calls demanding its return, but their reluctance to put anything in writing told me that they didn't want an obvious record of my connection to their organisation, so I sat tight, and gradually, as the weeks went by, the threats tailed off and I felt more relaxed about dipping into what was a very substantial sum of money. And I deserved it. I had been through bloody hell to find Alison Wolff. From the outset, Finn had presumed that she was already dead, so, really, nothing had changed.

In one way, there had been a positive outcome: two gang leaders, with differing, but nevertheless ambitious, plans to dominate the city, had been removed. According to Sara – who I started meeting regularly for lunch, even though she didn't believe that I too had been deceived over the meeting point for Alison's handover – the scramble was on to fill their boots. Alexa, as we now knew her, slowly, slowly, came out of her shell, partly because of the first-class treatment I paid for her to have, but mostly, I think, because of the care Trish lavished on her. She was very good with seemingly hopeless cases, which gave me cause for optimism. Eventually Alexa, real name Olga Alexa Litvenyenko, was well enough to fly home to her family in the Ukraine.

Being relatively cash rich also meant that there was no need to work for a while. I spent a lot more time with Bobby and the ever-expanding Lol, and in the Bob Shaw, but gradually boredom drew me back to the office. I ordered a complete re-fit and sat behind my expensive desk in my executive chair and twiddled my thumbs while I waited for the next case to turn up. And waited. My only distraction was Sara. As well as our lunches, we would text, relentlessly winding each other up, or chat on the phone. About six weeks after Thomas Wolff flew out of Belfast, Sara called me but, as I was already on with Trish, she tried to leave a message. My voicemail was full, so she texted to say as much. I'd neglected to delete my saved messages, so spent twenty minutes going through them. I'd forgotten about one of them, from Jonathan, my contact in the strip of bars out at Ballyhackamore. He'd said he had something to show me but, with all of the madness, I'd never gotten back to him. I deleted it, but then that raw nub of journalistic curiosity that would always be part of my DNA kept gnawing at me during the afternoon. Having nothing better to do anyway, and with the hour approaching beer o'clock, I took a drive out to see him at Culchie's Corner. He said I was lucky because, once a year, they had a regular clear-out of the CCTV footage they recorded inside the bar and that was due in a couple of days, so I'd timed it just right. He brought me into a back office and put a DVD in a player and then fast-forwarded to the bit he wanted to show me. He slowed it down and then paused it, and we both studied the screen. After a bit, I said, 'Nah, I don't think so. And, anyway, it has all been sorted out.'

He said, 'So you don't want it?'

I told him no, that he could throw it out.

I drove back into town and parked outside my apartment. I had another couple of pints in the Bob and then sauntered across town to Botanic. I slipped into the Empire and its Tuesday-night comedy club, and had a few more and didn't laugh at anything, mostly because it wasn't funny, but also because I was distracted.

I finished my drink about forty minutes short of closing time and then wandered up Botanic Avenue. The New Seekers had set up their regular camp near the entrance to Botanic Gardens and were busy preparing for this night's influx of alcoholics and crushers. Prim Simon was there, setting out chairs and tables. I took a seat and he said, 'Make yourself at home, but the coffee won't be ready for a wee while.'

'Fine by me,' I said.

He gave me a big smile and continued his work. After a bit, two female Seekers emerged from the bus, pristine now in their gowns and wimples but destined to be covered in coffee and juice and vomit as the night wore into early morning. One of them gave me a wide smile and said, 'I remember you!'

'Jane,' I said, 'how're you doing?'

'Fabulous,' she said. 'Can I get you a coffee . . . Andrew . . . wasn't it?'

'Orange juice,' I said, 'and you have a good memory.'

'I do . . . but then there was also something happened with you at Ballyferris . . . wasn't there?'

'Oh, yes,' I said. 'I got thrown out for sedition.'

She laughed and went to get the juice. When she came back with it, she asked how I'd been and if I was still in that bad place with my life, and I said no, everything was fine and dandy; I had just spotted the bus on the way home and wanted to call over and say hello and thank the New Seekers for their support, and her, in particular, for helping me.

'Ah, it was nothing. Sure, that's what we're here for.'

'Well,' I said, 'I appreciate it.'

I lifted the orange juice and drained it in one. 'Better be getting home,' I said, and handed her the glass.

'Good night, Andrew,' she said as she took it from me. 'And may God be with you.'

She gave me another smile and turned away.

'And may God be with you, Alison,' I said.

It stopped her in her tracks, but just for a moment. Then she continued on into the bus. I followed her progress along the inside to the small kitchen area. She began to wash the glass. She did not look towards me.

I smiled to myself and turned away.

She had been right there with me, right at the start, and I hadn't noticed. But a colleague of Jonathan's in Culchie's Corner had picked up the photo I'd left and remembered her from a rumpus in the bar when she was collecting for the New Seekers and someone pulled her headdress off. I had no idea how she had ended up with the Seekers, if the trauma of the Wellington Street massacre had caused her to turn to them or they had picked her up, broken or shot, from the street and then slowly brainwashed her, or, indeed, if she had simply been converted because she believed in Eve, just like thousands and thousands of others. Ultimately, it didn't matter. My job was done: I'd been paid handsomely, the puzzle was solved and Alison was alive and free to live that life as she saw fit.

Perfect.

As I walked away from the New Seeker bus, my phone began to ring.

'Well,' Sara asked breezily, 'what's happening?'

'Funny you should ask,' I said.

Love
BATEMAN?

Read more from one of the best writers around

www.headline.co.uk

The Prisoner of Brenda

Bateman

When notorious gangster 'Fat Sam' Mahood is murdered, the chief suspect won't say a word. Incarcerated in a mental institution, he's known only as The Man in the White Suit. That is until Nurse Brenda calls upon the investigative powers of Mystery Man, former patient and owner of No Alibis, Belfast's finest mystery bookshop . . .

Mystery Man enters the asylum undercover. But before his investigation can even begin, the suspect is arrested for the murder of a fellow patient. Is The Man in the White Suit a double murderer or a helpless scapegoat? Intrigue, conspiracy, and ancient Latin curses all combine to give the Small Bookseller with No Name his most difficult case yet.

Bateman: The Word on the street:

'I've been a fan of Colin Bateman ever since his first crime novel and he just seems to get better and better' Ian Rankin

'Bateman has a truly unique voice . . . He is a dark and brilliant champion of words' James Nesbitt

'Sometimes brutal, often blackly humorous and always terrific' *Observer*

978 0 7553 7869 2

headline

The Lost

Claire McGowan

NOT EVERYONE WHO'S MISSING IS LOST

When two teenage girls go missing along the Irish border, forensic psychologist Paula Maguire returns to the hometown she left years before.

NOT EVERYONE WHO'S LOST WANTS TO BE FOUND

As Paula digs into the cases the truth twists further away. What's the link with two other disappearances from 1985? And why does everything lead back to the town's dark past – including the reasons her own mother went missing years before?

NOTHING IS WHAT IT SEEMS

As the shocking truth is revealed, Paula learns that sometimes, it's better not to find what you've lost.

Praise for Claire McGowan:

'A knockout new talent' Lee Child

'Ireland's answer to Ruth Rendell' Ken Bruen

'This thriller is fresh and accessible without ever compromising on grit or suspense' Erin Kelly

978 0 7553 8640 6

headline

Three Dog Night

Elsebeth Egholm

In the small town of Grenå, once the murders start, no one knows who to trust . . .

Ex-convict Peter Boutrup is trying to build a new life. But then a young woman goes missing on New Year's Eve, and Peter discovers the body of Ramses, an old acquaintance from prison, on the beach.

When a woman is found in the harbour – naked, attached to an anchor with her face torn off – Peter must accept that the truth lies hidden in the past he is trying to forget.

Populated by a cast of characters from the underbelly of Danish society, *Three Dog Night* is a fast-paced thriller that paints a picture of a rarely seen side of Denmark.

Praise for *Three Dog Night*:

'Denmark's Queen of Crime' *Dagbladenes Bureau*

'Thrilling and brutal' *Ekstra Bladet*

'A highly recommended, bleak and captivating crime novel' *Information*

978 0 7553 9783 9

headline

The Unquiet Grave

Steven Dunne

The past can't stay hidden forever . . .

The Cold Case Unit of Derby Constabulary feels like a morgue to DI Damen Brook. However, in disgrace and recently back from suspension, his boss thinks it's the safest place for him.

But soon Brook uncovers a pattern in a series of murders that date back to 1963. Baffled that a killer could stay undetected for so long, Brook delves deep into the past of both suspects and colleagues unsure where the hunt will lead him. What he does know for sure is that a significant date is approaching fast and the killer may be about to strike again . . .

Praise for DEITY by Steven Dunne:

'DI Damen Brook is one of the most memorable characters in recent British crime fiction' Stephen Booth

'A well-placed, dark thriller from an author who's clearly going places' *Irish Independent*

978 0 7553 8372 6

headline